The Adventures

of Walt and Sparky

HUNKERING DOWN

Stephen Long

Sparky

Man's best friend

CONTENTS

Introduction

The Adventures os Walt and Sparky - Hunkering Down is the story of a retired Army veteran who moved to the mountains, bought some forest land, and built a homestead. They say that trouble comes in threes but for Walt and Sparky, trouble came in fours, fives, and sixes.

With very little help Walt built a nice log cabin, a woodshed, woodshop, and a garage. Walt was an avid ham radio operator, webmaster, amateur prospector, and a die hard prepper whose motto was "Be Prepared."

Living in the mountains, he was ready and to deal with the usual hardships like cold heavy snowfall, cold weather, downed trees, high winds, lightning storms, power outages, and forest fires, flooding, and dangerous animals. But one year Walt and Sparky had to face a hard winter with a nearby volcanic eruption, live months without sunshine, cope with three inches of volcanic ash on the ground, experience a large earthquake just south of town, extended power outages, road and bridge closures, down cell phone towers, food and gas shortages, and a federal government shutdown, and well armed home invaders.

As crime in the area increases, Walt designs out-of-the-box ways to enhance his home security and defense while preparing for trouble on his homestead. Living alone with Sparky he knows that he lives too far from town to count on any help from police in an emergency. He organizes a group of likeminded neighbors who talk with each other using citizens band radios and help each other and to combat local crime.

He meets a new neighbor who is both a ham radio operator and a deputy sheriff who joins the CB radio group and is both helpful and sympathetic to the plight of rural residents trying to survive the natural disasters a local crime wave, and food shortages, without the modern conveniences we all depend on.

Living without power is hard enough for a few days or a week but when the power is off for months, life's problems start to snowball. You can get by without refrigeration in the winter but no power means no hot water, and since rural residents depend on water wells, no water at all. Well houses and water lines can freeze without power, Ovens, stoves, and microwaves cannot work without power. Most phones, computers, internet modems, battery chargers, electric lights, cannot operate without power as well.

Road closures mean that you cannot get to town to buy food, gas, or propane. A federal government shut down means that many people must go without social security or retirement checks. Food and supply shortages mean the stores either aren't open, or do not have anything to sell.

When people get hungry, it is not surprising that they quickly get desperate. Law and order breaks down when people must struggle to just to survive. The rule of law becomes the rule of the lawless, and people must protect themselves. When this happens, all that people can do then is to hunker down, shelter in place, and hope that things get better soon. When things do get better, people understand that they need to do a better job of being prepared, because the unexpected is the rule and not the exception.

Chapter 1. October

"Blow Up Your TV, throw away your paper
Go to the country, build you a home
Plant a little garden, eat a lot of peaches
Try and find Jesus on your own"
John E. Prine

It was a beautiful day in the neighborhood. There wasn't a cloud to be seen and the blue sky was unusually intense. The air was crisp and clean and the fall colors were peaking. The subtle green colors of the evergreen forest were accompanied by the yellow Birch and Cottonwood leaves. The golden glow of Larch trees making the view spectacular and electric at the same time. Larch trees (also known as tamaracks) are deciduous conifers native to the cooler climates of the northwest, Canada, and Siberia. Unlike other conifers they lose their needles every fall, but first turn golden and bright yellow before falling off the tree. During this time the needles look bright yellow in the sunshine and on a cloudy day the trees glow as if they were plugged in, and radiate a bright yellow and golden color. Typically larch trees grow sixty to one hundred fifty feet tall. When the needles fall off before winter the trees are often mistaken as dead stands by greenhorns, who do not know better, and they cut them down for firewood. Of course the trees are dormant and not dead and the wood won't burn well until it is seasoned. But on a day like today the bright fall colors mixed with the evergreen trees and blue sky were a sight to behold.

The old Ford pickup slowly came up the hill from the creek and stopped at the woodshed. Walt got out of the truck and so did his little dog Sparky. He walked back to the tailgate and, one by one, he unloaded ten five gallon buckets from the bed and placed them on the ground behind the truck. Each bucket contained about four gallons of sand that he had shoveled from his sandbar along Rapid Lightning Creek. One at time, Walt carried each bucket into the woodshed and dumped out the sand in the corner of the shed that was partitioned to hold the sand in place. He had framed out a 10' x 16' space with plywood sides and added a gate so that he easily could walk into the framed area and keep the sand confined. With this last load Walt estimated that he had hauled about 10 cubic yards of sand into the woodshed since early in the summer.

During this time Walt had been worried that someone would ask him what he was doing with the sand. He had been lucky that nobody questioned him about this. If they would have asked, Walt planned on telling them that we was using the sand to mix concrete and also to use on the icy paths during the winter. He was relieved that his summer project hadn't drawn the attention of any nosey friends or neighbors. If anyone found out why he was collecting sand from the creek it would have been a big problem.

Walt had turned 51 this year and bought his 20 acres of tree-covered land shortly after he retired from the military. He enlisted in the Army when he was 19 and was able to retire at age 39 with a pension equal to one half of his base pay for the rest of his life, For $5000 down and $200 a month he finally had a place to call home and to build a homestead. Although the land was on a hillside there were several large level building sites on the property and an old logging road running through the middle of the 1320' x 660' property. A logger had estimated that there were about one thousand trees per acre on the place so Walt knew that he had all the firewood and timber resources that he would ever need.

Building a homestead on raw land by himself was a big challenge and a lot of work. He knew that it would have been a lot easier if Kathy would have been with him to help, but he lost her a few years ago in a car accident involving a drunk driver. She was the daughter of the U.S. Ambassador to the Philippines and he was not please that his daughter had married an enlisted man. Walt was still angry to think that Kathy died and the drunk driver lived. They were only together for two years and Walt knew that she would have loved to live in the

8

mountains and missed her too much to think about getting married again.

On the bottom edge of the property a large year 'round creek ran along the boundary of the property and contained lots of gravel. It looked like an excellent trout habitat. Rapid Lightning Creek had deposited well over 500 yards of gravel on Walt's property before it changed its course years ago. Fortunately Walt's property lines were determined by a survey but in the old days property boundaries were often marked by the location of a river or creek. If the water would change course, one property owner's land would be increased and the other neighboring owner's land would be reduced. He had heard of one case where an owner lost 700 feet along his property line when the creek changed course, so at least the property lines were well marked and set in stone by a survey.

Walt's place was located about 20 miles north of Sandpoint, Idaho and he named his stump ranch/tree farm, Idahome. He bought this land because it had lots of trees, a creek, a southern exposure, and bordered a paved county road. Sandpoint was a small town with a population a little over 8,000. It was located next to Lake Pend Oreille and the Pend Oreille River. It had been historically a logging town but recently attracted retired people and outdoor enthusiasts, both young and old. Located near the Canadian border, the area had a four season climate, great hunting and fishing, and a nearby ski slope. About half the people expected Sandpoint to become another Jackson Hole and the other half cherished the small town atmosphere and didn't want it to ever change. You could still spot the occasional bumper sticker that read, "Have a nice trip back to California."

Lake Pend Oreille is a treasure and is 1150 feet deep in spots. In fact it is so deep that the US Navy uses it for submarine research and it is one of the largest bodies of fresh water, in terms of volume, in the United States. At one time it was fished commercially and is still home to record Gerard Rainbow trout.

Schweitzer Mountain Resort is only eleven miles from Sandpoint in the Selkirk mountains and is a very popular ski resort. It overlooks Lake Pend Oreille, and has views of the Bitterroot and Cabinet mountain ranges with a summit elevation of 6400 feet above sea level and gets an average of 300 inches of snowfall a year. It has 92 named runs with the longest being 2.1 miles long and is the most popular ski area in the region. This was another reason that Walt chose to live here, he loved to ski.

It took Walt five years to build his log cabin and out buildings. Although he did this mostly on his own, he did get help clearing about 2 acres and leveling the building site and putting rock on the driveway. The trees from the clearing were sent to a local mill that cut them into rough cut boards measuring 2" x 6" x 18' long. He hired people to put on the roofs, install the septic system, drill the well, and do the wiring to the cabin and outbuildings.

Otherwise he was quite proud that he did everything else by himself. Walt took the time to dig out the foundation area to a depth of six feet so that he could have a useable crawl space underneath the log cabin and poured a concrete footer before completing the foundation with concrete blocks. This gave him a solid perimeter foundation with room to stand up under the cabin floor.

The cabin was built with vertical logs that he cut from nearby Lunch peak. These were dead standing Alpine Fir that had been killed in a fire. He cut and hauled the ten foot long logs himself and it only cost him $10 for a 10 cord permit from the State for enough logs to build the entire house. The dry standing logs had lost their bark and were brown and gray in color. Each log was drawknifed to expose the natural blonde wood color and make the cabin lighter and nicer looking on the inside. A drawknife is a horizontal knife blade with two small wooden handles that is pulled along the log to remove bark, shave wood, and also to shape wood.

After the cabin was completed on the outside with windows and doors there was still lots of work to be done. He installed the toilet, shower, and sinks and all the plumbing using copper pipe. He did all of the interior wiring and poured a hearth for the wood stove. Once this was done he was able to buy a large wood stove and install the chimney. Finally after all this time the place was looking like a home and not a construction site. For the first time he could be as warm as he liked regardless of the weather.

After completing the cabin he built a large woodshed and a shop building with two adjoining covered carports. One thing he had learned in his first few years on the property is that you could not have enough covered space in north Idaho. It rained a lot in the spring and fall and in the winter it snowed as much as five feet.

All of the power lines were underground. Besides being more reliable than above ground lines, they were not an eye sore. But when you looked around the clearing there were still several black cables to be seen leading to the cabin. Walt was a ham radio operator and had half a dozen antennas scattered throughout the clearing with overhead cables that lead to the house. The satellite internet dish in the yard gave his old style log cabin and outbuildings a twenty first century look.

Walt had a few chores to do before winter but he knew that there weren't going to be many days as nice as this one before the weather turned. He picked up two empty dog food bags from the pile and his grabber tool. The grabber is a device that old people use to pick up their socks and other items off the floor without bending over. It is about three feet high with pinchers at the bottom and a squeeze operated handle at the top. When the handle was squeezed the pinchers at the bottom would close together so things on the ground could be picked up.

He called his little dog Sparky who was always eager to go for walk. Sparky was half Red Healer and half Australian Shepherd. She was mostly black and with a coat that was soft as a bunny. She had one brown eye and one blue eye. She was very fast and agile and had a bark that was much bigger than her size. She was very sweet to Walt but could be the barking dog from hell if she didn't know you.

Together they walked up toward the west end of the property on a search for White Pine cones that were found on the forest floor. The White Pine trees have large pine cones which are often removed from the upper branches by squirrels and dropped to the ground. When dry the cones open up and are usually between six and eight inches long. Walt collected fifteen bags of dry cones every fall and used them to start fires in the wood stove. To start a fire in the stove all you needed was two pieces of firewood spaced about six inches apart. Then one pine cone is placed between the firewood pieces and six to ten pieces of kindling is put over the pine cone. When a lit match is held under the cone for five seconds or so you can start a perfect smoke free fire every time. Then after waiting five minutes or so a larger piece of firewood is placed on top of the burning kindling. Dry Birch bark works the same way so Sparky and Walt were on the hunt for pine cones and Birch bark.

Usually the pine cones were found in a group near the bottom of a White Pine tree but sometimes you could find them well away from the trees. Maybe they blew in on the wind or maybe a squirrel got tired of carrying them, nobody knew for sure. As they walked along the deer trails and foot paths Walt kept his eyes on the ground and soon he had two bags full of cones to take back to the woodshed. Two bags and the grabber was all that Walt could carry anyway so for now their walk was over.

Needless to say there was a good chance that they would see some wildlife when they went for a walk. There was lots of deer around this time of year and a few rabbits and squirrels too. In addition sometimes they would see turkeys, ravens, woodpeckers, and other birds as well. Every now and then they would stumble on a grouse. These birds try to stay hidden as long as possible and when they finally flushed a few feet away from you and flew away, the noise and surprise was enough to make your heart stop for a second. Sometimes they would see bear sign and once in a while they might get a glimpse at a fully grown bear or bear cubs. Moose could be seen on the property later in the winter when they would come in to eat low hanging cedar boughs but it was very unusual to walk up on a Moose in the summer or fall, especially if Sparky was present. This could get ugly in a hurry since Moose do not take kindly to a dog barking at their feet.

That night after dinner Walt checked his email and found that he had a little web work to do. He had taken some courses in town and learned how to edit photos and build websites. He had a website of his own that advertised mines and mining claims for sale and he did the web work for four other people who needed web work done from time to time. The owner of the website that sold hand forged knives sent him a picture and description of a new knife that he just completed and needed it added to his site. It was an easy job and it took less than an hour to do the work and get this loaded up to the server. After this was done he watched a few You Tube videos, checked out some news sites and went to bed.

The next morning Walt got up about 5am as usual and after a trip to the bathroom he lit a fire in the woodstove, made coffee, fed Sparky after she came inside and made himself a big breakfast. He put the large cast iron pan on the burner and sliced up a potato. He put the sliced potatoes in the microwave on high and nuked them for two and a half minutes. By then the pan was warmed up and he spread a slice of butter all over the pan and carefully laid the potato slices in the pan so they were not touching each other. By microwaving the potatoes first they didn't take long to cook so he sliced up a couple of pieces of ham and some red onions and nuked them for sixty seconds. By this time the potatoes were done on one side so he turned them over and dumped the ham and onions on top of the potatoes. Next he added five pieces of sliced cheese over the potatoes and cracked an egg in the unused portion of the pan. While this was cooking Walt pulled out a heavy paper plate and put six spoonfuls of chilled applesauce on the plate. He flipped over the egg, turned the burner off, poured a fresh cup of coffee and enjoyed one of the best breakfasts anyone could ask for while listening to the local news on the radio. If Sparky was lucky, and she usually was, she got a small piece of ham while Walt finished his breakfast.

By this time the woodstove needed a few more sticks of wood, Walt got a fresh cup of coffee, and they both sat down by the radio. Sparky was a good radio dog. That is to say that no matter how much amplified noise came over the speaker, she slept at Walt's side while he was on the radio

Walt had a pretty nicely equipped ham radio station with two one hundred watt HF transceivers for long distances, two QRP 10 watt HF transceivers that he had built from kits, two 2 meter FM transceivers for local communication, a CB transceiver, a SDR all band receiver, a police and fire scanner, a 600 watt amplifier, and several tuners, and a boat anchor. A boat anchor is an older radio tube radio that weighs a lot because of the built in transformer. Even though he hadn't used this radio in years he kept it on the radio table because it looked cool and he loved it too much to get rid of it. Each radio could be easily connected to several different antennas with switches depending on what frequencies he was going to be operating on.

Licensed amateurs are allowed to operate their radios on several different bands which are small ranges of frequencies throughout the radio spectrum. The bands refer to the wavelength of a particular frequency. The lower the frequency, the longer the wavelength. The 160 meter band for example is located just above the AM broadcast band between 1.8 and 2.0 Megahertz. This band behaves like AM broadcast stations and have a relatively short distance during daytime but can be heard at a much farther distances during the night. Each band of frequencies has its own behavior and characteristics under normal conditions depending on the time of day. To contact a radio station in Europe, Africa, Asia, or Australia during the daytime hams would normally use the 20, 17, 15, or 12 meter bands but these bands are not normally open late at night.

Walt discovered a group of hams a few years ago who got together on the air from about 9:30 – 11:30 every morning on 3.988 Megahertz to talk with each other on SSB (Single Side Band). This was the most popular mode of voice communication used today because it allows more people to communicate within the same bandspace than (Amplitude Modulation) because SSB signals have a smaller bandwidth.

The group had five or ten regulars and twenty or more people who would stop by to talk with the group on an occasional basis. Walt got along well with them all because there was no subject that was off limits. Of course they talked about radios and antennas but also talked about fishing, hunting, UFO's, giants, ancient archeology, politics, current events, religion, guns, cooking, pets, other hams, cars, weather, history, books, music, movies, liquor, tobacco, food prices, airplanes, military experience, camping, mushroom hunting, gold panning, trapping, you tube videos, and just about anything else that you could imagine. When Walt turned on his radio that morning a coupe of people were already talking.

"We got some rain last night here. Looks like .25 inches or so. Did you get any rain Dennis? (AU7PM)

"No rain yet Frank but I can see it is coming according to my weather widget. How is my signal? You are just above my noise level." (AR7QRN)

"You have a good signal over here in Blaine Washington, a solid S8. What is your noise level? (AU7PM)

"I've got you about an S6 but I have a really bad noise level at an S5. Let me see if I can pick you up a little better on the web SDR. (AR7QRN)

"Morning guys, AP7ZMT here" Walt broke in.

"Morning Walt. Dennis is in here and he is trying to find a web SDR that will work this morning. This is AU7PM." A web SDR is a receiver in another location that can be accessed using the internet.

"OK Frank, I know that it is hard for him to hear anything over the noise level that he has over there. I hope he gets the power company to take care of that soon." (AP7ZMT)

15

"What's the temp over there? Did you get any rain? (AU7PM)

"Not yet but it is supposed to get here this afternoon. They say we could get some lightning to go with it. I hope not. It's pretty dry over here. 35 degrees right now" (AP7ZMT)

"I can hear you both on the Winthrop machine. Morning Walt." (AR7QRN)

"Morning Dennis, you've got a good signal in here this morning. Have you talked to the power company yet?" (AP7ZMT)

"I'm going to call him a little later." (AR7QRN)

"Did anyone check out the higher bands this morning? (AU7PM)

"I heard Spain, Italy, and Germany on 17. They weren't real strong. Don't know if I could have worked them or not. Nothing on 15 yet." (AR7QRN)

"It's nice to hear that the bands are coming back. Heard an Australian station on 12 meters the other day but he was the only station I heard on the band. (AP7ZMT)

"AU7PM for ID"

"AR7QRN"

"AP7ZMT. Did anybody listen to Alex Jones last night? He was warning people that the CDC was going to lock us down again."

"I don't think people will fall for that again." (AR7QRN)

"I don't think so either. The Johns Hopkins study proved that masks or lockdowns didn't work anyway." (AU7PM)

"I can't believe they are not in prison. Morning guys, Alpha Yankee Seven Oscar Mike."

"Don't worry Ray. Even if they don't go to prison they'll probably rot in Hell. What's going on?" (AU7PM)

"Not much. Going to take one last ride today and then get motorcycles ready for winter. (AY7OM)   "It's hard to think about winter when it is this nice out." (AR7QRN)

"There are two seasons in Idaho. Winter, and getting ready for Winter. Got your wood in Frank?" (AP7ZMT)

"Got the last load in last week. All covered up and ready to go. How about you? (AU7PM)

"The wood shed is full but I still need to get a few more bags of pine cones and kindling. If it doesn't snow until December it will be fine with me. I plan on putting the chains on the tractor and attaching the snow blower in the next week or two. I hate putting on chains when it's cold outside. (AP7ZMT)

"Got my deer tag yesterday but I am going to wait until it cools down a little. I see them every morning down in the hay field." (AR7QRN)

"Are there any bucks in the group or all they all does? (AU7PM)

"I've seen one big buck but he doesn't seem to be interested in the does, YET. (AR7QRN)

"It won't be long now. Thanksgiving seems to be the peak of the rut around here. (AY7OM)

"I know a guy who never bothers to go hunting until Thanksgiving because of the rut. I understand that most seasons he is back home by lunchtime with a nice buck to show for it." (AU7PM)

" Good Morning everyone, this is AM7DX."

" Morning Jeff." (AR7QRN)

" Morning Jeff. Good to hear you in there." (AU7PM)

" Hey Jeff What's going on? (AY7OM)

"Got your wood in yet? Good signal into Sandpoint." (AP7ZMT)

"Good looking day over here. The wood is in, just have to pick up some hay and we'll be all set. 32 degrees this morning." (AM7DX)

"You get those big round bales don't you? How are you going to haul it? " (AP7ZMT)

"Normally we get it delivered but the guy had an accident and his truck is in the shop. So they will load it in our truck and when we get here we'll put a rope around it and drive out from under it. Then we can roll it it into the hay barn. Not as easy as usual but we've done it before." (AM7DX)

"I'll be right back. Need to get some more coffee and put another log on the fire." (AU7PM)

"Hey Joe, how are you doing? Ready for winter? (AM7DX)

"I need to get the studded tires on the car but they aren't legal until next month. Also need to get some propane but otherwise I am pretty well set. I'm kind of looking forward to winter so I can spend more time on the radio." (AN7HM)

"Did you guys here about the UFO sightings in Seattle yesterday? Happened in broad daylight. (AR7QRN)

"I saw the news report on You Tube. They didn't look like weather balloons to me. They are not ours, that's for sure. (AM7DX)

"I saw this too. I could not believe the media was finally talking about this. What about you Ray, did you see this?" (AU7PM) Ray didn't believe in UFOs.

"Yes I saw them too and don't know what it was but until I see a little green man for myself, I still don't believe it. (AY7OM)

" If one comes over here, I'll bring him over for coffee." (AM7DX)

"Call first so I can make an appointment with the taxidermist. It would make a great conversation piece." (AY7OM)

"I guess I'm going to pull the plug this morning. Going to take Sparky for a short walk and then I going to town to pick up my batteries and the inverter." (AP7ZMT)

"OK Walt, how many batteries are you going to get? (AU7PM)

"I have ordered 12 group 27 deep cycle sealed batteries and a 4000 watt sine wave inverter. I am going to charge them off the grid and use a generator for back up. Solar cells don't make sense right now because we can easily go 45 days in the winter without seeing the sun. (AP7ZMT)

"Roger, it sounds like you'll have a really nice system when you're done. Talk to later, AU7PM."

"Ya Walt, sounds good. 73 AY7OM."

"73 Walt, this is AM7DX."

"73 Walt, Talk to you later. AR7QRN."

"Yes it should be a really nice day to go to town. Catch you guys later. This is AP7ZMT clear." Walt turned off the radio and power supply and got up to check the fire and get another cup of coffee. Sparky was getting excited knowing that they would be going for a walk very soon. Walt finished about half of his coffee and they departed for their pine cone hunt and dog walk. When they filled up two more dog food bags it was time to go to town. Normally Walt would leave Sparky at home to watch the place but he could tell that she really wanted to go along so they got in the truck and headed to town. Walt cracked the passenger window just enough to give Sparky lots of fresh air but not enough to stick her head out of the window which is what she really wanted. It was a twenty mile trip to town and traffic was very light for this time of day. Since the county had paved Rapid Lightning Creek Road a few years ago the trip was much more enjoyable than dodging pot holes had been in the past. At least now with a paved county road you could wash your car and it would still be clean when you got home.

It was about six miles down to the school and fall colors on the Selkirk mountains and the crisp and clean air had everyone in a good mood. The temperatures were summer-like so people didn't need jackets or coats and they seemed happy to be outside. School was still in session so the stores were not full of kids.

Walt pulled into the Farmland and left Sparky in the truck. He wasn't worried about her getting too hot like he would have been on a summer day. He had placed his order on the phone so everything was ready when he entered the store. Two employees helped him to get everything to the truck and get it loaded. He had twelve deep cycle sealed batteries, a large inverter/charger, 6 and 10 gauge insulated wire , a switch box with a 30 amp breaker, two dozen battery connectors, ten electrical outlet boxes, outlets, and outlet covers. Fortunately it was a nice day and everything could be loaded in the bed of the truck without the need to cover the load with a tarp. He felt a little light headed thinking that he was finally going to get his emergency power system together and he felt a little light in the wallet too since he had just written a check for a little over $4800 with tax.

Before driving home he pulled into the drive through window at burger King and ordered a whopper and fries and took the time to eat this in the parking lot. Naturally Sparky got some of Walt's hamburger, so she didn't feel left out. Walt drew the line and didn't give her any French fries because he told her that they were, "Too salty."

The drive home was uneventful except that they saw two deer grazing in the shade on the side of the road. The two does were busy eating the tall grass and didn't even look up at the truck as they passed by. Sparky barked at them but the deer paid no attention to the little barking dog in the truck.

When they got home Walt stepped out of the truck and Sparky jumped out right behind him. She immediately started to look the place over for any new smells that might indicate that they had visitors while they were gone. Walt lowered the tailgate and set one of the batteries on the porch. He unlocked the cabin door and went inside to get his battery charger. Each of the twelve batteries would need to be charged before he could install them. You would think that a new battery would have a full charge, but usually they don't. The batteries that Walt had purchased were 12 volt, 100 amp hour, Gel cell, deep cycle batteries. They could be discharged and reused 750 times and when charging they did not emit toxic gasses like lead acid batteries so they were perfectly suited for back up systems and could be safely installed in his crawl space.

It took nearly 30 minutes before the battery would not take a charge anymore and Walt was able to get six of batteries topped off before dinner and charged the rest the next day. One thing that Walt was never any good at was estimating how much time a job would take. Walt thought he could have this done in two days but it took a week to complete the project.

Because he was working in the crawl space everything had to be brought in through the trap door in the cabin floor. First he had to build a long sturdy table to hold the batteries which weighed almost six hundred pounds. Then he covered the table with a piece of two inch thick styrofoam and arranged the batteries in a row.

The batteries were connected in parallel and he needed to assemble lots of short cables to connect the array to the bus bars. The bus consisted of two steel pieces of flat bar about 30 inches long. They were mounted in parallel and spaced about 6 inches apart. Each bar had a hole in the middle every 2 inches for the length of the bar. Both bars were mounted one and one half inches above a solid back board with wooden spacers at the top and bottom of each bar. Then quarter inch bolts and nuts were placed in each of the drilled bar holes. This allowed thirteen different 12 volt circuits and devices to be attached to the bus.

The sturdy rack had to be built to hold the inverter three feet off the ground. It was important that the batteries, the bus, and the inverter all be off the ground in case the crawl space flooded. An inverter is an electronic device that converts 12 volts DC to 110 volts AC. This particular inverter produced a pure sine wave like normal power from the grid and this is required by many sensitive electronic devices like computers. Also this inverter had the ability to correctly charge the batteries from grid power, or from a generator.

After this was done Walt wired five outlets in the cabin and one outside on the porch. These were connected to a plug in that crawl space that could be plugged into the output of the inverter. These outlets had specially marked outlet covers so that they would not be confused with the normal 110 volt outlets throughout the cabin. In addition he wired 4 more outlets in the cabin for 12 volt DC and these were connected directly to the bus. He painted these outlet cover plates red so that they would never be confused with the 110 volt outlets,

He ran a ten guage wire with a plug from the porch down to the inverter and installed a plug so that he could charge the batteries with a small generator from the porch if grid power was not available. Then he wired an outlet from the well house and ran a wire into the crawl space. to a 30 amp switch. In the event of a power failure this allowed Walt to go into the crawl space and switch the well from grid power to the inverter. This was important because the well house was heated during the winter with two 40 watt 110 volt incandescent light bulbs and he could switch from grid power to battery power without going outside. Although it took longer than he thought Walt was very happy with the project.

In the event of a power failure Walt had plenty of light inside the cabin using 12 volt LED bulbs. He had running water from the well and could use his computer, operate his radio station, use the microwave, and even run his refrigerator. The only things he couldn't use during a power failure was the water heater, electric heaters, the electric stove, and the air conditioner.

Walt decided not to buy solar cells to charge his batteries because it was common in the months of December and January to never see the sun at all. Also solar cells do not work when they are covered with snow so, for now, he planned to keep the batteries charged using grid power or with a generator when needed.. He estimated that, depending on usage, he could go at least a week without power before his batteries would need to be recharged.

Feeling good about completing his project Walt and Sparky went on one last pine cone hunt. They walked to a new section of the property and returned with two full bags of cones in less than an hour. Sparky got her dinner and Walt checked his email to find that he had a little more web work to do in the morning.

The local weather forecast predicted rain by next weekend and Walt made a list of the things that needed to be done before the rains came. He needed to get his log splitter undercover, service the tractor, install the tire chains, attach the 5 foot wide snow blower on the back, and get gas, diesel, and propane. He knew from experience that once the rains came, Indian summer was over. He was always relieved to see this annual change in the weather because the threat of forest fire was over for the year.

Over the past few days Walt was able to get his chores done. He also stocked up on groceries and bought two big bags of science diet dog food for Sparky. He was able to get his web sites updated and added a new listing to his goldandsilvermines website. It was a 20 acre patented placer mine in Montana for sale with an asking price of $500,000. The owner was offering terms and wanted $100,000 down with the balance spread over three years at 9 percent interest. This seemed to be priced right and Walt thought he could sell it. If he did, then he would earn a 5% commission. The biggest problem Walt could see would be finding a buyer before the weather turned cold.

After that, nobody would bother to look at the mine until spring when they could do their own testing. No buyer in his right mind would buy a mining property without doing their own testing no matter how good the geologists report sounded. Also Walt knew that most mines that were sold were not sold for the asking price and the final price was subject to negations. The geologist report estimated that the mine had 10,000 troy ounces of mineable gold reserves which, if accurate, would be worth about 20 million dollars. Walt was excited about this new listing and gave the seller a free banner ad on the home page in addition to the web ad.

He had operated the website for several years and one thing that he had learned was that selling mines and mining claims wasn't easy. As a rule, banks would not loan money to anyone who wanted to buy a mine because mining was considered to be a risky business. Even if someone had a good mining property it was still likely that they would fail due to bad management, equipment failure, or running out of cash.

Big mines can burn 10,000 a day in diesel fuel alone not counting wages or other expenses. So most mines were purchased with private money so the number of buyers that could actually buy a mine was quite small. If you asked a buyer if he had the money, he would say that he did. What the buyer often meant was that he could get the money from his wife, brother in law, or other family member. When one of Walt's listings did sell, it usually resulted in a nice payday. However not all of Walt's mine listings were subject to commission. Some owners chose to advertise their mines for an $1800 flat fee and, in this case, any sale would be commission free.

Walt didn't claim to be a miner although he had learned a lot about mining since he started the website. He did have a little succcess panning for gold in Montana. Anyone who has ever done this will tell you it is a lot of work. Most miners only pan for gold to test samples to see if there is any gold in the sample or not. If there is, then they might consider bringing in equipment. If there were fewer than 5 colors per pan, they would look elsewhere.

Chapter 2. November

"Well, I live on a ridgetop
And, Lord knows, I like it just fine
Where it's windy and foggy
And quiet most all the time"
Jesse Colin Young

Walt was feeling good because all his work was done before the rains came. As he looked out the window he could see the water drops dripping off the roof. The fire danger was over and he got paid on the first of every month. It sure was great to look at the calendar and know that there was more money in the bank. With all the money he spent last month, he was pretty well tapped. But now Walt and Sparky could look out the window and watch the trees grow. He didn't have to go back to Sandpoint for several weeks if he didn't want to and he reminded himself that he was retired. He finished his coffee and breakfast and told himself that it was a good day to relax and play on the radio. His email could wait awhile and now he was just going to take it easy and have fun. He lived on a hill and it could rain for a month or more, it didn't matter and he didn't care.

Walt sat down at the radio desk and turned on the power supply and radio. He bypassed the tuner and switched to his hexbeam antenna. The hexbeam looked like an upside down umbrella and was mounted on a wooden pole about 32 feet above ground. The antenna was directional and could be pointed in any direction using a controller inside the shack. He pointed the hexbeam toward Europe, turned on his amplifier and began to listen around to see which bands were open. Sometimes the bands were dead and other times they had lots of traffic. Ten, Twelve, and Fifteen meters were quiet but Seventeen meters had some traffic so the band was at least partially open. He began to transmit.

"Q R Zed, Q R Zed, is this frequency in use?" He didn't hear anyone come back so he tried this again. "Q R Zed, Q R

Zed, is this frequency in use?" It was always a good idea to ask if the frequency was busy because it is common to hear only one side of a conversation. Since nobody indicated the frequency was busy, he began to transmit.

"CQ, CQ, CQ, calling CQ, CQ, CQ. This is AP7ZMT located in Idaho calling CQ and standing by for a call." He waited 10 seconds or so and called CQ again. "CQ, CQ, CQ, calling CQ, CQ, CQ. This is AP7ZMT located in Idaho calling CQ and standing by for a call." In a few seconds someone was calling him.

"AP7ZMT this is DK19GF. How do you copy?"

"DK19GF this is AP7ZMT. Thanks for coming back. The name here is Walt, Whiskey Alpha Lima Tango. I am located in the northern panhandle of Idaho near the Canadian border. I will give you a signal report on the next go around. Over."

"Roger that Walt. I have you in Munich Germany at a 5 x 8. My name is Hans, Hotel America Norway Sierra. I am running a FTDX 5000 with about 1000 watts into a 2 element cubical quad antenna up at 55 feet. How copy? Over."

"OK Hans. You have a great signal into Idaho. 5 x 9 with great audio and armchair copy. I should tell you that I was stationed in Augsburg about 20 years ago while in the Army. I really enjoyed myself and visited Munich many times to attend beer fests and music festivals. Over."

"I am glad that you enjoyed your stay over here. The age here is 72 and I have been a ham since 1978. Were you a ham while you were in Germany? Over."

"No I didn't get licensed until about 20 years ago Hans. I did know a sergeant who was a ham and visited his station once. He is the man who got me interested in the hobby to begin. He helped me talk to my folks using a phone patch as long distance rates were quit high at the time. Over."

"Did you get to travel around Europe when you were here?"

"I did go to Amsterdam and London a few times and that was fun. Our barracks in Augsburg had a bar so we didn't have to go far to get a beer. Later I moved into an apartment in Longweid and I remember that we lived on the third floor and every week a delivery man would climb the stairs with two cases of beer for us. Then he would walk down to the truck and bring up more beer for the other resident. I am sure that he was in great shape after climbing stairs all day."

"Yes I am sure that he was in really good shape. Do you think that you will ever get back to Germany? If you do you should come see me. Over."

"Thanks Hans but I don't travel much any more. I live in a log cabin in the forest and only go to town once a week. In fact I travel so little, my 10 year old truck only has 30,000 miles. Over"

"I understand. My traveling days are over as well. That's why I like the radio. I can stay home and talk to people all over the world. Over"

"Yes it is a great hobby that's for sure. One reason I look forward to winter is that I can spend more time on the radio. I really enjoyed this QSO. So many contacts are just quick signal reports and that's it. But I am afraid that I have to go for now to meet a group on 75 meters. I am sure that there are lots of people who would like to contact you so I'll leave this frequency to you. Hope to talk to you again soon Hans. 73, This is AP7ZMT. Hope you make lots of good contacts today. I'll be clear on your final. "

"OK Walt it has been fun talking to you today. Check out my QRZ page and you can see some pictures of my station. Talk to you again soon I hope. 73 This is DK19GF clear and Q R Zed. North America."

Walt stood up and stretched his legs and put another log in the stove. He got a fresh cup of black coffee and sat down at the radio desk. He switched to the 130 foot end fed wire antenna and switched the tuner out of bypass. He switched bands on the amplifier and put it on standby and then tuned the radio to 3.988 Mhz. Nobody was on frequency yet so he recorded the details about his contact with Hans in his log book. He thought that he would send Hans a QSL card later. He had talked to Germany many times in the past but thought it would be nice to get a card from Hans.

QSL cards are the size of a post card with a ham's call sign and a picture of his place, antennas, or equipment. They include a space to write the date, frequency, signal report, mode, power level, and a short personal note. They certify that the contact has been made so that people can get different awards like DXCC (worked 100 countries), WAS (worked all States), etc. Most hams display their favorite cards on the wall of their shack. They also serve as a reminder of the QSO (conversation) years afterwards.

"Good Morning this is AU7PM. Is anybody on frequency?"

Walt put down his pen and pushed the switch on his desk microphone. "Good morning Frank. Raining over here. How is it going this morning? AP7ZMT."

Dennis broke in. "Good morning guys. AR7QRN."

"Morning Walt. Morning Dennis. It rained all night. 43 degrees here. How about you Dennis? (AU7PM)

"Light rain here but I have low noise level here." (AR7QRN)

"Hear any DX this morning Frank?" (AP7ZMT)

"I worked Italy, France and Finland on CW on 15 meters about an hour ago."(AU7PM)

CW is a tone about 1000 hz and this is sent in combinations of short dits and a little longer dashes using international morse code to send letters and numbers. CW signals take up less space on the band than SSB (single sideband) or AM (amplitude modulation) modes and generally they allow communication at farther distances than voice modes.

"I talked to Georgia and Texas this morning on 10 meters." (AR7QRN)

"I had a nice QSO with a station in Munich on 17 meters before coming down here. AP7ZMT."

" It's nice to see that the bands are opening up. AU7PM."

" Morning everyone. AN7HM."

" Morning Joe." (AU7PM)

" Good to hear you this morning." (AR7QRN)

" Hey Joe." (AP7ZMT)

"I'm getting tired of all the political ads on TV. Glad to know the elections are coming up soon." (AN7HM)

"I voted absentee since my vote didn't count last time." (AP7ZMT)

"So much fraud everywhere you looked but the attorney general and courts refused to consider it. AR7QRN for ID."

"President Joe Bama wasn't elected. He was installed to ruin the country and to personally take the blame. AM7DZ."

"No kidding, people think he is stupid and in mental decline. The truth is that he is doing exactly what they wanted him to do, and in that sense, he is doing a great job, AP7ZMT."

"Amen." (AU7PM)

"Morning everyone. Maybe this will be the end of the democrat party. AY7OM."

"I hope so. You can't find anything that he has done right in the last two years." (AR7QRN)

"I wonder if anything will change even if the Dems lose the house and the senate?" (AN7HM)

"We are all old and very lucky we don't have to watch the country go to hell for much longer." (AY7OM)

"If I was God I would have flushed the whole mess down the toilet by now. AM7DX."

"I know what you mean. Is everyone ready for winter?" (AU7PM)

" I am. The wood is in and the plow is on the truck. AN7HM."

"I am ready. (AR7QRN."

"I am ready too. We got our hay under cover yesterday. " (AM7DX)

"All I can say is that if there is anything you need you better get it now while you can. AP7ZMT."

"And before the price goes up. AU7PM."

"I am glad that I am not trying to buy a house or a car right now. The prices are insane." (AM7DX)

"I am really glad that I am retired right now. I don't know how I ever found the time to go to work. AY7OM."

"With band conditions getting better I am planning to spend more time on the radio and less time listening to politics and the news." (AR7QRN)

"Me too. AN7HM."

"Going hunting this weekend. Saw some nice bucks on the game camera." (AU7PM)

"Well good luck with that. Be sure and email us a picture if you get one." (AD7DX)

"OK Jeff will do." (AU7PM)

"Hey guys I am going to pull the plug. It's been fun to hear everybody this morning but I have to get up and stretch my legs. Going out with with Sparky to walk the dog. I'll say 73 and catch you guys later. AP7ZMT."

"OK Walt, have a good day. AR7QRN."

"73 Walt." (AN7HM)

" 3, see you in the morning." (AM7DX)

" See you Walt. AN7OM."

Walt turned off his radio and power supply and Sparky woke up and was eager to go for her walk. Walt decided to walk in the woods close to the boundary lines along the sides and back of the 1320 x 660 foot property. Walking in the woods, and not on the open roads or paths would keep them drier than walking out in the open. Once the snow came they wouldn't be able to walk this way until spring.

Because it was raining the skies were darker and the lack of sunlight was noticeable in the woods. The leaves that were still on the birch, cottonwood, and the alder trees but had lost much of their yellow and red colors. The tamarack needles were still on the trees and they were now a dull yellow color and no longer glowing like they had been a few weeks before. Along the way they encountered several upset squirrels who let them know that they were not happy to see visitors. Sparky barked at them even though she could not see them in the trees. A woodpecker could be heard nearby pecking loudly on a rotted tree hoping to find a meal. There were three different kinds of woodpeckers that lived in this forest, the downy, the hairy, and the pileated, and that was the largest and the model for Woody

Woodpecker in the cartoons. Since he could see exactly where the knocking sound was coming from he could not be sure which type of woodpecker he was hearing. In any case the woodpecker did not seem to care that Walt and Sparky were moving through the woods and he never missed a beat.

When they got close to the corner Walt caught a glimpse of something that didn't look right in one of the trees. When he got closer he could see that someone had put up a tree stand on his land. He had not been in this part of the property since the summer before last so he wasn't sure how long this was up. The property lines were clearly marked with orange survey tape and the tree stand was about 25 feet from the line. Sparky was busy sniffing the area around the tree while Walt took a closer look at the stand.

It was a pretty nice looking commercial tree stand made of green colored metal with a wide padded bench seat that could accommodate two hunters at the same time. It had two metal support bars under the seat, padded shooting rails, and two harnesses to safely hold the hunters. The metal ladder to access the shooting platform was 18 feet long and this would give the hunters a great view and keep the scent well above ground.

Walt was pissed. He had never given anyone permission to hunt on his land. He guessed that the tree stand had been installed by bow hunters because bow season was months earlier than rifle season, or maybe by poachers who did not care about hunting regulations anyway. He figured that whoever installed the tree stand just walked up the survey line, and noticed the nearby deer trail before he chose this spot for his tree stand.

Walt cut the walk short and took Sparky home and put her in the fenced yard behind the cabin and returned with some tools. It took him close to an hour to disassemble the stand and altogether it weighed about 60 pounds. Then he hauled it out to one of his tractor trails used for firewood gathering and brought it back to the cabin that afternoon with his tractor and stored it in the woodshed.

Walt didn't have any use for a tree stand now but thought it might be useful later. It was found illegally placed on his property and as far as he was concerned, it was finders keepers. If he ever found out who put the thing up in the first place they could expect some dental work instead of the return of their property. He knew it wasn't his neighbors to the south because they weren't hunters. He didn't think it was any of the other neighbors either because they all had property of their own.

Walt put the tractor under cover and let Sparky in the house. She was glad to see him of course and wondered why she had been excluded from the rest of the adventure. Walt checked his email and found that he had some more web work to do. One of the websites that Walt managed was owned by a couple who were toymakers. They had four new toys that they wanted to add to their website in time for the Holiday season. Unlike their other toys which were mostly wooden cars, boats, trucks, and blocks, the new toys were reproductions of popular American Folk toys that many young parents had never seen. The toys had to demonstrated using short online videos if they were going to sell. Each new toy would need to have its own web page with pictures, descriptions, and demonstration videos. Each new toy would have to be linked to their shopping cart and each new toy page had to be linked to their home page.

One of the new toys was a wooden toy acrobat that measured 13 inches high. The painted gymnast was suspended by twisted fishing line and appeared to be hanging from a high bar and suspended in a wooden frame. He was held in one hand and pointed vertically. When the bottom of the frame was given a pinch, the painted acrobat would jump over the "bar" to the other side. With a little practice and a lighter controlled pinch, the acrobat would land on the "bar" in a variety of trick positions. Sometime he would do the "spilts" with his legs. Other times he would get both toes caught in the bar and so on. With a little luck and technique he could do about 20 tricks. Historically this toy was called a jumping jack.

The next toy to be added was a spinning top. This style of top used a launcher so it did not require throwing skills. Young children could learn to spin the top in about four or five tries. The launcher was placed over the top, a short string had to have one end inserted through a hole in the stem of the top, the top was slowly turned until all of the string except for a loop at the end was wound on the stem. Then the launcher and top were held over a table or flat surface, all the string was quickly pulled out and away from the launcher, the launcher was lifted off the top and the top was spinning. Once spinning little colored paper circles resembling records could be placed on the stem of the spinning top so that the colors of the paper "records" blended until the top finally stopped spinning.

Another new toy to be added to the website was the dancing man. This was an articulated wooden man with swinging curved arms and moving legs that were attached at the knees with a wire joint to his feet with painted boots. A stick about 12 inches long was inserted into the back of the man. The toy was operated by sitting on a chair, inserting the tail of a thin wooden paddle under your leg, tapping the end of the paddle with a steady beat, and then lowering the man down until his feet touched the bouncing paddle and the man began to dance. With practice this toy could make anyone the life of the party. Historically he was called a limber jack.

One of the newest of the old toys to added to the website was called tiny tennis. It was a small tennis court that you held in one hand and volleyed a ping pong ball back and forth across the net. It was colored green with white lines and a white net made of gauze. Like the other toys it took practice and this toy was originally seen in a Charlie Chaplin movie,

The last of the new old toy ideas to be added to the website was called a flipperdinger. This was carved stick about 8 inches long that was held up to your mouth like a whistle. Near the end of the stick was a small dowel about one inch high that pointed straight up. The dowel was drilled with a hole in the center so that when you blew through a long hole in the horizontal stick, air would come out through the hole in the dowel. About five inches above the dowel with the drilled hole was a wire hoop that looked like a basketball hoop. A small styrofoam ball with a wire hook at the top and a stem of wire at the bottom which had been inserted through the ball.was placed into the hole in the dowel. The object of the toy was to blow through the carved stick causing the styrofoam ball to float above the small dowel and eventually hook the wire hook on the wire hoop above the dowel (before running out of breath)

Since the videos the toymakers had provided needed editing Walt estimated that this web work would take him four to five hours to complete. So in his mind Walt thought that he had made one hundred dollars or so by checking his email (even though this work had not been done). Walt liked counting his chickens before they were hatched and he liked doing this kind of easy work to supplement his retirement. He could do it whenever he wanted working from home while sitting in his underwear and without driving to town. There was no shipping to worry about and no sales tax to collect or pay. He was paid online with PayPal so his earnings were directly deposited into his bank account. His customers didn't know how to do this themselves and they were happy to find someone who would maintain their websites at a reasonable cost and in a timely manner.

Walt decide to go ahead and do their web work right away. He edited the four demonstration videos so that they were only two minutes long. He resized the photos of each toy and completed the four new web pages and linked each toy to the shopping cart. Then he linked the new pages to the home page and loaded everything up to their server. It took him a little over four hours as he had estimated and notified the couple that their new toys were online.

While he was doing this web work he couldn't get the tree stand out of his mind, He had been on the property for ten years and never had trouble with trespassers, poachers, or thieves but maybe the times were changing. He was distraught to think that big city crime was coming to the area and that maybe he should take security a little more seriously. Maybe he thought that he was immune to crime in his mountain homestead. Or maybe he was in denial and didn't want to think about this because he had never had a problem before. He had never bothered to lock the woodshop or the garage, even when he went to town.

Before he turned off his computer he decided to look on Online World for some driveway announcers. To his surprise these didn't cost a lot of money. For $35 he could buy a unit that had two wireless sensors that would work up to 400 feet away and ring an alarm inside the cabin. He didn't hesitate to click on the add to shopping cart button.

Then just for fun he searched for a home security camera system and couldn't believe what he found. These systems used to be expensive but they were certainly affordable now. For $176 he found a system with four 1080p indoor/outdoor weatherproof cameras, a 1 TB hard drive, with 80 feet of night vision, and motion alerts. He already had a spare monitor to go with this and the whole system would work with or without the internet. He couldn't help himself and added this to his cart.

Walt hated what the lockdowns and mandates had done to the country but he absolutely had learned to love the Online World business model. With just a few clicks, whatever you wanted was on its way. His debit card was on file so he could buy things without removing his wallet. And if he was unsatisfied he could return items easily for a full refund.

Walt powered down the computer fed Sparky, made dinner and streamed a spy movie to relax for the evening. The movie was OK but Walt kept thinking about home security and getting better prepared to defend his home. Walt used to believe that he never wanted to be more than 10 feet from a loaded gun. He had several revolvers, which were always kept loaded and a shotgun at the door. In addition he had a shotgun in the woodshop and garage and a .357 revolver in his truck. Whenever he went to town he usually had a small .357 in his coat.

Walt was lucky that he lived a State that had constitutional carry laws. Any adult could legally carry a weapon either in plain sight or concealed without the need for a concealed weapons permit. When this law was passed some people were concerned that it would lead to higher crime rates but the opposite occurred. Criminals had to assume that everyone was armed and capable of defending themselves.

This reminded him of the old joke where a cop stops an old lady who was speeding in her convertible on an Arizona highway. The cop walked up to the car and asked to see her license and registration. She hands this to him and he asked if she had any guns in the car. She tells him that she has a 9mm in her purse, a .38 special in the door, and a .44 magnum in the glove box. He was quite surprised to hear that she was so well armed and asked what the hell she was afraid of? The old lady replied, "Not a damned thing!"

That night Walt couldn't get to sleep and then he got an idea. He would start a local neighborhood net using CB radios so the neighbors could notify each other if they experienced any thefts or had seen any strangers or suspicious activity in the area. Walt didn't like nets on the ham bands but he had to listened to enough of them he knew how they should be run. He would get as many neighbors as possible to check in by radio every Sunday night from 6:30 – 7:00 to start with, and once everyone got used to this schedule they could talk to each other evenings to chat. They could look for things they wanted to buy or trade for, or advertise the things they had for sale. In other words they could network with each other.

The next morning before radio time Walt made some flyers describing the neighborhood CB radio net and offering to help people to shop for CB radios and low cost antennas. On the flyer Walt suggested that people consider powering their radios with batteries so that they would work during power outages and listed his phone number in case anyone had any questions. Over the next few days he planned to deliver some flyers to neighbors and post this information on the Flume Creek road community mail boxes on Rapid Lightning Creek Road and the bulletin board at the Country Store about 6 miles down the road. He thought the net would be slow to get started but once people knew about this, the net might become quite popular and a regular part of the neighborhood.

The Country Store was a local treasure and now had become a legend. It was started about 50 years ago as hillbilly convenience store. Over the years it added more products and services like showers, washers and dryers, pay phone, gas pumps, and propane refills. It was a place you stopped by on the way to and back from town. The current owners really made it special by offering a lot of great homemade food to take out or eat in. The food was so good they did a lot of catering and then the owner's son took over. He was an experienced and talented chef and he made the store even more popular by adding lots of high end menu items and more table space. The catering business exploded and people would drive for miles to eat lunch or dinner in the middle of a country store. The store had a north Idaho motif with some tables next to the beer coolers but the food was great and everybody loved the place. Where else could someone buy mouse traps, wasp spray, wine, and homemade lasagna? If you chose to eat at a table, you were likely to see people you knew shopping for beer and catfood. There was no other place like it.

CB (citizens band) radios operate on the 11 meter band (27 Mhz) and have 40 different channels. Most CB radios are AM but some are SSB. Depending on terrain, power level, and antenna they usually operate line of sight with a range of 3–20 miles. When conditions are favorable they can also skip signals off of the ionosphere and can communicate hundreds or even thousands of miles. Legally they are restricted to 5 watts and no license is required.

CB radios can be purchased for as little as $50 and antennas can be purchased for $20 and up for a 3 foot magnetic mount that can be easily attached to the roof of a car or the metal roof of a building. Larger antennas can be used to increase the range and they can be made at home to keep the cost down. Many hams got interested in the radio hobby by starting with CB transceivers. CB radios also work well to communicate on family farms or ranches where no cell service was available so these radios are quite popular.

Walt looked at the clock, added some wood to the stove, and got a fresh cup of coffee before he turned on the radio. He didn't have to change the frequency or antenna so he could start transmitting right away once he determined that nobody was using the frequency.

"This is AP7ZMT. Is anybody on frequency this morning?"

"I've been listening for 15 minutes or so and you are the first person I have heard so far. Good Morning Walt. This is AU7PM."

"Hey Frank. Good signal in here this morning. How's it going today?" (AP7ZMT)

"Pretty good The cats have been fed. A little cool this morning. 55 degrees in the house when I got up but it's warming up fast." (AU7PM)

"Heard the weather forecast and we might get snow this weekend. I was hoping it would hold off until after Thanksgiving. The big news here is that I found someone's tree stand on my property if you can believe that. Over." (AP7ZMT)

"You mean somebody put up a tree stand without permission?" (AU7PM)

"Roger that. I have no idea who did it or when they put it up. Needless to say I took it down. Over." (AP7ZMT)

"Was it homemade or commercial?" (AU7PM)

"It was a really nice metal tree stand with bench big enough for two hunters with a padded seat and shooting rest and an 18 footmetal ladder." (AP7ZMT)

"I can't believe that Walt. Good morning I have been listening for a few minutes. AN7HM."

"I couldn't believe it either. I took it down and put it in the woodshed. I am just hoping someone comes here to ask for it back." (AP7ZMT)

"I'd like to see that. Morning Walt. Morning Frank." (AN7HM)

" Morning Joe." (AU7PM)

"Morning Joe. The tree stand was in the back corner of my property. I figure that someone walked up the survey line to get there." (AP7ZMT)

"Some people either have a lot of nerve or no brains whatsoever. Oh I have some news for you guys. I heard my first Mayday call!" (AN7HM)

"I've never heard one. What happened? (AU7PM)

"Last Monday I turned on the radio about 2 in the afternoon. The radio was tuned to 80 and the band scope showed that the band was dead except for a weak station down at 3.7 Mhz. So I tuned down to see who it was and heard a Mayday call. I couldn't believe my ears. I kept listening and when he stopped transmitting I came back to him and gave my call." (AN7HM)

"Could he copy you? What was going on?" (AP7ZMT)

"Yes he was glad to hear me and said that he had been calling for awhile. It turns out that he and his wife and daughter were on a sailboat and the mast and antenna had been damaged in a storm the night before. His cell phone wasn't working and the auxiliary motor quit working. He was dead in the water and getting pushed toward shore, He was worried that their boat would be torn up on the rocks."

"So what did you do Joe? (AU7PM)

"I got his position which was 43 km south of Forks and I told him to stay on the radio and that I would notify the Coast Guard and get back to him in a few minutes. Then I broke into the maritime service net on 14.300 Mhz and relayed the information. He was off Ruby Beach in Washington State. Then Net control asked if there were any boats nearby but the closest was more that an hour away so he notified the Coast Guard and I went back down to 3.7 Mhz and told him that the Coast Guard had been notified and I stayed on frequency until they got there. Over. (AN7HM)

"Did you get the coordinates. I'd like to look that up on Google maps? (AU7PM)

"I've got them right here 47 degrees 42'39" N by 124 degrees 24'56"W AN7HM."

"How long did it take for help to arrive? AP7ZMT"

"A helicopter arrived in 30 minutes and a boat was there in about an hour. We had a nice chat until the boat showed up. His name was Carl. His call was VE17QM. They were from McCloud Lake British Columbia and the name of their sailboat was *Only For Sail*. His radio was only putting out 45 watts because of the damaged antenna. The boat was a 30 foot Moon Dancer. Needless to say he was very glad I picked him up and told me to expect a QSL card. AN7HM for ID."

"AU7PM for ID. Wow that's some story."

"That's pretty cool Joe. AP7ZMT for ID."

"I've been reading the mail. Way to go Joe! AY7OM."

"Thanks Ray. It was pretty exciting until I knew that they were safe. (AN7HM)

"I've never heard a Mayday call either but I called one in once on my two meter handheld. One of the neighbors had a slash fire run away on him and couldn't connect with his cell phone so I called Mayday on the Hoodoo Mountain repeater and a guy came back and took down the location and he called the fire department who sent up a couple of trucks."

"So many people today don't know anything about ham radio and can't imagine it being better than their cell phone."

"I'll bet that Carl guy never goes sailing again without a radio, and a spare radio just in case." AN7HM.

"This was a lot more fun today. I thought that we would be talking about the election results." (AU7PM)

"Those scum bags got their butts kicked. I thought it was great." (AP7ZMT)

"It's hard to imagine that a new congress can fix the damage that was done to this country in the last two years. AY7OM."

"Can you imagine letting 20 million illegals cross the border and thinking that was a good thing?" (AN7HM)

"I don't know anyone who was happy with any part of the Joe Bama administration."

"I would rather be governed by people who were chosen at random out of the phone book. Where do these people come from?" (AY7OM)

"At least now that the election is over maybe they'll take down all those campaign signs. They really bother me. Talk about littering." (AU7PM)

"The bummer is that the new people don't take over until January. So the current Congress still has a month and a half to destroy the country and steal as much as they can." (AN7HM)

"Got some interesting Covid news for you. Over 400 CDC employees have refused to get vaccinated. What does that tell you? (AY7OM)

"I'll bet that when the data is known the vaccine will have killed more people than all our wars put together. And now they are trying to get approval to vaccinate babies as young as 6 months old!" (AN7HM)

"That's a sobering thought Joe. There is a special place in hell for these control freaks. It's been fun this morning but I am going to have to sign off now. Got a few things to do. 73 Everybody. This is AP7ZMT. You guys have a good day and hope to see you in the morning."

"73 Walt. AU7PM"

"Talk to you late Walt AY7OM."

" Later Walt. AN7HM."

Walt powered down the radio and put another log in the woodstove. Sparky didn't care if it was raining. The radio was off and it was time to go for a walk. Besides she knew the smells were better in the rain and must have wondered if Walt knew this or not. They walked down the driveway and looked for a good place to install one of the driveway announcers when it arrived. Walt found a good spot where someone coming up the road would not see the sensor unit until they had already passed it. Then they walked up past the house site and found another good spot for the other sensor. By this time Sparky was pretty wet so they came back to the cabin to warm up and dry out.

Walt had been thinking about ways to show some of the more distant neighbors that they were in range of a CB radio. He positioned a tape recorder near his CB radio that would turn on and start recording anytime it heard a sound. Then after 20 seconds of silence it would stop recording and turn itself off. This would allow him to drive around the neighborhood and use the CB in his truck to transmit back to his cabin. He would indicate where he was calling from and move to another location. After trying this about 20 or more times he could return to the cabin and play back the recording get a good idea of the area that a CB could be expected to cover. If any neighbors were uncertain if they were close enough to have this work, he could loan them the CB radio out of the truck and a magnetic mount antenna to be sure that they were not wasting their money.

Snow finally arrived at Walt's cabin on Thanksgiving day. It was snowing hard enough that he thought it would stick and it would be several months before he could expect to see the ground again. There was something magical about the first good heavy snow of the year. It was so quiet you almost hear the snow flakes falling. Since it was a holiday there wasn't much traffic on the road and Walt thought it was a little like being inside one of those toy snow globes. Since he was prepared for winter he was totally stress free. The people who worked at the Schweitzer ski resort were pleased since the ski hill would be open soon and they could start drawing a paycheck. Of course the kids were excited too as were the hunters who could finally track the deer.

However anyone who didn't have their firewood in or their snow tires installed, was under a lot of stress. Also people who had to drive to be with family and friends for the holiday were not happy about the snow and ice on the road. It seemed that when winter started about half the people welcomed it, and the other half did not. But at the end of winter four months later, about everyone agreed that they were tired of snow and ice and could not wait for spring.

Walt did not have any plans to go anywhere until the following week. He had no interest in cooking a turkey but who said that you have to eat turkey on Thanksgiving anyway? His choices for dinner were a steak and potatoes or a homemade Pizza. He knew that Sparky would have chosen a steak dinner but he decided on Pizza, a nice warm comfort food perfect for watching the snowstorm.

The next morning Walt looked out the window and guessed that he had nearly a foot of snow on the ground. Sparky had to go outside to do her business but when he opened the back door she saw how much snow was on the ground and she wasn't sure if she really wanted to go outside or not. She eventually stepped out into belly high snow and then remembered just how much fun it could be. After running around a little and chomping at the snow she was more than ready to come inside. After making a fire and cooking breakfast Walt decided to check his email. He had no connection and then remembered one of the chores associated with winter. He had to put on his pack boots and stomp through the snow to clear the satellite dish with a broom before he could get online. He checked the local weather and saw that the Cascade mountain passes had almost three feet of snow which stranded many people who traveled to Seattle for Thanksgiving and now, were having a hard time getting back. Other than a few personal emails that needed to be answered he didn't spend much time online and turned his computer off for the day.

Then he turned his attention to winter's version of mowing the lawn, snow removal. It was a good idea not to bother with the driveway after the first snow because the frost was not in the ground yet and using a plow or the tractor's snow blower could actually tear up the road. So he shoveled the snow off of the steps and ran the walk behind snow blower in the yard. Snow blowers worked pretty well when the snow was cold and could throw the snow 20 feet or so. But if you tried to blow snow after it warmed up a little the snow coming out of the chute might only go five feet and resemble ice from a snow cone. Then it would be so thick and heavy that it would plug up the chute so it was a lot better to get this done while it was cold. It took Walt nearly an hour to clear the area by the cabin and buildings but it looked really good when this was done.

Walt had an early supper Sunday and was ready to launch the Rapid Lightning Creek Neighborhood CB Net. He had already heard from a couple of neighbors who had seen the flyers and didn't know what to expect. The net was supposed to run every Sunday night between 6:30 pm and 7:00 pm. He turned on his CB and didn't hear any stations on any of the 4o channels so he tuned the radio to channel 20. He was a little early and began transmitting at 6:15 pm.

"This is Walt, net control, looking for early check-ins to the Rapid Lightning Creek CB Net." Nobody came back so a couple of minutes later he tried again. "This is Walt, net control, looking for early check-ins to the Rapid Lightning Creek CB Net." He got a response.

"Walt, this is your neighbor Stan. Gloria and I are checking in. Good to hear you this evening. You have a good strong signal over here."

"OK Stan thanks for checking in. Hi to Gloria you are booming in here too. We'll try to get started at 6:30." " This is Walt, net control, looking for early check-ins to the Rapid Lightning Creek CB Net."

"Good evening Walt, Stan and Gloria. This is Robert and Nancy on the Gold Creek cut off road. Do you copy OK?"

"Yes Robert. Hi to Nancy. You are coming in fine. We'll get started in a few minutes."

"Count me in Walt, This is Steve up Flume Creek. Good to hear everyone tonight. Thanks for starting this net. I think it will be a lot of fun and a good chance to visit with the neighbors."

"OK Steve good to hear from you I am glad to see this kind of response for our first time out." It was 6:25 pm. "Calling for early check-ins to the Rapid Lightning Creek CB Net."

"We're in here too Walt. This is Tony and Sherri. We are about 2 miles from the Country Store. How is our signal?"

"You are not quite as strong as the rest but perfectly readable, Thanks for checking in. We are just about ready to get started. Any more early check-ins for the Rapid Lightning Creek CB Net?" No Other early check-ins were heard.

"OK let's get started. This is the Rapid Lightning Creek CB Net. We are going to meet on this channel every Sunday night from 6:30 pm to 7:00 pm. Are there any more check-ins before we begin?"

"We're in here as well Walt. This is Mary and Beth down the road from you on the Snipes Road."

"OK Mary I have you and Beth checked in. Good signal over here. Are there any more check-ins? Nothing was heard.

"Thanks everyone for checking in. Tonight we have Stan and Gloria on Rapid Lightning Road, Robert and Nancy on the Gold Creek cut off road, Steve up Flume Creek Road, Tony and Sherri on lower Rapid Lightning Creek Road, and Mary and Beth on Snipes road. The first thing I would like everyone to realize is that because we are on the radio anyone can be listening so be careful not to say anything like, We are going to town tomorrow morning and we always leave our house unlocked. Just kidding, but you get the idea. So lets only use our first names or you can use a CB handle instead if you like. The next thing to mention is that I would like you all to send me an email with your name(s), address, and telephone numbers so that we can contact each other if necessary. I am also a ham radio operator and my email is AP7ZMT at gmail.com. It doesn't sound like any of you people need any help but if you ever have any questions about radios or antennas don't hesitate to contact me. Also I wanted to mention that if you like, you might consider leaving your radios on this channel from time to time so that you can talk with each other more often. And I suggest that you consider running your radios on battery power so that they will work during a power outage. With that lets hear from each of you in the order that you checked in. You don't have to say your name or say over when you are done transmitting but it helps if you do, to avoid confusion, at least until we learn each others voices. So come in Stan and Gloria, tell us what is on your minds. Over"

"This is Stan and Gloria, nice to meet everyone. We are located on Rapid Lightning Creek Road near Walt and have lived here for about 5 years. We want to thank Walt for starting this net and we think it will be a great asset to the community. Also we should mention that we have quite a few chickens so if you are looking for home grown eggs, give us a call. Back to net control. Over."

"Ok Stan. Once I get everyone's contact info I will forward this to you all so that you have each others email addresses and phone numbers. Back to you Robert and Nancy.Over."

"This is Robert and Nancy on the Gold Creek cut off road. We have been here over 20 years and really appreciated seeing the road get paved. If you ever drove on the potholes connected with gravel, you'll know what we are talking about. Nice to meet everyone tonight. Back to net control. Over.

"Very good Robert. I only had to put up with the gravel the first year that I was here. Big improvement. Cut 15 minutes off the trip to town. It's you turn Steve. Over."

"Yes this is Steve. I am about 2 miles up Flume Creek. I wish we would have had this net last year when we are all threatened with evacuation from the Trestle Creek fire. I'll be contacting you Stan about some eggs. I usually have firewood for sale if anyone is interested. Back to net. Over"

"Real Good Steve. I am sure that you'll be able to find some customers for your wood. Tony and Sherri, tell us what is on your minds. Over."

"Good to hear all of you. We weren't sure if we were too far away but copy everyone just fine so far. I like the idea of leaving the radios on often so that we can talk to each other more than just once a week. Over"

"Yes I think this will be very useful for all of us. Mary and Beth, you are last on the list. Go ahead. Over."

" This is Mary and my partner Beth. We are located on the Snipes Road and agree that this net should be great. It is nice to meet some new friends. Over."

"Real Good. Glad to hear that everyone can hear each other. Are there any late check-ins? This is Walt, net control for the Rapid Lightning Creek CB net. Over"

"I've been listening. Got here a little late. This is George and my wife Carla. We live up on the Moonfire road. Over."

"Well glad you could make it George, Did you copy my email address?"

"Yes Walt, I got that part. Nice to hear everyone. We'll be on time next week. Over."

"OK I just wanted to thank everyone for participating in our neighborhood net. As soon as I get your emails I'll send everyone names and contact information for net contributors. Always happy to help with questions and concerns. With that I'll close the net for tonight but of course you are all encouraged to stay on frequency and visit with each other. Really appreciate you all tonight. The more regular participants we get on board the more useful this net will be. We can talk about anything you want. We can share information about forest and slash fires, road conditions, lost pets, area wildlife, speed traps, suspicious activity, neighborhood thefts, things for sale, local events, contractors, builders, snow removal, anything you want. I'll leave you tonight and sign out. Hope to hear from you all next Sunday on this channel and I'll say 73 to all. This is something ham radio operators say to each other that means best wishes. 73 This is net control signing off."

After Walt signed he could hear that a few people were staying on frequency and chatting with each other. Lots of people made new friends tonight and he could not be more pleased with the turnout for this first night of the neighborhood net. Walt left his radio on just to "read the mail" (listen in) while he got up to let Sparky out for one last time before she went to bed.

Within the next few days everyone's emails were in and Walt made a contact list to share with everyone. He reminded people that some subjects were best covered by email or telephone for security reasons. Also he mentioned the idea that nobody owned the frequency and sometimes channel 20 would be busy so they should have an alternate. He suggested that their alternate channel simply be the date. If it was the first of the month the alternate frequent would be channel 1, and so on.

Also he pointed out that they may encounter a kid or other loudmouth who would try to interfere with people by jamming, swearing, or playing music on the frequency. If this would happen Walt suggested that everyone turn off their radio for 30 minutes and then turn on their radios to the alternate channel. By this time the jammer, having heard nothing but dead air, would be off the radio and they could all communicate as usual. If the alternate channel was busy then they could use the channel above that.

The next day there was about 3 inches of new wet snow on the ground so it wasn't worth the time to run the snow blower. The snow on the driveway from Thanksgiving day had been driven on several times so it wasn't worth dealing with that either. So after shoveling the steps and sweeping the snow out of the satellite dish Walt took Sparky out to play in front of the cabin. They played a game called snow cookie where walt would make a snowball and throw it so that Sparky could chase it. When she caught up with it she would chomp it and there would be nothing left of the snowball. After about a dozen snowballs Sparky had enough and wouldn't bother to chase them down any more. It was a good way to see that she got some exercise on a cold winter day since this time of year their walks got shorter and shorter. She was happy to settle down by the woodstove and soak up a little heat.

Walt turned on his computer and connected to the internet to check out a few news sites just for fun. It wasn't fun at all since all the headlines were gloom and doom. There were more supply chain issues, bare shelves in some grocery stores, another two hundred thousand illegals crossed the border last week, LGBTQ grooming of young school children, infanticide where 3 more States said it was OK to kill babies after they were born, and the government was establishing a ministry of truth, Walt couldn't take it anymore and clicked on Spotify to listen to some classic rock. At least that brought his blood pressure down. He couldn't believe that he had fallen for it again. Legacy media was harmful to his health. Like a junkie, he just couldn't kick the habit.

That afternoon he heard a truck coming up his driveway. When it pulled in the yard he could see it was the UPS truck. He put on his coat, left barky Sparky in the cabin and went out to meet the truck in the yard. His Online World order had

48

arrived with his security system and driveway announcers. He thanked the driver for coming up in the snow and made sure that the driver had his phone number so that if the road was bad he could call and Walt would meet him at the road. The driver thought this was a great idea and wished that all the people on his route were that thoughtful.

As soon as Walt got back in the house he opened the package and examined his new toys, After reading the manual he cleared out a space in the radio room for the hard drive and his spare monitor. It looked like he only had enough cable to install two cameras for now but he would see how much more he needed and get it ordered right away.

The next morning Walt installed the driveway announcers on the upper and lower driveway and two cameras out the front door. Since he didn't get much company it would be awhile before he could try them out. Even though it was still November having some new toys made it seem like Christmas.

Chapter 3. December

"I'm always waking up to bad news in the morning
Yeah there's bad news going round
I get the feeling that we're not gonna make it
Cause our time's running out"
Warbly Jets

After completing his morning chores Walt got online to check his email. He had two requests for more information about gold mines and forwarded the owners names to the interested parties. He also had an email from the Pacific Northwest Remote Viewers Group. They wanted Walt to post some new target coordinates for the month and to post results from the last month's targets on their website.

Walt got started doing their web work a few years ago. He knew a little about remote viewing and had taken the Major Ed Dames Technical Remote Viewing home study course for two years. He knew that remote viewing did work, and almost anyone could learn to do this, to some degree, but had not practiced this himself for years.

It is important to understand that for most people, remote viewing is not viewing at all. This should have been named remote knowing. Clairvoyants such as Nostradamus, Edgar Cayce, and Ingo Swann were natural remote viewers who could see pictures in their minds, but most remote viewers cannot really see pictures in their minds. Instead they can learn to perceive details about people, places, and events in the past, present, and future, hence knowing and not viewing. Major Ed Dames refers to remote viewing as an attention management system.

Ingo Swann was an artist and clairvoyant who taught the military how to teach people how to do this when he worked with the Stanford research project and the Stargate project. If you ever get a chance to see some of his paintings of deep space I think that you would agree that they look like photographs taken from the Hubble telescope but they were created before the Hubble. In any case the military spent a lot of time working with Ingo Swann and perfecting remote viewing protocols.

Nobody know exactly how this really works especially when we are looking at people, places, or events in the future but it is often explained as retrieving information from the Hall of Records (aka Akashic records) which are said to contain information about everything that has ever been or ever will be. Remote viewing does have two major limitations. You can't usually retrieve details about numbers or time by using basic remote viewing techniques.

Remote viewers, however can narrow down information about time by discovering if something happens before or after a known event. Also some remote viewers have had some success determining numbers by using associative remote viewing techniques which assign objects like fruits and vegetables, for example, to represent numbers. But most remote viewers believe that the reason that time and numbers are so elusive is that these are not important enough to catalog in the Hall of Records. Because Nostradamus was also an astrologer he was able to use astrology to help him pinpoint time in many of his predictions.

Basically remote viewing is done in the following manner: First a manager or handler decides what information he is looking for and creates a target on a clean piece of paper something like; "(8734/2197) Noahs Ark / present location".

Then the paper is put in a sealed envelope. On the front of the envelope the target numbers are written in two lines, one above the other on the center of the envelope. 8734 on the top line and 2197 on the bottom line. These numbers are totally random and used to identify the target. The envelope is then put aside.

Next a remote viewer (or viewers) who have never seen the envelope, and do not know what the target is, sit alone without anything on the table except a few blank sheets of paper. Then the remote viewer spends about 15 minutes or so trying to clear his mind and relax using meditation or musical tones to lower his brain wave state. When ready, the remote viewer puts his pen to the top left corner of the paper and the manager reads the two target numbers aloud. The remote viewer repeats these numbers as he writes them down, 8734 on the top line and 2197 below it. Immediately, the remote viewer puts his pen to the paper and produces an ideogram. This is an automatic small scribble produced by the subconscious. Sometimes the shape of the ideogram can give a hint about the target and sometimes it does not. But this odd shaped doodle represents the target.

At this point the remote viewer touches his pen to the ideogram to connect with the target and silently asks himself a series of questions about the target and writes down the first thing that comes to his mind about each of the following; textures, colors, smells, tastes, temperatures, sounds, dimensions, and hardness (or softness). This must be done quickly and without thinking. Finally the viewer records how he would feel if he was actually at the target by using only one word. At anytime during the session the remote viewer can touch his pen to the ideogram to reconnect with the target.

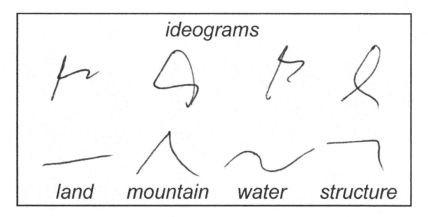

After this is complete the remote viewer produces some kind of rough sketch depicting the target. At this point the remote viewer gives his work to the manager who does his best to make sense out of the data and come up with possible conclusions about the target. Complex targets may require multiple sessions from multiple viewers to glean useful information.

Obviously there is a lot more to remote viewing than this but this is how a basic session works. Most remote viewing targets take multiple sessions and more sketches from different perspectives including interior views, and details about the target's motion and rotation to fully understand the target. With practice, remote viewers can work alone without the need for a manager to cue targets or analyze the results.

When people had questions about remote viewing Walt would suggest that they take a home study course from Courtney Brown at the "Farsight Institute" or Ed Dames at "Learn Remote Viewing" to prove to themselves that remote viewing works.

Walt knew from experience that the data was almost always valid and if something went wrong with a session it was usually in the analysis phase. For example if a remote viewer perceived that the target was colored yellow and shaped like a hot dog was it a banana or a yellow submarine? By examining the size, hardness, and taste perceptions this would makes it easier to make this determination.

It didn't take long for Walt to update the Pacific Northwest Remote Viewers Group website. He got this done in less than an hour and would only bill them $25. He tried his best to keep his customers happy and same-day-service was a good way to do this.

Walt put a couple of logs in the woodstove, and got a fresh cup of coffee and sat down at the radio. He was a little early for radio time but he turned the radio on 3.988 and began to transmit. "Q R Zed, Q R Zed, is anyone on frequency this morning? AU7ZMT."

He didn't have to wait or call again. "Hey Walt just got back from checking out the upper bands. Pretty dead so far. How is it going this morning? AU7PM."

"Quiet here this morning. Just finished doing some web work and thought I'd get on the radio. 28 degrees here but no moisture in the forecast today. What's going on over there?" (AU7ZMT)

"Got your email about the CB net. Sounds like a good idea and that you are off to a good start." (AU7PM)

"Yes I never thought I would get excited about Chicken Band Radios but I think it will be a good way to meet the neighbors. Six check-ins the first night. We'll see how many we get in the next few weeks but I can see that with more people I'll have to extend the hours. Over" (AU7ZMT)

"What are the hours now? (AU7PM)

"Went 30 minutes last time and then closed the net and encouraged everyone to stick around for a round table. Listened for awhile and don't know how long people were on. Over." (AU7ZMT)

"I think that it is a good way to do it, keep the net short and then turn it into a roundtable." (AU7PM)

"Roger that, the important thing is to get people used to using their radios. AU7ZMT."

"Morning Guys. Good signals this morning. AY7OM"

"Morning Ray. What's new? (AU7PM)

"That I was robbed yesterday." (AY7OM)

"What happened Ray? (AU7ZMT)

"I got gas yesterday. That's what happened. Cost $160 to fill up my truck." (AY7OM)

"Things are looking up now that Joe Bama is president. Food prices are up, inflation is up, interest rates are up, and energy prices are up." (AU7PM)

"You're right Frank. Things are looking up. AY7OM."

" We might have won the house and the Senate last month but we'll be stuck with President Alzheimer for two more years." (AU7PM)

"Americans will suffer from his so called leadership years after he is gone. (AU7ZMT)

"I am really glad I have never posted anything on social media now that the Ministry of the Truth is looking over our shoulders." (AY7OM)

"I have cancelled my accounts since they started this. Good thing we have ham radio. AR7QRN."

"I think that's what they wanted. If they can't kill you with the vaccine, they can shut you up. Morning Dennis." (AU7PM)

"Morning Dennis. Good signal this morning. AY7OM."

"Morning Dennis. What's the temperature over there? " (AU7ZMT)

"Twenty Three here now. Had a clear night last night. Got my brakes fixed on the car yesterday. The parking break was toast but now the car will go forward and backwards!" (AR7QRN)

"Were you able to fix this yourself? AU7PM"

"Sure did Frank. Checked it out on YouTube and it was an easy fix once I got it apart." (AR7QRN)

"Anybody work any DX lately? (AU7PM)

"I made a quick contact with Bulgaria the day before yesterday on 15 meters. Got a 5x7 report. He was 5x9 here with a small amp and a 3 element yagi." (AY7OM)

"What time was that Ray?" (AU7PM)

"About 10:45 local time. Over." (AY7OM)

"I plan to spend some more time on the radio now that I am in hibernation mode for the winter" (AP7ZMT)

"Know what you mean about hibernation mode. The days are getting shorter and shorter. It's hard not to sleep in" (AU7PM)

"I heard on the news that New York City spends $30,000 a year on each public school student but only about half are proficient in reading or math when they graduate. Do you believe that? AR7QRN."

"Maybe if they weren't spending so much time teaching them that there were over a hundred genders, and that men can give birth to a child, there would be some time to teach them how to read." (AY7OM)

"For $30,000 they could give each student a private tutor." (AP7ZMT)

"Our tax dollars at work. Anybody who has their kid in a failing public school isn't doing them any favors. AU7PM"

"Finally got my first copy of CQ magazine yesterday." AP7ZMT)

"How do you like it? (AU7PM)

"I think that I'm going to like it better than QST but time will tell. Lots of contest info, not near as many ads, some QRP radio plans, 6 meter stuff, RTTY, international short wave frequencies, and even a cartoon. And there was a story about some young hams with a picture of a 15 year old boy from Peru running his radio at home while wearing a mask." (AP7ZMT)

"Are you kidding me? (AU7PM)

"I can scan it and email it to you if you want." (AP7ZMT)

"No, I don't want to think that anyone is that stupid." (AU7PM)

"So much for public education." (AR7QRN)

"Has anybody read *The Real Anthony Fauci* by Robert F. Kennedy Junior? The subtitle tells the story. I have it right in front of me. It reads Bill Gates Big Pharma and the Global War on Democracy and Public Health. It proved that Fauci and a few other NIH scientists have been making Big Pharma a fortune for fifty years." (AY7OM)

"I have heard nothing but good about the book. It has something like 2100 foot notes. Over." (AP7ZMT)

"Remember those 15,000 pages of vaccine data that the drug companies wanted to keep secret for 75 years? Now we are finding out why. They knew in the first few months that it wasn't safe or effective and went ahead with it anyway. The U.S. had the worst body count and the highest death rates of any country in the world. AY7OM."

"I heard they made over 100 Billion dollars selling vaccines to the government. I always wanted to get in the drug business. (AR7ORN)

"The drug business I always wanted to be in was coffee. I can't believe how much people pay for coffee these days. AM7DX."

"Morning Jeff, it's not just the money. Some people wait in line, idling their cars for 30 minutes until they get their fix." (AP7ZMT)

"Morning Jeff. Speaking of fixes, I am going to get another cup." (AU7PM)

"Morning Jeff, How much snow do you have on the ground? AY7OM"

"We had about 16 inches but the rain has taken it down to under a foot now." (AM7DX)

"Well now that December is here I am going to sign off and order a Christmas present, for me. Over." (AP7ZMT)

"At least that way you'll get what you want. What are you shopping for? AR7QRN."

"I'll tell you all about it next time. Anyway 73 to all and hope that everybody has a good day. We'll be clear and catch you later.. AP7ZMT.

"73"

"73"

"Later Walt. AM7DX."

Walt turned off his radio and booted up his computer. He had been looking at several similar units online and finally decided on the one he wanted. You know what they say about boys and their toys. Walt decided on the Desert Fox Automatic Gold Panning Machine.

He had stockpiled about 10 yards of sand that he dug from the sandbar along his creek frontage and he knew that it contained some fine flour gold. He also knew that if anyone found out about this, it would be big trouble for everyone. They don't call it gold fever for nothing. If anyone knew that he was taking gold out of the creek drainage he would have more than just a few fishermen to deal with.

Even in Idaho you had to have a permit to mine whether it was on your own property or not. Besides the local authorities, the State Fish and Game Dept. and the EPA would have something to say about this. So Walt had kept his mouth shut despite the fact that he had been thinking about this since he first saw a few colors in his gold pan.

The Desert Fox Automatic Gold Panning Machine was designed to capture extremely fine gold. The unit consisted of a a water proof plastic tub about 24" x 20" x 15" deep. Above the tub sat a round gold catching wheel with seven separate spirals that pick up gold seven times with each rotation of the wheel at up to 105 rotations per minute. The spirals run from the outer edge of the wheel to a hole in the center of the wheel. The spiral wheel can be adjusted to operate up to 80 degrees above the tub or at lower angles if desired. A small 12 volt motor rotates the wheel while water is pumped from the tub into the wheel. Gold works its way to the center of the irrigated rotating wheel gets deposited in a small cup. The excess material dumps out of the bottom of the wheel and is directed away from the water filled tub. This works well in the desert because the water in the tub is recycled. Walt figured that he could put the whole unit in his five foot Otter plastic sled so that he could do this in the comfort of his cabin without making a mess. The panning machine would be fed a cup of sand at a time so this wouldn't be fast but it should be fun and if he was lucky, profitable.

He planned to tell the guys on the radio about this but he wasn't planning on telling anyone where the material came from. The whole unit only weighed thirty pounds and sold for $435 with free shipping so Walt figured that it would pay for itself sooner or later. Walt had panned gold the old fashioned way in Colorado and Montana and looked forward to a less labor intense method of gold recovery. After re-reading the info about the machine he clicked on the "Buy Now" button and wished himself a Merry Christmas.

Walt hadn't been down to check his mail for a few days so he put on his pack boots. These goofy looking oversize boots were often seen in Sandpoint during the winter. The bottoms were made of rubber that was usually about three inches high. The upper part of the boot was leather. They had removable liners and were great for snow, ice, and mud. Half the time Walt didn't bother to lace them up tightly and he thought of them as a North Idaho slippers.

Walt's mailbox was at the bottom of his driveway on Rapid Lightning Creek road. He seldom got anything important in the mail so he didn't feel the need to check his mail everyday. Anytime somebody sent him money it was usually directly deposited into his bank account or via PayPal. Sparky was never allowed to go down to the county road unless Walt was with her and she always enjoyed the short walk and discovering new smells. Because the driveway was on a hill Walt usually took a ski pole in case the road was icy. When they got to the mailbox all he found was a couple of bills and some advertisements by some of the local businesses. Then he remembered that he had to pay his property tax by December 20. Idaho property tax bills are due June 20 for the first half and December 20 for the second half. If someone cannot pay this, they can delay payment for up to three years without fearing the seizure of their property. When he bought his twenty acres the taxes were very reasonable but over they years they increased to $1500 per year. Part of this was because of the improvements that he had made but the other factor was the number of new people moving to the area causing real estate prices to rise. Idaho was now the second fastest growing State. Lots of people agreed that Idaho is what America used to be.

Walt and Sparky spent a lot of time together and the only thing that would make her a better dog would be if she could play checkers or cribbage to help pass the time. She was young and there was still time to learn a few new tricks. Sparky loved to lie down on the carpet in the radio room and didn't seem to mind the noise, static, and occasional screeching sounds produced by the radio. In fact over time she had learned to recognize some of the voices that she heard almost every day.

That night Walt decided not to stream a movie he normally did on Saturday night but to spend some time watching videos instead. He liked BCP (Black ConservativePatriot), Amazing Polly, and a few others. He also liked to watch videos about gold panning, firearms, and of course ham radio. He used to be a big fan of the NFL but once the kneelers disrespected the flag he swore off pro football and would only look at college football games or MMA whenever he watched sports.

When Sunday morning came Walt tried to catch up on a few chores like doing dishes, laundry, and bringing in firewood before it was time for church. That's what he called listening to the Alex Jones show on 9.350 Mhz on one of his shortwave receivers. He liked Alex Jones because he was usually way ahead of the legacy media and sometimes he would break a story five years before anyone else. Most of the conspiracies he talked about turned out to be true.

After the show was over he had time to take care of Sparky, make himself supper, and get ready for the Rapid Lightning Creek CB net. At 6:15 he turned on the CB set to channel 20 and began to transmit. "This is Walt are there any early check-ins for the Rapid Lightning Creek CB net?" to his surprise somebody came right back.

"This is Robert and Nancy. We're ready to go.'

"That's great Thanks for checking in. Is there anyone else who would like to check-in tonight. Over."

"We are here too Walt. This is Stan and Gloria."

"Very good guys. Glad to have you in here."

"I'm here too Walt. This is Steve up Flume Creek."

" Sounds good Steve. We should have a good group tonight. We'll get started in a few minutes. Is there anyone else who would like to check in?"

"This is Scott down by the store. Do you copy me OK?"

"Sure do Scott. Thanks for checking in."

"Tony and Sherri are here too Walt."

"Real good. We'll get going in a few minutes."

"This is Tom up Flume Creek. Count me in too."

"OK Really loud signal over here."

"Mary and Beth are too. Good Evening Walt."

"Really good crowd tonight. Thanks everyone. We'll get started pretty quick."

"This is Fly Boy. I am also located down the road by the PR Store. How copy? Over."

"Good signal here. Are you a pilot?"

"I take pictures of people's places with a drone, mostly for realtors. Over."

"Hey that sounds fun. Glad to have you in here tonight."

"We are in here too. This is George and Carla. Over."

"Got you in here. Is there anyone else who would like to check-in to the Rapid Lightning Creek CB net tonight? Nothing was heard. "I guess that's it for now. First I'd like to thank everyone for participating and mention to Scott, Tom, and Fly Boy to please email me your name, address, and telephone number when you can. My email address is AP7ZMT at gmail.com. I am also a ham radio operator and that is my ham call. Is there anyone else before we get started? Over."

"This is George and Carla up Moonfire road. We just wanted everyone to know about the burglaries up Trapper Creek road. Has everyone heard about this?

"No George I haven't heard of this. Tell us more. Over" Walt seemed anxious and wanted to hear more details.

"We heard about this down at the store. Two cabins were broken into and some things were stolen. Both were owned by snowbirds who left for the winter and when a neighbor saw snowmobile tracks in their driveways he went to check things out and found the doors were kicked in so he called the Sheriff who came up to investigate. The owners were notified but they were both in Arizona. The neighbor temporarily fixed their cabin doors but cannot say what was taken. The Sheriffs Dept is not releasing that information. Over."

Walt responded. "Thanks for telling us this George. This is one of the purposes of our net, to share information so that in some cases we can defend ourselves and our property. Hopefully this is an isolated incident but it reminds us all to keep our eyes open. I wanted to mention that with more people joining the net we will try and run the net a little longer in the evening. What I would like to do is let everyone have a chance to speak to the net and then to turn it into a roundtable. A roundtable format allows everyone to talk to the group and then to turn the conversation over to the next person in the order that they have checked in without turning the radio back to net control after every transmission. I would like to see each person have at least two turns at the microphone and after that people can stay on frequency and chat as long as they want. Are there any questions or comments for the net?

Walt waited for a moment and having heard nothing he said "OK, then lets start the roundtable chit chat. The order will be first Robert and Nancy, then Stan and Gloria. After that it goes to Steve, then Scott, Toni and Sherri, Tom, Mary and Beth, Fly Boy, George and Carla, and then back to me. After that we'll go again in that order for at least one more time around. Go ahead Robert and Nancy. Over."

"This is Robert and Nancy. Not much going on here. According to Farmers Almanac we are supposed to have a cold winter, especially in early January. Over to San and Gloria."

"I never could understand how the Almanac was more accurate than the national weather service. At least they say that they are. The coldest it's been since we got here was 23 degrees below zero. Over to Steve."

"I haven't been here that long but anything below zero is cold enough for me. Question for Fly Boy, how far will your drone go and how long can it fly on a battery charge? Over to Scott."

"Hello everyone. Nice to meet you all. I am really excited about meeting you. I don't get up the road very often but I have heard that the side roads can get pretty bad during mud season. Back to Toni and Sherrie. You must live pretty close to me. I am only a quarter mile up from the store."

"We must be pretty close to each other. We are on the right hand side of the road just past the Johnson place. We think the net will make the winter more fun. Over to Tom."

"This is Tom. I am about a half mile up Flume Creek and I can tell you that during mud season I park near the mailboxes and walk in because I don't like chaining up in the mud. Over to Mary and Beth."

"Hello every one. Beth and I are looking for a contractor to build an addition to our house. We would like to find someone that lives in the Rapid Lightning area. If anyone has a suggestion please let us know. Over to Fly Boy."

"Hello everyone. Nice to meet you. To answer Steve's question I can fly my drone about 5 miles, and take pictures of the site and safely return home on a fully charged battery. I can see from the controller what the drone sees, and can fly 500 feet above the ground. If the drone runs low on a battery charge, it will return to me automatically. Normally a full charge lasts up to 40 minutes.. Back to Walt"

"Wow that sounds really fun. I am sure you'll have lots of customers once the word gets out. Who wouldn't want some overhead pictures of their place. I built my cabin myself and can't suggest any contractors. Back to Robert and Nancy."

"I can't think of any contractors who I would recommend to anyone but if someone knows of a local tree climber we would like to hear about them. We have a couple of trees close to the house that need to be cut from the top down. Over to Stan and Gloria."

"We know two local contractors and would recommend either of them. One is Rick Higgens and he has done some work for us. The other is John Casey and we hear that he is pretty good as well. Both advertise in the yellow pages. If you can't find their numbers let us know and we'll get these for you. Over to Steve."

"Thanks for the info about your drone. It sounds like a good one for sure. I'll contact you later in the year. I would like to have some video of the place to send back to some of the relatives. Back to Scott"

"The drone sounds very fun. It would have been nice last year to send up and take a look at the forest fire on lunch peak. I do a lot of fishing and always thought it would be fun to have a drone to drop the lure in an area where I can't get the bait. Over to Toni and Sherri."

"I've thought about that too. Also might be useful to look for elk just before hunting season. Also Walt, we are interested in getting into ham radio and would appreciate your help and advice. How much does this cost? Over to Tom."

"Scott, I have never tried fishing with a drone but I do have a remote controlled boat that works pretty well if you can keep it out of the weeds. The line is attached with Velcro and when you get a strike the line breaks away from the boat and you can play the fish. It makes fishing fun even if you aren't catching anything. Back to Mary and Beth."

"Thanks Stan and Gloria for the contractor suggestions. We'll be in touch if we have trouble finding their numbers. Obviously we are looking for some who could get the work done next summer before the rains come in the fall. Over to Fly Boy"

"I can tell you that during last year's fire, it was prohibited to fly a drone in the area because it might endanger the helicopters and aircraft dumping water on the fire. Also as long as you were not harassing the elk, it would be useful to locate them just before hunting season. Back to Walt."

"Toni and Sherri, give me a call and you two can come over to see the shack and I'll give you a chance to see ham radio in action. I am mostly interested in HF Single Sideband and this can regularly contact people all over the country and sometimes all over the world. You'll have to get licensed but this isn't very hard as all the questions and answers are published in the study guides. As far as cost goes a person could get started with used equipment and a homemade antenna for $500 or so. But like any hobby you can spend a lot more than that if you want. Also I would suggest that you both get licensed because then you can talk with each other at much longer distances than CB radio. Anyway give me call anytime you want to play radio. With that I am going to pull the plug for tonight and I want to thank you all for making this net possible. If you have any friends or neighbors who might be interested please invite them to join in. Wish you all the best and I encourage you to stay on frequency after I sign off and visit among your selves. It's been fun. I'll say 73 and this is Walt signing off and going QRT. That's ham radio talk for going off the air. Take care and see you next week. Over."

Walt signed off but left his radio on to see how many people continued to visit and exchange information with each other. He was please about the growth in the net and especially glad to hear about the burglaries up trapper Creek. Walt didn't get the newspaper and might not have heard about this except for the net.

The next morning after lighting a fire in the woodstove and letting Sparky out, Walt turned on his tablet computer to watch the Spokane KHQ channel 6 news on their website. He noticed it was December 7 and he expected to hear that it was Pearl Harbor Day. Instead the local news had been pre-empted by the NBC national news feed. Overnight there had been a massive eruption of Kilauea, the Hawaiian volcano. This was the most active of the five volcanoes that make up the big Island of Hawaii. Kilauea had been acting up for years and erupted almost continuously 1983 – 2018 completely destroying over 700 homes, two towns, Kalapana and Kaimu, in addition to Hawaii's largest freshwater lake. During this time lava completely filled Kapoho Bay and created new lava land one mile into the sea. The volcano is thought to be over 200,000 years old and emerged above sea level nearly 100,000 years ago. Its magma plumbing system extends from the surface more than 60 km deep into the earth.

This recent eruption was bigger than anyone had seen before with explosions emitting ash up to 60,000 feet in the air, 30,000 feet higher than before. Although this happened during the night, the video coverage was spectacular but soon observers and reporters realized that this was far more than an ordinary light show. It was dangerous. Flowing lava was pouring into the ocean and the steam it created was hot enough to melt your skin. This caused littoral explosions that occur when hot lava meets the ocean and looks and smells like Atomic bombs with rock fragments everywhere. Nearby boats in the water were set on fire. And the sulfur dioxide made the air so bad it was hard to breathe and very dangerous because the hot steamy air mixed with sulfur dioxide was acidic and burned a person's lungs on contact. Much of Hawaii was destroyed in hours where temperatures reached up to 3000 degrees F.

Walt could not take his eyes off of the screen. This was hell and he was watching this in real time and living color. He didn't know it at the time, but when this was over it would kill nearly 100,000 people on the Big Island alone.

Over the next few days it became obvious that the horror and devastation was not limited to the Hawaiian Islands. The prevailing winds would carry the ash to the Jerupa Valley, known as the Garden of the World, about 40 minutes west of Los Angeles, California. The winds carried ash and sulfur dioxide which when combined with the seasonal rains produced a very strong acid rain that was harmful to animals, people, and plants. Hospitals were overwhelmed within the next 30 days another 100,000 Americans on the mainland would likely die from drinking water poisoned by sulfur and acid rain. The damage to farms and agriculture was so severe, nobody could predict how long it would take these business to return to normal. Walt realized that this event might have been predicted by Michel de Nostradamus almost 600 years beforehand when he wrote in Quatrain 265 about a time in the future when Mercury was in Sagittarius when Saturn was Fading.

"Great Calamity
To be done through the
Lands of the West.
Fire in the Ship
Plague and Captivity"

In Quatrain 49, Century 10, Nostardamus also wrote:

"In the path of the
Hollow mountains
Garden of the World,
Near the New City"

When Nostradamus was talking about the Hollow mountains was he referring to Hollywood? Nobody can be sure. A lot of people did not take Nostradamus prophecies seriously, but Walt wasn't one of them. As far as he was concerned Nostradamus was one of the greatest remote viewers of all time. He predicted 911 and got the date pretty close when he wrote:

"The Year 1999
the seventh month
From the sky will come
A great King of Terror"

1999 is only two years from when this really happened The attack on the Trade Center didn't happen in the seventh month as Nostradamus predicted, but occurred on September 11, 2001. Sept is Latin for 7. Walt felt that his prediction was pretty close considering it was made over 500 years ago.

Because of the prevailing winds Walt did not think that this would directly affect him right away although, eventually, it would affect everyone in the northern hemisphere. It made him realize that at any moment could be our last, and that we should be thankful for all of our blessings all of the time. He could not escape the irony that Pearl Harbor Day and the recent Kilauea volcano occurred on the same date and both were in Hawaii!

He spent the next few days monitoring some of the ham emergency service nets on 20, 40, and 80 meters depending the time of day. Much of the cell phone system in Hawaii was destroyed and what was left was spotty at best. Some of the landlines still worked. People who used satellite internet still had service but cable and cell phone internet no longer was working. Otherwise the only communication from the Islands was by satellite phone and ham radio.

One of the main functions of ham radio was to provide emergency communication. Normally this worked in conjunction with the phone system but without reliable telephone service, relaying message traffic was more difficult.

Nonetheless thousands of hams were ready and eager to do what they could to help out. Most people on the Islands who survived had friends or family on the mainland who were worried about them. It was unreasonable to assume that the postal service would resume normal operation anytime soon.

There was little Walt could do to assist but monitored the emergency service and maritime nets so see if there was any message traffic to or from Sandpoint. Otherwise all he could do was think of how many people lost everything in the blink of an eye. He intentionally avoided the temptation to get on his ham radio for HF recreational contacts in order to save the bandwidth for people who really needed it. In addition to the radio he kept his tablet nearby and monitored news sites to keep as up to date as possible. When he did feel the need to talk to other hams he used his 2 meter FM rig which had a distance limited to less than 100 miles and didn't interfere with emergency communication.

For the next few days Walt kept in touch with his ham radio friends on 3.988 by email and they all agreed to resume their regular morning radio schedule the following week. This meant that they would have lots of catching up to do when they all got together again. Also it would give everyone time to process what had happened in Hawaii.

On the morning of December 10th Walt got an email from the Pacific Northwest Remote Viewers Group. This was not expected because he normally only heard from them once a month. They wanted him to post the results from the last website update to read; "Target 8734/2197 – Noah's Ark / Present Location." They also included the paperwork of three of their remote viewers to be posted who had worked on this target showing all of their data, sketches, and conclusions that determined that Noah's Ark was located near the top of Mount Ararat.

Walt looked this up online and found that it was the highest mountain in Turkey. It was the largest of two volcanoes at 16,854 feet above sea level and often had snow at the top all year. It was a popular destination for mountain climbers during the summer. Possibly a Lidar survey would help to determine its exact location. Lidar is a lot like radar but uses laser light instead of radio waves and is often used to create 3D maps of the earth's surface or the ocean floor.

The group also wanted Walt post the following; "Priority Target – Please work as soon as possible. 8659/1523." This seemed odd but Walt got this done right away and then emailed them an invoice for his work.

That afternoon Walt got a phone call from George, one of the neighbors on the CB net. "Walt, this is George up Moonfire Road. Got a minute?"

"Sure George, what I can I do for you?"

"Carla and I just got back from town and spotted some poachers just up from your place. Two guys in a red RAM pick up with a black grill guard. They had shot two deer right off the road and were loading them in their truck."

Walt knew that rifle season was over a few days ago and besides it was illegal to shoot anything from the road. "Did you get a plate number?"

"No, didn't have time to think about confronting two men with guns."

"Thanks George I'll see what I can do. Gotta go." Walt thought about this for a moment and decided to call Scott. After Scott did not answer the call, Walt called Fly Boy. "Hey this is Walt, are you busy? Can you do me a favor?"

"Sure Walt, what can I do for you?"

"I just heard from George that there are a couple of poachers that will probably be heading down the road any minute now. Could you use your drone to get some pictures of their truck and their license plate number?"

"I can do that. What kind of truck am I looking for?"

"A red RAM pick up with a black grill guard."

"I'll get right on it and give you a call later." Fly Boy put on his coat and grabbed his drone and controller. In less than a minute the drone was in the air and hovering on the side the county road. Fly Boy had a good look up Rapid Lightning Road and saw two cars coming down the road. A minute or two after that he spotted the truck. Fly Boy's drone was hovering about 30 feet high and he got a good look at the passenger side of the truck as it rolled by. Then he followed the truck and got some video of the two dead deer in the truck bed and the license plate as well. As far as he could tell, the two men didn't even notice the drone.

When Fly Boy got back to the house and down loaded the video. It looked really good and when enhanced and magnified in Photoshop, it was no problem reading the license plate. He called Walt. "Hey I got some video of the truck with the two deer in the back, I think that you'll be really pleased with the quality. I will email this to you right now."

Walt was really excited to hear this. "That's great. I really appreciate it. When I get this I will notify Fish and Game. Can't thank you enough. I guess you can add private detective to your list of drone services. Talk to you later."

When Walt got the video he really was impressed with the quality of Fly Boy's camera. It didn't really need any enhancement or sharpening, and just a little magnification was needed to read the plate number. Walt called Fish and Game to report this and emailed them a copy of the video. They thanked him and told him that they would investigate this and get back to him. Then he called George and told him that Fly Boy was able to get video confirmation of the two dead deer and the plate number. George was glad to hear this and they both agreed that this was a big win for the CB net.

After thinking about this for awhile Walt decided to send everyone on the net an email and tell them about what just happened and asked them not to discuss this on the radio. He knew there was a slight chance that the poachers would find out about this and retaliate against Fly Boy so this was a matter of protecting the members of the net.

The next morning Walt saw that he had about 8 inches of new snow on the ground so he had to sweep off the satellite dish to get his internet working. After checking his email and looking at a few news sites to get information about the volcano and the mess in southern California, Walt took a look at dry survival food on Online World. He found a deal with 167 different dry meals for $270. Even though his pantry was full he clicked on the Buy Now button anyway. The dried food meals were supposed to last up to 20 years and he thought this sounded like good insurance. He had no plans to actually eat any of this unless he had to but thought that he might be able to trade some meals in an emergency.

Then he fed Sparky and let her outside and made some pancakes for himself. With a good breakfast behind him, he let Sparky back in the cabin and went out side to shovel the steps. Once this was done Walt started the tractor and blew the snow off of the driveway and the parking area at the bottom of the road. The snow was cold so the blower handled this easily and when he was done with the driveway he cleared out the parking area by the cabin, woodshop, and garage. Even though the machine was doing the work, this took several hours and Walt was tired of backing up all the time that was necessary when he ran the rear-mounted snow blower.

The snow blower cleared a path five feet wide but it was a slow process because the tractor had to be run in 4WD and in low range. When he was done he had to clean out the snow blower with a shovel before it could be put away. If he failed to clean it, the snow blower could be iced up and not work the next time he needed it. Over the years Walt had learned that using a machine was fun for about two hours and after that it was work.

All the time that he was dealing with the snow, Walt couldn't stop thinking about the new remote viewing target. What could be a Priority Target and why was it so important? Walt decided that he could remote view this on his own to satisfy his curiosity. Since he was tired he decided that he would do this the next day.

The next morning after lighting a fire and taking care of Sparky Walt got ready to do some remote viewing. He had not actually done this in a long time so he wanted to give it the best chance possible to succeed. First he cleared the kitchen table of everything except a few blank sheets of paper and a pen. Next he prepared a remote viewing work sheet and wrote the words "date and time" on the top left hand corner. The he drew two lines about 2 inches long from left to right with one line spaced about three quarters of an inch below the other. In the top right hand corner of the page he drew the outline of a square box that measured about three inches on each side.

Then about an inch under the two lines on the left side of the page he wrote the word "textures". About an inch below this he wrote the word "colors". Under this he wrote "smells" and continued writing more words below the others with about one inch spacing between all of the words. When he ran out of room he continued on another blank piece of paper so that after the word "smells" the list continued to include the words "tastes, temperatures, sounds, dimensions, hardness, and feelings." On the third piece of blank paper Walt wrote the word "sketch" at the top.

Walt was nearly ready to begin the session. He turned on his laptop computer and booted up an audio tone generator program and set it up to play a sine wave tone of 100 hz on the left stereo channel and 107.5 hz on the right channel. He set this to play on a continuous loop and clicked on play. Then he put on a set of stereo headphones and adjusted the volume to a low and pleasant listening level. He sat at the table with his pen in hand and the work sheets in front of him and listened to the tones and tried to relax,

This technique produces an altered brain wave state of 7.5 hz, the difference between the two tones. Humans cannot hear a tone this low, but by using two slightly different tones, the brain can be fooled into aligning the brainwaves to a frequency that is too low for humans to hear.

After about 15 minutes of listening to the tones and trying to relax Walt was ready to begin. He put his pen to the top left corner and wrote down Dec 12 and 0915. Next he read aloud the numbers, "8659" and "1523" and wrote them on each line under the date. Immediately after writing the last number he moved his pen to the box at the top and produced an ideogram in the box. This was spontaneous and done without thought.

Then he started down the list of words that he had prepared and immediately and without thinking wrote whatever came to mind next to each word. Next to "texture" he wrote the words smoke and foggy. Next to "colors" he wrote black and gray. Next to "smells" he wrote hellfire. Next to "tastes" he wrote nasty and gritty. Next to "temperatures" he wrote hot and steamy. Next to "sound" he wrote loud, exploding, roaring. Next to "dimensions" he wrote huge, enormous, expanding. Next to "hardness" he wrote steamy. Next to "feelings" he wrote "frightening".

The sketch he produced next was rough and violent and resembled the cloud from an atomic bomb or mushroom that was larger at the top and expanding with altitude. Then he looked at the clock and wrote "end 0955". After looking at the ideogram, his initial impressions, and the sketch Walt wasn't exactly sure what the target was. Maybe it was a bomb or some type of explosion, he wasn't sure, but he knew whatever it was, it was big and it was powerful. He didn't know where it was located, or when the event had happened (or would happen). It would take several sessions by experienced remote viewers to sort this out. But he knew this target was important and he was glad that he decided to take a look. He took off the headphones and shut down his laptop. Finally he could have some breakfast and enjoy the first cup of coffee of the day.

Walt and Sparky spent the day stoking the woodstove and listening to the emergency service nets. The TV news out of Hawaii was beginning to show the extent of the damage and the Red Cross and FEMA kept finding more badly burned bodies and the local hospitals were filled to capacity. The U.S.S. Mercy hospital ship would be there in a week or so and people were being evacuated to nearby Navy ships and stateside burn units. Communication and power had not been restored to the Big Island and those that could were fleeing to other parts of the State.

The news was equally grim out of southern California and continuous acid rainfall and dense fog had knocked the economy to its knees. Most people were sheltering at home and the national guard wearing gas masks and hazmat suits were assisting with food delivery and other emergency calls.

About three o'clock in the afternoon Walts driveway alarm went off. Sparky echoed the alarm and added to the alert. He got up and saw that there was a UPS truck in his yard and he went out to greet the driver. It was Walt's lucky day. His Christmas present to himself had arrived and he was anxious to try out the new Automatic Gold Panning Machine. That afternoon he unpacked it and assembled everything he would need to get started on the project.

Just to be safe he spread a sheet of plastic on the floor and placed his five foot otter sled on top of the plastic, Then he put the unit together and put the Desert Fox machine inside the otter sled. He brought in a battery and put a trickle charger on it and planned to try it out the next morning..

After morning chores had been done Walt went out to the Woodshed and brought in two half full buckets of sand and added 3 gallons of water to the tub. He connected the battery and turned it on and it seemed to be working. The spiral wheel was turning and water was being pumped through the nozzles into the wheel. He watched the way it was working and experimented with the angle of the pan. The instructions said that the material should be sifted to 10 mesh or smaller so he sifted about a half bucket of sand using the 10 mesh shifting pan and only came up with a few larger pebbles and stones.

Now he was ready to try the machine. He slowly added one cup of sifted sand to the rotating wheel and adjusted the overflow shelf on the tub so that the tailings from the tub would spill onto the plastic covered floor and not end up in the tub full of water. When this was working well he added one cup of sifted sand at a time until the material was gone. Next he turned off the machine and looked in the center collection cup and saw that it contained about 20 colors of very fine gold. A color is a piece of gold large enough to see but too small to pick up with your fingers. Any piece of gold that can be picked up with your fingers is called a picker.

Walt was ready to jump out of his skin. The machine worked as advertised and recovered very fine gold without depositing any black sands or foreign material in the collection cup. As long as he was set up Walt went out to get another bucket of sand and when it was sifted to 10 mesh, ran it through the machine. Merry Christmas, Amen, and Hallelujah. It worked and Walt was looking forward to processing the sand stored in his woodshed over the winter. Walt cleaned up the overflow tailings sands and put them in a bucket to dry. He would use this to cover the ice on the steps and paths later in the winter. He carefully took the unit out of the otter sled, put the collection cup in his bookshelf, and put everything away and back to normal.

Most people took Sundays off but Walt was retired so he could arrange his schedule any way he liked. Walt did his usual morning routine and checked his email before doing dishes, laundry, and cleaning up the cabin. He expected Toni and Sherri to stop by around 11:30 to talk about ham radio. When they arrived Walt went out to meet them and Walt asked them what they wanted to use ham radio for. They told him that they wanted to talk to family and friends in California, Texas, and Colorado. Walt explained that in that case they would need to get a general class license and operate on the HF bands. Before they went inside he showed them his antenna farm and he pointed out that each antenna could operate on several different bands.

This would mean that they would want to primarily use the 80, 40, 20, and 17 meter bands which could all be used with one wire antenna configured as an end fed long wire, a dipole, an inverted V, or an off center fed dipole. These antennas were easily made at home and could be supported between two trees. He showed them examples of each and then pointed to his hexbeam. The hexbeam looked like an upside down umbrella and it was directional. It had gain over a wire antenna and was turned with a motor to aim it. It needed to be mounted on a pole or tower and was only useful on the higher HF bands like 20, 17,15, 12, 10, and 6 meters. The wire antennas would cost about $200 and the hexbeam would cost about $1000. He went on to explain that wire antennas were the most bang for dollar and that he used his end fed almost everyday.

When they went inside he got them both a chair and they all sat in front of the radio table. He turned on his old Yaesu FT-900 which was a 100 watt SSB, AM, FM, and CW transceiver with a built in tuner and selected his end fed antenna. Walt started his demonstration on 17 meters and tuned up and down the band to see how many stations he could hear using Single Sideband. He heard a station coming in on 18.130 calling CQ.

"CQ CQ CQ calling CQ. This is AZ5NL calling CQ and standing by for a call." Walt pointed to the S meter on his radio and showed Tony and Sherri that he was coming in about an S5. Since there was noise on Walts receiver he was perfectly readable. "CQ CQ CQ calling CQ. This is AZ5NL calling CQ and standing by for a call."

"Walt grabbed the microphone and began transmitting. "AZ5NL. AZ5NL this is AP7ZMT. How copy? Over."

"Yes AP7ZMT this is AZ5NL. Thanks for coming back to my call. I am located near Waco, Texas, The Name here is Rick. Over"

"OK Rick. I have you into Sandpoint Idaho an S5 with armchair copy. I am running a FT 900 with a 100 watts into an end fed antenna. How do you copy me Name here is Walt. Over"

"Real good Walt. I have you about 5 by7. I am running a FT DX10 with 100 watts into a GAP vertical. The weather here is 68 degrees. What is it like up there? Over."

"It's a long way from 65 degrees. It looks like we are about 32 degrees now with a little more than a foot of snow on the ground here. I have a couple of visitors in the shack and they are thinking about becoming hams. Would you mind saying Hi to Tony and his wife Sherri?

"AP7ZMT this is AZ5NL. Hello Toni and Sherri. I encourage you to get your tickets and get on the air. You'll meet a lot nice people on the air. I have been a ham for over 40 years. Over."

Walt handed the microphone to Tony and encouraged him to reply. "This is Tony. Nice to talk to you Rick. We have family in Austin. I don't know his call though. That is one of the reasons we want to get on the air. Over."

"Well I think that you'll find that the path between Idaho and Texas is usually open on several bands. I hear Idaho stations often. Over."

"Thanks we are having fun so far. I'll turn the microphone back to Walt now. Over."

"OK Tony. I encourage both of you to get licensed. It's nice when everyone in the family can use the radio. Back to you Walt."

"Thanks for helping out Rick. I am sure that these two will get on the air soon. I think we'll look around the bands a little and let them see that there are a lot of people to talk to out there. I'll say 73 and hope you make some good contacts today. I'm listed on QRZ.com if you ever want to reach me. Have a good one. We'll be clear on your final. AZ5NL this is AP7ZMT. Over."

"I think it's great to help people get into the hobby. I have really enjoyed myself as a ham. 73 from Texas. This is AZ5NL clear."

Walt looked at Tony and Sherri and suggested that they tune around to see what else they could hear. Walt went down to 20 meters and began to tune up the band. They heard a station from Florida talking to a station in Canada. They heard a station in Puerto Rico talking with a ham in Mexico. They heard a QRP station in Colorado calling CQ. It was Sunday and there were lots of stations on the band. Then Walt powered down the FT 900 and turned on his Icom 7300. This was a newer radio and had a lot more bells and whistles than The Yaesu. The most noticeable feature was the band scope where all the signals on the entire band could be seen at once. Instead of tuning up and down the band you could see a strong signal and tune to it right away.

"Then he selected his hexbeam antenna and pointed it to Europe. He heard a French station calling CQ. "CQ, CQ, CQ this is F17DMC calling CQ North America and standing by."

Walt pulled up his desk microphoe and gave him a call back. "F17DMC this is AP7ZMT located in Idaho. How copy? Over."

"The AP7 station you are a little weak. Come again please. F17DMC"

Walt turned on his solid state amplifier and brought his power up to 400 watts. "This AP7ZMT located in Idaho. I turned on the amp. Is this any better? Over."

"Yes much better." While the French station was transmitting, Walt was able to point the hexbeam more in his direction. "The name here is George. Germany, Echo, Romeo, Germany, Echo. I am 25 km south of Paris. Over."

OK George. The name here is Walt. Whiskey, America, Lima, Tango. I am located in Idaho about 75 miles from Canada, Running an Icom 7300 at 400 watts into a hexbeam. Over."

"OK Walt. I am running a Icom 7600 with 800 watts into a 3 element Yagi up 55 feet. I have you at a S7. What is my signal report? Over."

"I have you at a S9 into Sandpoint, Idaho. I don't want to keep you and can hear other stations trying to work you so I'll say 73 and let you make a few more contacts. Thanks again for picking me up. 73 George. This is AP7ZMT."

"OK Walt nice to meet you. I am glad to see the band is holding up well tonight. 73. and QRZed. This is F17DMC."

Tony and Sherri could hear three or four other stations calling George. Then Walt turned the radio off. And turned on a smaller radio on the top shelf. That was HF SSB. I thought I would show you some 2 meter FM. This is about 45 watts and I'll be going through a repeater on Hoodoo mountain. "This is AP7ZMT testing." The repeater came back with a CW ID att full signal strength. He explained that by themselves 2 meter radios could only reach out 40 or 50 miles but by going through a repeater or series of repeaters you could talk to

Seattle using a line of sight low power FM radio. Then he turned off the 2 meter rig.

"Well I hope you got a taste of what ham radio is like. Do you have any questions?" They asked about the cost and once again Walt explained how they could get started on HF with used equipment for $500 or so and that his 7300 costs about $1200. A wire antenna could be built for less than $200 including the feed line and they might need an external tuner as well. He explained that it was not a good idea to cut costs on an antenna because this was more important than the radio.

He gave them some back issues of QST magazine and some radio catalogs to take home and showed them where they could order some study guides to prepare for the tests. He explained that the tests were not that hard since the study guides listed all the multiple choice questions and all of the answers. Also there were several websites that had practice tests and this was a great help preparing for the tests. He encouraged them to get the technician study guide and the general study guide and that many people take both tests on the same day. Once they passed the technician test they would have to wait for the FCC to issue them call signs, He wanted to be realistic and encouraging and thought that it would take a month to be able to pass the test if they studied one hour a day. Also he wanted to mention that he would help them set up their station and shop for radio gear once they established a budget.

Naturally Tony and Sherri had a lot to absorb in one day and were suffering from information overload. When they left Walts they had a lot to talk about.

When Tony and Sherri were gone Walt took Sparky for a quick walk and grabbed a bite to eat. It was almost time for the Alex Jones radio show on 9.350 Mhz on the shortwave. Walt really wanted to hear the latest news about the Volcano and its aftermath so he expected that this would be an especially good program.

Once again, it was another great show. Alex talked about the history of Kilauea and how it had been active for such a long time that people almost took it for granted and a tourist industry had been centered around the volcano. Restaurants, Hotels, and daily tours went to the rim to see the red hot lava.

He also talked about the likely long term health effects and the damage to southern California agriculture. He pointed out that there were lots of earthquakes occurring on the other side of the world at the same time and how these might be related.

Alex mentioned the fact that President Joe Bama warned of a world wide food shortage and that 18 months after his warning over three dozen food processing plants in the U.S. have been destroyed by mysterious fires. He said that although this wasn't getting much press coverage these fires did not appear to be accidental and that creating a food shortage was in his opinion by design.

He mentioned that a new study by the U.K. government showed that there were more people who died from the Covid vaccines than were saved by the vaccines. This alarming statistic suggested that this was by design as well. And that more black and brown skinned people were harmed by the vaccine than white people. He pointed out that when the government told people that the vaccines were safe and effective what they really meant was that the vaccines were safe for them because many of the elites were injected with saline. And that it was effective because they worked exactly as intended, to cause excess mortality.

Alex also mentioned that it was by design that most abortion clinics were placed in black and brown neighborhoods and that this was by design as well. He made the point that our welfare system was designed to tear families apart since poor women could not get welfare if there was a father living in the home.

This is why Walt listened to the Alex Jones show. He talked about things that the mainstream news didn't want to mention. After two hours the shortwave broadcast was over and Walt turned off the radio.

Later that night Walt ran the CB net as usual and it went very well. Five new members joined in so this totaled 14 including himself. He had never imagined that the net would grow this quickly but it showed that there was a strong demand for local information and communication. The neighbors also liked the net because they could meet and talk to neighbors who they never would have met. Tony and Sherri thanked Walt for the ham radio demonstration and said that they had ordered both amateur radio license study guides and hoped to be ready to take the tests in a few months. Although this was not Walt's intention when he started the net it was an unwritten rule that hams helped anyone who was interested in the hobby become hams. A lot of hams got their start in the radio hobby with CB radios.

The next morning Walt got on 3.988 to visit with his radio friends. This was the first time that they had spoken with each other on the air since the volcano erupted and they all had lots to talk about. Walt told them about his new Gold Panning machine and what he heard the day before on the Alex Jones show. Frank wondered if the California calamity would lead to a food shortage in the Northwest. Ray was concerned that more Californians would move to rural areas of Washington and Idaho. Joe had friends in Hawaii and had not heard if they were OK. Mike assisted in passing radio traffic from people worried about their families in the Seattle area.. Steve wondered how this would affect our weather and if we would see acid rain as well. Dennis said that he spent some time listening on the ham bands but had been inactive until now. It was really good to hear from everybody but Walt got a phone call and had to sign off.

Walt looked at the caller ID and saw that it was from Idaho Fish and Game. "Hello this is Walt"

"Walt this Travis White with Idaho Fish and Game."

"Yes Travis, what can I do for you?"

"We wanted to give you an update about the two poachers that you reported."

"Great, were you able to track them down?" Walt asked.

"Even better than that. The video you sent us will help us to get a conviction on the poaching violations for sure. It turns out that they were from Oregon and one of the men was a convicted felon so he wasn't allowed to have firearms in the first place. The other guy had a warrant out for his arrest. When the SO (Sheriffs Office) came to investigate they found some stolen property including items reported stolen from two cabins up Trapper Creek."

"That's really good news Travis. Thanks for the update."

"Yes your tip got some bad guys out of here. Our jobs are a lot easier when we get good info from the local citizens. Thanks again Walt." Travis hung up the phone.

"Glad that we could help and really appreciate the update. We don't get the newspaper." Wow that was good news, Walt thought to himself. He was sure the folks up Trapper Creek would be happy to get their stuff back. He logged onto his email account and notified everyone on the CB net about the call from Idaho Fish and Game. In the subject line it read, "Won one for the Good Guys." The CB net had taken some bad guys off the street. How cool was that?

Over the next week Walt kept busy. It seemed like it snowed everyday so snow removal took a lot of his time. He made sure to see that Sparky got some exercise outdoors and he spent a lot of time on the radio as well. He made sure to say "Merry Christmas" to radio contacts and didn't believe in safe and politically correct "Happy Holidays" bullshit.

The following Saturday Walt attended a neighborhood Christmas Party at Robert and Nancy's place on the Gold Creek cut off road. He had never met them in person or been to their place but he was glad that he went. He got to meet some new neighbors and some of the people from the CB net as well.

Walt used to drink a lot of beer but lately he kept this to a minimum and gave himself a two beer limit for the night. This was difficult because once Walt started drinking he had a hard time stopping. In any case Walt had a great time because Robert and Nancy were playing some good music on their stereo and they had a billiard room. It was made from a converted carport and had hydronic heat in the carpeted floor. Walt had played a lot of pool when he was in the military and he wasn't shooting too badly considering that he had not played in awhile.

Playing pool was a little like playing golf, where every great shot is followed by a miserable shot and that is why it is such a fun game. Just as you think that you are pretty good, you find out that you aren't. Walt told himself that someday he was going to build a room like this and have his own table. Since Robert and Nancy played all the time they both won easily but everyone had a great time.

On the Sunday before Christmas Walt did his usual routine of housework, listening to Alex Jones, and running the Rapid Lightning Creek CB net. Life was good and it sure felt good to be inside and warmed by the woodstove instead of fighting with the snow trying to drive home from town.

When he woke up Monday morning Walt looked out the window to see how much snow had fallen overnight. He couldn't tell exactly but he knew it would be easier to deal with while it was cold so he lit a fire in the wood stove, fed Sparky, skipped breakfast and started the tractor. In a few hours he finished snow blowing the driveway and parking area and put the tractor under cover. Then he shoveled the steps and swept off the satellite dish.

Sparky was glad that he was back in the cabin and she was hoping to have some fun but Walt told her that this would have to wait. He made a pot of coffee and a quick breakfast and then checked his email and turned on the radio to chat with his friends. Jeff and Frank were already on the air. "I saw the documentary *2000 Mules* last night. It was fabulous. Anyone who still claims that the 2020 election wasn't full of fraud is brain dead. AM7DX."

"I have heard of it but haven't seen it yet. Its that good huh?" (AU7PM)

"It basically showed absolute proof that the election in Pennsylvania, Michigan, Wisconsin, and Georgia was rigged big time. The illegal votes in those States were enough to turn the election." (AM7DX)

"I guess that's what Nancy meant when she said to wait until the next morning because they had the votes. (AU7PM)

"Exactly. First they showed that many of the voters were not legit. Either dead, felons, or out of State residents. Then they proved that the drop boxes were stuffed with video and electronic geo-tracking data. They showed the same people returning to the drop boxes with stacks of ballots and wearing surgical gloves that they immediately discarded in the trash. They also pointed out that the drop boxes were illegal because they were not approved by the State legislatures and that none of these States bothered to check the signatures on the ballots. It was amazing." (AM7DX)

"Makes me wonder why I bother to vote. AP7ZMT."

" Morning Walt." (AU7PM)

"Have you seen it yet?" (AM7DX)

"No but I have heard it is really well done. Too bad the lame stream media is afraid to talk about it. They won't even mention it on Fox." (AP7ZMT)

"Just like Hunter's laptop. They are all afraid to even mention it. Remember 10% to the Big Guy," (AU7PM)

"Fake News is Good News, that's their business model." (AM7DX)

"A.G. Barb said that he hasn't seen any evidence of election fraud. That's understandable, considering where his head is."(AN7HM)

" t's in a dark and stinky place up there, that's for sure. Morning Joe" (AP7ZMT)

" Does anybody have plans for Christmas?" (AN7HM)

"Nothing special here. Plan to fire up the hot tub and shoot off some bottle rockets. That's about it. AP7ZMT. Over."

"The grand kids are coming over and that should be fun. They haven't been here in awhile. AM7DX."

"That should be fun. I think my son will come for a visit. I need him to help me with my computer anyway."(AU7PM)

"We'll be going over the pass to see my daughter. Hope the roads aren't too bad." (AN7HM)

"I thought the DHS Disinformation Board was canceling Christmas this year. AY7OM."

"Morning Ray. The Government tried to cancel it the last two years with Covid." (AU7PM)

"They tried to shut the whole country down, that's for sure. Even banned going to Church. Do you think anyone in government has actually read the Constitution?"(AY7OM)

"Why bother, it was written by old white slave owners anyway." (AP7ZMT)

" Makes you proud to be a tax payer doesn't it?" (AM7DX)

" At least when I graduated from High School I could actually read my diploma." (AY7OM)

"Back then we didn't have Tampon machines in the Boy's Room." (AU7PM)

"And boys didn't have menstrual cramps either." (AM7DX)

"That's progress. Nowadays boys can get Mother's Day cards." (AN7HM)

"Maybe we are all stuck in a dream and after Christmas we'll all be back to normal. What do you think AP7ZMT?"

"We're in a dream all right. A bad dream," (AY7OM)

"As usual we have solved the world's problems this morning." (AU7PM)

"It's easy if you are as old as we are. AN7HM."

" t's been fun as usual guys but I've got a few things to do. See you all later and have a Merry Christmas. Remember that it's not legal to shoot a reindeer with a red nose and the fat old man in the red suit probably is not a home invader. 73 guys. AP7ZMT clear and going QRT for awhile."

"OK Walt, you have a good day today. AU7PM."

"See you later Walt AN7HM."

"Merry Christmas Walt. AM7DX."

"Later Walt. AY7OM."

Walt turned off his radio but the rest of the group stayed on the air for another 30 minutes or so. As soon as the radio was off, Sparky was on her feet and giving Walt the look. He knew that she wanted to go for a walk so he put on his pack boots, coat and sheepskin cap and they walked down the cleared driveway to the mailboxes. It was too early to even think about checking the mail so they came back up the hill. Walt took one of her toys out of his pocket and they played fetch with her ropey football. This was a football shaped rubber toy similar to a Kong with a short rope tied to each end. He would throw it but she was so fast she would often be under it before it hit the ground. Then she would run around and shake it back and forth until she was a little tired then Walt would take it from her and try another throw.

Soon they both went into the cabin and Sparky took a long drink of cold water while Walt took off his hat and coat. Cow dogs have a lot of nervous energy and if they don't get a little exercise everyday they will look for something to chew so Walt tried his best to give Sparky the attention that she needed. Sometimes if the snow was too deep they would play a similar game in the cabin but it was better if they played outside. Walt spent the rest of the day catching up on his emails and sending out Christmas greetings with a few pictures to friends and family.

That afternoon the postman drove up his driveway to deliver the dried food that he ordered from Online World and a package from his sister. The postman knew people wanted to get their packages in time for Christmas so he made an extra effort to get things delivered before the holiday. If a package would not fit in the mailbox, he would usually leave a note asking Walt to schedule the delivery and meet him at the road or pick up the package at the Post Office.

Walt opened the package from his sister and put the sausage and jerky in the refrigerator and a box of oranges in the mud room so that it would stay cool and not freeze. He hoped that the gifts that he had ordered online for his sister and brother in law had arrived but wouldn't know for sure until he talked to her on Christmas Day.

The next day was Christmas Eve and Walt and Sparky drove to town. Nothing a dog loves more than going for a ride so, even though it was cold, he cracked the window just enough so that her nose could get some fresh air. He got a few groceries at Locals Grocery and then they went to Burger King where he picked up two large Whoppers and French fries. He put these in the tool box in the back of the truck so they both did not have to suffer smelling this on the way home. By then it was 11am and he picked up Christmas dinner at Papa Murphy's take and bake pizza shop and drove home.

When they arrived home Walt put the pizza in the refrigerator and took the hamburgers out of the bag. One of the burgers was for Sparky and he pulled the meat out of the bun and scraped off the ketchup and mustard. After breaking the burger up in small pieces, he put them in her bowl. Sparky took care of the burger in no time and was hoping the other burger was also for her. Walt heated this and the French fries in the microwave and sat down to eat his lunch. It had been a long time since he had gone to a burger joint and he savored every bite.

That afternoon he played ham radio had some good long chats with a dozen or so hams from around the world. Lots of people were off that day so the ham bands had plenty of stations to talk to. He actually heard a station on Christmas Island in the pacific but there were so many stations trying to make contact with him that he didn't even try.

The next day Walt got up about 5am as usual and he played some Christmas music on the stereo until lunch time and after calling his sister, he went outside to prepare his hillbilly hot tub. The wind was not blowing but it was lightly snowing and the trees were decorated with snow making it look like a Norman Rockwell postcard outside. His hot tub was a little crude but it worked like a charm. The tub itself was a six foot round galvanized steel stock tank with two foot sides. Underneath the tank was a 55 gallon barrel without a top or a bottom. He filled the topless barrel with firewood and then filled the tank with fresh water using a garden hose. On the far end of the stock tank a six foot piece of stove pipe stood upright that was the exhaust. After the tank was filled with 42 degree well water he lit the fire in the barrel. The fire easily caught and the smoke went up and out of the stovepipe.

It took about two and a half hours to heat the water. He had a floating thermometer in the water to tell him when it was done. While the tub was warming Walt took the pizza out of the refrigerator so the crust would rise. When the tub was about perfect Walt went out to the tub and climbed it. The bottom of the steel tub was quite warm so he had to sit on a one inch thick board to keep his butt from getting burned. There was plenty of room to stretch out and relax in the perfectly heated fresh water. Christmas music was playing on a small portable radio that was sitting on the deck around the tub. When he got in the water he realized that he had forgotten his bottle rockets but that was OK since he planned to use the tub again on New Year's Eve and they looked cooler at night anyway. After about 30 minutes he was cooked and ready to go back to the cabin. The funny thing about using a hot tub in the winter is that when you strip down naked you are freezing and shivering as you get in the tub. But after thirty minutes in the 105 degree water, when you get out of the tub you don't feel the cold at all.

Walt got out of the tub, opened the valve to drain the water, put on his robe and pack boots, and slowly walked to the cabin without objecting to the fresh snow falling on his head.

When he got back to the cabin he dried off the best that he could while Sparky liked his wet legs, got dressed and preheated the oven. While the oven was warming he added some extra cheese and mushrooms to the pizza. When the pizza was cooked he let it cool for a few minutes before cutting it into six slices. Then he took three of the slices and ran them under cold running water all over the top and all over the sides and bottom. This was his secret. Nobody else in the world knew about this easy way to improve a pizza. Next he micro-waved the three slices for 85 seconds and then put them a plate. This made the cardboard tasting dry pizza crust come to life and become so tender and moist that the pizza could be cut and eaten with a fork. This trick worked well with left over pizza as well. It would turn a cheap five dollar frozen pizza into a work of art, Walt ate half the pizza and put the other half back in the refrigerator for later. Sparky wondered why she didn't get any but Walt told her that it was too spicy for her. Sometimes being a dog was great and other times it wasn't.

Over the next few days it snowed everyday. With colder temperatures the snow was no longer wet and sticky but pure white powder. It was so light ad dry that you could clear the deck, steps, and paths with a leaf blower (if you could get one to start). On days like this Walt wished that he had an electric leaf blower to try this but his gas powered leaf blower was hard to start even in the summertime. When it snowed like this is was so quiet you could not hear the traffic on the road. This time of year was wonderful if you didn't have to go anywhere. There was no wind whatsoever so the snow just piled up on itself. The snow covered wooden fence posts appeared to be wearing pure white top hats over 12 inches high. Every few days Walt would deal with snow removal but he didn't bother to do this everyday. When it was cold the dry snow wasn't icy or slick.

One extra chore this time of year was knocking the snow off of his antennas so they wouldn't carry too much weight. This meant striking the coax feed lines with a shovel or a snow rake and the shock would clear most of the snow. If he didn't do this on a regular basis, and it rained and turned icy, the additional weight could bring them down and they might not be able to be repaired until spring.

When Sunday evening came Walt was ready for the last Rapid Lightning Creek CB net of the year. It had been a pretty good year as far as he was concerned and he was optimistic about the future. His Gold Panning Machine appeared to be working well and in a month or two he would have a better idea of how much gold might be in his sandbar. He had made a lot of improvements to his place and both he and Sparky were in pretty good health. He only had two years to go before his land was paid off and otherwise he was debt free. Of course he had a few bills like telephone, internet, electricity, property taxes, and insurance but these could easily be covered with his military retirement check.

It was 6:15 pm and he turned on the radio. He didn't hear anyone talking so he keyed the microphone and began to transmit. This is "Walt on the Rapid Lightning CB net looking for early check-ins. Over."

"This is George and Carla, I guess that we're first tonight.Over."

"Roger that, hope all is well."

"Had a nice Christmas and hope that you did too."

"Are there any more check-in for net? Over"

"I'm in here too. This is Peter on Thunder Alley. Over."

"Good to hear you Peter. Are there any more check-ins? Over"

"We are here too Walt. This is Tony and Sherri. Over."

"Real good. Did you get you license manuals yet? Over."

"Sure did, We've been studying the technician manual for about a week now."

"Sounds good Toni. Anybody else in here tonight?"

"This is Robert and Nancy. Log us in Walt. Over"

"Got you in here. Taking check-ins for the Rapid Lightning Creek CB net. Come on in. Over"

"This is Jane on Wellington Road. Evening Walt."

"Good signal in here tonight. Are there any more check-ins?"

" This is Fly Boy. Good to hear everyone tonight. Over"

"Got you in here Fly Boy. We'll get started in a few minutes. Any more check-ins come now."

"Stan and Gloria are here Walt."

" I'm in her too Walt. This is Steve up Flume Creek."

"This is Scott down by the store."

"OK Scott, good signal tonight. Anyone else please come now. Over."

"This is Susan on Rapid Lightning. Hello everyone."

"This is Charles and Megan on the High Road. Copy OK Walt?"

"Loud and clear Charles and Megan. Got you in here."

"This is Brett on Rolling Thunder Road."

"OK Bret, anyone else?"

"This is Mary and Beth, We're in her too Walt."

"Me too. This is Tom up Flume Creek."

"That's great. It looks like we have a full house tonight. Are there any other check-ins before we get started?" Walt waited a bit and then continued. "OK I count 15 stations in here tonight including myself. Really happy with the turn out and thank you all for checking in. As I told you all in my email the net was very successful a few weeks ago and I think the neighborhood will really benefit from your continued participation. If there is anything any of you want me to cover you can call me on the phone, shoot me an email, or bring it up on the air. I want to take this moment to wish you all a Happy New Year and I thought it would be fun if any of you have any New Year's Resolutions that you would like to share with the group. I haven't thought about this myself but before the net is over I am sure that I'll think of something. Thought we'd go to a roundtable again with two go rounds each by check in number. I have the order as George and Carla, followed by Peter, then Tony and Sherri, Robert and Nancy, Jane, Fly Boy, Stan and Gloria, Steve, Scott, Susan, Bret, Mary and Beth, Tom, and me. Go ahead George and Carla. Let the roundtable begin." That was a handful but Walt hoped that he got the order correct.

"This is George and Carla up Moonfire Road. We'll take this opportunity to wish everyone a Happy New Year. My resolution is to read a new book every month. Carla hasn't thought about hers yet. Maybe next time around. Over to you Peter."

"OK I haven't thought of any resolutions either but I guess that mine will be cutting more firewood next year. I can see I'm going to need it. Over to Tony and Sherri."

Walt jumped in ahead of Tony. Just to make it fun I am writing these down and we'll read them next year like they used to do on the Art Bell show. Sorry Tony back to you."

"OK I guess that our resolution is to pass the ham tests and be on the air with our General Class licenses next year at this time. Back to Robert and Nancy."

"Oh boy is it our turn already? I guess my resolution will be to put a deer in the freezer next year. Nancy wants to learn how to make her own yarn and learn to weave. Back to you Jane."

"I can help you with that Nancy. I have done this before and used to be in the craft business. Actually my resolution is the same as Robert's, to put a deer in the freezer. Over to Fly Boy. Over."

"My resolution is spend next winter in Arizona playing with my drone instead of shoveling snow. Over to Stan and Gloria."

"You catch on fast Fly Boy. It took me 10 years to start dreaming about escaping the winter. My resolution is to spend more time fishing on the lake and less time picking up slash. Gloria would like to expand her garden. Over to Steve."

"Well mine would be the same as last year's, to lose some weight and keep it lost. Over to Scott."

"I know better and have made that one before. I would like to learn to play the banjo. I heard there is a guy in town who gives lessons. Since I live alone I won't be bothering anyone while I practice. Back to you Susan."

"That's a good one Scott. I would like to build a kiln and start making pottery like I used to do in college. Over to Charles and Megan."

"I guess our resolution would be to finish the cabin and get a well and running water. Over to Bret."

"Amen. That's the best one I have heard so far. Nothing changes your life like plumbing and a hot water shower. I used a bucket shower for a few years and really celebrated having all the hot water I wanted. My resolution is to put some rock on the driveway and get rid of some of the mud in the spring. Over to Mary and Beth."

"We would like to get that addition built that we were talking about earlier. I think we've found a contactor who is willing to do this on our budget and schedule. Over to you Tom."

"I have heard some great resolutions tonight. I plan to start making bird and bat houses and selling them at craft fairs. I've got the tools and a place to work and have a deck of cedar logs ready to be cut into lumber. Over to you Walt."

"You guys are a tough act to follow. My resolution is pretty small potatoes compared to some of yours. I want to get a legal limit linear amplifier for my ham station but I'll have to earn a little more money first. My other resolution is to get my code speed up to 20 words per minute. Like I said I have recorded these resolutions in a notebook and it will be fun to see how we all did next year. Back to George and Carla.Over"

"This is George. Carla has decided that her resolution is build a greenhouse. Nothing fancy, basically a plastic covered box with raised beds. One of the neighbors has one and leaves the sides up all year and just puts the plastic roof on for the summer. Oh and I wanted to mention that we'll be monitoring this cannel on Wednesday evenings if anyone wants to chat. Over to Peter."

"This is Peter up Thunder Alley. Just wanted to mention tht I was almost run off the road the other day by a kid driving a bright yellow Bronco. I'd like to find out where he lives if anyone knows. Back to Tony and Sherri."

"Sounds good about Wednesday evenings I'll try and remember this. Oh I wanted to mention that we were in the Sub Shop yesterday about 15 minutes before they were supposed to open and they had 5 people making subs all at once. They are great sub sandwiches and it must be a really good business to have that many employees early in the mornings. Over to Robert and Nancy."

"We get two 12 inch spicy Italian subs every time we go in there and it's $21.20 with tax. Then we eat half for lunch and the other half for dinner. He's been there for years and delivers a lot of sandwiches over the lunch hour. Over to Jane."

"I've see the Bronco you are asking about Peter but don't know who he is or where he lives. I'm sure you'll see him in the ditch soon. I've never been to the Sub Shop but I'll give it a try. Over to Fly Boy."

"I don't know why people think that just because they have a 4wd they can drive as fast as they do in the summer when the road is covered in ice. I remember seeing a Toyota truck just bounce off the road while I watched him in my rear view mirror. I didn't stop to help him. I figured that he drove in the ditch so it was up to him to drive out. Back to Stan and Gloria."

"We think the greenhouse sounds like a great idea Carla. It's the only way to garden in North Idaho and it keeps the deer away as well. I have heard that it can sometimes even snow in August if you can believe that. Over to Steve."

"I stopped by the Sub Shop the other day and had to parallel park by the credit union. Hadn't done that in years. I am normally only in town early in the morning before it gets busy. Back to Scott."

"Sandpoint is a zoo anytime after 11am. When I first moved here the population was about 4000 but now it has doubled and of course lots of the traffic is from people who live out of town. I know that people from Montana actually shop in Sandpoint. Over to Susan."

"I know a guy who gets angry if he has to stand in line at the Post Office. Not a big line either. If he is behind two or three people he threatens to come back later. Over to Charles and Megan."

"I don't think we would do well in a big city any more. We've been talking about having a party for the net sometime this summer when we can have a cook out. Keep this in mind. We'll have to work around everyone's busy schedules. Back to Bret."

"Sounds good about a party for the net. And George I like the idea of getting together on the radio Wednesday evenings as well. I'm going to write this down. Over to Mary and Beth."

"We like both ideas, A Wednesday get together on the radio and a party in the summer. It will be fun to put a face on the people we have been talking with on the radio for sure. Somebody was telling us that summer starts on the fourth of July around here. Over to Tom."

"That saying about the fourth of July isn't exactly true. It's usually the fifth of July. There is another saying I like a lot about Bonner County. There are two seasons here, winter and road construction. Don't you agree Walt?"

"I haven't been here that long but I think there is a lot of truth to this. I'll keep an eye out for the Bronco and a summer party sounds fun. Also I think adding Wednesday for CB chit chat is a great idea. The more people get used to contacting each other on the radio, the more useful this will be for everyone. I guess I'll say Happy New Year to all and clear out of here for the night. It's been fun for sure. And since we ripped off Art Bell's idea of making new years resolutions maybe next week we can each make a prediction of something that will happen in the year and write these down too, Maybe there is a psychic among us. I will be in the hillbilly wood fired hot tub shooting off bottle rockets around 9pm on New Years Eve. If any come over your house you'll know they came from me. I am too cheap to celebrate with gunfire since ammo is so expensive. Take care and hope to talk to you all next Sunday if not before. This is Walt, signing and saying 73."

"Before you go Walt, tell me a little about your hillbilly hot tub." Peter asked.

"Well it is six foot round metal stock tank that has a firebox and stovepipe built underneath it. It is filled with fresh water every time so there is no chlorine and it takes about 2 and a half hours to warm up the water. I'll send everyone a few pictures. Not as neat as a commercial hot tub but the price is right and there is no electric bill to worry about."

"OK Thanks Walt. Sounds like something I would be interested in. We'll let you go. Talk to later." Peter thought that a hot tub to soak in every now and then was a great idea.

On New Years Day Walt got up about 5:30am and lit the fire in the woodstove. When he turned on the yard light to let Sparky out he could see that there wasn't any fresh snow and he was pleased that he did not have any snow removal chores. He let Sparky back in and she finished her breakfast kibble in no time and was hoping Walt would drop something while he made his breakfast. After breakfast and a few cups of coffee he booted up his computer to check out some news sites and the local weather forecast. Then Walt checked his email and found some Happy New Years wishes from friends, a few ads for after Christmas sales, and an email from the Pacific Northwest Remote Viewers Group. They wanted Walt to post the results from the last website update to read "**Priority Target 8659/1523 / Next Volcanic Eruption / Location**." They also wanted Walt to post the copies of the remote viewing sessions and subsections of five of their remote viewers and to show all of their data, and sketches, along with the remote viewing manager's analysis. In addition they wanted the following warning displayed in large text on their home page,

"**WARNING – MAJOR VOCANIC ERUPTION PREDICTED IN YELLOWSTONE CALDERA IN THE NEXT 30 DAYS.** December 31 - Seattle Washington. The Pacific Northwest Remote Viewers Group has issued a high confidence alert that a major volcanic eruption will take place in the Yellowstone Caldera sometime within the next 30 days. This is expected to be massive eruption with certain loss of life and destruction of property. The Pacific Remote Viewers Group recommends that people evacuate the area as soon as possible."

This Warning was to be linked to the "**Priority Target 8659/1523 / Next Volcanic Eruption / Location**." Which linked to the session reports, sketches, and the mangers analysis. And of course this needed to be done as soon as possible. Four hours later, Walt finished this work, loaded up the new pages, sent them an invoice, and wished them a Happy New Year. He also sent them a personal note thanking them for their work and explained that he would do what he could to publicize this for them.

After a shock like this he needed a break and took Sparky for a walk out in the snow to try to clear his mind. The cold fresh air and the virgin white snow helped to get his heart rate back to normal but he couldn't stop thinking about what he just learned. He knew from his own effort to remote view the target that it was big, explosive, and scary. Imagine being told that within 30 days it would be the end of the world for anyone who was near the super volcano when it erupted. After all, the images of the Kilauea volcano and cloud of acid rain to hit southern California were fresh in his mind. But these tragic events happened in far away places. Yellowstone was pretty close to home and this would be a big problem for Walt and all his friends throughout the inter mountain area and the pacific northwest.

Because of the New Years Eve and New Years Day Holidays he couldn't really warn anyone about this until January 2 nd. So Walt decided that he had some time to decide exactly what to do. He brought in firewood and kindling and then made a nice dinner. After supper he filled the hot tub with fresh water and loaded the firebox so it was ready to light. Because it would be dark soon he brought some extra firewood to the hot tub. He planned to light the hot tub fire at 6:00 pm so that it would be ready around 8:30. He took his bottle rockets and lighter out to the deck so that he wouldn't forget them. His plan was to shoot off his bottle rockets around 9 pm because this would be midnight on the east coast. This is how most of the locals celebrated New Years Eve. They watched the ball drop in Madison Square Garden at 9 o'clock Pacific time and then shot off their guns and fireworks, By midnight Pacific time the neighborhood was usually pretty quiet and most people had gone to bed.

When it was time to hit the tub Walt took his portable radio with him to listen to music and to keep track of the time. The warm water was very relaxing and for a few moments he forgot about Yellowstone. Then it was time to shoot off some bottle rockets. He always bought the ones that made a boom (or pop) when they reached their peak. This made it possible to aim them so that they would explode over a neighbor's house and this added to the fun. He kept a stash of bottle rockets for use in the hot tub in the winter and sometimes he would shoot them in the direction of moose to scare them out of the yard. If a moose is camped out in your yard it is not a good idea for you or your dog to go outside, so this is a good and safe way to scare them away. For some reason a 12 gauge shotgun fired in the air doesn't scare moose but a bottle rocket does. When Walt was thoroughly cooked he got out of the hot tub and opened the valve so it would be empty (and not frozen) in the morning.

Chapter 4. January

"Let me hear ya now
I don't know, I don't know
I don't know where I'm a-gonna go
when the volcano blows"
Jimmy Buffet

Sparky was glad when the sounds of gunfire and bottle rockets were done last night. They both slept in longer than usual but that's one thing that holidays were for. Rather than taking the day off and watching parades and bowl games Walt had a full days work ahead of him preparing to warn as many people as possible about the Yellowstone volcano. He prepared the following press release:

"FOR IMMEDIATE RELEASE:

WARNING – MAJOR VOCANIC ERUPTION PREDICTED IN YELLOWSTONE CALDERA WITHIN THE NEXT 30 DAYS!

January 2 – Seattle, Washington

The Pacific Northwest Remote Viewers Group has issued a high confidence alert that a major volcanic eruption will take place in the Yellowstone Caldera sometime within the next 30 days. This is expected to be massive eruption with certain loss of life and destruction of property.

The Pacific Remote Viewers Group recommends that people evacuate the area as soon as possible. If evacuation is not possible then residents are encouraged to prepare for wide spread volcanic ash that can damage buildings and block roads. Power outages are expected. Cell phone and internet outages are likely.

People would be wise to prepare for major disruptions that could last for weeks, months, or even longer. It is recommended that drinking water, food, medicines, and pet food be stockpiled. People should know that breathing volcanic ash is extremely hazardous and good quality face masks will be required. Vehicles should not be driven in the ash because this can cripple auto engines in just a few miles.

It is also suggested that people keep their bath tubs, and covered hot tubs filled so that they can have water on hand to flush toilets and for cleaning.

This is not a drill. We hope that we are wrong but we are over 90% certain that an eruption will occur.

For more information contact the Pacific Northwest Remote Viewers Group at TPNWRVG.org. "

Walt planned to send this press release by email to every newspaper within 1500 miles of Yellowstone the next day when people went back to work. He would be sending this to every TV station in the same area as well. He would also be sending this by email to all of his personal, family, and radio friends. In addition he would pay out-of-pocket to have the press release sent by Issuewire to over 300 locations.

He knew that it was human nature and most people would ignore this warning and laugh at the idea that anyone could predict the future. But there was nothing Walt could do about this. It was his duty and obligation to warn as many people as possible but it wasn't his problem if they did not believe in the warning and/or chose to ignore it.

On the third of January Walt took his only credit card out of the office and put it in his pocket. His Visa card had never been used but it was going to get a workout in the next few days. Walt kept the card for emergencies and if a volcano in his back yard wasn't an emergency, he didn't know what was. He left Sparky at home and drove his truck to town.

His first stop was the Northland store which was both a farm and sporting goods store. He bought 8 fifty pound bags of dog food which was all the Science Diet that Sparky liked in stock. He also picked up six five gallon plastic gas cans, and three five gallon plastic water jugs. Next he stopped at Import Tools store and bought $100 worth of AA, AAA, 9 volt, and C cell batteries. After this he filled up the six new gas jugs with regular gas and drove home to work on his list. When he got home he ordered another dried food meal selection like the one that he got a few weeks ago.

The next day he went to town again to make a major food buy. He only bought foods that he could store long term like canned meats, tuna, peanut butter, canned peaches, salsa, rice, pasta, dried milk, powdered eggs, flour, yeast, etc. While he was checking out he remembered something his grandmother had told his father, "Get it before the hoarders do." After leaving the grocery store he bought 5 more plastic gas can at the Farmland and filled them with gas before driving home.

When he got home and put things away he started working on another list. It was impossible to purchase, or even think of, everything he would need for an entire year but he was trying to plan ahead. The next day in town he bought vitamins D3, C, and Zinc. He picked up some Ibuprofen, shampoo, toothpaste, wooden matches, some gallon propane cylinders, paper plates, paper towels, zip lock bags, toilet paper, sea salt, wax paper, freezer paper, freezer tape, garbage bags, coffee, and coffee filters, until his cart was filled. He asked himself if he was going crazy as he drove home but he justified this behavior as planning for the worst and only buying the things he would need later anyway.

By this time he was getting lots of feedback from people about the press release. Some people were prepping as he was, and others thought that he spent too much time listening to Alex Jones. Come to think of it he remembered that he should pick up some tin foil the next time that he went to town and a hundred pounds of potatoes to go with it.

Another thing he thought that he might need was a pitcher pump and some PVC pipe in case the electric pump in his water well failed. This cost him another $300 but the peace of mind it gave him was worth it. This kind of manic behavior was common among people who are convinced that danger is around the corner and after remote viewing this himself, Walt knew that he had every reason to be concerned. Even though he had plenty of guns and enough ammunition to start a revolution, he thought that he should stop by the Sandpoint Gun Shop and pick up some more.

Besides prepping for the Yellowstone Super Volcano Walt tried to learn as much about this as he could. The more he read the worse it sounded. The only good part about an eruption this time of year would be that there would be fewer tourists in the park. Yellowstone National Park hosts 3 million tourists a year mostly in the summer and fall.

The last eruption of the Yellowstone Caldera happened over 600,000 years ago and ejected an estimated 200 cubic miles of magma, granite, dust, gasses, and volcanic ash into the atmosphere. The caldera was created when the molten rock was ejected so rapidly that the land above it collapsed into the chamber that held the magma.

An eruption of this size could spread a three foot layer of molten ash as far as 1000 miles and start fires which would add to the destruction. The area would be completely closed to ground travel and be closed to air travel and rescue operations as well. Some experts predicted that the entire U.S. would experience a "nuclear winter" and the country would not see much sunshine at all for quite sometime. Sulfuric gasses would be mixed with the water vapor in the atmosphere and the haze that would blanket the country would rapidly cool the northern latitudes and drastically impact crops and the food supply. In addition the acid rain and large amount of ash would poison surface water for years.

Experts have suggested that the Yellowstone Super Volcano would kill as many as 90,000 people immediately and countless numbers of farm animals and wild life. Eventually the casualties could be well into the millions.

He learned that there were up to 20 super volcanos around the world and 4 super volcanos located in the United States mainland and one in Alaska. The biggest known super volcano eruption was called the Great Dying and known as the Permian Extinction which occurred in Siberia 250 million years ago. This put so much CO_2 in the atmosphere that it killed 80% of marine life and 70% of vertebrates on the planet. The last recent super volcano eruption occurred 26,500 years ago in Lake Taupo, New Zeland.

One thing Walt noticed about all the experts and their predictions about a volcanic event of this size was that none of them bothered to point out how society would suffer a complete melt down if something like this would happen. Most Americans live paycheck to paycheck and cannot afford an unforeseen expense of as little as $500. Most people don't have two weeks worth of food, water, cash, or anything else for that matter. If the power goes out, people cannot use their credit cards to buy food or gas. If the power goes out they would have no heat in their homes and could not prepare meals at home even if they did have food and water.

It wouldn't take too long before people would get desperate, lawless, and violent. People would begin to take whatever they wanted, whenever they could. The rule of law would be quickly replaced by the rule of the jungle, where only the strong survive. The large population areas would quickly become a hell on earth and eventually this would spread to rural areas like Rapid Lightning Creek Road where criminals would try to prey on people who they viewed as easy targets. Knowing this, Walt was more concerned about security than ever before.

That evening Walt turned on his CB radio and heard some of the neighbors already on the air.

"I don't know about this. What do you think? It sounded like Scott but he couldn't be sure.

"I have heard of remote viewing on the radio and I think there could be something to it. But even if nothing happens it's a good idea to be prepared as much as possible for any emergency." This was Fly Boy for sure.

"That's a good point. I think that most people who live up here in the woods are better prepared than people in the city."

"If you live in town it's just a few minutes to go to the store but for us it's more of an adventure especially in bad weather. I feel sorry for the people in Hawaii and southern California too. One minute you live in paradise and the next minute you are living in hell."

"I don't know what is worse, watching the calendar and waiting for a disaster or having it hit you by surprise."

Walt jumped in and joined the conversation. "Evening guys This is Walt I've been reading the mail. I don't know what to expect up here but from what I have read, if Yellowstone blows it could be one for the record books. Some experts predict as much as 3 feet of ash on the ground for a 1000 mile radius."

"Hey Walt this is Scott. Ash like that would be a lot more to deal with than the same amount of snow."

Fly Boy jumped in. "I don't think a snow blower would do much good. Besides the ash would fry the engine in no time."

Walt remembered seeing a documentary about the Mount Saint Helens eruption in 1980. "I guess the ash would destroy cop cars and emergency vehicles in less than an hour. When Mt. Saint Helen blew they finally resorted to putting panty hose over the air filter just to keep the rigs running."

Scott thought this sounded like a good idea. "That's a good idea. Don't have any panty hose at the moment but maybe I'll get some."

"They are also useful if you plan to rob a bank." Fly Boy joked.

"Well if something does happen I am sure that we'll be glad to have our radios. The big thing is to have them hooked up to a battery. I wouldn't expect the power grid to be too reliable."

"That's for sure, and if the sun is blocked, we'll need generators to charge the batteries. And we'll have to remember to protect the generators with panty hose too." Walt suggested.

"I guess in a case like that it would be better to run the generators in an out building to minimize their exposure to the ash." Fly Boy had given this some consideration.

"Sounds like a good idea. I never would have thought about this. Been listening in. This is George. Over."

Walt added, "If you think that things are expensive now just wait until the stores are out of food and there is no power to pump the gas. I was thinking that cash might not be much good and it might be better to have some things that you could trade."

"Like what," Fly Boy asked.

"I don't know. Besides food, water, and gas, maybe firewood, coffee, and liquor," Walt replied.

"How about toilet paper? We all saw how crazy that was with the lock downs," George replied.

" just ordered a variety of dried meals from Online World. 167 meals for about $280. That might be good trading stock as well." Walt was trying to get people to think about prepping.

"If the volcano erupts, a lot of people will go nuts without their Online World fix." Scott said. " Get it now while you still can."

Walt threw out this idea. "Another thing that we need to think about is our own security. I would expect looting and home invasions to become common even in rural areas."

"I never thought about that but you're right Walt, this could be a big issue for sure. You couldn't even call the cops if the phones were out." Fly Boy responded.

Walt replied. "I have a radio that will broadcast on police frequencies. It is illegal to do this except in an emergency."

George added, "Even if you could get through to the police they probably couldn't get here in time anyway.

"You mean the government can't always save us? Say it's not so." Fly Boy said jokingly but it got everyone thinking that security could be a problem and if they needed help, it probably wouldn't arrive in time, if at all.

Walt didn't say anything about this but he just thought of something that he would pick up if he could. He wanted to get a good air cleaner for the cabin in case of forest fire smoke but with the threat of an ash cloud, this might be a good thing to have. "Gotta go finish my list. Fun talking with you guys tonight. See you Sunday." Walt turned off his radio but everyone else kept talking with each other for awhile longer.

The next morning Walt did his morning chores and he and Sparky had breakfast while the woodstove was warming up the cabin. He checked his email and then started looking for an air cleaner online. He looked at several and then ordered a Blueair Air Purifier for large rooms. It removed 99.97% of pollen dust viruses and came with a Particle and carbon fiber filter and 2 washable pre-filters. The ad said that it was very quiet and only needed 60 watts of power. The unit cost $279 and Walt clicked on the Buy Now button. He hoped that it would arrive in a week or so and that this would be in time. He looked at the clock and saw that it was almost time to get on the radio.

He selected his end fed antenna, turned on the power supply and his Icom radio. It was already tuned to 3.988 and he didn't hear anyone on and he started transmitting. "QR Zed, QR Zed, Is there anyone on frequency this morning? This is AP7ZMT."

Dennis came right back to him. "You're the first person I have heard this morning. AR7QRN."

"Morning Dennis, how are things today?"

"Not bad Walt, just waiting for my coffee to cool down so I can drink it. What's new with you?"

"I have been prepping for the volcano. The more I read about it the more concerned I get. Over."

"Do you really think that is going to happen? AU7PM."

"I think it will happen for sure Frank, the questions I have are when will it happen and how bad will it be?"

"One thing I know about people who predict the future is that they are almost always wrong." (AU7PM)

"Like they say, even a broken clock is right twice a day."
(AP7ZMT.

"Unless it's digital and then it's never right." (AR7QRN)

"We're always ready for anything up here at the ranch.
AN7HM."

"That's a good way to be." (AP7ZMT)

"Morning dudes. Wish I could say the same thing. I just hope that I have enough firewood for the rest of the winter. AY7OM."

"Morning Ray. I ran out of wood once and vowed never to let it happen again." (AU7PM)

"Yes Frank, I know what you mean. (AY7OM)

"We ran out of wood last spring and had to bring back 20 sticks at a time from our daughter's place. Since we usually see her everyday this worked but it wasn't fun. AM7DX."

"If the volcano blows I wonder if we will have global warming or global cooling? (AR7QRN)

" I think the jury is still out on that one but I am leaning toward warming at first and then cooling. Over. (AP7ZMT)

"I am topping off my gas tanks and keeping my batteries charged just in case." (AM7DX)

"Just looking at the pictures of Hawaii makes me wish that I had built an underground house out of concrete." (AR7QRN)

"I think an underground house would be great. Easy to heat and no stairs." (AP7ZMT)

"How's your CB net coming Walt?" (AU7PM)

"It's working out pretty good. We've got 15 people so far and we just started meeting twice a week. One couple is even studying for their ham licenses."

"I've been thinking about trying to start something like that over here. We have a lot of neighbors close by." (AR7QRN)

"Besides meeting some new neighbors it is a good way to network. I think I told you that we are able to help catch two guys who were breaking into cabins. One of the guys used his drone to get a plate number." (AP7ZMT)

"Sounds like you are off to a good start. Has anyone worked any DX lately?' (AU7PM)

"I worked a few stations in Europe the other day on 17 meters. AN7HM."

"I worked Ireland and France this morning on CW before coming down here." (AU7PM)

"I haven't worked much on the radio. Been listening to the emergency service nets out of California and Hawaii. AN7HM."

"Some of those people went from living in paradise to living in hell in the blink of an eye Joe. AM7DX."

"And some went to living in Heaven." (AP7ZMT)

"Roger that Walt. AN7HM."

"This is Ruby, AN6RST. I've been listening for awhile. Is there another volcano I don't know about? Over."

"This is Walt, AP7ZMT. I do the web work for the Pacific Northwest Remote Viewers Group and they are predicting that Yellowstone will blow in30 days or so. Over."

"Oh my, I hadn't heard about that." (AN6RST)

"You can see their press release at TPNWRVG.org, that's Tango Papa Norway Whiskey Romeo Victor George dot org, if you like. AP7ZMT.

"Roger, I'll take a look at that." (AN6RST)

"Where are you located Ruby? This is Frank AU7PM"

"I am living south of Portland, Oregon right now. Got my call about 12 years ago in Sacramento, California. Over."

"Hope you didn't lose anyone southern California. It still looks pretty bad down there. AM7DX."

"Not that I know of but I have heard some of the hams I know from down there talking about this. It's a real mess. Over."

"Just wondering if you know AN7ICM Ruby. He works net control on the Marine Services net on 40 meters? AN7HM. The name here is Joe. Over."

"I have listened to the net a few times and recall hearing him but I have never checked in there. Over."

"Roger. By the way we are here about every morning from 0930 to 1130 and you are welcome to join in anytime. With a lady on frequency, we'll have to mind our manners. By the way are you a YL or an XYL? Over." (A YL means a young lady and an XYL means a married woman)

"I am a YL. You can see me and my station on my QRZ.com page Over."

"That's great we can use a fresh viewpoint around here Ruby. We are all OM (Old Man/Men). This is Jeff AM7DX."

"Speak for yourself Jeff. Some of us are older than others. This is Dennis, AR7QRN."

"Morning everyone. This is Howie operating mobile with 100 watts. Do you guys copy OK? AS7MB."

"Morning Howie. You are sounding good over here. Got you an S5-6. AP7ZMT."

"Well glad to hear that I am making it into Idaho. When you run mobile, you just never know how it will go."

"Coming into Blue Creek just fine Howie. AR7QRN."

"Heard that you guys actually had some snow the other day. Over"

"We had about 4 inches on the roads around Port Townsend. A lot of accidents. Most people here do not have snow tires or any idea how to drive on the snow, Over."

"The trick to driving on snow is to put the gas peddle all the way to floor and go as fast as you can. AU7PM."

"That's what people were doing alright. Some of the roads looked like a demolition Derby. Oh Walt, I got your email. Thanks for the heads up. Over."

"Roger that I sent it to as many people as I could. I hope it doesn't happen but the remote viewers group is pretty certain that it will. Keep your batteries charged up just in case. Over." (AP7ZMT)

"Good idea. AS7MB."

"Besides the obvious, I think that society will go to hell in a hand basket if people have to go for more than a few days without grid power or the internet. Over."

"That's why I got my concealed weapons license years ago." (AN7HM)

"Roger that. It's just so hard to hide my machine gun under my trench coat. Over." (AP7ZMT)

109

"They just don't make trench coats like they used to.: (AU7PM)

"I keep a face mask in the car in case I need to stop by a bank and make a withdrawal." (AY7OM)

"Do you see what you got yourself into Ruby?" (AR7QRN)

"You guys are fun. I am tired of talking about radios and antennas all the time." (AN6RST)

"There isn't much that we don't talk about from time to time that's for sure. " (AU7PM)

"Well I hope everyone had a Happy New Year. Has everybody made a New Years Resolution already? Mine is to learn how to grow mushrooms. Over. (AU7PM)

"I haven't though about this but I would like to upgrade to Amateur Extra, AS7MB."

"I would like to get a directional antenna like a hexbeam up this year. AN7HM."

"I would like to finally write that Children's book that I have been talking about. AM7DX."

"I am just hoping that there is a next year, if you know what I mean. AP7ZMT."

"My resolution is to get the power company to get rid of my RF noise so I don't have to cut down their power pole. AR7QRN."

"My resolution is to get a new car or I should say, to be realistic, get another car. AY7OM."

"I guess my resolution is to grow a garden now that I have the space. AN6RST."

"Jeff, Howie, Joe, and myself are big gardeners Ruby. We are always happy to talk about this. I can send you a few seed catalogs to look through. AU7PM."

"Thanks Frank, that would be nice. I have grown flowers before but I am new at vegetable gardening. AN6RST."

"It's been fun everyone. My little dog is giving me the look so I better stretch my legs and take her for a walk. She is my security system and I want to keep her in tip top shape. 73 and talk to you all later. This is AP7ZMT signing off and going out to play in the snow.

Everyone in the group said, "73, and Happy New Year" and Walt turned off his radio and put on his Pack boots. Sparky couldn't wait for Walt to get his coat and sheepskin cap and was jumping at the door as he opened it. There were fresh deer tracks around the cabin and garage and when they walked onto the driveway they saw that one large moose had walked up the road. Besides being much larger, moose tracks are shaped totally different than those of deer and elk. They are even more impressive when seen in the mud. Sparky stuck her nose in the tracks and gave them a good strong sniff. Walt could only imagine that the smell was strong enough for her to taste.

Although the lower driveway had been maintained and had little snow, the upper driveway had about 24 inches of powder snow making it difficult for both of them to walk through. Walt tried his best to walk in the moose tracks and Sparky decided that breaking trail and going first was too much effort so she let Walt take the lead. After they got about half way to the property line they turned around and headed home. Walt knew that the next time they walked this way he had better be in snowshoes.

Sparky was a little tired when they got back from their walk and that was the whole point of the walk, to get some exercise and lot of fresh cold air. The nice warm cabin felt great when they got inside. Walt got Sparky some fresh water and he poured himself a hot cup of coffee.

Walt wasn't sure what to do for the rest of the day. While on their walk he had decided that there was no use ordering anything else online because it was doubtful that he could actually get anything he wanted shipped in time. Any last minute supplies that he needed would have to be purchased in town. He was surprised that the stores still had lots of things on the shelves and that there hadn't been a rush to buy supplies since the press release about the predicted eruption at Yellowstone had been published in the paper. He tried to tell as many people as he could about this but most people did not take this nearly as seriously as he did.

For a moment he understood how the clergy must feel when people didn't respond to the teachings of the church and make an effort to change their attitudes and behavior. Like Paul Revere all he could do was to try and warn people that danger was coming. If they didn't choose to believe him, there wasn't anything else he could do about this so he tried not to think about it. In the game of life, nobody gets out alive anyway.

Walt decided to get his Gold Panning Machine set up and process some of the sand from the sandbar. He got everything together and turned on his radio to the local FM station, rock 103. As he started to run some sand through the machine he felt good to be doing something fun and productive in the comfort of his warm cabin on a cold snow covered day. The radio was playing some classic rock and roll when a Jimmy Buffet song began to play.

"Now, I don't know
I don't know
I don't know where I'm a-gonna go when the volcano blows
Let me say now
I don't know
I don't know
I don't know where I'm a-gonna go when the volcano blows

Ground she's moving under me
Tidal waves out on the sea
Sulphur smoke up in the sky
Pretty soon, we learn to fly…"

Walt was able to relax and not think about the volcano until he heard this on the radio. Then as he continued to add sand to the rotating spiral wheel he kept singing to himself, "Now I don't know, I don't know, I don't know where I'm a-gonna go when the volcano blows." He smiled as he recognized how preoccupied he had become with this thought. Then they played one of his favorite songs by Jesse Colin Young, Ridgetop.

112

"Now, when I built my house
I cut six trees to clear out the land
But there's thirty or more left
And you know that they're gonna stand

It's a squirrel sanctuary
They think this woods is their home
And as long as I'm here
I'll make sure people leave us all alone..."

After hearing this song and singing along, Walt stopped thinking about the volcano for awhile and remembered how lucky he was to live in God's country away from the rat race and the pollution and the crime that he left behind in the city. It was so relaxing and satisfying to be running sand through the gold panning machine and watching the small pieces of gold getting washed into the catch cup. For the rest of the afternoon nothing bothered him and all the stress was lifted out of his body. He was at peace in his warm and comfortable cabin with his little dog Sparky who was stretched out and sleeping on the carpet by the stove.

He had processed five half buckets of sand that day and felt like he had accomplished something for the day. Then he picked up everything, fixed supper, and called it a very good day. He was pleased that his machine was working well and that he was catching a little gold.

That night Walt didn't get much sleep. He was thinking about how he might be able to make some devices to help defend against home invasion. It must have been something that he had for dinner because no matter how hard he tried it seemed that this was all that he could think about all night long.

His idea was to build a small wooden miniature claymore mine that fired 12 gauge shotgun shells. It could be set off with a tripwire but he had to find a way to remotely activate this so it would not fire unless it was armed. He didn't want wildlife or Sparky or anyone but the bad guys to be able to trigger the device.

He thought the mini mine could be built out of wood to hold the shotgun shell and a mouse trap (that when tripped) could be used to fire the shotgun shell. The hard part would be to design something that would prevent the spring trap bar from contacting the rear of the shotgun shell unless it was remotely armed. Possibly a radio signal could be used to arm the device but he wasn't sure exactly how to do this. It would take some thought and some experimentation to perfect the idea but he thought that it could be done.

Another idea that he had been thinking of was to make a cylinder that held a pistol shell. This could be attached to an arrow so that when the arrow was shot from a bow and the loaded cylinder struck the target, it would cause the shell to fire at point blank range. This would have the advantage of not giving away the shooters position because the sound would not be coming from the direction of the bow. Maybe he had been watching too many movies but this is what he was thinking about when his mind wandered.

After thinking about both of these ideas for awhile Walt decided that they were stupid, impractical, and not necessary.
The mini mines would be dangerous and the idea that they could be armed remotely with a radio signal meant that any spurious RF signal could arm the mines at any time without his knowledge. The idea of a bang stick head on an arrow was silly as well. The first time it was used, everyone would hear the shell go off and it would defeat the purpose. It would be better to use a normal arrow anyway because you could get off a few shots before anyone noticed that you were shooting at them.

But after discarding these two bonehead ideas he had come up with something that was workable. He went out to the wood shop, started a fire in the stove, and began making some stock to make birdhouses using some cedar boards that he found under the workbench. The boards were rough cut 1" x 10" x 6 feet long so he ran them through the planer on both sides. Then he cut two of the boards down to 6" wide and then cut these in half on the band saw so they measured a little less than 1/2" x

6" X 6 feet long. After that he planed the long thin boards down until they were each about 1/8" thick.

The next day Walt drove to town and got some Tannerite at Northland. He was able to get 10 two pound target jars for $170. They were labeled extreme range (200 yards or more) and were the biggest ones they sold. This is the brand name of a popular binary mixture to make exploding targets. It is made with Ammonium Nitrate and fine aluminum power. When this is thoroughly mixed and packed in a confined space like a plastic jar with a lid, it can produce quite an explosion. It was pretty safe to use because it can only be detonated when struck by a high powered rifle bullet. While he was at the store he also purchased four jumbo packs of .177 caliber BBs. Before returning from town he topped off the gas in his truck, which he planned to do from then on, every time he was in town.

That afternoon Walt cut the cedar pieces to make birdhouses using the thin cedar boards for the face, and the one inch thick wood for the other pieces. Then he drilled a one inch diameter hole through the thin face boards and placed them face down on the workbench. He put a piece of black tape over the center hole and then spread a thick coat of yellow glue over the backs of each face board. When the glue set up for a few minutes and became tacky he carefully put as many BBs over the backs of the thin face boards and let them dry overnight.

His plan was to place a plastic jar of mixed Tannerite inside each birdhouse as it was assembled. Because he cared about the trees he made a U shaped metal backing for the target jars so that the blast would be concentrated outward toward the face of the birdhouse. He planned to install each birdhouse on trees in strategic locations around his parking area outside the cabin. He guessed that installing them about 8 feet above the ground would make them easy to hit and provide excellent killing power. In the case a home invasion he could fire his rifle at a birdhouse and the exploding Tannerite would send the BBs out through the thin face boards and toward the bad guys. Because the explosives were inside birdhouses they were protected from the weather and did not look out of place. Any birds that investigated the houses would be discouraged from choosing the house as a nest because of the black tape blocking the hole.

The next morning he assembled one and mounted it on a dead habitat tree on the upper driveway. He put some 4 foot high sticks in the snow at 8, 10, and 12 feet from the birdhouse and attached sheets of cardboard to the sticks to act as targets. He stepped back 50 feet or so and shot the birdhouse. When the birdhouse exploded Walt new that he had a winner. There was a very loud kaboom and there was very little left of the birdhouse. Even if the shrapnel wasn't an issue, just the noise would nearly scare a person to death. When he examined the cardboard targets, they had at least 20 BB sized holes in each of them. After the cardboard was removed from the sticks he could see that the BBs had embedded themselves well into the wooden sticks so he knew that this would be a very effective weapon.

The next thing Walt had to do was to decide exactly where to put the birdhouses. He imagined where and how he would attack the cabin and where he would take cover if he was one of the bad guys. Using this data he installed them in key locations that would be effective and that he could hit from the cabin. He had six birdhouses in the front of the cabin and three outside the back door. When he was finished it looked like he was quite a bird lover.

Earlier when Walt had been in town he was tempted to get a sign that read, "Insured by Smith and Wesson" but he decided against this and bought one that read, "Private Drive." It wasn't as threatening as the Smith and Wesson sign or as obnoxious as a "No Trespassing" sign. After all, he wasn't trying to discourage visitors, just explorers. When it was time to check the mail he and Sparky walked down the driveway and installed the new sign at the road.

When they were walking back up the driveway Walt still had security on his mind. He had seen a WW2 movie awhile back and remembered that the people in London used heavy curtains to block out the light at night from inside their homes. This would be a good idea if the power was out and he didn't want to advertise that he still had power. He couldn't think of anything that he had that would work for this but he would try to get something in town.

That afternoon Walt was going through his receipts to see how much he had put on his credit card and how much credit he had left over. He couldn't think of much else that he really needed to spend on emergency prepping so he took the card out of his wallet and put it back in the desk. He looked out the window and noticed that it was snowing again. Since he didn't have to go anywhere or do anything else outside for the day, this was fine with him.

Getting ready for the volcano was a little like studying for a test, At some point you just can't study anymore and you just want to get it over with. The prepping was stressful and satisfying at the same time. He knew that it was impossible to anticipate everything that he would need in an emergency but he thought that he had most of the bases covered. If he needed anything that he didn't have already, he would just have to get by without it. Walt put some more wood in the stove, made a quick dinner, and turned on his radio to listen to some of the news.

The big news was that there had been three mass shootings that day. A fifty year old black man fired over 30 shots on a New York City subway and killed 4 people and wounded 10 others. The suspect was in custody and his social media showed that he was a black nationalist. An 18 year old white kid shot and killed 11 black people in a grocery store in Buffalo, New York. They had him in custody as well and it turned out that he had been on a watch list for threatening to shoot up his school. In Los Angeles an Asian man shot 5 people and killed 2 of them in coffee shop. Some customers jumped him and prevented him from doing more damage.

Naturally these stories were followed by politicians calling for gun control even though there were very strict gun laws in each of these locations. Walt had always wondered why so many people went crazy and chose their victims at random. After all there were plenty of people that one could argue

"Needed killing" so why didn't they target them? Alex Jones had been warning about more government false flag attacks in order to start a race war and eventually confiscate firearms. It wasn't out of the question that these three attacks could have had government involvement considering how many "incidents" had been proven to have had so many FBI infiltrators.

The other thing that Walt wondered about is why so many of these mass shooters gave up without a fight and didn't go down shooting? The obvious answer would be that these people were cowards but maybe this was for another reason. Walt had learned that the government lied to the people all the time and the so called news covered this up. Only six people controlled 90% of the media. No wonder so much of the news was either fake or slanted.

The other story on the news was about a School District who was prosecuting three high school students for hate crimes because they used the wrong pronoun to refer to another student. Walt couldn't stand it any more and turned off the news and turned on his CB radio. A few of the neighbors were talking and Walt was just planning to listen.

"I just got some solar cells, a deep cycle battery, and some LED lights the other day. I think will this be nice when the power goes out." Walt could tell by her voice it was Jane.

"This time of year the power can go out any time. I hate looking for a flashlight in the dark. Over." This sounded like Susan.

"What I hate is when the power goes out when you are cooking dinner."

"I know what you mean. I keep a small camping cook stove in the house just in case. Another thing I hate is waking up to find the power out and not being able to get a cup coffee."

"Jane, are your solar cells putting out any power on these cloudy days? This is Scott. Over."

"The controller says that the solar cells are charging the battery but only at 25%. Over."

" That's better than I thought. I didn't expect them to work at all unless it was in direct sun."

"I also have a trickle charger to keep the battery topped off when the power is on."

"Do you have your CB connected to the battery?"

"I sure do but I have to disconnect the trickle charger whenever I have the radio on because it causes interference. Over."

"I've got to get some battery power and a few LED lights around here."

"LED lights are great. Before I got some LED lights I used kerosene lanterns. They hardly put out any light at all. This is Susan. Over."

"It really cracks me up to see those things in the movies, One kerosene lantern lights up the whole room. What a joke."

"I know exactly what you mean Jane. What else is new?"

"I can't believe the new snow plow driver. He just dumps a pile of snow in my driveway so I have to shovel it before I can drive in or out."

"That's one thing I like about my Jeep. I can drive right through it." Scott sounded like he didn't enjoy shoveling snow.

"I guess that you have to make a choice between gas mileage and not getting stuck in the snow."

"What I have noticed since I moved here is that they don't bother to plow if school is not in session."

"You've got that right, At least put a teaspoon full of sand down at the intersections."

"Since they are not using salt the cars don't rust."

"You've got a point there. In Wisconsin, a car will be rusted out in four or five years."

Walt turned his radio off and was glad to see that people were using their radios more often. The next day Walt looked out the window and saw that he had about 8 inches of fresh snow on the ground. He fed Sparky and let her out and cleared the parking area with the walk behind snow blower before breakfast. He thought he would do the driveway later with the tractor when it was time to check the mail. He wondered if he spent more time mowing the lawn and controlling the weeds or dealing with the snow. Either way it was part of the joy of being a home owner.

When Walt was done clearing the snow in the parking area outside the cabin he came in to warm up and get some breakfast. After so much exercise and fresh air he decided to have some scrambled eggs and fried potatoes with a couple of pieces of fried spam. He felt a little guilty eating canned meat that was intended to be saved for an emergency but it sure was delicious. After breakfast and a few cups of hot coffee he checked his email and then turned on his radio to 3.988. and heard a couple of people talking.

"I really need to get my 4wd car fixed, it's been sitting for seven months." (AY7OM)

"What's wrong with it Ray?" (AU7PM)

"It's the fuel pump. I have had two installed already. The problem is that it mounts in the gas tank and it's full of gas. I don't want to have to drop the tank so I am thinking about cutting a trap door in the floor board to make this easy to install."

"That sounds like a good idea. I wonder why they keep going out?" (AU7PM)

"Don't know for sure. I bought another one but I am not thrilled about working on the car in a snow bank and I don't have a garage." (AY7OM)

"It sounds like a big job. I don't have a great place to work on cars either." (AU7PM)

"Morning guys. I have a friend who had the same problem with an Ford Explorer and that's what he did. Once you get the trap door done it's not that bad of a job. Besides when you do get it fixed you'll have a full tank of gas and that is really worth something these days" (AP7ZMT)

"No kidding it's over $5 a gallon here." (AY7OM)

"I know it's just terrible. I'm glad I don't have a diesel. That's $6.50 a gallon." (AU7PM)

"Signals aren't too bad this morning. Anybody check the upper bands?" (AP7ZMT)

"Not this morning, just turned on the radio and heard Frank

tuning up." (AY7OM)

"I've been playing with my gold panning machine I told you about and having a lot of fun. (AP7ZMT)

"That does sound fun and are you getting anything?" (AP7PM)

"I haven't got enough to weigh yet but I got some colors in the collection cup. It's nice to be able to do this indoors on a cold winters day.Over." (AP7ZMT)

"Anything else new over there?" (AY7OM)

"I shot a 2 pound jar of tannerite. Boy does that make some noise." (AP7ZMT)

"My neighbor got some of that and you could hear it 1/4 mile away." AY7OM)

"How much is that stuff Walt?" (AP7PM)

"The 2 pound jar was $17 but you can get it in a lot smaller amounts. They even make 1/4 pound packs for paper targets. I guess that you can save about 50% if you make your own. I saw a video about that." (AP7ZMT)

"I am going to take off guys. Good talking with you this morning. I have some stuff to do. 73 AY7OM."

"OK Ray I am going to pull the plug as well. 73 Frank and Ray. I am out of here. AP7ZMT."

"OK guys if everyone is leaving early I'll find something to do. This is AU7PM listening out."

Walt turned off his radio and got set up to use his gold panning machine. After running this for a few hours he put things away, let Sparky out, and went out to get the tractor started to blow the driveway. It was perfect timing since the mail man was just driving off when he got down there. He could only blow the snow downhill so after the first pass he drove to top and widened out his path. When he got back up to the cabin with the mail, he cleaned out the blower and put the tractor away.

About an hour later he heard his driveway announcer alarm and looked out the window. It was the UPS truck. Walt was surprised that he got two packages that day, another dried food assortment and the air filter and cleaner so Walt was lucky that he cleared the driveway just in time. One of the extra bonuses of getting packages this time of year was that the cardboard boxes made excellent fire starter material. He put the food container away and found a place for the air cleaner in the living room.

The next few weeks went by quickly and Walt found the time to process about half the sand from the sandbar that he had stored in the woodshed. Walt hadn't weighed his gold so far but could not stand the suspense any longer. It looked like a lot but he wouldn't be sure until it was weighed. Gold is measured in troy ounces and there are 32 grams per troy ounce and not 28 as you might think. He placed a small paper cup on his postage scale and zeroed out the scale. Then he carefully dumped the gold from the machine's collection cup onto a clean piece of paper and slowly poured the gold into the paper cup. He was quite surprised to find that he had 1.18 troy ounces of gold already from (about) 5 yards of sandbar sand. This was fantastic! About $2000 worth of gold. How cool was that? He could almost pay off his credit card with the gold he had already collected and if he was lucky he might be able to double that amount. Just to be safe he put the small paper cup in a zip lock plastic bag and put it in the cupboard. Like they used to say on TV, " He loved it when a plan came together."

This was worth celebrating. Walt had been very good about controlling his drinking lately but there was a time and a place for everything. He went down to the crawl space and brought up two of his homemade beers. They were made from a European Pilsner recipe and had aged for about two years. They were pretty cool from being in the crawl space but Walt didn't want to take a chance on the beer being too warm so he went outside and filled a large mixing bowl with snow and placed the two bottles of beer in the snow.

Within 15 mutes the bottles were ice cold. He carefully poured the beer into the side of his glass and it only had a slight head. The beer itself was colored of course but clear as glass with no sediment whatsoever. It was perfect. Better than anything you could buy. He savored each sip and he was glad that he had waited and was not tempted to drink this before it was ready. "Here is to me," he toasted to himself, "Master Brewer and Gold Miner."

Walt left for town early the next morning. He wanted to pick up some small items that he had overlooked. As he pulled into the Box Mart parking lot he heard the radio break from it's normal programming. "We interrupt this program to bring you the following News Bulletin. A massive eruption of the Yellowstone Volcano has just been reported at 9:32 Mountain Standard Time. Please stay tuned to this station for further developments."

Walt couldn't believe what he heard even though he had been expecting it. He also couldn't believe his luck to already be at the store before the panic buying began. He only needed a few things and didn't expect to be in the store very long. He picked up some panty hose and this took a little longer than expected because he was not used to shopping in the women's underwear department. Then he found some flexible HEPA filters by the vacuum cleaners, HEPA stands for High Efficiency Particle Air and thought that these would both come in handy if the air quality was bad. As he walked by the light bulb aisle he grabbed some 110 volt LED light bulbs. He was headed for the check out line when he thought that he might as well get 4 dozen eggs, a large dinner ham, and a couple of loaves of rye bread. As he left the store he could see that the parking lot was filling up quickly. He topped off his gas tank and headed straight for home.

Walt knew that, depending on wind speed and direction, it would only be a few hours before the ash cloud would arrive in Sandpoint because of the stories he had heard about the Mt. St. Helens eruption. When he got home he parked the truck in the garage and made sure that all the doors in were tightly closed. He took everything inside the cabin and let Sparky outside. Then he brought a weeks worth of firewood inside the cabin and put another weeks worth of wood on the porch. Finally he got Sparky inside and locked the doors and turned on his computer to watch the news and turned on his local radio station, and police scanner as well.

He learned a lot about the Yellowstone super volcano while reporters were waiting for more updates. The TV reporter said that Yellowstone had erupted three times before over the last two million years. The caldera measured 35 miles by 45 miles and that, before the blast, scientists predicted that almost 2 million tons of sulfuric acid could be projected into the atmosphere in addition to the CO_2 and ash and magma. The last time Yellowstone went off it deposited 10 feet of ash and magma in 1000 miles in every direction and ash clouds could be over Europe within 72 hours.

When a recent volcanic eruption occurred in Iceland, over 100,000 airline flights were grounded because flying through these clouds can destroy a planes engines even at high altitudes where the ash cannot be seen with the naked eye. The last mini ice age which lasted for several years was believed to be caused by volcanos and this resulted in poor harvests, cold climates, and famine.

The reporter continued to say that an area around Yellowstone of 100 miles had been completely destroyed and that the intensity of the blast could be equal to thousands of nuclear bombs like the one used in Hiroshima. That hurricanes of pyroclastic super heated lava and ash were flowing away from the blast at temperatures over 400 degrees centigrade and speeds over 100 mph.

The reporter went on to say that there were many ways besides the blast and intense heat that the volcano could impact us all. The ash is heavy and can collapse roofs. It will destroy auto engines. It doesn't melt or wash away. The ash is composed of tiny pieces of frothy magmatic glass and rocks as small as the thickness of a human hair that can easily become trapped in our lungs. The sulfur dioxide can cause acid rain poisoning crops and water supplies. Thick ash clouds can cause temperatures to fall as much as 15 degrees in the winter and summer crops would not survive in deep ash deposits.

The local radio station was reporting that the ash cloud could now be seen approaching Boise in the south and

Lewiston in the west. So far it looked like a nice winter day in Sandpoint with cold temperatures and blue skies. A few hours later it was beginning to get dark outside even though it was shortly after noon. It kept getting darker and darker and it was eerily quiet as the ash cloud moved in. Walt let Sparky outside about 4 pm and when she came in she had been covered with a light coat of ash. Walt washed her off and made dinner while watching the end of the world out the kitchen window. Fortunately the wind was not blowing outside and soon it was dark. When he switched on the porch light he could see that his snow covered landscape had turned completely black. He listened to the local news and watched TV news on his computer until the power went out about 8 pm. Rather than switch to emergency power he and Sparky turned in for the night.

In the morning he looked out the window as soon as he got up and estimated that there was about 3 inches of ash on the ground. The power had not been restored and he went to the crawl space to plug in the inverter and connect the water pump to his system. He didn't know how long he would be without power so he used as little battery power as possible. After breakfast he emptied his refrigerator and put the contents into boxes out in the mud room where it was about 40 degrees or so. He thought that he could go a day or two before he would have to get some generator power to the chest freezer in the woodshop. Walt then thought to fill some water jugs with freh water and he filled the bathtub before disconnecting the inverter. For the rest of the day he would only be on 12 volt DC power.

When it was time to let Sparky out she didn't want to go. She took one look at the ash on the ground and didn't want any part of it. So Walt let her out on the front porch where she reluctantly did her business at the far end of the deck and quickly came inside. By then the ash had stopped falling so at least the air quality wasn't too bad. Walt wasn't taking any chances and placed a face mask near each door. Since he was only running on DC power for the day his driveway announcer, security system, and satellite internet modem was not working.

He replaced his cordless phone with an old style phone and to his surprise found that he still had a dial tone. He turned on his CB radio, police scanner, and QRP ham radio to listen knowing that these battery powered radios used very little power anyway. The local AM radio station was still on the air and giving weather forecasts and area ash accumulation reports. They reported that Spokane had six inches of ash on the ground and about 2 inches in the Seattle area. In terms of the ash flow the northwest got lucky. The prevailing winds were blowing from west to east and this meant that much of the country was not that lucky. The ash was reported to be about one foot deep in Nebraska and only about four inches deep in Ohio. But almost every State in the lower 48 reported some ash on the ground. It was way to early to tell but initial estimates speculated that something like 100,000 people, and an enormous amount of wildlife, had been killed so far.

Even though the Pacific Northwest Remote Viewing Group's prediction was on the money, Walt wished that this was not the case. Many Americans have died so far and many more people worldwide will suffer because of the Yellowstone super volcano. Humanity has survived these kinds of events in the past so it is a stretch to think of this as an end of the world event. Nonetheless many people who were warned in advance, either did not take the warning seriously, or could not relocate to save themselves. The Jimmy Buffet song kept going through Walt's mind, "Now, I don't know, I don't know, I don't know, where I'm a-gonna go when the volcano blows."

Walt gave a few calls on 3.988 using his QRP radio but nobody came back. Maybe, since he was using such low power, nobody heard him. Or most likely other people in the group were out of power and could not operate on battery power. He left the radio on in case he heard somebody and Gave a call out on the CB. It was still morning so he didn't really expect anyone to have their radios on but it was worth a try. "This is Walt, is there anyone on the radio this morning?"

"This is Jane. What happened to our winter wonderland?"

126

"This black frosting on our vanilla ice cream is really something isn't?

"It is surreal for sure. I am glad that we didn't get any more of this stuff. I wonder how long it will be before we get our power back?" Jane asked.

"I have no idea but I doubt that it will be anytime soon. Even though we have hydropower here I am gussing that a lot of the substation transformers are fried and maybe some of the lines are down as well. Over."

"I am sure glad I got the solar cells, that's for sure."

"I think it would be a good idea to carefully wash off the ash instead of trying to sweep it off."

"I think you are right this stuff must really be abrasive."

"Roger that. So how are things doing over there, Do you think that you can hold out for awhile?"

"I think so Walt. My plan is to eat everything in the freezer first before it goes bad. I think I can get some clean snow to put in the ice chests until I can get through it all."

"Good idea Jane. How about cooking? Do you have a propane stove?"

"I have a propane camp stove but I don't have a propane oven."

"That is the same story up here. Let me know if you need anything. I'll try to keep the radio on more often. And at least for now, the landline works if you have an old style rotary of push button telephone."

"Good idea, I haven't tried that yet. Will talk to you later. Have some things to do outside."

"Be careful not to breathe this ash, I heard that it is bad news if you get it in your lungs."

"Good idea. Thanks for reminding me."

"Oh one more thing. It will destroy your car engine and cripple a generator if ash gets in the air cleaner. You can protect this by putting some panty hose over the air intake. I bought some yesterday."

"Really good idea. I don't wear it anymore but I have some!"

"OK take care. I'm signing off now. 73." Jane had a good idea about eating the food in the freezer first. Nobody had any idea how long they would have to live without power and it didn't make sense to run the generator every few days to keep it cold. Walt tried to think of things he could use as ice chests until all his food was gone. At least they had plenty of snow in the winter. If this had happened in the summer they would all be out of luck. He had thought of building a smoke house awhile back but he never did and this would be a good idea for the future, if there was a future.

Chapter 5. February

"I see the thunderstorms up ahead
Dont know it but we're already dead
What was meant to be heard, never was said
Since the beginning of time, been misled"
Chronic Future

It was a few days before he got a chance to chat with some of the guys on 3.988. Walt was still using his QRP radio to conserve power. His battery power system was holding up well and he thought that he could wait a day or two before charging it up with the generator. He still had not heard any traffic on the road but he had talked to most of the people on the CB net. Everyone seemed to be holding out well but Scott and some of others were using their car batteries to power their radios and re-charging them by putting them back in their cars. Walt heard Frank calling, "This is AU7PM running QRP on battery power. Is there anybody on frequency?"

"Hey Frank good to here you. Are you running QRP? AP7ZMT."

"Roger. How about you? I have you about S5. Over."

"I have you about the same. Three inches of ash and 29 degrees over here. The sky is pretty dark but it doesn't look like any more ash is falling at the moment. How about you? " (AP7ZMT)

"We have about two inches of ash over here. I heard lots of places got dumped pretty good. Over."

"How about your phone, power, and internet?"

"We lost power and internet the first night. I haven't tried the phone yet. Over." (AU7PM)

"We have a landline and it is till working but it requires a push button or rotary phone that will work without power. I am not sure if any cell phones are working or not. I haven't tried calling anyone but we do have a dial tone. Over."

"I'll try that. I am pretty sure I've got an old phone around here somewhere. (AU7PM)

"Have you heard how everyone else is doing?" (AP7ZMT)

"I talked to Joe last night and he is doing OK. He said that he heard from Jeff and they are doing OK too."

"That's good. I sure am glad I invested in the battery bank and inverter. I've got a feeling that we'll be out of power for awhile." (AP7ZMT)

"Yes I've got about a half dozen batteries and charge them with my little Honda generator. I've got a full tank of gas in the other car so I should have some gas for awhile."

"I'm pretty well prepared over here but I put a good sized dent in my credit card getting that way. Over."

"Roger. I still cannot get over how powerful that volcano was. And I thought Mt. St. Helens was something." (AU7PM)

"I guess there is no such thing as a small volcanic eruption. We are both lucky that we didn't get buried in ash. I don't think that I will have to shovel the roof or anything but I plan to shovel the parking area and driveway." (AP7ZMT)

"That ought to take awhile."

"I don't think that I have a choice. Over."

"Probably not. You could always wait until Ash Wednesday." (AU7PM)

"That's a good one, but I would like to get it done before that. We'll just have to see how much snow we get on top of the ash. The only good part about the ash is that when it solarizes it will help melt the ice underneath."

"I never thought of that. It could be a problem here too. Let's just hope it doesn't trigger any more volacnos over here on the coast" (AU7PM)

"You've got a lot of them over there, that's for sure. From what I have heard the world could be in a nuclear winter for years." (AP7ZMT)

"Hey guys this is AY7OM."

"Good to hear you Ray. How much ash did you get?" (AU7PM)

"We got about three inches here. What a mess. Over."

"We are on battery power Ray, how about you? AP7ZMT."

"I am running the generator right now so I'll only be here for a few minutes since the battery charger wipes out the radio. Over." (AY7OM)

"Do you have enough gas and supplies to hold out for awhile?" (AP7ZMT)

"Not really. I never expected anything like this. I don't know how long it will be before they get the roads cleared." (AY7OM)

"Walt was just talking about having to dig out with a shovel just to get to the road." (AU7PM)

"I am in the same boat over here. I don't think anybody is on the roads yet." (AY7OM)

"Has anybody heard anything about getting the power back? This is AR7QRN."

"Haven't heard a thing Dennis. My internet is still out too." (AP7ZMT)

"Same here . Good thing we have our radios." (AR7QRN)

"Has anybody heard how things are on the east coast? I haven't been on much." (AU7PM)

"I heard that everything is out there too and the stores that are open don't have anything left to sell." (AR7QRN)

"When people get hungry enough things will start getting ugly."

"What are people going to do without the Super Bowl?" (AP7ZMT)

"That's the least of their worries. No food, no heat, no water, no gas, no internet, no cell phones, no nothing. I better get going and get my batteries charged. Hang in there and 73 This is AY7OM"

"OK Ray,we'll talk with you later> AP7ZMT"

"See you Ray. AU7PM."

"73 Ray." (AR7QRN)

"When this is over I'll bet that there will be a bunch more people into prepping." (AP7ZMT)

"I think that you are right about that. I'd better save my batteries too. See you all later. AU7PM listening out."

" OK Frank I'll be out of here too. AR7QRN."

"Same here. Good talking with you guys this morning. AP7ZMT clear and QRT. 73 all." Walt was glad to hear that people were OK for now and that they only got a little bit of ash. He couldn't imagine dealing with ash a foot deep like they got in Nebraska. And he was really glad that he had prepped as hard as he did. Hard times were going to be here for awhile, maybe years. Nobody wanted to talk about this on the radio but it was on everyone's mind. This had to be really hard on the deer and fish population and there would be more hungry hunters and fishermen this spring than ever before. The only gardeners who had any hope were those with seeds and a greenhouse to go with it. Until things got back to somewhat normal, every resource, every match, every gallon of gas and water had to be conserved. Back to the days of waste not, want not.

During the great depression there were things to buy if you had the money but this looked like it would be different. Just having money would not necessarily mean that a person could get whatever they wanted.

From now on we would no longer be a throw away society. We would be savers, scroungers, and fixers. More of our time would be spent trying to survive. The days of sitting on our rear ends and being entertained were over. We would no longer be bored, instead we would be tired.

Walt thought he had it made when he found some gold on his property but what good is gold if there is nothing to buy? If you can't eat it, then what good is it? All the rats would be competing for scraps. You would have to be brave in this brave new world.

That afternoon Walt put on his N95 face mask and went out the fenced area in the back yard and shoveled out a place for Sparky. The layer of ash sat on top of about six inches of snow. He shoveled the snow into his otter sled and hauled it to the fence line and then dumped it in a pile. This was a lot of work but at least he could see his progress. Now Sparky had a nice white shoveled area for herself and she didn't have to wade through the ash.

The next morning Walt found 5 inches of wet snow on top of the ash. He decided to run the walk behind snow blower to clean out the parking area in front of the cabin. With the snow before ash, the 3 inches of ash, and the 5 inches of new snow on top of the ash, the parking area resembled a giant ash sandwich on white bread. He carefully put a piece of panty hose over the air cleaner and then started the machine. Because the ash would be airborne he made a effort to fit his face mask tightly and began to run the machine. It did a great job removing the snow and ash and because the new snow on the top was wet, it did a good job keeping the ash from turning into a cloud as the machine deposited it 25 feet away. This worked really well and Walt was glad that he didn't have to shovel this.

The next day Walt set up the generator on the covered front deck and hooked up the wires to the inverter/charger. He carefully covered the generator's air cleaner with two layers of panty hose and started it. The generator would run about four hours on a tank of gas but he planned to be back in two hours or so. Walt ran the walk behind snow blower on the driveway and made two passes, side by side, to the road. When he got back to the cabin he checked the battery bank and the batteries were completely charged. He was pleased to see that he could easily go a week or more without the need to charge the batteries in his new system.

On the following day he was able to complete clearing the driveway to the road. The county road had not been plowed and the mail had not been delivered but at least the parking area and driveway was a nice white snow floor and this put Walt in a much better mood. Looking at all the ash in the yard and the driveway had been depressing so it was worth it to clean this up. With the new snow covering the ash on the roofs, the place looked almost normal.

Just for fun he turned on the inverter and turned on his satellite modem. He didn't expect that it would work but it was worth a try. When the modem connected to the internet he was thrilled to be able to get on the internet. First he checked his email and he had quite a backlog to deal with. Forty five minutes later he checked out some of his favorite new sites to get information about the super volcano and how it was affecting the rest of the country.

People were still digging out and most of the country was closed. If there were no more eruptions or after shock earthquakes, the federal government offices were expected to re-open within the next two to three weeks. The power grid was still in bad shape but, because of hydropower in the northwest, power in the Sandpoint area could return on a limited basis, by the middle of March. Bonner County Highway Districts expected to have the main county roads open by the end of the month and rural mail delivery should be able to resume two weeks after that. Once the power was restored and the roads were open schools and businesses could slowly get back to normal.

This was really good news for the Sandpoint area but many other areas were still in very bad shape and might take years to fully recover. Food and supply chain issues would still be a problem for everyone in the lower 48 for the foreseeable future. Overall the reports that Walt was seeing were optimistic and he was glad to see that he had his internet service working again. He unplugged the modem, and disconnected the inverter and went back on battery power.

Walt couldn't believe that the government and legacy media really believed what they were saying. Either they didn't really understand the long lasting effects of the volcano or they were lying to the people in order to maintain control. Did they really think that people were that stupid, that uninformed, or that forgetful? Apparently they did because they continue to tell us bedtime stories to control us. The list was a long as your arm, Roswell, the start of the Vietnam War, the JFK assassination, the Ruby Ridge, Oklahoma City, Waco, Texas, 911, weapons of mass destruction in Iraq, Afghanistan, the Russia hoax, Corona Virus, face masks, lockdowns, school and church closures, free and fair elections, safe and effective vaccines, the list goes on and on. There was no way we would be getting back to normal in just a few weeks, or ever for that matter. The best we could hope for was to get somewhat back to normal.

Walt knew that Sparky needed to have some fun so he put on his pack boots and face mask and took her for a walk down to the road. She really appreciated getting to stretch her legs and walk on the snow covered ground looking for new smells. She seemed to know that there was something very wrong about the sulfur smells in the air and the dark clouds in the sky. It was a short walk but better than no walk at all. When they got back to the cabin Walt brought in several more loads of firewood and four half filled buckets of sand to process later. The smell of sulfur still lingered in their nostrils when they went inside so he plugged in the inverter and turned on the air purifier. In 30 minutes or so the air seemed a lot fresher so he turned off the air cleaner. As long as the inverter was still on Walt micro-waved a baked potato and a couple of the last few slices of ham for dinner. Then he remembered that he had forgotten to listen to Alex Jones that afternoon but that it was almost time for the Sunday night CB net.

Walt turned on his CB radio and heard a couple of people already talking. "We're hanging in there. This ash is really nasty looking stuff. Over." It sounded like Stan.

"I've never seen anything like it but the old timers tell me that it was like this in the 1980s with Mt. Saint Helens."

"We weren't here for that either Tony but I have heard the same thing."

"Have you tried plowing it yet?"

"No I haven't. I didn't want to run my truck until the roads were open."

"Me neither. I am just thankful that we didn't get any more of it. I don't know how those people in Nebraska can deal with it."

"A foot of ash has got to be a real strain on the roof. That's probably like 10 feet of snow."

"No kidding. How are you guys getting along without power?"

"It's kind of like winter camping except we have the wood stove. We've only got 2 batteries and have been charging them with a generator."

"The longest we have been without power before is about a week. Over."

"A week is a long time to go without a shower. But after more than two weeks now, we smell like a couple of bears over here?

"Yes Stan it would be a little easier to deal with it in the summer when you could just jump in the creek."

"You know I haven't even thought of using the hillbilly hot tub since the power went out but that's a pretty good idea. How are you both holding up? This is Walt. Over"

"Hey Walt this is Tony. We are holding up OK. It would be easier to read the license manuals if the lights were on. Over."

"Yes you have a point there. I just found out that my satellite internet is working. How about you Stan?"

"Haven't been able to try it because I don't want to run the computer on the generator. How about you Tony?"

"I get my internet through my cell phone and that is not working, I can tell you that."

"Well its about time for the net. We'll try to keep it short to conserve on battery power. Is there anyone who would like to check into the Rapid Lightning CB net Over?

"This is Jane."

"Got you in here Jane. Anybody else?"

"This is Scott."

"OK Scott."

"Fly Boy is here too,"

"OK Fly Boy."

"I'm here too. This is Susan."

"Bret here"

"Peter on frequency.

"OK, I have Susan, Bret, and Peter. Thanks for checking in. Is there anyone else?" Walt liked the rapid check ins.

"Robert and Nancy here."

"Deal us in. Mary and Beth."

"This is Steve,"

"George and Carla"

"Charles and Megan"

"OK I've got George and Carla, and Charles and Megan. Is there anyone else?" Nobody else was transmitting. "OK that's everyone but Tom. I hope that he's alright."

"Sorry I'm late. This is Tom."

"OK that's everyone. Are there any new check ins? Walt waited a few seconds and didn't hear anyone else. "Well I guess this is it. Thank you all for checking in. I thought we'd try to keep it short tonight to help conserve battery power. I hope you are all hanging in there. Please let us know if there is anything you need or anyway we can be of help. I heard that the roads may open up in a few weeks and that will make it easier for all of us. Let's go around once in order and tell us how you are doing and what is on your mind. Also let us know if you have telephone and internet service. Well start with Stan and Gloria, then Tony and Sherri, over to Jane, then Scott, then Fly Boy, Susan, Bret, Peter, Robert and Nancy, Mary and Beth, George and Carla, Charles and Megan, Tom, and back to me. Go ahead Stan."

"Hello everyone this is Stan and Gloria. We are hanging in there except for a hot shower. We have not tried the internet or the telephone because the power is down. We hope you are all doing well. Over to Tony and Sherri."

"We are doing OK No phone or internet. Staying warm and the pantry is holding up so far. Over to Jane."

"I am doing fine so far. I really enjoyed seeing the last snow cover up the ash but I haven't started any clean up yet. I've been catching up on my sleep. No phone or internet, Over to you Scott."

"Scott here. My cell phone is out and so is my internet. The only battery I have is out of my truck so I have to put back to charge it. Doing OK so far. I needed to lose weight anyway. Over to Fly Boy."

"Yes being locked down in volcanic ash is a good weight loss program for sure. I have satellite internet and can use it when the generator is on. I am siphoning gas to run the generator. Good thing I can walk to the store, whenever it opens again. Go ahead Susan."

"Well I am glad to hear that we are all hanging in there. I guess as long as we have heat we are doing better than lots of people. I do have a working landline but no internet at this time. I have started shoveling a little each day so when the road is open I can get the car out. Over to Bret."

"Roger that Susan. I guess we are all in the same boat. Been eating mostly pancakes and peanut butter but I do have plenty of wine over here. No phone or internet. Over to Peter."

"OK on the wine. I ran out of beer yesterday. I can tell you that when this is over I am going to take prepping a little more seriously. No cell phone or internet yet. I am starting to dig out as well. At least the firewood is holding out. Back to Robert and Nancy."

"We are hanging in there as well and playing lots of cribbage. I haven't checked the phone. We do have a landline but need 110 volts to use the phone. We have pretty well cleaned out everything in the freezer but have the pantry to fall back on. I guess we'll start to shovel out our access as well. Good to hear you all. Take it away Mary."

"This is Mary. Beth and I are doing OK. We have just started our fourth jig saw puzzle. We keep checking the local news on our portable FM radio but otherwise it is pretty quiet around here. I haven't tried to see if the phone is working. We have plenty of firewood and gas for the generator. Up to George and Carla."

"OK Mary. We are pretty well set for awhile since we try not to go to town often in the winter anyway. This reminds us how nice it is to have our radios so that we can talk with each other. Our internet works off the cell phone so we are out for awhile. Next summer we plan to get a landline. Having the wood cook stove really paid off these last few weeks. Over to Charles and Megan."

"Megan has been able to do some baking on the wood stove. She wraps some metal chain in a circle and puts the pan on the chain and has made a few cakes for us. How's that for old time cooking? Otherwise things are OK here. We've got about everything we need for now. Go ahead Tom."

"I can't believe how quiet it has been around here. Almost like going back in time. Except for being out of beer and cigarettes I am doing fine. Needed to quit anyway. Glad to hear everybody this evening. Keep your batteries charged. Talk to you later. Go ahead Walt."

"I am really glad everyone is warm and healthy. I ran my generator and the walk behind snow blower and used pantry hose over the air cleaners. I bitched about wearing a face mask during the Covid but it is important to wear a mask with this ash. This is what killed the dinosaurs.

This is just my personal opinion but I don't think that things will ever get back to normal, so as soon as we can, I think that it is a good idea to prep as much as possible when we get the chance. Especially when it comes to food supplies. I hope I am wrong but to quote Winston Churchill, *This isn't the beginning of the end, it is the end of the beginning.* Feel free to contact me if there is anything I can do to help. I'll say 73 for now and thanks again for coming on the air."

Walt turned off his CB radio and let Sparky out one more time for the evening. He turned on a shortwave receiver and listened to some international shortwave broadcasts to see if he could get any news about the ash cloud over Europe and Asia. Airlines were still grounded and news from overseas was sparse on U.S. media. He couldn't find much interesting at the time so he turned off his shortwave receiver and thought it would fun to listen to some hams overseas. The bands were not open to Europe that night so he turned on his inverter and satellite internet modem. Then he turned on his laptop computer and connected to the internet using WiFi. Next he opened his bookmark file and found the link to a web based SDR (Software Defined Radio) located in London. This opened up a screen that resembled a radio so that he could tune to any band and any frequency on any mode and listen over the internet to exactly what the SDR receiver was picking up in

London. Since at that time it was very early in the morning in London he selected the 80 meter ham bands and listened in LSB (Lower Sideband). Then he tuned up and down the band to listen in on some of the European hams. This was very interesting and he heard several QSOs (conversations) about the ash clouds and cooler weather that they were experiencing. Then he selected the AM broadcast band in the AM mode and tuned up and down the band. This allowed him to hear some of the local broadcast stations to listen for some news shows. One in particular was taking phone calls from people who were commenting on the effects of volcano. After this he tuned to a web based SDR receiver located in Italy and repeated the process. Most of the hams he heard were speaking Italian, French,, or German but a few were speaking English. One in particular was a U.S. army sergeant who was stationed at the American embassy and he was talking to another soldier stationed in Germany. They were comparing notes about the light dusting of volcanic ash and the effects of the weather so far.

After a couple of hours Walt turned off his laptop, internet modem, and the inverter and went to bed. The next morning he woke up an saw that there was no new snowfall. Both he an Sparky were glad this was the case and she went outside while Walt lit the fire. He listened to the local AM radio station while he made breakfast and didn't hear anything new so he got set up to process some more sand to pass the time. When it was 9:30 he listened for the guys on 3.988 but didn't plan to check in until he was done using the gold panning machine.

Frank and Mike were comparing notes and wondering when the power would come back. Joe joined in and was thinking about clearing his long driveway. Ray was wondering if he had enough wood for the winter and complaining that the Postal Service was not up and running. Dennis was worried that the deer weren't finding enough to eat since he normally saw fifty or so in his field every morning. He reported that they were trying to clear the snow and ash with their feet hoping to get down to the dead grass underneath.

140

Walt's police scanner came to life and the police were being called to a report of several men trying to break into the Northland store that had been closed for weeks. Walt wondered if this was the start of a crime wave? Things like this just didn't happen in a sleepy ski town like Sandpoint, especially in broad daylight. He turned off his ham receiver and turned on an AM radio to KLXY 920 out of Spokane. They were reporting a stand off at a grocery store between a man with a rifle and the Spokane Sheriffs Department. Walt thought to himself that people were beginning to crack under the stress. He decided that he could spare the battery power and turned his inverter, security system, and driveway announcer back on.

To minimize the power use by the security system Walt turned off the monitor. If the cameras detected any motion the unit would turn on and keep recording until 30 seconds after the motion stopped. He didn't expect that anyone would drop by, of course, but he wanted to mentally start thinking about security. He told himself, that from now on, if he went outside, he would be packing his concealed carry gun. This was a Ruger LCR, 5 shots with a 2 inch barrel in .357 magnum. It was one of the lightest revolvers of its kind and could easily fit in a pocket although sometimes he carried this in a fanny pack.

When he would practice with this gun he usually shot .38 specials because they didn't kick as much. Walt thought that carrying a gun was a pain but he made the decision to start carrying it anyway. When driving, he had a larger .357 with a six inch barrel with him in the truck. He had never needed a gun but the way things were going, he thought it would be a good idea to get into the habit.

For home defense he had a couple of 12 gauge shot guns and several rifles from .22 cal up to 30'06. He had never worried about bear or mountain lion around his place. The dangerous animals he wanted to be ready for only had two legs. His motto was, "Be Prepared," and did not want to "Be Sorry." Some people call it paranoia but others call it a keen sense of awareness.

Walt spent the afternoon running his gold processing machine. He was getting pretty comfortable with the machine and he processed all the sand that he had brought inside earlier. Before he put the machine away he wondered what would happen if he ran a little volcanic ash through the machine? He emptied the collection cup into the paper cup that he had kept in the zip lock bag and went outside and collected a half bucket of volcanic ash. It was much heavier than the same amount of sand and it was so fine it didn't need sifting. He ran the half bucket of ash and then looked in the collection cup. He couldn't believe his eyes. There was a small amount of fine gold in the collection cup! He wondered if anyone else had thought about this or not? He would have guessed that a small amount of gold would have been detected with a spectrographic assay but to find recoverable gold in the ash was unbelievable.

With three inches of ash containing fine gold spread over his 20 acres, maybe he was rich. Or, if people found out about this, and enough people processed the ash to recover gold, maybe this would drive the price down so far that gold would become nearly worthless!

He decided to grab one of his homemade beers from the crawl space and think about this for awhile. The first thing he promised himself is that he would keep his big mouth shut and not say a word about this to anyone. The beer went down so quickly that he went in the crawl space and got another.

Several scenarios went through his head. He could lease some acreage near town and get the city to dump their ash trucks on the leased land. They might require him to keep it covered or wet to minimize the ash from blowing away. To do this he would need to have a plausible reason for stockpiling this much ash. He could always say that he was going to make pottery with it like people did with ash from Mount St. Helens.

He could offer locals a place to dump their ash in one of his clearings. But he would still need to have a reason to do this. Maybe he could say that he wanted to sell this as a garden amendment or to package this as a souvenir.

Maybe he could say that he wanted the ash to mix with concrete or that he planned to sell it as an abrasive. He was sure that the county would rather dump the ash at his place rather than haul it away but in the winter this wouldn't be possible. Possibly he could go into a partnership with one of his friends who had a good spot to stockpile this, but it would have to be with someone he could trust and someone who could keep his mouth shut. Gold does funny things to people, it's a sickness, and that is why they call it gold fever. Walt realized that this was the worst idea that he had so far.

He finally decided that he didn't have to solve this problem until later. His first instinct was best, to keep his mouth shut. Walt finished his beer and put the gold panning machine away. As he was cleaning up he couldn't help but think of all the gold laden ash that he blew off the parking area and driveway with the snow blower. At least he hadn't touched the upper driveway, he would be a lot more careful with that.

Walt was just about finished eating the thawed contents of his freezer. He was thankful that the cold weather allowed him to keep things cool and he didn't have to throw any food away. He wished that he would have been able to build a smoke house to preserve meat and fish but he never got around to it. One reason for the delay, is that for best results, some kind of fruitwood is needed and he didn't have any.

Besides smoking meat and fish the old timers would can this in jars but it was a time consuming process. He remembered some of the home canned meat dinners that he had eaten in the past. Adding a baked potato or two and you had a meal fit for a king.

Meat and fish could be dried in a food dryer like jerky but this didn't have a very long shelf life. The modern freeze dryers were wonderful but they were expensive and the process took more time and effort than you might think. However when this was done the food looked good and lasted for years.

When the food from the freezer was gone, Walt thought that he would mix his dried meals with the canned goods from his pantry. He has lots of rice, peas, and flour as well, and like Bret mentioned, there was always pancakes and peanut butter.

Walt liked shooting but he wasn't a hunter. Maybe that's why he forgot that he had a tree stand in the woodshed. In a month or two the snow would be melted and he should locate some good game trails before that and put up the tree stand just in case. He knew that deer season was closed until late October but, if he was hungry enough, he would consider poaching a deer. He didn't care for poaching but if it meant the difference between eating and not eating he wouldn't feel too badly about it.

He had considered that the fish in the creek might be a good emergency food source but thought that the ash and acid rain might have impacted the fish. Even if the trout survived, the creek would probably be fished out in no time. Walt wasn't a gardener either but he did have carrot, radish, and lettuce seed and he heard that these were pretty easy to grow, He might be a able to trade a few things with the neighbors for some other vegetables. In a normal year there were plenty of huckleberries on the mountain but after the ash, picking berries would be challenging.

He had thought about getting some laying hens awhile back and this would still be a good idea. However if he had to buy food for meat birds, this could get expensive in a hurry, if you could even buy the food in the first place.

When people thought that things were getting back to normal they might not think to restock their pantries, or they might not have the money to do so, but this was Walt's plan, He would be going into maximum prep mode as soon as he could. He couldn't help but think of the old Tennessee Ernie Ford song, "Sixteen Tons, with a minor adjustment to the lyrics, "If the last one didn't get you, the next one will."

Sparky reminded Walt that it was time for her afternoon meal. Walt got her some cold water from the mud room and a cup of kibble. Then, like every afternoon, she needed to go out for a few minutes. Although Walt had been thinking of food, he wasn't hungry and had about a dozen saltine crackers topped with peanut butter.

Walt remembered that he had left the security system on so he turned this off, the driveway announcer off, and the inverter off just as it got dark. He remembered that he wanted to install some kind of light blocking curtains on the windows and thought that he better work on this the next day. Once the roads were opened, this would be an important part of his security protocol. Now there was no one on the road but soon there would be, and he didn't want to send any strangers an invitation by advertising that he had power when nobody else did.

The next morning Walt woke up to see Sparky watching him from the foot of the bed. He stuck his hand out from under the covers and she came over to lick his hand. He thought of the old Folgers coffee commercial and how it would have been better if the jingle said that the best part of waking up is getting to pet your pup. He got out of bed and let her out right away. It was still dark out so he used his flashlight to look out the door to see if there had been any new snow overnight. He didn't see any new snow or any new ash either.

After starting a fire and putting a tea kettle on the stove for coffee he let Sparky inside and she laid down by the stove. It wasn't putting out any heat yet but the sound of the wood catching fire made her think it would be warming up soon. When the water in the tea kettle was hot, Walt got to make his first cup of coffee by pouring the hot water onto a drip cone with a filter and ground coffee. Then he got his last yogurt from the mud room and had this for breakfast. During this time Sparky was sitting in front of him waiting for her turn to lick the cup. She loved yogurt and licked every speck of yogurt Walt had left. Then she got busy cleaning off her face and had a big smile after that. Walt guessed that she was thinking that the best part of being a pup was getting to lick the cup.

By this time the stove was kicking out some heat and Walt turned on the local news on his portable radio and dripped another cup. The news reporter was reading the police report from yesterday and even though Sandpoint was closed, the Sheriffs Department was busy. Two businesses in town were burglarized and deputies responded to a domestic dispute. The weather forecast for the day did not call for any precipitation but the chances of seeing the sun were slim to none. The ash clouds were solid at about 6,000 feet and there was only light winds predicted for the day. It was 29 degrees and expected to climb to a high of 35 degrees. Not a bad day, but not a good day either.

Walt had been thinking about his plan to stockpile ash and recover the gold but he decided against this. He had plenty of ash on his property and really didn't want any more. He was retired and he didn't want to spend the rest of his life chasing gold or money. A stockpile of ash would be an environmental issue and if people started to do this it really could drive the price of gold down to near zero. He had some gold on his property so it seemed like a good idea to process this at his own pace and sell it while the price was high. Gold was selling for about $1900 a troy ounce before the volcano and likely would go up when the markets reopened.

The reporter on the radio mentioned that Bonner County Highway Districts would be starting to get the county roads cleared next week. With 900 miles of county roads this was going to take some time and they would be announcing their clean up schedule soon This would be a bigger job than just sending out snow plows. Some of the ash would be loaded into trucks and hauled away and then the roads would be washed off so that the remaining ash went into the ditches. Unfortunately this meant that eventually the ash would flow into streams and rivers and eventually into the lake. Overall this was expected to take about a month.

The city of Sandpoint had its own road department and they would be busy clearing the streets in town so that the city could open for business. The local power companies were discussing a plan to restore power to Sandpoint, and nearby Ponderay, so that businesses could reopen. But because of power sharing agreements with other utilities their plan was to provide power north of town on one day and south of town the next. No estimate was given about how long these rolling black outs would last. Walt thought that this was better than nothing and at least people would know what to expect.

The cynical side of Walt was thinking that when people could get to town then it would be logical to assume that people would come up Rapid Lightning from town. He expected people to be heading for the hills for a variety of reasons. Besides the locals, he thought that there would be a lot of people who were displaced by the volcano moving in the area when spring came to North Idaho, and that more people meant less of a quality of life. A few years ago new people who moved here would often leave the area shortly thereafter. They would find out that they couldn't earn a living here or that the winters were too harsh. But now more people would come here and stay for the clean air and country lifestyle and also to escape big city crime. He thought once again about the local bumper sticker that read, "Have a nice trip back to California."

Walt brought in a few days worth of firewood while Sparky got some fresh air in the back yard. He also brought in 6 half buckets of sand to process a little later in the day and got the gold panning machine set up.

It was a little early to meet the guys on 3.988 so he listened up on the higher bands. Fifteen meters wasn't open yet but 17 meters was wide open into Europe and the Midwest was coming in strong as well. He heard a station in Nebraska calling CQ and decided to give him a call. "AM0KQJ this is AP7ZMT. How copy? Over."

"Yes AP7ZMT, thanks for coming back. You have a nice signal into Nebraska. Name here is Alex. Over."

"OK Alex, I have you 5 by 9 into Sandpoint Idaho. The name here is Walt. I am curious how much ash you got and how everyone is dealing with it. Over." (AP7ZMT)

"Well what can I tell you Walt. Things are really nuts here. We are out on a farm and have almost a foot of ash on the ground. We are strictly farmers and didn't have any livestock

147

to lose. We are out of power but keeping things running with a large diesel generator over." (AM0KQJ)

"Oh boy I know that you got hit a lot harder than we did. We have about 3 inches of ash up here. I am guessing that you have some equipment if you are on a farm. How does it run in a foot of ash? Over." (AM)KQJ)

"We haven't tried to dig out yet but I can tell you that it is going to be a big job when we do. We have a big loader and a dump truck but we haven't decided what to do with it yet." (AM0KQJ)

"How many acres do you have and what crops do you grow Alex?"

"We have 320 acres and lease another 160 acres next door. Mostly we grow corn and some soybeans. Over."

"Is there any chance that you'll get a crop in? What are you going to do? AM7ZMT."

"We do have some corn in the silos but we have no idea if we can plant this year or not. Over."

"I don't claim to know anything about farming but I am curious if a little bit of ash would be beneficial or harmful to your soil? Over."

"I don't think a little ash will hurt the soil at all but the acid rain could be a real problem. AM0QKJ."

"How about your roofs did you have to clear the ash or did you lose any buildings?" (AP7ZMT)

"We had to shovel the roofs on the house and the machine shed. This was a big job and took us four days."

"Wow that's about as close to the end of the world as it gets. I am really sorry to hear about this. And we thought that we had problems up here. Is the army or national guard helping to clear the roads?"

"They just started but it will be awhile Walt. We've been hit with big ash dumps before. There is a very famous old water hole with hundreds of dinosaurs that were buried under 20 feet of ash. Maybe in a half a million years we'll have some really great soil to show for it. Over."

"Is there any chance that you can bury it. I know that would be a big job but I have been watching some of the mining shows on TV and sometimes they strip off 50 feet of over burden before they can get to the pay zone. AP7ZMT."

"That is probably our only option. Over."

"How about your cell service and internet. Is any of that working?"

"We did get our cell service back the other day but without power we don't have the internet working. Really glad to have the radio."

"Roger that Alex. It has helped me keep my sanity here as well. Running an inverter to power an Icom 7300 into a hex beam. Over."

"I am running an Icom 7600 here barefoot. Don't want to use the amp on the generator."

"I don't blame you. I hate to run sensitive electronics on a generator. Well I have sure enjoyed this QSO Alex but I've got a schedule down on 75 meters. I wish you the best of luck with the clean up and hope that you and all the other farmers are able to get your crops planted. It's a hell of a thing. That's for sure. Hope you make some good contacts today. I'll say 73 and be clear on your final. AP7ZMT."

"OK Walt, it's been nice talking to you today. You take care yourself. 73 this is AM0KQJ clear and QR Zed."

Walt got up to add wood to the fire and to drip another cup of coffee. Before he sat back down at the radio he turned on the driveway announcers and swapped over to his QRP radio. He couldn't imagine dealing with problems like Alex was facing. One thing about farmers, they know how to solve problems and are used to hard work.

When he tuned down to 3.988 some of the guys were already on the air. Dennis was talking to Ray. "I know what you mean. I never thought that there was a chance this would happen. AR7QRN."

"I thought remote viewing was a joke, Who would have guessed that anyone could have predicted a thing like this. Over." (AY7OM)

149

"Almost to the day too. I wish that I had stocked up beforehand." (AR7QRN)

"The only reason I have gas for the generator is that my car hasn't been running. It's pretty hard to get the siphon tube past the nozzle restrictor." (AY7OM)

"I know what you mean. I am tired of hauling this battery back and forth, that's for sure." (AR7QRN)

"I am doing OK so far but I need to get to a grocery store pretty quick. AU7PM."

"I know what you mean Frank. Good morning. AY7OM."

"Morning Guys, Another day in paradise. Over. AP7ZMT."

"That's right Walt, how are you doing? (AU7PM)

"I'm doing pretty good compared to a guy I just talked to in Nebraska. He has about a foot of ash on the ground on a 480 acre farm. Doesn't know if he'll be able to get a crop in this year or not. Over." (AP7ZMT)

"What is he going to do with the ash?" (AR7QRN)

"He is thinking about burying it. He had to clear the ash off his house and machine shed. What a mess. Over." (AP7ZMT)

"Things don't seem so bad over here after hearing about this guy. What is his call?" (AU7PM)

"Let me look, it is AMOKQJ. Over."

"I don't think I have ever talked to him. What band were you on?"

"17 meters just before I came down here."

" I think that a lot of people are in bad shape over here with no heat, no food, and no water. Over." (AU7PM)

"It sure is quiet in town. I miss not being able to walk to the store to get a sandwich and a cup of coffee." (AR7QRN)

"That would be nice, I am sure that I would miss that too." (AY7OM)

"Morning everyone. This is Ruby AN6RST."

"Good morning Ruby, we haven't heard you in awhile. How are you holding up?" (AP7ZMT)

"Pretty good Walt but I am out of cat food. Sometimes my cat likes what I am having for dinner, and other times she doesn't. Over."

"I guess that cats are more picky than dogs. My dog will eat almost anything. Over." (AP7ZMT)

"Any word over there when they are going to clear the roads and turn the power back on?" (AR7QRN)

"Haven't heard about the power but I know that they are working on the highway. I can hear the trucks and the loaders." (AN6RST)

"What are they doing with the ash?" (AU7PM)

"I am not exactly sure. All I know is that they are hauling it away." (AN6RST)

"Wish they would haul mine away. AN7HM."

"Morning Joe. What is going on?" (AU7PM)

"I heard that the fish were dying in the reservoir. I really hate to see that." (AN7HM)

"That's a shame. I'll bet the hatchery has got the same problem." (AR7QRN)

"I haven't heard but I'll bet you are right." (AN7HM)

"I never thought that we would see anything like this. It's kind of like living in a movie." (AN6RST)

"I sure wish the remote viewers group would have been wrong. AP7ZMT."

"I would have bet on it." (AY7OM)

"Most people felt the same way, I'm sure." (AP7ZMT)

"No matter how bad it gets here, it's a lot worse in a lot of places. I can't imagine living in the big city when something like this happens." (AN6RST)

"The elevators wouldn't work. You might have to go up and down 50 flights of stairs." (AU7PM)

"I never thought of that. AN7HM."

"Wish I had a good book to read." (AN7RST)

"Wish I had enough power to use the radio all day. It's amazing how people are running QRP lately." (AR7QRN)

"I know what you mean. A lot of guys laugh at QRP operators but look who is laughing now." (AY7OM)

"I have not heard anyone running an amp since the volcano blew, except for some of the emergency service nets." (AN6RST)

"Come to think of it you're right Ruby. I'd better get off here myself and save a few electrons." (AP7ZMT)

"OK Walt, you have a good one. We'll talk you later. AU7PM."

"Good to talk to you today. See you later.73. This is AP7ZMT. We'll be clear."

Walt turned off his radio and let Sparky out for a minute. When she came in Walt sat down and turned on his AM radio to local FM rock station and started the gold panning machine. He had enough experience with the machine by now that he didn't have to think about running it. He could listen to the radio and make money at the same time. He was almost three quarters through his stockpile of sand and running the machine was a good way to pass the time. Three hours later he was done with the sand he had in the house and was cleaning up his mess,

After a quick lunch he started to work on his window light blankets. He started with the three windows that could be seen from the county road. Walt chose to use old army blankets for these. He didn't have any curtains or curtain rods for that matter because they weren't usually needed when you lived out in the country. He attached the blankets over the windows with dry wall screws and had them rolled up with bailing twine when they were not in use. When he wanted to deploy them he could lower them into place so that there were no gaps at the bottom with a one foot overlap past each side.

For the bathroom window he used a small carpet and installed it the same way. The two windows in the bedroom were covered with custom fit pieces of cardboard that could be pushed into the window frame so that they fit tightly.

The kitchen and living room needed to have light shades that were easy to put up and take down and easy to peek through while they were up so these would take a little more thought.

After it was dark Walt turned lots of his LED indoor lights and went outside to look for leaks. The light blocking shades that he had put up so far worked perfectly.

The next morning he found some old beach towels that had been stored in the garage and sewed some black plastic onto the back of the towels to block the light and then installed them in the kitchen and living room. They could be raised and lowered like the other light blocking shades and he easily could peek through them. He would test these when it was dark but felt confident that they would do the trick. He wanted to have the cabin look like nobody was home if anybody came by after dark no matter how many lights were on inside. If someone approached the cabin and his security system was working, the motion detectors would trigger the night vision cameras that worked in the dark. If he was looking at the monitor he would be able to see them on the monitor. If he wasn't looking at the monitor, their pictures would be recorded on DVD anyway.

Just before lunchtime his telephone rang. He hadn't heard the old phone ring in sometime so it startled him at first. When he answered the phone it was Susan from the CB net. She found an old style telephone and wanted to be sure it was working. She wanted to get Walt's advice because she wanted to buy a gun for self defense and didn't know anything about them.

Walt wanted to know if she wanted to carry a gun in the car or in public or if she just wanted something to defend herself at home. She hadn't really thought about this but decided that some kind of pistol would be the best all around choice. Walt told her that using a pistol took a little more practice than a shotgun but it would give her the most all around protection since she could carry it anywhere she went and also have it handy when she was home.

He told her that he was no expert but he suggested a small revolver because they were very reliable and easy to conceal. Also they didn't jam like automatics and that you could keep one in a drawer for 100 years, pull it out, and it would still fire. He told her that when the road was open she could come over and try some of his revolvers or better yet he could meet her at the Sandpoint Gun Shop and try out a couple on the spot at their indoor range. She liked that idea and jokingly asked if she could get a pink one? As soon as the road was open Walt told her that he would give her a call.

This got Walt thinking that he would bring up the idea on the CB net that, in his opinion people should be prepared to defend themselves and that he would help them pick up a gun and give them some free advice if this would be useful. Walt never thought about this before because it was well known that most people who lived in the country for awhile had several guns.

He remembered Randy Weaver when the government stormed his house at Ruby Ridge a few miles up the road and killed his teenage son and his wife while she was holding her baby in the doorway. The media painted him as having an arsenal but when they showed his guns spread out on a sheet of plywood his "arsenal" was typical of the number and type of guns that you would find in any country home. He had a couple of rifles, a couple of shotguns, and a couple of pistols, and nothing more, No assault rifles, no automatic weapons, and no large capacity magazines. Rather than being punished, the agent who approved the assault on Randy's family was promoted to the head of the FBI!

Another thing Walt wanted to impress upon Susan was that she should be certain ahead of time that, if she needed to defend herself, she would not hesitate to kill someone if there was no other choice. This decision would have to be made ahead of time because there would be no time to think about this if she found herself in a life or death situation. Unlike the movies, an inexperienced shooter has no business trying to wound someone because they don't want to kill them.

In Walt's opinion the idea was to stop the threat. You stopped the threat by aiming for the head or the center of mass. A bad guy on drugs might not be stopped if he was shot in the shoulder or leg and could easily hurt you before he knew that he had been shot. Besides, you can't be sued by a dead man, and if he's not dead you'll probably be sorry.

Walt thought it would be a good idea to take Sparky for a walk that afternoon. He put on his rubber bottomed boots, grabbed his ski pole and they walked up the upper driveway. This had quite a bit of snow on it since he had not done any snow removal on this part of the road all winter. He wanted to give her some exercise and was looking for a good place to put the tree stand. He didn't see any deer tracks except those going up and down the road and he had hoped to see some tracks crossing the road. He did see a couple of places that looked like they might be good but thought he would wait until most of the snow had melted and more deer tracks were visible. When they got close to the property line they turned around to see something that he had never seen before. His boot tracks were black and in sharp contrast to the white snow cover. His boots had sunk down to the ash layer underneath. Sparky's tracks didn't sink down that far so they looked normal in the snow. This was so unusual that he wished that he had taken his camera along for the walk. Maybe they could get some pictures of this the next day if they didn't get any new snow to cover the tracks. It was too bad that these were boot tracks and not some oversized fake Bigfoot tracks instead.

After they got back to the cabin and walked by the wood shop Walt started thinking about his first security system. He had wired an electric fence unit to the metal door of the shop. He had mounted a single switch box outside the door and when anyone touched the door they would get a nasty shock if they didn't know to turn off the switch beforehand. He hadn't used this except when he went to town because it produced a very loud pulsing noise on his ham radio receivers. It was too much trouble to walk outside each night before bedtime to activate the fence charger and also to go out in the morning to turn it off. He could hard wire this so that he could turn it on and off from the house but this didn't seem to be worth the effort. Then he thought of putting the fence charger on a timer. He rarely operated his radios after 9 pm or before 6 am so the timer seemed like a good solution. Why hadn't he thought of this before?

This gave him another idea. He could easily extend the wire from the woodshop door to the garage man door and cover both buildings at once. When he went to town, he could bypass the timer. He wondered how long it would take before he forgot about this and shocked himself good and proper. He guessed that would only happen once and he would no longer be so absent minded that he fell for his own trap.

After Walt fed Sparky and let her out for the last time of the evening Walt wanted to have something good for dinner. He opened a can of Spam from the pantry and cut off three big slices that he fried one at a time while making some pancakes. Most people wouldn't call this dinner but it was quick and easy and really quite satisfying. A lot of people in the U.S. joked about Spam and said that it wasn't good for you because of the salt. But hunters and fisherman know that this is great chow to take on a camping or boat trip. It's also excellent when cut into small cubes and fried and then mixed with rice. In fact the people in the Philippines like it so much they even have an ice cream flavored with Spam.

That night Walt deployed the light shades in each window and left the driveway announcer alarm on just to get into the habit. He logged on to the internet and checked his email and got an email notification from PayPal that he had been paid for his work by the Pacific Northwest Remote Viewers Group. So he logged into his PayPal account and had the money transferred into his checking account. He was glad this was all they wanted and didn't have another Priority Target to post. What would it be next time, Mt. Rainier, Mt. Baker, Mt. Shasta? At least for now, no news is good news.

While he was online he checked out some of his favorite news sites and noticed several stories about the "new virus" monkey pox. There were only two known cases in the country so far and for some reason the government ordered 13 million doses of vaccine. Nothing to see here folks, (monkey) business as usual, isn't that special?

He was more interested in stories about the volcano than politics and focused his time and attention to reading stories about the ash cloud and how people were coping with this worldwide. Reporters were speculating that the coming food shortage would impact third world countries the most and that this would lead to a massive relocation of emigrants to Europe, Canada, and the United States. Walt hoped that governments didn't spend too much money trying to figure this out. People who only make $3 a day are the most likely to be affected by a worldwide food shortage and cannot be expected to stay at home and starve.

One story that he found particularly interesting talked about the fact that although the super volcano had erupted, it wasn't nearly as bad as it could have been. This could either mean that the worst was over for now or that there would be another larger eruption in the future. No one really knew for sure. Nonetheless there were many deep aftershocks being recorded in the area everyday.

Walt turned off his computer and went to bed for the night. He had the volume on the driveway announcer maxed out and, if it went off and he didn't hear this, he knew that Sparky would. He had the best and oldest form of danger alert ever known, a good dog with a loud voice.

The next morning the local radio news reported that the Bonner County Highway Districts were beginning to clear the roads. They would start with Highway 95, Highway 2, and Highway 200 today and that other County roads would be started after that and the schedules and progress of the work would be reported on their web site. The City of Sandpoint and Ponderay had already started and they were expected to be done by the end of the next week.

The news also said that the local power companies would be restoring power to Sandpoint and Ponderay within the week and, for the time being, rolling blackouts would occur every other day for the areas north and south of town. The schedules for blackouts would also be posted on their web sites.

This was really good news and Walt felt that now he could uses as much power as liked. After breakfast he ran the well pump using his inverter and cleaned out the hillbilly hot tub and filled it with fresh water. Next he got some firewood and prepared the firewood in the hot tub to be lit sometime in the afternoon. He attached the inverter/charger to his generator and ran it for a couple of hours to charge up his battery bank. He had used about 6 or 7 gallons of gas to use the snow blower and generator all this time and he couldn't complain about this.

Once the power came on he could plan which days to cook with the stove and which days to eat leftovers. The refrigerator could be run on days with power and, if needed could be run using the inverter and battery bank. He could start running his radio at full power and use the linear amplifier as well. He could get on the internet more often and use his 110 volt lights every other day. He could put a battery charger on his truck and even work out in the shop if he wanted.

Once he could get to town he could start buying food again depending on what was available. He could start using his chest freezer when needed and it would be fine only getting power once a day until the weather warmed up. He could meet Susan at the Sandpoint Gun Shop and so that she could try out some guns and decide what she wanted.

Walt thought of an experiment that he could try. He put Sparky out in the fenced backyard and turned on a small digital tape recorder and placed it near the driveway announcer alarm. Then he bypassed the electric fence charger and walked down to the mailbox. When he returned he put the fence charger's timer back online and went back into the cabin. He listened to the digital tape recorder track as it played back until he heard the driveway announcer's alarm. He did hear the pulsing noise from the fence charger but this wasn't a problem, the alarm worked fine. He didn't really think this would be an issue but he wanted to be sure.

When he heard the pulsing noise from the fence charger it wasn't the end of the world. By using the noise blanker feature on the radio, most of the pulsing noise could be eliminated but it was more pleasant to use the radio without the noise. However his QRP radios did not have a built in noise blanker so they could not be used when the noise blanker was on.

Later that afternoon he lit the fire in the hot tub and took Sparky for a short walk and then played fetch with her and with a couple of tennis balls. Soon she was tired and they went inside to get her some supper. A few hours later Walt was getting ready to take a bath in the hot tub. Normally he didn't use soap but he added some shampoo and an extra towel to the pile of stuff he planned to take outside. He also took a bathrobe, rubber slippers, an electric lantern, some bottle rockets, a lighter, a portable radio, and, just to get into the habit, he also took his fanny pack with the .357.

He went out to check the temperature and it would be a few more minutes before the tub temperature was perfect. He didn't want to be early and he didn't want to be late. He turned on the security system, installed the light blocking shades in the windows, and left Sparky in the house when he went out to the tub.

The tub was 102 degrees when he got in the water. He liked it a little warmer but it would warm up soon. He turned on the radio and listened to some classic rock at and started to relax. As the tub got a little warmer he shot off a few rockets and really stretched out. He waited until he was done to wash his hair because it was not fun sitting in the tub with a wet head in cold weather even if the water was hot. He wrapped the towel around his head and remained in the tub for awhile longer before getting out, putting on his robe and slippers, and slowly walking back to the cabin. He felt great. The well-deserved hot water bath took away a lot of stress from the last few months. Sparky was relieved that Walt was back in the house and showed her affection by licking his feet and legs.

Just because some things were on the verge of getting back to normal did not mean that things were getting back to normal. The weather sucked. It was colder than normal and nobody has seen sunshine since the eruption. The skies were dark and it always looked as if it was going to rain or snow. But the air didn't smell bad as it had before and the wet snow and it kept the ash from bowing and getting in the air, Although the people in the northwest still had lots of problems, they had it better than most areas of the country so Walt was thankful for this.

The next morning Walt was so relieved about the power coming back soon that he made his coffee the old fashioned way, using his Mr. Coffee electric coffee maker. If he would have had some bread he probably would have used the toaster as well. He pulled the light shades from the windows and got ready to celebrate another day of living. Even though it was pretty gloomy looking outside he couldn't help but think that things were looking up. When he checked his email he found that he had another set of target coordinates to post for the Pacific Northwest Remote Viewers Group which was fine with him. He liked making money while sitting at home by the fire. After the last target, he was a little curious about this one but he wasn't curious enough to try to remote view this himself. If it was bad news, he didn't want to know about it.

He hadn't heard anything since Christmas from the other websites he worked on so he sent them all emails hoping that they were all right and had weathered the storm. Most retail websites were traditionally slow after the holidays so he had no reason to assume that anything was wrong but wanted to say Hi anyway.

Maybe Walt watched too many movies but he had been thinking about how he would react if bad guys with guns were outside his cabin. They would almost certainly be coming up the driveway and if he was lucky he would have some warning. If they came in the yard waving guns their intention would be obvious but maybe they would be more cunning and lure him outside. Or maybe they would think he was not home and knock on the door to see if he was home. In any case he didn't want to get in a gunfight while trapped inside the cabin. There were no good shooting positions from the cabin anyway and on top of that the cabin wasn't what you would call bulletproof.

If he had the time and opportunity, he thought that he would go out the back door in Sparky's fenced area and come around the side of the cabin to confront armed invaders. Without cover this would not be a good idea but what if he had cover?

He came up with a plan. The side of the cabin had a seven foot fence made of field fence box wire two tiers high and strung between treated 4" x 4s" that stood 8 feet above the ground. His plan was to put an old piece of plywood on the outside of the fence running 4 feet high and 8 feet long. This was a good idea anyway because Sparky could not see who or what was in the yard and bark. So this would look perfectly normal for a place in North Idaho.

Walt planned to build a shooting position on the inside of the fence behind the plywood. He would use old plastic dog food bags and fill them with the sand he had left over from the gold panning machine. He guessed that the bags would weigh about 100 pounds each and thought that he could stack them four feet high and six feet across behind the fence and hidden from view behind the plywood. If he also stacked them so that they protected him from the side it would leave him a protected area about 4 feet by 4 feet and make a perfect shooting position. Unless the bad guys had .50 caliber weapons, sand bags like these should provide excellent protection.

In a pinch he could shoot from inside the cabin by cracking open the kitchen window but this would only be good for the first shot or two and offer him no protection whatsoever.

If something like this did happen and he chose to go out the backdoor it would be best to have a rifle and ammo pre-positioned so that he did not have to grab a weapon on his way out the door. Ideally he would build a secret , weatherproof, and camouflaged locker so he could leave a few guns out there all the time.

In addition he would make sure that there was a loaded gun in the woodshed, woodshop, and garage just in case he was caught away from the house. It took all day to put this together but he was very pleased with the result. It was functional but he needed to think of a way to decorate it and to conceal its' true intention. He wasn't sure how he would do this and had to give this some thought. Walt hadn't decided which guns to put in the secret sandbox locker either but ideally he would want one rifle and one shotgun. He had been so busy that he didn't get on the radio all day but he had made a lot of progress. Walt would have loved to discuss this with his radio friends but knew enough to keep his mouth shut, no matter how hard it would be. Talking about his prepping and defensive plans might be considered premeditation if he ever had to go to court.

Another security improvement he thought would be worthwhile would be to add high intensity lights that could be turned on from the outdoor shooting position to flood the parking area with light. This would have to wait until he could get some LED light bars and wire, whenever he could (finally) get into town.

That night after dinner Walt felt like being entertained so he tuned into a AM radio station from Salt Lake City that came in pretty well at night. They had an old radio show on called Radio Mystery Theater and it was always a lot fun. Radio was so much better than TV drama he didn't understand why it wasn't more popular today. When you listened to radio you could be doing other things besides staring at the screen. At the same time your imagination took over filling in the details of the characters, scenery, and story line. The writing was better than it is today and when you heard a radio drama you remembered it more vividly than you ever would if you saw it on TV. Movies and television relied on action and special effects. Radio drama relied on writing and actors with unforgettable voices. It didn't matter if the show was a western, a mystery, science fiction, or an adventure, it was just more fun and exciting on the radio.

Walt had always been fascinated by the magic of radio. The idea that a voice, data, or music could travel thousands of miles into your mind was still spellbinding to Walt. Sending information through space (and in some cases time) was mystical, mind-blowing, and astonishing. The only thing more impressive would be long distance telepathy. Maybe this is why he was so intrigued by remote viewing. No power, no wires, no gadgets, no gismos, nothing but the power of the mind.

Walt spent the next week processing the remaining sand left in the woodshed. It was easy work and he was anxious to see how much total gold he had recovered. It was repetitive but satisfying at the same time and it gave him something to think about besides politics or the volcano. When he finished the last bucket of sand he couldn't wait to weigh the gold and he emptied the gold into the paper cup holding all the gold he had recovered so far. He placed an empty paper cup on his scale and zeroed out the weight. He set the scale to read troy ounces and carefully poured his gold into the empty paper cup. When he looked at the scale it read 2.64 troy ounces. This was outstanding. Quickly he did the math in his head and calculated that if gold was selling for $1800 an ounce this would be worth over $4,000. He should have kept a log to determine how many hours it took to process the sand but he hadn't thought to do this.

One thing nice about gold is that it was not taxed until it is sold. He could hold onto the gold until he needed the money or the price went up. But considering what he knew about the ash containing gold he thought it best to sell this as soon as possible. The pawn shop bought gold and he planned to sell his gold as soon as possible.

The next morning he heard a back up alarm and truck traffic on the county road. After breakfast he and Sparky walked down to take a look. The country was using a grader to pile the ash onto the center of the road, Then a loader was scooping up the ash and loading it in a dump truck, When a truck was filled it would go down the road and an empty truck would position itself to be loaded with ash. As they worked their way up the road, a water truck was washing the road so that the remaining ash was washed into the ditches. This was fantastic. It was like the French people must have felt in WW2 when the allied troops had come to save them.

When Walt and Sparky got back to the cabin Walt telephoned the Sandpoint Gun Shop. They didn't open until 10 am but someone answered the phone anyway. Walt found out that they were open Tuesday through Saturday from 10 am – 5 pm. Then he called Box Mart and they had been open for the last week. After this he called the pawn shop and found that they would be open as well.

After this he called Susan. When she answered he said, "Hello Susan, this is Walt. It looks like they have the road open. Just wondering if you would like to go to the Sandpoint Gun Shop tomorrow?"

" Hey Walt, thanks for calling. Sure I can do that what time are you thinking?

" How about 10 am. I can meet you at the gun store. If you see something you like you can try it out at their indoor shooting range."

" That would be great, I'm not sure where its located."

" They are on the left side of hwy 95 about a mile north of Box Mart. Can you meet me there?"

" Yes that will be great. How will recognize you? She asked.

" I'll be driving a Ford pick up truck with a tool box in the back. What will you be driving?"

" I have a red Toyota Tacoma."

" OK that will work great for me I have a lot to do it town but I'll be there at 10. See you then. It should be busy in town."

"Yes I think so too. Really appreciate it. See you tomorrow."

Chapter 6. March

"I feel the earth move under my feet
I feel the sky tumblin' down, a-tumblin' down
I feel the earth move under my feet
I feel the sky tumblin' down, a-tumblin' down"
Carole King

Walt left Sparky at home and got an early start to town. He hadn't been anywhere in over a month and he was glad to be on the road. The sky was still dark and threatening and the snow and ash covered trees were eerie and in sharp contrast to the snow cover on the ground. The ditches were stained with volcanic ash but the roads were in good shape. Northern Elementary School was not in session and no lights were visible in the windows. None of the north side of town had power. When he got into Ponderay the traffic lights were working and this was a good sign.

First he stopped at Box Mart and the parking lot was already half full. Walt noticed that about one third of the cars were clean but the rest were filthy. He could tell which cars slept in garages and which ones did not. Nobody washed their cars in the winter anyway. The shelves in the store were not bare as he feared, however there were signs advising people that there were limits on some items. Customers could only buy 2 dozen eggs, 1 package of chicken or hamburger, 1 pound of bacon, 2 pounds of cheese, 1 case of beer, 2 loaves of bread, and a few other items were also limited until they could be restocked. Some items like toilet paper, paper plates, and paper towels were completely sold out but this was understandable. After being closed for more than a month there was a lot of what economists call penned up demand.

Next Walt stopped by the gas station and topped off the gas in the truck and then headed to Import Tools which opened at 8 am. He found two high power LED light bars like those used on off road trucks and also picked up some wire.

165

He still had time to go to the pawn shop and see about selling his fine gold. The pawnshop was just opening its doors and they were glad to have a customer as soon as they opened. The spot price for gold that morning was $1838 an ounce. The owner looked at the gold and saw that it did not have any black sand or other impurities. Then he tested it and found it to be 87% fine gold, so this reduced the total value. Factoring in the purity, Walt really had 2.29 troy ounces. With a spot price of $1838 an ounce, the gold was worth $4209.02. The owner was willing to pay 85% of the total value, which amounted to $3577.67 cash. This was Walt's first experience selling gold but he understood that the owner had to make money to stay in business so he happily took the money. Normally he would have snooped around looking for deals but he was pressed for time.

It was just about 10 o'clock so he drove past Box Mart and pulled into the Sandpoint Gun Shop parking lot. He spotted the red Tacoma pick up and parked next to her. Walt got out of his truck and walked over the Toyota and said, "Are you Susan? I'm Walt."

She got out of her truck and said, "Nice to meet you Walt. Thanks for helping me out."

Walt had never met Susan except for on the radio. She was pretty short but most people were short in comparison, he was six feet 2 inches when he stood up straight. She was an attractive woman, he guessed in her late 30's with blond hair and a slender build.

Walt asked, "Before we go inside I wanted to ask you what you want a gun for? Protection, home defense, hunting?"

"I want something I can carry with me for self defense and protection."

"OK, that's what I needed to know. One other thing, have you ever fired a gun before?" Walt thought this was a fair question.

"No I never have." she admitted.

"Well in that case lets go inside and look at a few small revolvers. I personally like revolvers better than automatics

166

because they are easy to operate, very safe, and extremely reliable. A lot of people like automatics because they hold more bullets and you often see them in the movies and on TV. But I think you will do a lot better with a revolver. I have brought one with me we can shoot at the range, Let's go take a look."

Walking into a gun store can be intimidating at first. There are guns on the wall, guns in glass cases, and lots of ammo and shooting supplies, and targets resembling animals or criminals. They walked over to the glass cases and Walt told the salesman that they wanted to look at small hammerless .357 magnum revolvers He saw two right away that he wanted her to look at.

" I have one of these Susan and it is an excellent choice. It is a Ruger LCR (Light Carry Revolver) in .357 magnum. This is a very powerful pistol cartridge and it does kick a bit. But you can also fire .38 special cartridges in it which are a little cheaper and they don't kick as much, so they are better to practice with.

This is hammerless which means that the hammer will not get caught in your clothing when you pull it out. It is a 5 shot, light weight, double action revolver with a smooth trigger pull. Because of the short barrel it is best used at a short range. Double action means that you don't have to pull back the hammer to cock it, just pull the trigger as many times as you want."

The salesman took it out of the case and handed it to Walt. Walt examined it to be sure that it wasn't loaded and carefully handed it to Susan, "Here see how it feels. It's not loaded and it is OK to pull the trigger. Just don't point at anybody."

Susan took the gun and got a chance to see how it felt.

"Walt added, these are highly desirable and if you ever wanted to sell it, it wouldn't be a problem. At nearly $800 I know this seems expensive, but if your life is on the line you want a gun you can depend on."

The salesman just smiled knowing that Walt was doing his job for him. Walt saw another gun nearby and asked to look at it as well. It was a Smith and Wesson M&P 340, 5 round. .357 Magnum revolver with a 1.8 inch barrel.

"This is another good choice Susan. It's about the same price and has a great reputation. It also has a Tritium front site which is easier to see at night."

When Susan examined the S&W she said, "They both feel pretty good. They are not as heavy as I thought they would be."

Walt saw one more gun he wanted to point out. It was a Bond Arms Snake Slayer. "This isn't a revolver but it is a very popular self defense weapon. As you can see it is a derringer but it has a trigger guard for safety. It is only two shots but with a 4 inch barrel it is more accurate than the other two guns and it is a little heavier. It can shoot either a .45 caliber Long Colt cartridge or a .410 shotgun shell that can be loaded with buck shot or bird shot for snakes, I am sure it has a kick to it but I have never fired one and it's a little cheaper than the others. Do you want to look at it?"

"No I like the idea of having more than two shots." Walt was disappointed because he had always wanted to shoot one.

"Ok lets go do some shooting." The salesman got them two of the same guns that had been fired before and a dozen rounds of .357 ammo and 25 rounds of .38 special ammo and asked, "Will this be enough? Walt said that it would be fine and then the salesman asked what kind of targets that they wanted? Walt told him that they wanted self defense targets. He got the targets and two sets of ear protection and pointed the way to the gun range.

Walt had never been in the range but it was nice to have an indoor range in Sandpoint. The Sandpoint Gun Shop also rented fully automatic weapons and Walt was glad to see that nobody else was using the range. This meant that they could talk to each other and then put on their ear protection was they were ready to fire. Walt attached one silhouette target to the holder and pushed the control button to take the target 20 feet away.

He turned to Susan and said, "This might not seem that far away but according to the FBI the average shooting takes place at a distance of something like 7 feet and less than two shots. So first I want to mention how important it is to always treat a gun as if were loaded and always point it down range."

He got out his note book and a pen and drew a picture of the rear sights and showed her how to align the rear sight with the front site. Then he drew a circle on top of the front bar sight so that she would know what a proper sight picture looked like. Next he loaded the LCR with two .38 special bullets and set the gun down on the bench. " OK the gun is loaded. Go head and put on your ear protection, pick up the gun, hold the gun firmly, aim at the target and fire it. You can use both hands to hold it if you like"

She picked up the Ruger and held it with two hands, aimed, and fired. She seemed surprised how easy this was. Then she fired again. She pulled the trigger one more time but the gun was out of bullets and then set the gun down on the bench pointed down range and pulled off her ear protection.

"Well what did you think?" Walt asked as he glanced at the target.

"I don't think I hit it but it didn't kick like I expected it to."

"You did great. It takes a little practice before you get the feel for where the gun shoots. OK let's try this again." Walt brought the target closer to within 10 feet and showed her how to remove the spent shells from the cylinder. Now go ahead and load it with five bullets and try it again."

Susan carefully loaded the gun, put on her ear protection, and fired all five bullets at the target and set the gun down.

"That was great," Walt said and he could see that she hit the target. He brought the target forward. She could see that she got two hits in the chest and one in the head and the remaining two on the paper. Walt put a mark on each hit with his pen and took the target back to 10 feet. "OK lets try this again, this time be sure to aim at the heart every time."

She reloaded and made sure her ear protection was on securely and emptied the gun at the target. She could see that she hit it three times in the heart area and pulled off two shots into the shoulder. "That felt pretty good" she said as she placed the gun back on the bench.

"I'd say that was pretty good shooting for your first time. Now lets try this with some .357 cartridges. Hold on tightly, you will hear and feel the difference."

Susan emptied the expired shells onto the bench and loaded up the gun with .357 magnums. She seemed a little nervous but she was having fun. After putting her headphones on she held the gun with both hands and fired one shot. She felt the difference in power but then pumped 4 more shots into the target, one right after the other. She could see that the first two shots were on target but the others drifted after that. She put the gun down and took off her headphones. "Wow I see what you mean. There is kick to the .357."

"Yes I agree. That's why I like to practice with the .38 specials. Now lets try this again with the .38 specials and this time hold the gun with one hand and take yor time between each shot." Walt brought the target forward and marked the new hits with a circle so that she would know which ones were from the .357 and returned the target to about 10 feet away.

Susan loaded the gun and took her time and shot one handed. She wasn't quite as accurate but the bad guy would have been quite dead full of that many holes.

"I think you are doing great Susan. Lets try the same thing with the S&W. here I'll put on a new target for you and let's start with the .38's." Walt showed her how to load the gun and placed it on the bench.

When she fired this for the first time she got all five bullets in a 5 inch group in the heart and couldn't believe it. "Not bad, I like this gun."

I can see that. Let me mark the hits and you can try it again with the .357s."

This time she didn't hold the same group but her shooting was pretty impressive for a beginner. Walt wanted her to try the gun he had brought from home. It was a Ruger SP100, This was a large .357 with a six inch barrel. He showed her how to pull back the hammer and fire this single action, For this he took the target out to 25 feet.

She slowly fired each shot single action and found it was pretty accurate. Then Walt reloaded the gun and had her fire it double action at the same distance. She could see that it wasn't as accurate when fired double action and this is what Walt wanted her to experience for herself.

"Well, what did you think? Asked Walt as he was retrieving her target.

"I can see what you mean about a longer barrel but I think it makes sense to get something I can carry a little easier. I can't imagine that big gun in my purse. I liked both guns but I like the S&W a little more. Lets go talk to the salesman."

Walt made sure that all the guns were unloaded and they went out to the counter displaying the handguns and targets. "She liked the S&W the best. What can you do for her?'

The salesman was glad to hear that he hadn't wasted his time and that he had made a sale first thing in the morning. "I'll write up the purchase order, waive the gun range and ammo fees, and she'll have to fill out the federal background check form and pay for the gun today. It usually takes a week to ten days but after this is approved she can pick up the gun and we'll throw in a free box of .38 specials. How does that sound?" He looked at Susan and thought that would be great.

As they left the Sandpoint Gun Shop Susan thanked Walt for all his help. He replied that she had made a great choice and handed her the targets. He also handed her his SP100 and the left over bullets and said, "Here, I'll loan this to you until you get your gun. Keep it loaded in the house in a safe place where you can get to it quickly. Guns don't do much good if they are not loaded. Oh and by the way, pretty soon you will be insured."

"Insured, what do you mean?" She didn't know what Walt was talking about.

" It's and old saying, Insured by Smith and Wesson."

Susan got the joke and got in her truck and thanked him again. Walt remembered something, "I almost for got I wanted to get some more ammo." He waived at her and went back into the Sandpoint Gun Shop.

When Walt walked back in the Sandpoint Gun Shop the salesman was surprised to see him. "Long time no see, is there anything else I can help you with?" he asked.

"I wanted to take a look at the Henry Big Boy. Is that a .357? Walt asked as he pointed to the rifle on the wall.

"Sure is." The salesman replied as he took it off the wall and handed it to him. This little carbine has everything you could ask for."

Walt looked it over. The salesman was right about that. It had a synthetic stock, mounting points for a sling, a rubber recoil pad, Pitcatinny and M-Loc accessory slots, fiber optic sights front and rear, a threaded muzzle to accept a suppressor, a seven round removable tube magazine, a side loading gate. "What no cup holder? Walt joked as he worked the lever action back and forth. "What are you asking for it?

"It is $899" the salesman answered, "If you take it today I'll throw in 2 boxes of shells."

"You know, I believe I will take you up on that."

"Let me write that up. With tax that will be $952.94."

"Sounds good. Walt reached for his wallet and handed the salesman $1000 in cash. Here is my CCW."

"That will be great. You'll still have to sign the background paperwork but since you have a concealed carry permit, you can take home the rifle today."

In Idaho you no longer have to have a concealed weapons permit to carry a weapon concealed but if you do, then you do not have to wait for the Feds to give you permission to buy a gun. Walt walked out of the store a few minutes later almost hugging it with joy and then he put it in his tool box and made sure it was locked.

It was almost noon and he thought that as long as he was in town he would stop by Locals Grocery and pick up some more groceries. They didn't have any signs regarding limits so he bought 20 pounds of potatoes, a canned ham, some more chicken thighs, hamburger, butter, peanut butter, canned tuna, a frozen microwavable lasagna, and some jerky. After he left Locals Grocery he stopped by Papa Murphy's and picked up a take and bake pizza. Walt was celebrating. It had been a good day and a worthwhile trip to town.

When he returned he stopped by the mailbox but it was empty and wondered when rural mail service would resume. When he pulled into the yard he could hear Sparky barking her head off. She missed him anytime he went to town but this had been a longer than usual trip and she was ready to get some fresh air. He put the groceries in the mud room to keep things cool until the power came back on and wasn't quite sure how he was going to cook the pizza. His inverter wouldn't handle his oven so he let it thaw, and cranked up the wood stove. This would be a first, he had never baked a pizza on a wood stove before but if he cut it in half first he thought that it would work. He put the pizza on a cookie sheet and balanced this all on a trivet. After an hour and fifteen minutes, it looked good enough to eat, and it was (delicious).

Walt couldn't wait to try out his new rifle. He got six paper plates and colored a one inch circle in the center of each plate with a magic marker. Then he put on his rubber pack boots, and took the paper plates and a staple gun outside and he took Sparky for a walk up the upper driveway. When they returned from the walk he let Sparky out back into the fenced yard and went out front and got six long thin boards about the size of yard sticks. He walked toward the driveway entrance and stapled a plate to a stick and stuck this in the snow. This would be his closest target and this was about 120 feet from the porch. He repeated the process about every 25 feet from the first target and he estimated that the farthest target was about 225 feet from the porch.

Next he took the rifle out of the tool box in his truck and loaded with six .357 magnum bullets. He worked the lever and chambered the first round and fired. He had no problem hitting the center of the paper without making any adjustments to the sights. He stepped back on the porch and fired at the five remaining targets one at time, His worst shot was the farthest distance from the porch and it was about an inch below the center. That was both fun and satisfying. Then he loaded five more bullets and shot the targets as quickly as he could. He was getting used to the lever action. He was impressed how quickly he could fire and, how easy it was to re-acquire the target in his sights.

When he was done firing, he set the rifle on the porch and picked up his paper target plates and put them in the woodshed. He carefully cleaned the gun and was admiring its construction. Walt had never owned a gun with a threaded muzzle. This allowed a noise suppressor (silencer) to be attached to the end of the barrel. Noise suppressors could not be used or purchased without registering the paperwork and paying a large annual fee to the ATF. Walt really had no interest in these but it was nice to know the rifle was built to accommodate one if he ever changed his mind.

This was his newest and best rifle and he was planning to make it sleep outside in the secret locker. It was the best choice. His other rifle was way more powerful. The bolt action 30 '06 could take down any animal in North America including a polar bear however it was not the best choice for home protection or any kind of fire fight. For tonight anyway, the new kid could sleep indoors.

When he checked his email later that afternoon he saw that power would be restored north of town in the morning and that people in this area could expect to have power every other day. This was a big relief at least from now on the outages would be short and they would be planned. Once the power came back on he would top off the charge on his battery bank with the inverter/charger and get the refrigerator going again. He didn't have enough food to justify turning on his freezer but he thought it would be a good idea to start freezing water bottles to act as ballast until the freezer was restocked with food.

As long as he was online Walt watched a couple of shows on YouTube highlighting how many people were having a hard time paying bills and feeding their families after the volcano. Gasoline and diesel fuel were at record high prices, inflation was over 10% year over year, and that the number of people unemployed had increased 45% in the last month. For the first time since the great depression some people had to stand in food lines just to get something to eat. The volcanos had impacted the whole country and things were much worse for the economy than the Covid lockdowns. The mood of the country was much like the skies, dark and gloomy.

Crime and suicide rates were rising quickly and there was little the government could do to help. The way that government had helped in the past was to give people money but if food, fuel, and housing were in short supply, more money didn't help. In fact more money added fuel to the fire and everything became more expensive in a very short period of time. During the Covid lockdowns, businesses and schools closed and people held on as long as they could. Then just as things were getting back to normal the volcanos changed everything, literally overnight. Lives were lost and dreams were shattered. America, it seemed, was on the ropes.

News like this was hard to take. Walt had spent a lot of time and money prepping for the worst so when it came, he was better equipped to deal with it than most people but it still affected him like everyone else. People are a little like volcanos, Walt reasoned, they can take a lot of pressure for awhile but at some point they are going to blow. (He could not believe that he still could not get the Jimmy Buffet song out of his mind... *Now, I don't know, I don't know, I don't know where I'm a-gonna go when the volcano blows.*)

The next morning Walt put the inverter/charger back on grid power and put the entire cabin and water well back on grid power as well. He reset the timer on the hot water tank knowing the power would be off the next day. He planned to use the oven to cook the second half of his pizza and was trying to think if he should plan on doing more cooking while he could use the oven and the stove. He planned to install the LED lights that he got from Import Tools in the after noon and was hoping to get a little time on the radio after that.

There was about 2 inches of fresh snow on the ground and

this did not require any work or effort except to sweep off the satellite dish. The sun was still hiding behind the clouds but it wasn't too cold outside and the wind was not blowing. By post volcano standards it looked like a pretty nice day. In a normal year the month of March would mean the end of winter when people put their snow shovels away and got ready for spring. So far the year had been anything but normal.

The cabin had warmed up nicely and Walt made a killer ham and egg breakfast and shared some of this with Sparky. He made twelve cups of coffee in his Mr. Coffee coffee maker and planned to leave this plugged in for much of the day. He had nowhere that he had to go and nothing that he really had to do. Life was good and, for him, things were looking up. For a moment he was living the dream and planning some the things he hoped to get done in the summer. He would bring in more sand from the sandbar. He would get the tree stand put up and build a smoke house. He wanted to build some cold frames and do a little light gardening. And someday he hoped that he would build a billiard room and a man cave. Come to think of it, he thought, his whole place was a man cave! Then his daydream stopped and Walt returned to the present. He looked at the clock and it was time to get on the radio.

Since the power was on Walt turned on his Icom 7300 and his linear amplifier. He tuned to 3.988 and selected his end fed antenna. He listened for a few minutes and didn't hear anything. Then he started transmitting with 500 watts, "Is there anybody on frequency? This is AP7ZMT."

"Your coming in strong this morning Walt. This is AU7PM."

"I've got power this morning so I am taking my amplifier for a walk. How about you?"

"We got our power back two days ago. It was sure out a long time. I am charging batteries this morning." (AU7PM)

"We are rationed over here. We are only scheduled to have power every other day for awhile. But we can work with that. Over." (AP7ZMT)

"Roger. Have you been to the grocery store lately?"

"I went to town yesterday. Box Mart had limits on some things so I stopped by another store as well." (AP7ZMT)

"I went to Winco and they were pretty well stocked but they had limits on ground beef and chicken. Over." (AU7PM)

"I am sure everybody wants to stock up as soon as they can. I know I do. The problem is that even if you could buy 300 pounds of meat you couldn't put it in your freezer all at once." (AP7ZMT)

"I know the quick freeze shelf in my freezer can only do about 10 pounds per day." (AU7PM)

"Mine is the same way. I am not going to try and restock the freezer until the power stays up on a daily basis. It would be too expensive to run the generator every other day." AP7ZMT)

"What did you see when you went to town, anything?"

"I saw a lot of dirty cars. You could sure tell who has a garage and who doesn't. Over." (AP7ZMT)

"Roger. Saw the same thing over here. It will probably change now that people are driving and the power is on."

"Oh I went to the Sandpoint Gun Shop and helped one of the neighbors pick out a new pistol. She had never fired a gun before but she did pretty well at the range. Over" (AP7ZMT)

"An indoor range or an outdoor range? AU7PM."

"The Sandpoint Gun Shop has an indoor range and they don't charge you anything if you buy something. Over." AP7ZMT.

"Did she buy anything? (AU7PM)

"She bought a Smith and Wesson M&P 340. It is a 5 shot hammerless revolver in .357. Over." (AP7ZMT)

"OK sounds like a nice gun. How much did that set her back?"

"It was 788 plus tax. They waived the range fees and threw in a box of shells. She won't be able to pick it up for a week or so. But I got a new toy too. It is a Henry Lever Action Big Boy carbine in .357. Shot it yesterday. It's a really nice gun. Couldn't live without it." (AP7ZMT)

"I know what you mean. Sounds fun, what are you planning to shoot with it? AU7PM.

"Home Invaders. Over." (AP7ZMT)

"It ought to be good for that. I have a Henry and really like it too." (AU7PM)

"I was surprised how much gun prices had gone up. A few years ago I paid about $500 for my Ruger LCR and now they are over $800, AP7ZMT."

"I know. The prices are through the roof. I am glad to hear that your neighbor bought a good quality gun. Lots of people are tempted to buy the cheapest thing they can find." (AU7PM)

"Years ago when I was in college I bought a new Iver Johnson .38 special 5 shot revolver for $67. I've still got and it still works but you can't hardly hit anything with it unless you are closer than 10 feet. And then it's a real pain to get the spent shells out to reload. AP7ZMT."

"Sounds like a Saturday Night Special." (AU7PM)

"That's exactly what it was and exactly why I got it. Over."

"Oh I heard a strange noise in the sky. The airlines are flying over here again. I guess the ash clouds are no longer a problem. Over." (AU7PM)

"I hadn't heard that but we hardly ever get any aircraft overhead. But maybe things are getting back to normal. Did you hear that another food processing plant burned to the ground? I think it was in Portland. Over." (AP7ZMT)

"No I hadn't heard about it. How many has it been now? AU7PM."

"I am really not sure, I know that it has been over 2 dozen in the last year. Don't those dead chickens know that smoking is bad for their health? (AP7ZMT)

"It's been too many in such a short time to be accidental. I wonder what's going on? (AU7PM)

"Remember when President Joe Bama said there was going to be a nationwide food shortage just after he took office?" (AP7ZMT)

"I do remember that. Sounds fishy to me. AU7PM."

"I can't figure it out either. You would think if it was a terrorist, they would have claimed responsibility by now. AP7ZMT."

"Morning Guys. AN7HM here. Been listening for awhile. I can't believe that both of you have power and I sitting here in the dark. Oh, Walt I have one of those S&W revolvers I carry everywhere. It's a really nice gun, I'm sure your neighbor will love it. Over."

"Yes Joe. I like the way it feels, I like the way the extractor is protected. And I like the tritium sight. She took to it right away. I loaned my SP100 until she can pick it up. Over."

"Is that a Ruger?" (AN7HM)

"Roger that Joe. It a six shot .357 revolver with a 6 inch barrel. It's a big heavy thing to carry around but it shoots straight. Over." (AP7ZMT)

"OK. Well Frank what are you up to today?" (AN7HM)

"Oh not much. I did get to town to get groceries. Like Walt was saying. There sure a lot of dirty cars out there. How about you?" (AU7PM)

"Just waiting for fishing season. I've been getting my gear ready and have a new fly rod I want to try out. I don't know when we'll get our power back," (AN7HM)

"Did you eat all the fish in your freezer. Give them away or what?" (AP7ZMT)

"We ate what we could but gave the rest away. I don't care I'll catch more, I'm sure. Over." (AN7HM)

"I wonder how fish will deal with all the ash. I heard that we have some dead fish in the creek." (AP7ZMT)

"I haven't heard anything one way or the other but is seems that the ash would not be good for the fish. Maybe they'll do better in larger bodies of water. AN7HM."

"I hope so. There are going to be a lot of hungry hunters and fisherman out this year. I wonder how the deer population will do as well?"

"I think the deer might be alright. They know enough to dig though the ash. AU7PM."

"I hope you are right Frank. I'm going to bail out of here and take Sparky for a walk. Good hearing you Joe. I hope that your power comes back soon. I'm going to take a long hot shower tonight. 73. AP7ZMT."

"Don't rub it in. We've really missed our hot tub. That's for sure. 73 Walt. AN7HM."

"Yes Walt we'll talk to you later. 73 AU7PM." Joe and Frank continued to talk and Walt turned off his radio and amplifier. Sparky overheard Walt talking about a walk and she was sitting up ready to go.

Walt put on his pack boots and took Sparky down the driveway and a paper grocery bag to bring up the mail. No tracks at the box meant no mail, so they walked up the driveway past the home site and kept an eye out for deer tracks crossing the road. He saw two sets of tracks and noted the location. He didn't have to decide right away but soon he wanted to settle on a spot to install the tree stand. Sparky had some fun for a change and got to bark at a squirrel who shot up a tree and then just scolded her from the safety of a large branch.

As soon as they got back, Walt started to preheat the oven for the other half of the pizza. When this was done he had a frozen microwavable lasagna that he bought the day before and thought he would cook it today in the oven and eat it tomorrow. When the power was off he could reheat this in just a couple of minutes by running the microwave on the inverter.. He thought he should check this everyday because mail service was supposed to resume any time. He had one of those jumbo sized mailboxes and he wasn't sure if all his mail would fit in the mailbox or not.

After lunch Walt installed the two LED light bars over the front porch deck and they were protected from the weather under the overhanging roof. He wired this so that they could be turned on from the sandbag shooting spot using DC power from his battery bank. He knew the lights would be extremely bright but wouldn't know for sure until dark.

The lasagna was meant for tomorrow but Walt had some for supper that night anyway. After dinner he caught up on doing the dishes, and then deployed the light shades throughout the house. He let Sparky out back and he tried out is new lights. They lit up the entire parking area and he could only imagine how blinding they would be if your eyes were used to the dark and they were turned on without warning.

Before bed he remembered to take a hot shower and it felt so good he stayed in the shower until all of the hot water was gone. After a shower like that he slept like a baby.

The next morning he remembered to transfer everything to inverter power. He didn't care how much power he used or how long he used it, since he knew the power would come on the next day. Before breakfast Walt turned on the local AM radio station to hear the weather forecast and was stunned by what he was hearing. At 9:15 am Eastern Standard Time a large jet plane had crashed into the Chesapeake Bay Nuclear Power Plant outside Washington D.C. It damaged the containment wall and the subsequent explosion breached the reactor and ruined the emergency cooling system. Radiation was escaping and the reactor was rapidly overheating. It was expected to explode. The entire area was being evacuated and only key government personnel were being admitted into the Doomsday Bunker.

Walt connected to the internet and started watching the coverage on a Fairfax, Virginia TV station. They were showing drone coverage of the scene and, except for a handful of emergency workers, the entire area was being evacuated. The highways were packed as people were fleeing. Nobody knew how far away would be safe. The explosion could be deadly for 50 miles in every direction. The radiation could be deadly for hundreds of miles. Nobody knew for sure. The prevailing winds would push the radiation cloud on shore. Power was out in much of the District. Because this was real, it was even more scary than a Hollywood movie. Walt couldn't take it anymore and shut down his computer.

First Kilauea, then Yellowstone, and now a runaway nuclear reactor in the nation's capitol, what could be next? He had always heard that trouble comes in threes. Maybe this was true. Even though he was thousands of miles away, this was a huge tragedy and would affect everyone in the country and beyond.

Like it or not, most people in the U.S.A. are completely

dependant on the Government. The States get money from the government, veterans and retired people get money from the government, schools and hospitals get money from the government, poor people get welfare and food stamps from the government, the list goes on and on. An event like this would bring the country's economy to a screeching halt. Who could know how long it would take to recover and how many people would die? It was unbelievable.

Walt remembered what it was like in the Ukraine when Chernobyl blew up in 1986. The entire area was sealed off and the Russians covered the reactor with dirt and concrete. Harmful radiation was detected as far away as Sweden. People all over Europe developed cancers and other health problems. It was and still is a nightmare. Even 50 years later the radiation levels are 1000 times normal in the nearby forest floors that are not covered by concrete. So anyone who thinks that the government can recover in weeks or months is a fool.

Obviously the people nearby in the District, Virginia, or Maryland will get the worst of it but things are going to be bad everywhere. How can people buy food if they don't have any money? There won't be stimulus checks and there won't be food stamps. People will have to get by on their own and this could not possibly end well. Walt's mind was running away on him. There would be trouble in River City and everywhere else as well.

Walt was lucky that he got to town the other day and bought some food and gas to replace what he had consumed so far. Maybe if he was lucky the power grid in the Northwest would not be too badly affected since 83% of the power in the area comes from hydroelectric plants. However when most of the people are without jobs and money the you-know-what hits the fan. Even if he didn't get his pension for awhile, he could get some money from gold and get by, but what was everyone else supposed to do?

Walt had been thinking about a way to improve his sandbag shooting area so it didn't look like something out of war movies. If he took it apart and built it with plywood on both

182

sides he could fill the double sided plywood L shaped barrier with sand. Then he could put a plywood counter top over it and put his propane grill nearby so that it looked like a Bar-B-Q area. He could also put a roof over this so that he could cook outside in the rain. He would have to wait a little bit before the snow melted but he thought that he would get the materials the next time he went to town. He didn't ask Sparky what she thought about this but he knew that she would approve. What dog wouldn't like a Bar-B-Q in her back yard?

Walt made a quick breakfast and got on the radio a little early to hear what the hams were saying about the plane crash. He wanted to hear the hams in the D.C. area so he pointed his hexbeam to the east and tuned the 20 meter band. The upper portion of the band was busy and it usually has the most traffic. This is because it is where the general class license holders must operate if they want to talk on SSB. He tuned to a strong signal to listen for a bit.

"I couldn't believe it either. The news is claiming that the pilot intentionally crashed his plane into the plant. They don't know why. AM4OKM. Over."

"Roger that I heard that he was going through a divorce and that may have pushed him over the edge. AS4TD."

"Could be. I am just glad to be down here in Florida and don't have to evacuate. How close are you? Over." (AM4OKM)

"I am about 400 miles south in Wilmington, North Carolina. I think I'll be OK too. But I have several friends in the area and have not heard what their plans are. I'll bet that they are in their motor homes right now. Over." (AS4TD)

"Roger that John. It's a good idea to have something like that in case you have to bug out in a hurry. My guess is that they would be heading south. AM4OKM."

"That would be my guess too." (AS4TD)

"Contact."

"Go ahead contact this is AM4OKM with AS4TD. Over."

"Thanks for picking me up. This is Charlie AZ1CHC mobile. We are in a motor home just north of Philadelphia and were on our way to visit our son in Annapolis when the plane crashed. Now we are headed back to Portland, Maine. Have you heard any more about the reactor. Has it exploded yet? Over."

"No I haven't heard that it has, Have you heard anything John?" (AM4OKM)

"It just went off as Charlie was transmitting. I hope your son is alright. Annapolis is pretty close to D.C. Over to you Charlie. AS4TD."

"Damn it, I was hoping they would get it under control. My wife is trying to call our son now but it went right over to voice mail. Over." (AZ1CHC)

"I sure hope they get those boys out of there. If anybody can do it, the Navy can. I heard that a lot of cell traffic has been busy all morning long. Good luck on this. Wish your son well. Over. AM4OKM."

"Roger and thanks, we'll keep trying to get through. Thanks for letting me in. I'll say 73 and keep heading for the barn. You guys have a good day. AZ1CHC mobile clear."

"OK Charlie I'll bet the roads are going to be jammed. Hope to talk to you later under better circumstances. AM4OKM."

"Yes Charlie. All the best to you and your wife. That's got to be tough. AS4TD. 73."

"Wow. What perfect timing. Do you believe that John?" (AM4OKM)

"Talk about bad news travels fast. That was something."

Walt tuned off to listen for anyone in the D.C. area but he couldn't find anyone. This was understandable. If he was located at ground zero, he wouldn't be on the radio either. He selected his end fed antenna and tuned down to 3.988. Nobody was on yet so he got a refill on his coffee. As he listened to the static noise Walt couldn't help but wonder if this was the end times or not? He decided that it may be the beginning of the end times but, from what the Bible and Nostradamus said, the end times would be even worse than this with famine and fire worldwide.

Walt remembered that he had some survival shield X3 in the medicine cabinet. This was a high potency and pure form of iodine sold by Alex Jones. He looked at the bottle and it was about half full. He set it on the radio bench in front of him and would start taking it if radiation was detected nearby. Iodine was essential to protect the thyroid and he wished that he had purchased another bottle but as his grandmother used to say, "If wishes were horses, beggars would ride."

Just then he heard a voice on the radio, "This is AU7PM."

"Morning Frank, have you been listening to the radio? AP7ZMT?"

"No I just got up what's going on?"

Walt told him about the plane crash and the reactor just blowing up.

"Oh, no. We're in deep do-do now. Over." (AU7PM)

"You got that right. Don't expect to see your social security check anytime soon. This is a bigger deal than people think. Over." (AP7ZMT)

"Roger that Walt. I do get another retirement check from the State and if that is affected I an SOL. Over." (AU7PM)

"I don't think I'll see any money from the VA for awhile. I think that we can expect big trouble in the streets when people can't afford groceries. Over." (AP7ZMT)

"I think I'll go back to town this morning and pick up some more supplies. What do you think? Over." (AU7PM)

"I think that's a good idea. I am going to go into town again tomorrow, if there is a tomorrow, Over."

"Roger. I am already gone. Talk to you later. AU7PM."

"I think that is a good idea. Remember to top off your gas tank and ammo supply. AP7ZMT going QRT."

Walt got back on the internet and took a look at the NOAA website. They had an interesting map posted that showed the status of the ash clouds across the country and their density, altitude, direction of travel, and speed. All you had to do was to position the cursor over any area you liked and the info came up in a little box that made the map very easy to use and informative. If you didn't want to see the ash clouds you could click and they would not be seen. Instead you would see radar images of clouds with moisture. You could make that disappear as well. They had a new overlay that showed radiation from the blast, where it was going, and how strong it was at any point away from the plant. So far it had traveled about 125 miles away, mostly in a northwest direction. He bookmarked this page and sent the link to everyone on his mailing list. He also included a personal note describing his fears that things would soon get out of control when people ran out of money and/or food and suggested that everyone take home security more seriously than ever before.

Just after lunch he took Sparky for a walk down to the mailbox. This time there were tire tracks indicating that the mailman had stopped. Walt took the paper grocery bag out of his pocket and filled it with mail. He could only guess how much trouble it had been for the mailman to stuff all of this mail into the jumbo sized mailbox. The mailman probably had a vary tough day since everyone on his route had over a months worth of mail to deliver that day. His little truck must have been loaded. Walt was glad that he had the paper bag with him. That is the only way he could have carried all the mail home in a single trip up the hill.

When they got back to the cabin it took awhile to sort the good mail from the junk mail, advertising flyers, newspapers, and magazines. He didn't mind the junk mail that could be burned in the wood stove. But the stuff printed on shiny paper did not burn well and made a lot of ash so he had to store this until he could take it to the dump. Now that the mail was being delivered again he would have to remember to check it everyday. If he didn't Sparky would do her best to remind him.

That night he microwaved his left over lasagna for dinner and installed the light shades as usual. Just for fun he turned on the CB and heard a few neighbors talking. "I'm sure glad that we don't have a nuke plant nearby. That must have been awful." Walt recognized Mary's voice.

"Some of those people will never be able to return home. Their neighborhoods will be radioactive for 100 years. Over." That was Susan. He knew her voice pretty well by now.

"I was thinking about something Walt said in his email. What are people going to do when they run out of money?"

"I think that the Covid lockdowns were a walk in the park compared to what will happen now. What do you think Mary?"

"I am afraid you are right. Have you got your gun yet?

"No, not yet. I should have it in a couple of days. I had fun shooting at the range. I'll feel a lot better when I have it with me all the time."

"I don't have a gun that I can carry but I have a double barrel shotgun here at the house."

"Walt says they are really good for home defense. I plan to get one someday. How big is it?

"It is a 12 gauge and I think the barrel is 18 inches long. Over."

"That sounds good. Hope you don't have to use it. Over."

"I had a raccoon that was a problem. I didn't have to kill it but I did scare it off and as far as I know it has never been back," Mary said.

"That's good. I wouldn't shoot one if I didn't have to either."

Walt turned off the CB. He was glad to hear the ladies were getting used to the radio and that Susan had a good time at the range. He hoped that she would get a shotgun soon and was pretty sure that she would.

The next day Walt went to town early to get more groceries and some plywood and some eight foot 2" x 3"s to build his Bar-B-Q area. The 2" x 3" boards are great for framing and less expensive then 2" x 4"s. When he was coming back from town he stopped at the Country Store for a sandwich and learned that the store had been burglarized the night before. They had security camera video of the thieves and just turned this over to the Sheriff that morning. The thieves got away with beer, cigarettes, lottery tickets and jerky but no cash. They broke a window to get in and the Sheriff told the owners that with the video, they had a good chance to track them down.

What a bummer. The owners were great people and they didn't deserve this. Walt always thought that if you were going to steal from someone, you should pick on someone who could afford it, and not Ma and Pa working stiffs. He doubted that the thieves were from the neighborhood, and he would be glad whenever he heard that they had been caught and convicted.

When Walt got home he noticed some fresh tire tracks on the driveway. When he pulled into the yard Sparky was barking. He knew that she would be glad to see him and he let her out right away He left the building materials in the truck and put the truck away in the garage. After the groceries were put away he checked the security system and saw that it had one fresh recording. When he played it back he saw that he had some visitors while he was gone. A red GMC truck pulled in the yard and two men got out of the truck. One came onto the porch and knocked on the door. After a few minutes he went back to the truck. The other man knocked on the door to the woodshop and Walt could see that he got a taste of the fence charger. They looked around a little and left. Walt could see that nothing had been disturbed and he figured that Sparky was doing her job and her barking scared them away. He noticed that the man on the porch had looked right into the security camera. The camera also caught the license plate of the truck and it was perfectly readable. Since nothing was taken there was no reason to be alarmed but Walt saved the recording in case he needed it.

Later that afternoon Walt emailed a screen shot of the GMC truck and the two men to everyone on the CB net and asked if anyone knew them. If they were local, maybe he could find out who they were and what they wanted. This gave him the idea to suggest that people consider putting inexpensive game cameras on their driveways so that they can see who is visiting when they aren't home.

It rained over the next three days and the temperatures never dropped below freezing. The snow pack was quickly melting and all the new snow over the ash was gone and the snow under the ash was melting as well. By the end of the third day Walt's driveway was mostly clear of ice and he could get up his road in two wheel drive. This was always cause for celebration and signaled that Spring was around the corner. Two Robins were caught on his security camera and this was another good sign. The skies were still overcast but someday soon everyone hoped to actually see the sun. Until then people would have to be happy that it wasn't quite as cold in the mornings.

It was Sunday afternoon and Walt made sure to listen to the Alex Jones radio show on shortwave. Most of the show dealt with the power plant breach and the evacuation of the Washington D.C. area that caused the government shutdown. People were just getting used to the fact that it would be sometime before the government could reopen. Rumors had circulated that the entire government would relocate to the Midwest but this was not official. It made sense to avoid both coasts but the Midwest cities still had problems too because of all the remaining ash from the Yellowstone volcano. From a practical standpoint Congress and the Supreme Court might relocate in one city and the other government offices could move to other cities. The entire Pentagon might be moved to a military base but this was still being discussed. Naturally there was a lot of politics involved and another word for politics is money. Under the best conditions government moves slowly but in this case it would be awhile before they could move at all.

After the show Walt took Sparky for a walk but without the snow floor on the driveway she was filthy when they got back. Fortunately it was a day that the power was on so there was warm water to wash her down in the shower. Naturally she didn't care much for this but at least she was clean and after an hour or so in front of the wood stove she finally was dry enough to give her a pet.

Walt was looking forward to talking with everyone on the Rapid Lightning Creek CB net. There were a lot of things they could talk about and he hoped the others looked forward to this as much as he did.

Walt had turned on his CB radio a little early that night and had everybody checked in by 6:30 pm. He had a full house again and was glad to see that the group was still enthusiastic about the net. "I want to thank everyone for checking in tonight. We have a lot going on and I am sure that we are all glad to have the power back on even if it is only every other day. Now that our road is open and we can finally get to town, I hope that everyone is re-stocked and ready for spring. I am sure you all heard about the break in down at the store. I am afraid that we will see more crime with the high unemployment, potential food shortages, and the disruption of government checks. Hopefully we can network together for our mutual benefit. Let's get started tonight in the order that you checked in. We'll start with Scott, then Tom, Stan and Gloria, Steve, Robert and Nancy, Mary and Beth, Tony and Sherri, Susan, Charles, and Megan, Peter, George and Carla, Bret, Jane and back to me, Tell us what is on your mind Scott."

"OK Walt. It's been a rough time the last few months but glad to hear everyone. I went to town today and saw that some things were beginning to sell out. I got your email and don't know those guys but will keep my eyes open for them. Sooner or later everyone stops at the store. I installed my game camera on the driveway and just have to remember to check it now and then. Over to you Tom."

"I've been watching the news out of Spokane and they are reporting that burglaries and car jacking is way up from last year. I was so glad to have the power come back so I could take a hot shower. I am planning on building a root cellar as soon as it warms up a little since I cannot afford to run my refrigerator every other day with the generator. And speaking of generators, do you believe the price of gas lately? Over to Stan and Gloria."

"We got some batteries yesterday for our game camera. We haven't used it for years. It was nice to see the driveway thawing out but seeing all this ash makes me sick. Also I was thinking that I would need a broom to sweep off the logs before I cut them into firewood. I'll bet the ash will dull a chain in no time. We are keeping everything locked up at night for the first time since we have been here. Sure hope they catch those guys who broke into the store. Over to you Steve."

"Good idea about sweeping off the ash and saving your saw chain. I paid over $30 for my last chain. I saw a couple of Robins today so maybe spring is on its way. I can't remember the last time I saw the sun. I thought the volcano was bad news but this government shutdown and relocation is going to hurt us all. I don't get any government checks but my customers do. Over to Robert and Nancy."

"We are going to miss our social security checks, that's for sure. We're not sure what we are going to do and have been thinking about getting our place logged. I don't know if the mills are taking logs now or not. Also I took a walk down to the creek and saw quite a few dead fish. I am assuming this was because of the ash. And I agree the price of gas is outrageous. We've got a real gas hog for a generator. It's your turn Mary and Beth, go ahead."

"We are doing alright but our plans for an addition to the house are up in the air. It just depends on lumber prices and the economy. Beth's folks live in Virginia and they have been thinking about moving out here. It would be a big change for them to move out in the country and also to put up with our two season climate. Otherwise we are doing OK. And I agree about having hot water. That's what I missed the most. Go ahead Tony."

"We are doing alright. The pantry held up but just barely. We are scheduled to take our ham tests the first of the month up at Bonners Ferry. I'll give you a call Walt and we can start looking for some ham gear. We are in the market for a pistol, if anybody has one for sale, give us a call. Over to you Susan."

"I just bought a new one and hope to pick it up this week. The guy at the gun store said that they are selling fast. My folks are on social security and they don't have a lot of hope to see their checks in the near future. I wish that I could help them but they don't live here. I just started some tomato plants and few other things as well. I hope we get some sunshine soon. I don't know if the ash will be good for the garden or not. Your turn now Charles and Megan."

"I am a retired federal employee so missing retirement checks is a big concern to us as well. We used to live in Maryland and we are so glad we moved up here. I cannot imagine what it is like back there now. Tony, I have a pistol you might want. I'll give you a call tomorrow. Megan just got her tomato plants started today and I agree about the lack of sunshine. Peter, go ahead."

"OK good to hear from everyone. I went to town yesterday and I have never paid $100 to put gas in my little car before. But I am afraid that everything will get more expensive the way things are going. My folks just sent me a game camera for my birthday and can't wait to put it up. It will be fun to see what kind of critters are stopping by. I saw some moose tracks on the road the other day. I am hoping to get a few more solar cells if I can find them. They have been hard to find lately. Up to George and Carla."

"I know what you mean about wanting more solar cells. I just hope we get some more solar to go with them. We've been thinking about getting one of those 12 volt camping coolers. They are about the size of an ice chest and might come in handy when the weather warms up. We've had a game camera up for years but I think it is a good idea to photograph the driveway. Also we have been thinking about getting a large potable water tank for days when we can't run the pump. Does anybody know if they would freeze in the winter? Over to you Bret."

"I think a water tank would be great but I think that you would have to insulate it with styrofoam or maybe straw bales that were covered in plastic to keep the straw dry and to keep the waater from freezing. Besides drinking water, it might be nice to have in case of fire as well. I need to get better prepared for emergencies around here. It's hard to do when you need a good supply of everything. I would like to find a better way to store gas. I have an old truck without a motor and keep it here just for gas storage. I'm getting better at siphoning. Guess it's your turn Jane."

"OK, good to hear everyone. Never thought I'd be shoveling ash in the winter. Also I never thought I would be using the Bar-B-Q this much during the winter but I'm glad I had it. Also I'll be in the market for firewood this summer if anybody knows someone with good wood for sale. I feel really sorry for everyone who won't be getting their retirement checks for awhile. A lot of my clients are retired and I'm sure this will affect me as well. They say that bad things come in threes. I'm not sure if we have had our three or if we still have one to go? What do you think Walt."

"I have asked myself that as well. I guess we'll just have to see but I think things will get worse before they get better. I have been told that I am a glass half empty kind of guy. I'll send you the name of my firewood guy Jane. He's not the cheapest in town but he always has good quality wood. I like the idea of the 12 volt camping cooler. You can only keep things cool in a root cellar, definitely not cold, and I guess they work as freezers too. I'll bet they are like solar cells, real hard to get nowadays. Back to you Scott."

"That is a good idea about the 12 volt coolers. I'll look online and see if I can find any. If I do, I'll let you guys know. I know a lot of people around here make extra money shoveling roofs in the winter. I'll bet that there are a lot of people who need help getting rid of their ash as well. There are a lot of retired people living here and I'm sure they need help in one way or another. Over to you Tom"

"I have done a lot of work for people over in Hope. It's a 30 minute drive but the people are nice and they tip pretty good too. Maybe a 12 volt cooler is a better idea for me than a root cellar. I'll check them out. I wonder if there will be a tourist season this year or not? What do you think? Back to Stan and Gloria."

"I think that people will be leaving the cities in droves and there will always be work for people who want to work. Up until recently people could sell a house they bought in Orange county thirty years ago for $50,000, and sell it for $2 million. I don't know how the market is today but my point is that there are people with money to spend. Back to you Steve."

"I agree that there will be lots of people moving here. Whether they have a boat load full of cash is another story. Also I think that if the sun ever comes out the tourists will follow. I can't imagine filling the tank on a motorhome these days. Over to Robert and Nancy."

"I'm not sure how that works anymore. I know the local 76 station's pumps will not pump more than a hundred dollars at time. So I guess you have to fill it three times in a row. We usually get a little help with chores during the summer but this year we'll be cutting back and doing things the old fashioned way, by ourselves. Over to you Mary."

"Well at least you know how to do things by yourselves. That really makes a difference. It is amazing how many things that you can learn to do by watching YouTube videos. If you ask me, they should get rid of the politics and focus on how-to videos. Go ahead Tony and Sherri."

"I think that's a great idea. I watch those myself and learn a lot. Most things are easy if you know how. Oh I don't know if you guys know this but we have a deputy Sheriff living on the Creek now. His name is officer Weldon and he seems to be a pretty nice guy. He is a ham operator Walt and works a lot of 6 and 2 meters. I didn't get his call but I'm sure you'll hear him on the air. Over to you Susan."

"That's good news about the new deputy living here. Maybe people will slow down on the road. I wish a few more cops would move in here too. I had a lady tell me that years ago the cops wouldn't even come up this road even for a report of shots fired. They would just wait at the store or the school and wait for the bad guys to come down the road. Over to Charles and Megan."

"I hadn't heard that before but we all have heard how bad the road was before it was paved. One guy told me it was so bad and the potholes were so deep you couldn't get out of first gear. And that the road was so muddy there was no use taking you car to the car wash because it would be dirty when you got home. Over to you Peter."

"Well it is nice that Rapid Lightning is paved but Thunder Alley is a bottomless pit of mud for most of the year. In fact the road is better in the winter than the rest of the year. And if you think that chaining up in the winter is a hassle, try chaining up in the mud just to get home. Back to George and Carla."

"That doesn't sound fun at all. Our road is on a hill and has had lots of rock over the years so we don't have to deal with the mud but I have seen the cars parked on the side of the road at Flume Creek during mud season and some of those folks have quite a walk. Usually some A-hole insists on driving home and ruins the road for everybody. Over to you Bret."

"Our road can get pretty soft but most people try not to tear it up too badly. Our biggest problem is the townies coming up here looking for real estate. We get a lot of hunters too. Sure enjoy talking with everyone on the radio and I'll try to leave mine on more often. Keep your heads low and your powder dry. Back to you Jane."

OK Bret. I'll try and keep my radio on more often as well. It would be a good idea to get the new deputies phone number so if anyone has this please email it to me. I guess we missed Fly Boy tonight. Hope he's all right. If anyone hears from him, say hi from me. I am going to see my sister in Spokane for a couple of days. I'll let you know what it's like over there. They usually have better weather than we do. I'm pretty sure they actually have some green grass showing. Over to you Walt."

"That's right, I can't even count. I thought we had everybody in here tonight. I'll send him an email and tell him that we missed him and we all hope he's doing well. Anyway it's been fun. You know what they say, misery loves company. Maybe we'll get some sunshine soon. Thanks for checking in and don't hesitate to call me if I can do anything for you. I'll say 73 and try to keep my radio on more often as well. You guys take care. Gotta go now."

Walt thought that the net went well and he would check up on Fly Boy in the morning to be sure he was OK. He turned off the radio and let Sparky out one more time for the night. His window light shades were in place, the security system was on, and the woodstove was about out for the night. If the weather was good he would try to get the new improved shooting bunker/Bar-B-Q area buit tomorrow. If the weather was bad he could precut the materials in the woodshop. He made a note to himself to meet the new ham in the neighborhood. He didn't work 6 or 2 meters often but he would try to listen for him.

The next afternoon Walt had completed the shooting bunker. It was perfect. Nobody could guess what it was really for. It has a very cool hidden storage area in the corner by the house. It was a little less than 2 feet thick and 4 feet high and it was completely filled with sand to the top. The plywood countertop could be used as a shooting bench and also would be useful when cooking outside. The Bar-B-Q was placed next to the sidewall and its' propane tank was protected by 6 feet of sand, The plywood roof kept the area dry and free of snow and it was perfect for outdoor cooking year 'round. The bare plywood sides weren't pretty but Walt thought that he would cover this with cedar shakes later in the year.

A few days later Susan was driving up Rapid Lightning Creek Road to return the Ruger revolver that Walt had loaned to her. The pistol was on the passenger seat and so was a peach pie that she had made for him to show her appreciation. She noticed two camouflaged colored four wheel ATVs quickly approaching from behind and slowed down a little to let them pass. The ATV in front pulled into the other lane and began to pass her. As it got even with her Tacoma the passenger in the ATV began to scream at her to get out of the way. He was waiving his fist and screaming at the top of his voice. She picked Walt's revolver up off the seat and showed him that she had a gun. Then she floored the truck and raced up the road thinking that she had lost them. When she got to Walt's red colored mailbox she turned and went up the driveway and pulled into his yard.

Walt was coming out of the woodshop when Susan pulled in, As she got out of the truck she handed Walt his pistol and thanked him for the loan. She reached into the truck for the pie And the two ATVs pulled into the yard and stopped behind her. Each ATV had a baseball bat mounted on its front like people used to do on cars with steer horns. Four men jumped out of the ATVs and one of the men started screaming at Susan. "Hey you dumb bitch, when you took off like that you threw rocks that broke my windshield!"

Walt stepped out from behind the Tacoma still holding the large frame revolver which was pointed at the ground. "Do you boys have a problem? He asked.

All four men could see that Walt was holding a pistol. Their attention was focused on the gun. The loudmouth yelling at Susan looked at Walt and said, "She cracked my windshield, I need to be paid." Walt pointed the Ruger at his face and asked, "Would you like to be paid in lead? Get the hell off my property."

Then one of the other men shouted, "Look Roy, that gun isn't even loaded." Walt looked surprised. One thing that was true about revolvers is that if you were close enough and looking down the barrel, you could tell if the gun had bullets in the cylinder or not. The men began to move toward Walt

Susan quickly set the pie down on the drivers seat of the Tacoma and pulled out her new Smith and Wesson. She pointed it right at the crybaby's head and said, "That gun might not be loaded but this one is." She had her finger on the trigger and was now carefully aiming at his heart.

Walt looked at Susan and said, "Good Job." Then he looked at the men and asked, "Are you still here?" The men got in their ATVs and quickly backed out of his yard and went down the driveway. As they were leaving one of the men shouted, "We'll be back."

After they left Walt asked Susan what that was all about and she described what happened down the road. They went inside and Susan met Sparky and they were immediately best friends. Susan and Walt had coffee and pie together and Walt thought that a pie for a gun loan was a really good deal. Walt gave her the tour of the place and showed her what his security camera had recorded. She was impressed at the quality of the video and Walt told her that he would make her a copy and email it to her. When it was time for her to leave Walt told her that he would follow her down the road. "That's not really necessary Walt, I have my insurance, remember?"

Walt replied, "That's OK, I was going to stop by the store anyway." When it was time for Susan to turn into her driveway she rolled down the window and waived. There had been no sign of ATVs but Walt thought that there was a good chance that he would see them again.

As Susan stepped in the house she got a phone call from Jane. She just returned from Spokane and found that her house had been broken into. The door was damaged and some things had been stolen including her stereo, TV, solar cells, and her grand father's deer rifle. She didn't have any insurance and didn't know how she could replace everything. The deputy sheriff had stopped by and taken her statement and that he had just left her house a few minutes ago. Susan told her how sorry she was to hear this and told her that if she needed anything to give her a call. As soon as she hung up the phone, Susan sent a email to everyone on the CB net advising them what had happened to Jane.

When Walt pulled into the store there was a Bonner County Sheriffs' SUV parked out front and the deputy was standing on the porch reading the bulletin board. Walt walked up to him and asked, " You're not officer Weldon are you?" The deputy tuned to Walt and said that he was. Walt went on to say, "Hi My name is Walt. I live up the road and hear that you are a ham. I wanted to meet you my call is AP7ZMT."

"Oh that's great. I heard there were a couple of hams up here. My name is Chip and my call is AY7COP. Nice to meet you."

"That's a really great vanity call sign. How long have you had it?" Walt asked.

"Believe it or not that is my original call sign, I've been licensed almost 15 years." Deputy Weldon replied.

Walt and Chip visited a little bit and Walt told him that he normally operated on HF and that he usually was on 3.988 in the mornings. He also told him about their new Rapid Lightning CB net and invited him to jump in anytime. They both agreed that it had been good to meet each other.

Walt went into the store and wondered what he would buy. The only reason he was there was to be sure that Susan got home OK. He decided to order a turkey sandwich and a small bag of chips. When he walked out of the store, officer Weldon was pulling out of the parking lot and heading into town.

As Walt was driving up the county road he was listening to the local AM radio station. They were interviewing the head of the food bank and she was saying that they were swamped by requests for food boxes and that demand had never been higher. She was asking people to donate whatever they could and especially needed canned goods, baby food, pet food and rice, pasta, and potatoes. She was describing customers who drove expensive cars coming to the food bank for the first time in their lives. She also remarked that she had seen more people with "Will Work for Food" signs in the supermarket parking lots than ever before.

Walt tuned to a music station and thought things must be getting bad if people were asking for food. He though that next time he was in town he would try to pick up something for the food bank and hoped that others would do the same. When he got home he got out of the truck and picked up his mail and drove into his yard. Sparky heard him coming and she was a lucky dog that day because Walt planned to share a small part of his sandwich with her. Of course she was hoping to get a few chips as well but he told her, "Chips aren't good for dogs." She had heard that a million times and knew that this is what people would say when they wanted something all to themselves.

Later that evening Walt heard AY7COP on the 145.59 Hoodoo Mountain repeater, "This is AY7COP testing." This was a common way to see if your signal was reaching the repeater. If it was the repeater would respond with a message identifying itself, "This is the XYZ repeater. When you heard the message and looked at the signal strength you had an idea about the strength of the repeater's signal.

Walt responded. With his 13 element yagi antenna he had no problem reaching the repeater. "Chip, this is Walt AP7ZMT. Over."

" Oh Hi Walt good to hear you. Would you like to switch over to simplex?" Repeaters operate duplex which use two different frequencies, one to receive from the repeater and another to transmit to the repeater. In simplex operation one frequency is used for both transmitting and receiving. Chip knew that they were so close to each they didn't need to use the repeater. Also there was no reason to hog the repeater in case anyone else needed to use it.

"OK, How about 147.00?"

"Sounds Good AY7COP QSY."

"AP7ZMT QSY."

"Well heard you in there and just wanted to say Hi. What is the set over there?"

"I've got a Kenwood radio and a Ringo Ranger antenna. What are you running?"

"I have an Icom 45H and a yagi antenna. I also have a Ringo Ranger that I use on the scanner. Speaking of scanners I hope that you guys aren't going digital anytime soon. Over."
Analog scanners can hear digital signals but they are unintelligible.

"I don't think that they have this in their budget. They would have to replace a lot of radios to do this. Besides if we have anything sensitive to talk about we just use our cell phones."

"That reminds me. Would you email me your telephone number? My email is AP7ZMT at gmail.com."

"Roger will do. I'll have to come over sometime to see your station. Over."

"OK just give me time to hide the still. Stop by anytime, I'm usually around and my name is on the red colored mailbox. Over."

"Sounds good Walt. I'm getting a phone call so talk to you later. AY7COP."

"OK See you later. AP7ZMT."

Walt wanted to ask Chip if there was any news about the Country Store burglary but he knew better than to ask about this on the air. He remembered that he told Susan that he would send her a copy of the security system video so he copied this to a thumb drive and logged onto the internet. When he checked his email he found the email from Susan describing what happened to Jane. His first thought was that this was bad luck but then he remembered that Jane had told everyone on the radio that she would be going to Spokane for a few days. Maybe it wasn't bad luck, maybe, he thought to himself, it was bad security. He thanked Susan for telling him about this and attached a copy of the security camera video.

He went through his other emails and saw that he had a message from Chip so he wrote down Chips telephone number and email address. Since Chip had not joined the CB net he decided that he would keep this to himself for the time being.

After going through his emails he checked the NOAA web site and saw that the radiation danger zone cloud had advanced another 150 miles or so to the northeast. The area east of Los Angeles wasn't getting much news coverage these days but people and agriculture were still suffering. The press hadn't bothered with many new stories about the Yellowstone National Park area either. It was fly over country and news coverage of the volcanos had been trumped by the nuclear disaster in Washington D.C.

Still no decisions had been announced about relocating the government but President Joe Bama had scheduled a speech to the nation a week from Monday at 6 pm PDT. The cynical side of Walt thought that this would give all the politicos time to act on their inside information and make ton of money. What a great time to be a real estate agent in the Midwest. Was America a great country or what?

Lately Walt was toying around with another security idea in his head. He was thinking of ways to make spike strips like the police use from time to time to disable speeding cars. At first he thought of using 20 penny nails but he decided that these wouldn't stop a car fast enough. If the nails could be drilled with a hole through them from top to bottom this might really do the trick but they would be a real pain to build. His best idea so far would be to make the spikes out of metal tubing which could be cut on a diagonal to make them sharp.

The spike strips the police use have a flexible base that can be easily unrolled across the road. He wasn't sure how to make something like this but maybe he didn't have to. After all he wasn't planning on unrolling them across a road. He could mount the spikes on 2" x 4"s and carry them in his truck. What would really be nice is if he could think of a way to deploy them on the lower end of his driveway by some kind of remote control. This is the kind of problem solving he liked to do when he couldn't sleep. He decided that he would think about this awhile.

The next day Walt couldn't get the burglary at Jane's out of his head. Maybe he could coordinate with Chip and they could set a trap for the thieves. If the bad guys were listening to the CB he could have someone else ask him on the air if he would be home the next day. He could causally mention that he had a doctors appointment in Coeur d'Alene that day and that he would be gone all afternoon. If anyone stopped by to rob the place, Walt could catch them in the act. If Chip was nearby, and the thieves got away, Walt could call Chip and tell him who to look for. Walt's security camera system would give them all the evidence that they would need. Maybe Walt watched too many movies, but except for Sparky, he lived alone and had a lot of time on his hands. Besides it just might work.

After supper Walt called Chip on the phone and told him the plan. Chip thought it was a good idea and suggested that Walt leave something valuable on the porch so that the thieves could steal this if they chose not to break into the cabin. He also said that he could not participate because of an entrapment issue, but that he would be standing by to stop the thieves if he got a call from Walt. Walt agreed and said that he would set the trap on Sunday night on the CB net and plan it for sometime Monday afternoon. Chip told him that this would be perfect because he would be off work by noon on Monday.

Walt refined the plan and decided to what to use on the porch as bait. He remembered that he had bought a new flat screen TV about a year ago. He still had his old TV in the woodshed in the same box that the new TV came in. He also had a box from Online World that was in good shape that he could fill with sand and seal it so that it appeared to be unopened. Walt decided that he would stay in the cabin in case they tried to kick in the door. If someone looked around all the buildings would be locked and he could watch them on the security camera system. If they didn't damage anything but took the items on the porch, he would give Chip a call. If they did break in the cabin, he would be waiting for them and give them 357 reasons that this was a bad idea.

When it was time for the CB net on Sunday Walt was all set to go. He had alerted Stan about the plan and he agreed to ask Walt on the air if he would be home the next day. As planned Walt said that he would be gone all afternoon because he had to go to Couer d'Alene for a doctors appointment and that Stan should come over the next day. He also mentioned that his name was on his red colored mailbox so that Stan wouldn't have any trouble finding the place. Otherwise the net went on as usual and Jane told everyone about the burglary. Chip listened to the net but did not check in.

Early the next afternoon Walt heard the driveway alarm and was in the radio room watching the security screen. An old International pickup pulled in the yard. To his surprise an older man and woman got out of the truck. They looked around as they approached the cabin and heard Sparky barking from the inside. They waited to see if anyone would come out to greet them but nobody did. They didn't know that Sparky was a little cow dog and sometimes Walt called her barky Sparky because her bark was bigger than her size. They must have decided not to risk breaking into the cabin and decided to leave. But they did take the bait. The woman took the TV and the man lifted up the heavy box from Online World. They put both items in the back of their truck and left. First Walt called 911 and reported the theft. He had a description of the people, the truck and the license number, 7B1278905. As soon as he hung up he called Chip on the cell phone and gave him the same information. By calling this into the Sheriffs Department first, it gave Chip some cover.

Chip saw the truck coming down Rapid Lightning about 5 miles from the Country Store. He was going up the road as they passed him. Chip turned his Sheriffs Dept. SUV around, turned on his lights, and pulled them over. They were very good actors and asked him why they were stopped. He said that he stopped them for reckless driving but after getting a call from the dispatcher, Chip was able to arrest them for suspicion of stolen property. Bonnie and Clyde were taken to the County jail and booked for trespassing and theft. Chip called Walt to tell him the good news and that he would need a copy of the security camera footage.

The next day Chip called Walt again but this time he had even better news. The Sheriffs Office had gotten a search warrant and when they searched the old couple's farm house they found some of Jane's property including her grandfather's deer rifle. This was great news and Chip said that Jane had been notified. He also said that it did not look like these people had anything to do with the burglary awhile back at the Country Store.

Walt was really pleased that the plan worked so well and that most of Jane's property had been recovered. He was glad that he didn't have to confront the couple and, as far as he knew, they didn't even know what he looked like. He was also glad that they didn't damage his property and that he didn't have to use a weapon to defend his home. As soon as Walt hung up the phone with Chip, he sent everyone in the CB net an email telling them that Jane's thieves had been caught and that some of her property had been recovered. He reminded people how important it was not to announce the fact that they would not be home over the radio because you never knew who was listening.

Walt went into town to pick up some 1/4 inch steel tubing and a 12 foot 2" x 4" for his latest project. On the way back he stopped by Locals Grocery to pick up a roasted chicken at the deli counter. As he walked through the store he was shocked to see all the bare shelves. He had never seen this before. It looked like the empty shelves of the old Soviet Union. When he asked the cashier about this she told him that everyone was having trouble getting restocked and all she could do was apologize. Walt topped off the gas in his truck and filled two 5 gallon plastic gas cans. He didn't bother to check any of the other grocery stores but he had no reason to doubt her.

As he was passing the Country Store he saw Chip's rig in the parking lot and pulled in to say Hi and thank him for his help. Walt learned that he was there on official business and that the Country Store had been robbed at gunpoint an hour earlier. Three masked men from Washington State had held up the store and tied the owner's hands and feet with cable ties and then locked him in his cooler. The men got a little cash and they filled up their van with gas, but the strange thing was that they had taken mostly food! They brought in hand trucks and boxes and took out canned food, frozen food, sandwich meats, bread, wine and beer. They didn't bother with snack foods, ice cream, or lottery tickets. The owner was found thirty minutes ago by a customer who was looking for beer in the cooler. This type of brazen robbery was unheard of in Sandpoint. Most of the burglaries in the area were done by sneak thieves in the middle of the night and not gun toting, mask wearing, criminals.

Walt could not understand this. If someone was going to risk committing a crime with a gun why not hold up a bank? That's where the money is. The penalty is the same either way.

It reminded him of the looters a few years ago who broke into a Dollar store. If you're going to be a crook, Walt thought, be a CROOK, show some ambition, and set your sights a little higher. It didn't make sense.

When Walt pulled into his driveway he stopped to get the mail and drove up to the house. He took the 12 foot 2" x 4" out of the truck and put it in the woodshop with the 2 plastic gas jugs. He had smelled the Bar-B-Q chicken all the way home so he didn't have to think about what he would have for dinner. After letting Sparky out he checked his security cameras and saw that there were no new recordings. The woodstove was nearly out and he added a couple of small logs. Then he brought in wood and kindling for that night and was finally able to sit down. What a day, he thought, getting Jane's property back, seeing bare shelves in the store, and finding out about the robbery at the Country Store down the road. It was a lot for one day.

When Sparky came in she could smell the chicken and was on her best behavior. Walt opened a can of baked beans to go with it and heated them in the microwave. Whenever he could he used paper plates to keep dirty dishes to a minimum. Walt ate almost half of the chicken that night and Sparky got some too.

After supper he turned on his portable radio to the local news and heard a story about the robbery. The police were still looking for the tan colored Washington van and were asking the public for help. They had a partial plate number which was SP946..... The weather forecast was for light snow that would taper off by midday tomorrow. March Madness was almost over and the final game would be Monday night. Gonzaga had made it to the Final Four but lost a close game to BYU.

The national news seemed like one bad story after another. Government closures, record unemployment, more inflation, and food supply chain issues continued to dominate the news. Walt couldn't help but wonder if more people would be listening to President Joe Bama's speech or the basketball game on Monday night? As far as he was concerned there was no contest. He would be listening to the game.

The next morning Walt got up and saw that the weatherman was right. It was snowing lightly and it looked like an inch or so was on the ground. Yesterday he had grid power but he would be running off his battery and inverter for the day. He got the woodstove started and let Sparky out, As he was micro-waving a cup of water to make coffee he felt the cabin shake. Sometimes the cabin would shake if it shed a lot of snow at once but with only an inch of snow on the roof it was something else.

Later that morning he learned that a 6.5 magnitude earthquake had occurred 5 miles south of Sandpoint. The quake was only half a mile deep and there was a lot of damage to area roads and bridges as well as buildings. The power had been knocked out and schools were immediately closed and the kids were sent home. Some kids could not get home by bus or car because the bridges over Lake Pend Oreille were no longer passable. They would have to get across the Lake and the Pend Oreille River by boat and be picked up on the other side. Authorities warned of possible aftershocks and people were on edge. Several fires had started from broken gas and propane lines and emergency crews were swamped and travel was difficult.

Some of the Californians who had moved here had been through earthquakes before but there had never been a recorded earthquake in northern Idaho. Most recent Idaho earthquakes were in the Challis area closer to Yellowstone. So much for the idea that trouble comes in threes. Lately it looked like troubles came in fours, fives, and sixes.

Walt put on his coat and went outside. He couldn't see any damage to the cabin or the antennas. He took a close look at the garage and the woodshop and they looked fine too. He walked to the driveway and looked down the road and could not see that any trees had come down. Then he went inside the cabin, took off his coat, and went down into the crawl space. This was made with a concrete footer and concrete block walls. He looked closely at the concrete blocks and there was no visible damage. His other buildings were pole buildings had no foundations so he had expected them to hold up well. But buildings with foundations were actually more fragile in an earthquake so he was glad he didn't have a foundation to repair.

He stepped up out of the crawlspace and went into the radio room. He turned on his 2 meter radio and tuned to the 145.490 Mhz repeater on Hoodoo Mountain southeast of Sandpoint He turned on his portable radio to the local AM station. He also turned on his police scanner and his CB radio. As an experience ham he could listen to them all at the same time without going crazy.

The scanner picked up police and fire department traffic so it was much busier than usual. He didn't hear anything at the moment on the 2 meter repeater of the CB. The local radio station was on the air with emergency power listing road and bridge closures throughout the County. He didn't hear anything about Rapid Lightning Creek Road so he was glad about that. There were only two short bridges on the road but if either one was out, people would have to the long way and drive over the Gold Creek cut off road to the Gold Creek road to go to town.

The two meter Hoodoo Mountain repeater was being used by two hams talking about Highway 2 between Sandpoint and Priest River. This was impassable because both the bridge coming into Priest River and the bridge just outside of Sandpoint were heavily damaged. Sandpoint had no highway access from the east because it bordered Lake Pend Orielle. This meant that Sandpoint was cut off to highway traffic from the south and the west. He hadn't heard about the Railroad bridges or if Highway 95 from Bonner Ferry was open or not. He turned his yagi antenna north and begun listening to the 146.96 repeater out of Bonners Ferry. "This is AP7ZMT from Sandpoint. Can anybody tell me the status of Highway 95? Over."

"AP7ZMT, this is Dick AN7LPG. How copy? Over."

"OK Dick thanks for coming back this is Walt, located 20 miles north of Sandpoint. I was wondering if you knew anything about Highway 95 between Bonners and Sandpoint? Over."

"As far as I know the Highway is closed at Naples. Over"

"Roger, thanks for the info. As far as I can tell Sandpoint is completely cut off by road. Not sure about the train tracks. AP7ZMT."

"I haven't heard about that either but it is hard to imagine that some of those bridges got out scott free. AN7LPG."

"So where are you located? Over."

"I am on the river just east of Moyie Springs. Over."

"How about Highway 2, what does that look like?"

"I am guessing that it's closed somewhere because I haven't heard any traffic on the road."

" Roger. Sandpoint is out of power. How about you?"

"Yes we are out of power here too. I have a small hydro generator that works pretty well as long as the creek isn't frozen so we are in pretty good shape. It is a homemade system with 60 feet of drop into the Kootenay River. How about you?"

"I have a battery bank with a dozen batteries that get me by but I have to charge them with a generator once a week. Your hydro system sounds really nice. I'd better get back to what I was doing. Nice meeting you and hope to talk to you again. This is Ap7ZMT. Take care Dick."

"OK Walt just when things were getting back to normal, they pulled the rug out from under us again. 73, AN7LPG."

"Oh, one more thing. Are you seeing any dead fish in the river?'

"I am afraid so Walt. It is a real shame. So many dead fish, the birds can't keep up. Over."

"I am sorry to hear that but I thought that might be the case. See you later. AP7ZMT clear.

"See you later. AN7LPG clear."

Walt left the radio on and turned on his SDR Play receiver on his laptop and tuned it to 145.490 so that he could listen to the Bonners Ferry repeater and the Hoodoo Mountain repeater at the same time.

Just as he was getting used to the idea of having power every other day he would have to start conserving power. He went to the sink to fill up a gallon water jug and he saw that the water was not clear, it was cloudy. The earthquake had shaken things up in his well so he decided to keep running the pump until the water cleared up. In about 45 minutes the water looked clear enough to drink. Running the pump through the inverter had put quite a draw on his battery bank so he set up the generator to charge up the system. As long as the generator was running Walt heated up the left over chicken and some baked beans in the microwave and had an early dinner. After the batteries were fully charged he left the security system on but turned off the monitor and all of his radios except for the CB. For the time being, he could get by without refrigeration but he was really going to miss his hot water and shower. He couldn't wait to talk to Chip and knew that he would have lots of stories to tell him about what was going on in Sandpoint. If the stores were having supply chain issues before, things were really going to get tough now.

Later that evening Walt turned on his computer and looked at some of the TV channel web sites out of Spokane to get some news. They had suspended their normal programming and had been running coverage and interviews about the quake damage all day. The Channel 6 website had terrific drone coverage of the Long Bridge on Highway 95 coming into Sandpoint. They also had pictures of the two bridges between Sandpoint and Priest River. The Channel 4 website had good pictures of buckled asphalt and large cracks in the road on Highway 95. They also had drone coverage of some railroad bridges that were heavily damaged as well as a mangled cell phone tower that had collapsed. They showed a map of power outages and all of Bonner and Boundary Counties were affected. The channel 2 website was showing children being ferried across the Pend Oreille River by private boats and a barge that could carry five cars per trip helping motorists to get south of town. It was more than unusual for the three Spokane television stations to devote so much of their programming to the Sandpoint area.

By this time it was getting dark so Walt put up the window light shades and let Sparky out one more time before bed. He hadn't heard anyone on the CB but thought that he would ask if anyone was listening. Fly Boy came back, "Hey Walt sorry I missed you guys the other night. How are you doing?"

"I'm doing pretty good. It's been one helluva day. How about you?"

"I've been flying my drone checking out the roads and two bridges on the Pack River. Both look fine to me. Over."

"You mean the one by the store and the one on Colburn Culver Road?"

"Yes I don't know about any of the others but we should be able to at least drive to Ponderay."

"That's good. Most of the time I don't go all the way into town anyway. I was watching the news coverage out of Spokane and they had some great drone shots of the Long Bridge and some railroad bridges."

"I wish I would have gone down that way but I wasn't sure the roads would be open."

"I heard the bridge at Naples was out so you can't get to Bonners Ferry and the two bridges are out between Sandpoint and Priest River. Over."

"Well it looks like nobody will be going too far for awhile. I think we'll really have to tighten our belts. At least I got groceries and gas the other day."

"I wonder how the Country Store is doing. I heard about the robbery. Over."

"I don't know I haven't gone down there because I didn't think that they would be open since the power was out."

"I am surprised nobody else is in here this evening."

"I think after supper a few more people will come on. What else are they going to do? They can't watch television," Fly Boy joked.

"That's for sure. I see the cell phones are out again. That's why I call them sell phones, to give people the idea that they should sell them and get a landline."

"After the last few months I am sure thinking about it."

"OK I guess I am going to listen to some shortwave for a bit and how the rest of the world is doing. See you later and say Hi for me if anybody else comes on."

"Will do Walt. I'll talk to you later. See you Sunday night for sure."

"OK have fun with your drone. Like they used to say, you can take a trip and never leave the farm."

"That's really true nowadays."

Walt signed off but left the CB on and started listening to the 2 meter repeaters to see if he could hear any locals talking about the quake. At the moment the repeaters were quiet so he tuned to the shortwave broadcast bands and listened to the re-broadcast of the Alex Jones show on 4.840 Mhz for awhile. He was predicting that martial law and gun confiscation was around the corner. Walt agreed that this is what the government wanted, but right now they couldn't find their ass with both hands. The fire in the wood stove was going out and the cabin was cooling down but rather than restart the fire Walt decided to turn off the radios and call it day. He wished that he had been keeping a diary for the past few months but it was a little late to start now.

The next morning Walt got up and pulled the light shades off the windows. He could see that they had about an inch of snow overnight and it looked dark considering the hour. After starting a fire and taking care of Sparky, Walt set the tea kettle on the stove to heat some water for coffee. He wasn't sure what he was going to do that day, but had been thinking about his tire shredder project. He had planned to mount the spikes on the 12 foot 2" x 4" that he got the other day. But two things about this made him change his mind. He was going to put this near the entrance to is driveway but he had not determined a good way to deploy this remotely. Also he thought that a 2 x 4s standing vertically (when not in use) would stick out like a sore thumb.

After he finished his coffee and breakfast he and Sparky went out and walked up the upper portion of driveway. Walt was looking for a small standing tamarack tree about 3" in diameter. He found one right next to the driveway and cut it down with a bow saw. The tree was about 20 feet long and he dragged it back to the woodshop. He put Sparky in the back yard and took his generator out to the woodshop so that he could have some light and use the tools. Walt changed the blade in the band saw to a metal cutting blade and cut 40 pieces of steel tubing into pieces 4 inches long. Then he cut one end of each piece with a diagonal cut to give them each a point. Next he marked a line on the small tree with a chalk line and drilled a 1/4" diameter hole every 4 inches up the tree starting three feet from the bottom. Each hole was 2 inches deep.

Walt inserted a sharpened 4" piece of tubing into each drilled hole with the pointed side up and admired how lethal this was looking. He drilled a ½ inch hole through the tree 90 degrees from the spikes about one inch from the bottom. Next he carefully dragged the log spike comb half way down the driveway and set the base next to another tamarack tree that was about two feet from the road. He attached the base of the tire shredder to the standing tree with a 3/8 inch lag bolt 8 inches long so the shredder would fit perfectly across the driveway.

He was ready for a break at this point but didn't want to leave the shredder across the driveway so he was determined to finish the project. He went back to the shop and retuned with a 12 foot aluminum ladder and leaned it up against the tree. He climbed the ladder and installed a eye bolt about 12 feet up the standing support tree and threaded some black paracord through the eye bolt. Then lifted the pivoting tire shredder up and inline with the eyebolt in the tree to visually mark this height.

He carefully laid down the shredder and tied the string in the proper position on the shredder tree. Next he lifted the shredder up and brought it almost vertical and nearly in line with the standing support tree and temporarily tied the shredder so that it would not fall down using 18 gauge mechanics wire. He also rigged it so that the shredder could not travel "over center" and back into the woods. Then he carefully strung the bailing cord through the woods and back to the cabin. He found a good spot in the back yard and tied this off to a young tree after pulling it tightly and gave himself another 20 feet of cord before cutting it free from the spool. He untied the cord from the young tie off tree and carefully gave the string some slack. After walking back to the driveway he could see the shredder laying perfectly across the road. It worked like a charm. Walt walked to the back yard, pulled the cord tightly and tied it to the small tree in the back yard. He walked back to take a good look at the installation. It was perfect. When standing up the spikes could not be seen from the driveway. It looked like a normal tree because it was. The pointed teeth of the shredder were only a few inches from the support tree so Walt thought that it was unlikely anyone or anything would be harmed when the shredder was in the upright position. When it was across the road, it was a different story. Walt knew that it was for emergency use only but if he ever needed it, it would destroy any set of tires that it encountered. Like the "A Team" always said, they loved it when a plan came together.

He put his tools away, locked up the woodshop and carried the generator back to the front porch and went inside to take it easy. Sparky had been out in the back all this time and that much fresh air makes a girl tired. Walt took a short nap in his chair and Sparky crashed out on the floor beside him. When he woke up it was almost time for supper so he turned on his portable radio to the local AM station to hear the news.

The lead story was about police being called to investigate a home invasion on Upper Pack River. A man had been wounded and his wife had been tied to a chair. The Sheriff declined to give any more details about the robbery pending further investigation.

The radio station reported that it was not known when power or cell service would be restored to the area and that two boats and one barge were operating from 6am –6pm from City Beach to take people and vehicles from Sandpoint to Lake Shore Drive and back.

They announced that the Senior Meal Delivery Service had been cancelled until further notice and that seven Churches in Sandpoint were offering free dinners, on a rotating basis, and that people could contact the radio station for more information.

Fifteen aftershocks had been reported by USGS but all were a magnitude 3.4 or lower and no new damage had been reported. The County had posted detour signs and a map on its website to help people bypass closed bridges. However these were restricted to light trucks and cars and private vehicles under10,000 lbs GVW. No heavy truck traffic could enter or leave town until further notice.

No precipitation was expected overnight. The low temperature was expected to be 31 degrees tomorrow with a high temperature of 44 degrees and cloudy.

After an exciting news broadcast like that Walt wasn't in the mood to make much of a dinner. He settled on peanut butter and crackers for the evening meal. Sparky wasn't pleased because "peanut butter wasn't good for dogs."

Walt turned on the scanner to the police and fire frequency bands and didn't hear anything. Then turned on his 2 meter radio and tuned to the Hoodoo Mountain repeater and this was quiet too.

However the Bonners Ferry repeater was busy so he thought that he would listen for a bit. Two hams were commenting that because of the earthquake they could not make their medical appointments at the Spokane Veterans Administration Hospital. Sandpoint had a small VA clinic but they couldn't get to that either and with the disruption in mail service they couldn't get their meds. Another vet was complaining about not getting his VA check and people were speculating about where the government would be moving and how long it would take to make the move. Another ham was wondering if it would be worth it to drive to Canada to shop for groceries but he was told that he could not cross the border without a vaccination card. Someone else mentioned that you could drive from Bonners to Sandpoint but instead a 40 minute trip, it was closer to 2 hours via all the detours.

Walt turned off the 2 meter radio and turned on the CB. It was quiet so he gave a call, "Anybody on the radio tonight. This is Walt."

Chip answered, "Hey Walt what's going on?'

"Not much, I have been trying to call you on the phone."

"I've been pretty busy lately. My cell phone is out anyway."

"Oh that's right. I forget that everybody doesn't have a landline." Walt hated cell phones and this is why.

"We'll have to get together. There's some stuff I want to tell you but can't do it on the air. Over"

"I understand. I heard about the deal on Upper Pack River. Over."

"That's just part of it. I moved here because it was a sleepy little town but I can tell you it isn't sleepy anymore."

"Roger that. I'm sure you miss the old days when a busy night was an open container."

"That would sound pretty good right now. I'll stop by when I get some time and fill you in."

"Roger that. I was getting used to having power every other day but I guess it will be awhile. Over."

"I am not sure about that. I don't think it will be too long but I don't know anything that you don't know Walt."

"I guess putting up wire isn't too big of a job, but towers, and equipment would be a much bigger deal. At least its not in the middle of winter when people need the heat. Over."

"That's for sure, what kind of emergency power do you have at the house?"

"I have a little Honda generator and three deep cycle batteries. At least I can get a shower at the office."

"That's what I miss the most, is a hot shower. I can use my wood fired hot tub but it's not what you call handy since I need to use the inverter to run the pump to fill it up, and then wait a couple of hours to heat it. Over."

"Roger. I understand. I'll stop by when I can."

"Sounds good. If you can we'll be here Sunday night for the CB net. We've got a pretty good group. Guess I'll go QRT for the night."

"OK Walt, I'll try and catch you on the net. See you later.73."

Walt had already taken care of the windows and was ready to call it a night. If he couldn't sleep in, he could always get up early and work some DX on the radio. At least the tire shredder project was done but it was the kind of thing that he couldn't talk about even to his friends. He was glad that he thought of using a tree instead of the 2" x 4s" anyway. By doing this you couldn't see his shredder for the trees.

The next morning Walt went out in the back yard with Sparky to make an improvement on the tire shredder control cord. He cut a small branch on the tree the cord was tied to so that only a six inch stem of the branch stuck out from the tree. Then he tied a loop on the end of the cord and another about fifteen feet from the end loop. This made it easier to deploy or retract the tire shredder depending on which loop was placed on the six inch branch. Walt had two diametrically opposed opinions about his homeboy projects, One was that if it is not broken, don't fix it. The other was that there is always room for improvement. There was something to be said for both. This reminded him of a Benjamin Franklin quote, "One To-Day is worth Two To-Morrows."

After breakfast Walt brought in a little more firewood for the day and got on 3.988 to talk to his friends. Two hams were already on the air. "I just barely felt it over here. But I did notice the bathroom door was moving on it own. Over." (AR7QRN)

"Roger. How far away are you? About 100 miles or so?" (AU7PM)

"I think that is about right. Over." (AR7QRN)

"Well when Walt gets in here we'll see if he felt it. Over."

"I felt alright. AP7ZMT."

"Well tell us all about it. AR7QRN."

"Morning Dennis, It shook the cabin but I was lucky. There was no damage that I can see and no trees came down that I can see. AP7ZMT."

"How far were you from the quake Walt? AU7PM."

"About 23 miles or so. It hit on the south side of the Lake just across from Sandpoint. It damaged bridges so Sandpoint is pretty well cut off by road except for some detours that are closed to truck traffic. Over." (AP7ZMT)

"Wow, that was a big one. Besides their politics the Californians brought their earthquakes with them too." (AU7PM)

"I guess that's right Frank. It took out the main cell tower and the whole area is out of power again. The railroad bridges are out too and I haven't heard anything about expected repair times. Over."

"Roger, the whole country is going to hell. AR7QRN."

"The country was dead before any of this started. Morning guys. AM7DX"

"That's a little harsh isn't it Jeff?" (AU7PM)

"I don't think so. Just take a look around. The Constitution doesn't matter, God is dead, criminals get released without bail, elementary kids are treated to drag time story hour, it's OK to kill babies even after they are born, men can compete in women's sports, we have to get vaccinated and wear face masks but illegals don't, the list goes on and on. Over."

"I can see what you mean. I'm just hoping things get better for my kids. AU7PM."

"Me too. Besides everybody knows that our biggest problem is climate change." (AM7DX)

"If that was true the elites wouldn't keep buying ocean front property! AR7QRN."

"It's always two sets of rules with these people. We can't have guns but they have armed security. AY7OM."

"Morning Ray, are you holding your breath for the Presidents speech on Monday?" (AP7ZMT)

"I can't wait to hear his plan." (AY7OM)

"I can't wait for them to start sending out checks. AU7PM"

"Amen, if they don't do this soon we are going to have another depression. Maybe they'll call it the build back better depression. AP7ZMT."

"Roger that. It's just part of the plan to get us all to buy electric cars." (AY7OM)

"If everybody had an electric car now, nobody could go anywhere." (AR7QRN)

"Part of the plan." (AY7OM)

"Moving the whole government is going to a big deal and won't happen overnight. Swamp creatures can't move that fast. Over." (AM7DX)

"Just think of all of the national monuments that nobody will ever see again. And what about the Smithsonian? How are they going to move that? Over." (AP7ZMT)

"I guess we'll have to wait until Monday. One thing is for sure a lot of people are going to make their fortunes selling property to the government." (AR7QRN)

"Maybe they'll just take it and give all the property owners IOUs." (AU7PM)

"I think they will do what they always do, print money. AM7DX."

"I sure that no one in government will profit from inside information. What do you think" (AR7QRN)

"I heard that a judge had ordered one of the vaccine makers to turn over their initial test data before the accident. Well now it turns out that something like 28 of the 34 pregnant women in the early tests, lost their babies." (AU7PM)

"Nothing to see here folks. Bring your 5 year old in for a Covid shot and get a discount on your kid's sex change operation." (AP7ZMT)

"These people are pure evil. AY7OM."

"I'd say Amen but somehow that doesn't seem appropriate." (AR7QRN)

"Hey Frank, what is gas selling for over there?" (AP7ZMT)

"Last week it was going for $7.58 for regular. Over." (AU7PM)

"I never thought I'd see the day it would be that high. I'm not even sure any stations are open over here yet, but usually it's a little lower over here. Over." (AP7ZMT)

"I heard that the strategic petroleum reserve was pretty well tapped too." (AY7OM)

"When they do fill it up again, it will cost more, that's for sure." (AM7DX)

"It looks like I have company. Got to go now. Will talk to you later. 73 This AP7ZMT clear."

"OK Walt see you later. AU7PM"

Walt turned off his radio and heard the driveway announcer. He turned on the security monitor to see that it was Chip. He wasn't in uniform and he wasn't driving the Sheriff's SUV so maybe it was his day off. By this time Sparky was barking at the front door and Walt let her out back. He went back to the front door and opened it just as Chip was stepping on the porch and said, "Good to see you Chip I don't think I have ever seen you out of uniform."

"It was my day off so I thought I'd be more comfortable in civilian clothes. Nice place you have here." Chip said as he was looking around. "Did you build this yourself?"

"I had a little help but did it mostly myself. Let's go outside and I'll show you my antennas and then we can check out the shack." Sparky was barking at Chip and trying to get him to notice her. They walked closer to the fence and Walt said, "It's OK Sparky this is Chip." Sparky went right up to Chip and started to sniff him through the fence. "She's a good dog, she doesn't bite, but as you can see she likes to bark."

Chip put his hand down and gave her a pet through the fence. "She's a good looking dog. How long have you had her?"

"It's been about 4 years now. I found her on Craig's List." Walt told him. "Don't know what I'd do without her."

Walt took Chip out to the center of the parking area and started to point out his antennas. He pointed to the hexbeam and said, "Just got the hexbeam last summer. I really like it a lot. I know there are better antennas but for the money this has been great." Walt didn't have to tell Chip that it was a directional antenna for 20 meters and up. "I didn't get the 40 meter loop for this because I didn't think it would do well with the snow and ice." Then he pointed to his 13 element yagi. "There is my main 2 meter antenna. The Ringo Ranger over there is used mostly for the scanner."

Next he pointed to his homemade rotatable inverted V dipole. "I use this mostly for CB but I have talked to Argentina with it on 10 meters." Then Walt pointed out his cobweb antenna for 20 – 6 meters and the Gap vertical for 80 –10. "There is my end fed wire for 160 an up. And that's about it except for the homemade rotatable loop and the longwire for receiving."

"Yes you have quite an antenna farm here. I am hoping to put up some wire this summer. How do you like the end fed?"

"I like it a lot. It needs a tuner but I use it almost everyday on 75 meters. When I first got it, it wouldn't load on 160 but once I grounded the match box , it worked great. I can get 500 watts with my ALS 600 on 160 with a pretty flat SWR."

"That's great. When I get some wire up I plan to work more on HF."

"Sounds good. Lets go take a look at the shack." For some reason hams refer to their radio rooms as shacks. This is probably because in the old days of ham radio, most wives didn't care for the noise so the hams would set up their stations in the garage, or outbuildings. Lot of hams stay up late or get up early to play with their radios and most wives appreciate it when hams are not operating in the house.

When they got to the radio room Walt gave Chip the grand tour and did not overlook any of his equipment. "This is my newest radio, the Icom 7300. As you know it is an SDR and it has a waterfall and touch screen display. The Yaesu FT900 I got from my father. The Kenwood 520SE was my first radio. I don't use it now because the meter is not working but I really like looking at it so I leave on the table. The 2 QRP radios I built from a kit. You can see the 2 meter radios, the scanner, the CB, and my little SDR Play. I built the active filters and amplifiers for the QRP rigs. And those are my crystal radios that I built a few years ago. It's amazing how much fun you can have with a crystal set. With the ham antennas and a little trap/tuner they work pretty well even on shortwave. And the portable electric guitar amp/speaker is high impedance so it's just like a regular radio. Listened to the Fiji Island soccer scores awhile back and the signal came in like it was right next door."

"I really like your set up Walt. Is that your internet set up?" Chip pointed to the security monitor.

"No that is my security system. I turned on the monitor when I heard the driveway announcer." He turned on the monitor and Chip could see his car parked out front.

"That's a great picture. I like the idea of being able to monitor the front door while you are on the radio."

"Oh I want to show you my power set. It's in the crawl space. Watch your step. Let me turn on the light." When they got down in the crawl space Chip was really impressed. The 12 batteries and the big inverter/charger installation looked great. Walt showed Chip how he could switch from grid power to inverter power to operate the water pump in the well. And he told him how he had wired alternate inverter outlets and 12 volt outlets throughout the cabin. Walt noticed that Chip was looking at his stash of homemade beer. "I make some really good homebrew beer. This is two years old. It's almost noon and I have a couple of cold ones in the cooler if you want one."

"You know it is my day off and a beer sounds great."

Walt and Chip went upstairs and Walt pointed to the living room and said, "Go ahead and have a seat, I'll be right back." He let Sparky in and grabbed his two bottles of beer, an opener, and two glasses and went in to sit with Chip. Sparky was doing her best to be a pest but Chip didn't seem to mind. Walt opened the bottle and handed Chip the beer and a glass.

Chip tilted the glass and slowly poured the beer. This kept the head to a minimum and he filled it to the top. Walt had already bragged about the beer so Chip sipped it slowly. "This is good beer," Chip said, "This sure doesn't taste like any homebrew I have ever had."

"Thanks, they have recipes for about any beer you like and good quality ingredients make it easier than ever. The trick is to let it age and not be in a big hurry to drink it." Walt was glad Chip liked his beer.

"I'm glad we have this time to chat. I couldn't talk about this on the radio and my cell phone is still not working. I thought that you would be interested in hearing about the recent crime spree." Chip told Walt about some of things that were not in the news. " We have been busy at the Sheriffs Department. I came here to be a cop in a small town but I never expected anything like this. We've had multiple break-ins, several home invasions, burglaries, a car jacking and even a case of cattle rustling on the north side."

"Thanks for telling me about this. Home security is always on my mind and I have expected things to get worse with the bad economy, food shortages, and the natural disasters. Now that the phones are out, people can't even call for help."

"Exactly, it's becoming a perfect storm for crime."

"I am sure the power outages don't help much either."

"With the power outages, lots of people can't go to work. And now with the government shut down, things are tough for lots of people." Chip poured another small glass of beer.

"I know, I am missing my retirement check that's for sure. But I have it a lot better than most folks. I have hardly any debt and this place will be paid off pretty soon. Then I'll be debt free. Also I have been prepping for a long time so I'm in pretty good shape."

"I wanted to tell you to be on the look out for a group up here that we are keeping our eyes on. They are a wanna be motorcycle club called the Batmen. Instead of bikes they drive ATVs. You'll know them if you see them, they have a baseball bat mounted on the hood." Chip could see that Walt was concerned.

"Actually I had a run in with them the day I met you." Walt told Chip how Susan had returned his gun and how they pulled into his yard yelling at them. He also told him how she convinced them to leave with her new .357 S&W. And how Walt followed her home to be sure they didn't bother her again and then met Chip down at the store.

"Well if they cause any trouble, we would like to know about it."

"I'll let you know. I'm just glad that Susan got to see how useful a gun can be to stay out of trouble."

"I'm glad to hear that you helped her pick out something that she'll feel good about carrying and glad that she did so well at the range." Chip was impressed that Walt took the time to give her some good advice and help her to get familiar with the gun. Even though he carried an automatic on the job, he thought a hammerless revolver was a good choice for a beginner. Chip finished the beer and said, "Really want to thank you for the beer and glad I stopped by to see your place. I'll try and be on the CB Sunday night."

"I think we've got some good people on the net and it can be a good experience for everyone. With the power and phone outages people realize how useful the radios can be."

"You know we monitor channel 19 down at the Sheriffs Office but we are too far away to hear you from up here."

"I'll mention that to people incase they want to take their radios mobile. Also I have everyone's email and they have mine too, and this helps if someone wants to share something that they don't want to broadcast over the radio."

"You mean like Jane?"

"Exactly. She learned her lesson and everyone else did too." Walt walked Chip to his car and thanked him for stopping by. Sparky approved and was always glad to meet another friend.

Later that day Walt received an email from Tony and Sherri. They had passed their two amateur radio tests and were now licensed General Class Operators. One problem was that they could not start operating until they received call signs from the FCC and the FCC offices were closed until they could reopen elsewhere. The other problem was that because of the earthquake damage they could not buy radio equipment and get it shipped into Sandpoint.

Walt said that he understood and had a radio that he could loan them so they could at least start listening to some hams until they got their calls. Walt invited them to come over the next day to pick up the radio.

When they arrived Walt took them into his shack and showed them a radio that he built from a kit, a version 4 uBITX QRP transceiver. This was an 80 – 10 meter 10 watt SSB and CW transceiver that ran on 12v – 13.8v DC. They told him that they would appreciate the loan so Walt showed them how it worked. It could be used as a general coverage receiver and could also transmit on any frequency that it received. After they got the short course, he disconnected the power cords and the antenna. He also gave them an active filter/audio amp for the radio and an external speaker.

They knew that they couldn't use the radio to transmit until they were issued call signs, but this would be a fun way to play with a radio. Walt also gave them a G5RV dipole antenna which was a 102' wire antenna with a ladder feed line and a match box. In addition he gave a 10 foot piece of coax cable with PL259 connectors to attach the antenna to the radio. "If you have any trouble, let me know. If you can, I would string the antenna north and south so that it will work best east and west. If you can try to get it 40 – 50 feet high and it will work great."

"Thanks Walt we really appreciate it," Tony said, "Have you got any ideas about what kind of radio we should get?"

"It really depends on your budget. You will need an antenna tuner to use this radio to transmit no matter what kind of radio you get. How much do you have to spend?"

"We talked it over and we would like to spend no more than $1500."

"In that case, I would first decide on a antenna tuner and see how much you have left over. You could get a tapped inductor tuner for $100 or so that would handle a couple of hundred watts. An automatic tuner in the same power range would run you about $250. I prefer a roller inductor tuner over an automatic one. You could get a legal limit tuner for $500 or a 300 watt version for about $300. If you think that you will ever want to get an amplifier and run high power, I would get the bigger tuner. Otherwise you could get a smaller one."

"OK we will talk it over and see what we have left for a radio"

"Either way you'll be able to get a nice 100 watt radio for that. There are lots of places to buy used equipment if you like, but you'll be able to go new if you want to. I will say that this hobby is like any other, you can spend as much as you want. For example you could buy a new version 6 of the QRP 10 watt radio I am loaning you for about $200 but it wouldn't have the features of a more expensive rig. It wouldn't have filters, a noise blanker, automatic gain control, and a few other things. Also at some point you'll want some other antennas as well."

"OK you've given us lots to think about. As soon as we get our calls we'll see what we can do." Tony was happy to have somthing to play with right way."

" One more thing. Since we live on Rapid Lightning Creek Road I shouldn't have to tell you to be sure and disconnect the antenna if there is a thunderstorm."

"That's right, they don't call it Rapid Lightning for a reason. Thanks again Walt. We'll talk to you later tonight on the CB net."

Walt felt badly about ignoring Sparky all day so he took her for a nice long walk. Spring was coming slowly to the Creek but at least the snow pack was on the run. As the snow disappeared the ash cover seemed to be more intense. At least when the rains came, some of the ash would be washed off the trees. Even pine trees breathe from their needles and could use some nice hard spring rains. The tamarack trees would soon begin to grow new needles and they didn't suffer like the other conifers did. If the winter snow was heaven, the ash was hell.

Who knows how long it would take before it wouldn't be an eye sore any longer.

This time of year it was natural to look at the woodshed and celebrate how much wood was left. But Walt knew from experience that he would be burning some wood right up until the first of June. When they got back from their walk Walt brought in some wood for the night and secured the light shades for the night. After dinner Sparky was trying to sleep in the radio room and Walt was getting ready for the CB net. He knew there was no use trying to catch any local news on the radio. It was the weekend and the local station never bothered to report the news on a weekend. About the best that he could hope for was a brief word about the weather. They predicted lows around freezing and no precipitation until the end of the week so gloom and doom was the order of the day and perfectly normal for this time of year.

Walt turned on the CB and gave out a call for early check-ins. To his surprise Chip was the first one in. "Hey Chip, thanks for checking in, it usually takes about 10 or 15 minutes to get everyone in here. Then we do a couple of rounds based on check-in order so you'll be first. Over."

"Sounds good I'll be here."

Walt took check-ins as usual and soon he had everybody ready to go. He checked his list twice to make sure that he didn't miss anyone and gave one last call. "Last call for check ins to the Rapid lightning CB net. Please come now." He didn't hear anything so he started the net. "Thanks again everyone we really do have a full house tonight. There's a lot to talk about that's for sure. I want to introduce you to Chip. He's new to the neighborhood and he's also a ham so he will be a big asset to our group. He is a deputy sheriff and a very nice guy. One thing he was telling me that I didn't know was that the Sheriff's department monitors channel 19 so if you ever need to contact them this might be a good way to do this if the phones are out. Some of us will probably be too far away but this might work for people who are closer to the store. And as long as I am at it we'll ask Chip if people can contact them via email or not. So lets get started. First we'll go to Chip, then to Bret, then to Mary and Beth, over to Charles and Megan, then to Scott, next will be Stan and Gloria, then Robert and Nancy, then to Peter, then Susan, over to George and Carla, up to Tom, over to Jane, then to Fly Boy, over to Steve, and then Tony and back to me. Go ahead Chip take it away."

"Nice to meet you in advance. Walt has told me about your net and I think it is a great asset to the community and especially helpful when the phones are out and the roads are a mess. To answer Walt's question, I am sure you can expect a timely response if you contact the Sheriff's office by email. The address would be BonnerCountySheriff dot idgov.org.
As I was telling Walt these tough times are breading more crime these days so be sure to lock things up. I guess it's over to Bret.

"Nice to meet you Chip. It's been a helluva year so far. I wonder if anyone has heard when some of the roads would be opened again so that we can get packages delivered. It seems like Sandpoint is pretty well cut off right now, Over to Mary and Beth."

"Hi Chip. Mary and Beth here. I am curious if anyone has tried the detours to Bonners or if there is a detour route to Priest River? I haven't heard anything about quake damage up here but if anyone knows anything about this, let us know. Charles and Megan how are things on the High Road? Over."

"We are doing OK considering. Sure wish the sun would come out that's for sure. Somebody might comment if the road is open all the way into Sandpoint and if not what is the detour? Welcome aboard to Chip and over to Scott."

"I am not sure about the road past Ponderay, but if there is no power in Sandpoint is there anything open anyway like gas stations for instance? I was hoping the Country Store would be open by now but I don't believe they are. Up to Stan and Gloria."

"We don't know anything because we haven't gone anywhere since the quake. I'd settle for power every other day again and hope we get this back soon. Also don't know if you have heard but the President will be giving a speech tomorrow night telling us about plans to relocate and restart the government. I sure hope he gets specific but I'll bet that he won't. Up to Robert and Nancy."

"I wouldn't guess there would be too many details. My question is will he be giving the speech from his basement or somewhere else. I don't see how we can avoid a depression if people don't start getting some relief. Down to Peter, go ahead."

"Hello to Chip it will be good to get some straight information about what's going on. Let us know if you hear anything. I am curious how much damage there was in Sandpoint besides the bridges? And I'll bet that Lakeshore Drive got hit pretty hard. Over to Susan."

"Good to hear you Chip. I haven't been anywhere either so I have no idea about the roads. I didn't know anything about the detours until I heard about them a few minutes ago. And I agree, it's a real good time to keep things locked up from what I've heard. Hope everyone is hanging in there. First the volcano, and now this. Go ahead George and Carla."

"Hello everyone. We've got a pretty good view of the road from our place and it would be nice to see something besides dark skies. If the power doesn't come back soon the lack of refrigeration will become an issue. We don't live near the creek. Down to Tom."

"I walked down to Rapid Lightning and Flume Creek the other day, and I can tell you there are a lot of dead fish down there. I don't think I would want to drink the water or use it for refrigeration either. When the bears wake up they'll be eating good for awhile. Down to Jane."

"I am sure you all heard what happened to me. Just locking your doors isn't good enough I can tell you. I don't think I'll be going anyplace for awhile. How about you Fly Boy?"

"I have been getting out a little bit trying to get some drone coverage. I wish we could get some straight answers but I guess if people don't know, they don't know. I do know that the Sandpoint Airport has been busy but I am not allowed to fly my drone anywhere near there. Oh I did hear that were are still having some aftershocks if that means anything. Up to you Steve."

"Think of all the stories we will have to tell our grand kids after this is over. If we were smart we'd all be working on some books right now. Maybe Hollywood would be interested. Oh, I forgot, after the volcano there isn't a Hollywood anymore. Over to you Tony and Sherri."

"Hello Everyone. Just wanted to tell you that we passed out ham tests and if you are interested you can borrow our study books. The tests really aren't that hard. Oh and Walt, got the antenna up and have really been enjoying listening to the radio. Over to Walt."

"You know I was thinking that it would be nice if those of us with landlines could leave our radios on more often. That way if someone needed help we could call it in. Also Chip, do you know if the Sheriff's office can copy a SSB signal on channel 19? I have a couple of radios that will work SSB on this frequency. Over."

"I think they can but I'll find out for sure and let you know. I have been getting into the Sheriff's office in Ponderay without a problem but I know there is a detour route that people are using to go to Sandpoint. When I get back to the office I will email everyone and list the detours that are in place right now. I don't know any more than you do about expected power, phone, and road re-openings but I'll let you know as soon as I hear something. Over to Bret."

"Thanks Chip this would be a big help. I would be especially interested in finding a gas station that was open. I have been using the gas from my truck to run my generator. Over to Mary and Beth."

"Tony, Beth and I would be interested in studying for our ham licenses. Send us an email and let us know when it would be a good time to stop by and pick up the study guides. We are about 3 miles up the road from you. Over to Charles and Megan."

"That's a good idea about siphoning gas from your car. I have had a hard time with this because of those nozzle restrictors they put in the filler tube. If anyone has a good idea to make this easier, let us know. Over to Scott."

"I found a good way to do this Charles. Get a short piece of pvc pipe that will fit past the restrictor and then put your siphon tube into the center of the pvc pipe and into the tank. This makes it easy to get the siphon tube out. Over Stan and Gloria."

"I have never tried this but it sounds like it would work. We are wondering how the ash will affect the garden. If anyone has any ideas about this, let us know. And Chip a list of the detours would be a big help. I am curious if the main Post Office in Sandpoint is open or not. I would like to order some things online and have it shipped to us General Delivery and pick up. Over to Robert and Nancy."

"That's a good idea Stan I would be interested in hearing about this as well. We did get our game camera up and have seen some pictures of two bear roaming the area at night. So at least some of them are waking up and I'm sure they are feasting on the fish. Over to Peter."

"I don't have a landline but I'll try to keep my radio on more often until the phones come back. It's kind of like a neighborhood intercom. And yes Chip thanks in advance for any info you can give us about the power or the phones. Go ahead Susan,"

"I'll try to find out when the Country Store is going to reopen. Even if they are low on food items people would still like to get gas and propane. Oh Walt I have been getting some practice with my new toy and thanks again, Over to George and Carla."

"OK Susan, we have got some fun pictures with our game camera as well. Saw a cougar sneaking around the other night. I am guessing that they like fish too. Over to Tom."

"Spring is kind of funny the way everything is hungry at the same time. I haven't seen a cougar since I've been here. Also if anyone has internet service now the Sandpoint News Paper website has had some good stories about the earthquake and has schedules posted with boat and barge crossings in case anyone has to get south of town. Over to Jane."

"Let me know what you find out about the Country Store Susan. It would be a lot handier for me to get propane than going into town. They must have a generator to keep their refrigeration and freezers running. Up to Fly Boy."

"I would really like to get some video of wildlife like bears and cougars feeding at the creek. I know I would have to fly high enough that the noise didn't scare them. Thanks for the idea. Up to Steve."

"Yes that would be great video and people would love to see this. I am guessing that you could also get some blue heron and eagle shots as well. I've been cutting a few dead stands for firewood and found that I have to clean off the ash before I stack the wood. Firewood is a dirty job anyway but this adds an extra step. Over to Tony and Sherri."

"No problem on the license manuals Beth. I'll send you an email after I get off the radio. Walt was right, you might as well plan on taking both tests at once. Oh Walt can you give me the shortwave frequencies and times for the Alex Jones show? Go ahead Walt."

"Sure Tony. Let me see. Weekdays he is on 12.160 Mhz from 0900 – 1300 local time. This is rebroadcast at 4.840 Mhz at 1900 local time. And on Sundays it is on 9.350 from 1400 – 1600 local time. And his website is infowars dot com. Unless anybody else has anything I guess we can call it a night. Anybody? Anything? Anyone? Go ahead."

"This is Jim on Thunder Alley. What time do you guys get on?

Well Jim we meet every Sunday at 1830 hours and lots of people are on the evenings other times as well. Feel free to check in next Sunday. This is Walt. Over."

"OK Walt thanks. I'll be here next week. Have a good evening everyone."

" All right well see you then Jim. I guess I'll call it a night. Feelfree and visit as usual if you like. And let me thank everyone for checking in and participating in the Rapid Lightning CB net. This is Walt. 73 everybody.

" Hey Walt, this is Chip, want to go down to cannel 15?"

"Sure meet you down there. Over."

"Just wanted to tell you how impressed I am with your net. I am going to tell some of the other deputies about this and maybe they can get something like this started in their neighborhoods too. Kind of like a neighborhood watch and listen. Go ahead."

"Thanks Chip, I am happy about this too. We got a good group here and it's nice to help people get together and help each other."

"Roger. I'll let you go. Maybe someday you can show me how to make some good beer. See you later."

"Be happy too. The hardest part is cleaning the bottles and then waiting for it to age. Later."

The next morning Walt woke up and saw that the weatherman was correct. There was no precipitation overnight and the outside temperature was 34 degrees and that was about normal for the end of March. Tonight Walt had two things to look forward to, the basketball championship and the State of the Union Address. This would be the latest in the year that this speech was ever given but considering the volcanic eruption and the nuclear accident at the nation's capitol, it was understandable. The speech was going to be held in Madison Square Garden which was far enough from Washington D.C. to be considered safe. Because of the size of the arena every politico who wanted a ticket could get in to see it. Unlike most State of the Union Addresses, public interest was high.

The national championship basketball game was scheduled at the same time as the speech so Walt decided that he would watch the game online and then watch a re-broadcast of the speech after the game was over. BYU would be playing Duke and Walt would be cheering for BYU even though they beat Gonzaga.

He spent the morning talking on the radio and worked three countries in Europe and one station in South Africa. After lunch he took Sparky for a walk and brought in several days worth of firewood and kindling. He got some of the last snow from the snow bank and put in the ice chest for later on. After an early dinner he got two beers out of the crawl space and put them in the cooler to chill. Even though it was early, he put the light shades in place so that he didn't have to deal with it later.

The game was close and Duke was leading at the half. Walt didn't really care because he wasn't a basketball fan, he was a Gonzaga fan. Championship games always had a longer half time than usual. This wasn't for the players and it wasn't for the fans, it was for the advertisers. When the game resumed Walt opened his second beer and sat back to enjoy the game. In the last few seconds BYU had a chance to win but a Duke player hit a half court shot and won the game for Duke.
Walt really enjoyed watching the game and he hadn't been that relaxed since he was in the hot tub. But all good things had to come to an end so he started to watch the speech on YouTube.

One of the nice things about watching a recording of the speech was that no time was wasted watching kids just out of school telling everyone what the President was going to say. The other nice thing about watching recordings was that you could fast forward through commercials.

The camera panned the audience. The congressmen and officials liked to get seats up front, not so they could see but so they could be seen by the cameras and by the voters. Unlike most State of the Union speeches the Democrats and Republicans were not separated on one side of the aisle or the other. This made it harder to perform stunts like sitting on their hands while trying not to applaud. Also the Speaker of the House and the President of the Senate were not seated behind the President, they were in the crowd like everyone else.

The President was about to enter. "Ladies and Gentlemen, The President of the United States, Joe Bama." He entered from the back and slowly walked up to the podium, squinting and trying to focus on the teleprompter as the crowd applauded.

"Thank you." The applause stopped. "I was told to come here tonight. They gave me some notes." Joe checked his pockets and found the note cards and began reading, "As you know we are planning to relocate the government because of the...well you know what happened. I know that you understand why the government has been shutdown. We have decided to..." Joe looks at his notes, "move all branches of the Federal Government to other temporary locations. It won't be..." Joe checks his notes..."easy and it can't happen overnight. They tell me that..." he flips over the note card, "I have made the decision to move all branches of Government to other locations. Their plan is to move the entire Legislative Branch of the Federal Government to Chicago because..."Joe checks his notes again, "it is the Windy City! Just joking, hey it has a large airport and Congressmen come and go all the time."

The Judicial Branch will be moving to Milwaukee and the Executive Branch will be moving to the Twin Cities. The Secretary of defense, Mr., I forgot his name but you all know him, and the Pentagon will be relocating to the Omaha area. They tell me that Government checks will start going out in the next 30 – 60 days..." Joe looks at his notes, "Experts tell me that the Washington D.C. area might not be safe to live in for the next 50 years or more." He looks at his notes, "At some point we will have to decide if it is worth it to build another Capitol City and where to build it." He looks at his notes, "This is a big job, maybe the biggest job in history." Joe looks down at his notes. "But we're going to get it done. You know why?" Joe whispers to the crowd, *Because I am the Commander AND Chief.*" Joe looks at his notes again, "It took the Lord six days to create the Universe. This will take a little longer." Joe hesitates a moment and then says, "We could get this done a lot sooner if Republicans would agree to spend more money. But they say this would lead to runaway inflation, and I say, who cares? *Your kids will be paying for it anyway.*" Joe smiles and says, "It's past my bedtime. Say your Prayers. No questions, Please." Joe turns to shake hands, but everyone else on the stage near him had already walked away. Joe Bama slowly walks back from the podium and out the way he entered.

The network reporters were stunned. This was the shortest State of the union Speech in history and he had to check his notes eleven times and then blames Republicans for not wanting to break the budget with more Federal spending. Not to mention having the nerve to tell people that government spending didn't matter because their kids would pay for it anyway. They didn't expect anything Presidential but they did expect more than this. Walt turned off his computer and thought to himself, "It's always someone else's fault isn't it Joe?" Besides, Walt thought, "The real reason that they didn't move the government to New York City was that they couldn't afford the rent."

Chapter 7. April

*"Step into the street by sundown
Step into your last goodbye
You're a target just by living
Twenty dollars will make you die"*
Alice Cooper

The first day of April would normally have been payday for Walt but after the President's Speech the other night it sounded like it would be a month or two or more before he could expect another retirement check. If people were hurting now they would certainly be feeling the squeeze in 30 – 60 days. It had been three months since anyone had seen the sun in North Idaho and it certainly did not look like Spring. Instead of green grass, people had dark gray ash days, one after the other, and dark clouds that had everyone in a "cabin fever mood."

Walt had received a list of detours from Chip but until the stores were open there was really no reason to even think of going to town. If it would have been raining Walt would have felt better about spending most of the day inside. There were a few things he could do but nothing that had to done right away so Walt spent most of the day on the internet and on the radio. He thought if he got lots of rest that night he would have more energy the next day so he turned in a little early on April Fools Day night.

He was sleeping soundly, and in the middle of a pretty good dream, when he heard the driveway alarm sound off. He sat up in bed and new what the sound was right away. Since the alarm kept beeping, Walt knew that it wasn't a deer or a moose, but that several vehicles were coming up the driveway. He jumped out of bed, put on his pants, locked Sparky in the bathroom, slipped on his pack boots, grabbed his coat, and slipped out the back door in the dark. The cold temperature on his face and a rush of adrenaline made him wide awake as his eyes got accustomed to the dark. He had planned what he would do in advance, and was squatting down behind his shooting table by the Bar-B-Q. He opened the hidden door on the inside of the shooting bench and pulled out his new Henry Big Boy rifle. It was loaded with 6 bullets and he hunkered down and waited. In case he needed to reload, he left the hidden door open.

Walt heard some vehicles come into the parking area and lifted his head high enough to get a look. There were 3 camouflaged colored ATVs, one behind the other and maybe a fourth behind them on the driveway. Although he couldn't see them well because of their blinding headlights, he was pretty sure they had bats mounted on their hoods. All but the first one turned off their lights and two men got out of the first ATV and stepped out 25 feet from Walt's metal front door. They each wore army fatigue jackets and one was carrying a bottle that looked like a Molotov.

The Molotov cocktail was invented by the Finns and used during the Winter War with the Soviet Union against their tanks. It was made with a glass bottle and typically filled with gasoline and had a cloth wick that extended out of the bottle neck. The wick was lit and when the bottle was thrown, and then when the glass bottle broke, the liquid would explode in a fireball. It got its name from the Soviet foreign minister, Vyacheslav Molotov and was a poor man's hand grenade.

Walt recognized both men from his earlier encounter with them when Susan had returned his revolver. The larger man was shouting at the house, "We're back, come out and get your beat down old man!" When he didn't see any lights come on in the cabin he pulled out his pistol and screamed, "I said come out of the house you piece of shit!" Still there was no response from the house. "Maybe your still sleeping, this should wake you up." Sparky could be heard barking from inside as fat ass fired four large bore pistol bullets through the metal door.

The other man held the Molotov and lit the wick. He was just about to throw it at the porch when Walt stood up from behind the fortified shooting bench and fired his Henry Big Boy .357 at the man before he released the Molotov. It was a perfect head shot and the man dropped instantly to the ground

238

before he could throw the fire bomb. The gas was leaking out of the bottle and had set the man on fire.

Fat ass, the loudmouth, turned toward Walt. As he turned Walt turned on the two LED light bars that were mounted under the porch roof and pointed directly at the man with the pistol. He looked at the lights for a second and possible thought that someone would be coming out the door. At that moment Walt shot him in the throat and he collapsed next to his burning buddy. Walt shut off the LED lights and gunfire erupted from the other invaders. Walt took cover for a moment and could hear several bullets striking the plywood sand-filled shooting bench. By this time someone had turned off the lights on the lead ATV. After a brief pause in the shooting Walt turned on the LED lights again and could see two men positioned behind the second ATV and using it for cover. Unfortunately for them, they were only 15 feet or so from a tree with one of the bird houses. The bird house was pointed at their backs. Walt aimed quickly but carefully and he hit the bird house in the sweet spot. The exploding bird house sent BBs and wood fragments through the two men and all over the side of the ATV.

More gunfire was coming toward Walt from four other men who had positioned themselves on the side of the woodshop and the garage. Both sides exchanged fire until Walt was out of ammo. Instead of a shot, Walt's rifle simply clicked, and Walt could be heard swearing, "Shit."

Two men near the garage must have figured that Walt was out of ammo and rushed at him firing wildly. By this time Walt had grabbed his pump shotgun and chambered a round. The two men caught without cover must have been scared because anyone who has ever heard a pump shotgun's action chambering a round would never forget this sound. Walt fired at the man in front and he went down hard. A close range hit from a 12 gauge shotgun loaded with buckshot is bad news for anyone on the receiving end. Walt quickly chambered another round and shot his buddy like dispatching a raccoon. Both men weren't dead yet but they would be very soon.

As far as Walt knew there were only two invaders left and they were using the woodshop for cover. The LED lights from the cabin were still on and Walt could see that one of the men was now near the garage. When he gave his position away by firing, Walt put a couple of more bullets in his rifle using the side loader. And waited. In a moment the man by the garage stepped away to get a better shot and Walt took aim at the birdhouse above and behind the shooter. His well placed shot detonated the birdhouse and dropped him like a sack of potatoes.

The lone invader didn't feel like fighting after seeing his friends on the ground and retreated back to the driveway. Walt could hear the ATV start up and Walt ran across the back yard and released the cord to lower the tire shredder. After a few moments Walt was pretty sure the threat was over and went back into the cabin. Sparky was going nuts but he didn't want her outside in case they were still in danger.

Walt looked at the clock and it was almost 4 am. He called the Sheriffs Department and reported the home invasion. He told them that shots were fired and that he was alright but there were a few invaders on the ground who might need some help. He gave them his name and address and told them that he would have the lights on when they arrived.

Sparky was still barking but he left her locked in the bathroom and turned on his computer and made a copy of the security disc because he knew the police would want the original. Then he went back outside and pulled the tire shredder cord and hooked the loop to raise the tire shredder before the cops got there. After this he turned on all the lights in the cabin and removed the light shades from the windows.

Walt put his unloaded rifle and his shotgun on the kitchen table and armed himself with one revolver and put his other pistol under his mattress for safe keeping. And waited for the Sheriff to arrive. A little after 4:30 am he heard the driveway announcer alarm and put his pistol in a drawer near the door. He heard the Sheriff's cars stop on the driveway and the doors slammed shut. They could not drive all the way in because 3

ATVs were blocking the road. Walt was standing in front of the porch with his hands up in the air when they entered the parking area. He wanted to be sure that they knew that he wasn't one of the bad guys and that he was unarmed. They patted him down checking for weapons and Walt gave them his driver's license which he already was holding in his hand. When they were sure that he was unarmed and the homeowner, they allowed him to put his hands at his side.

Even though it was till dark the parking area was well lit with the LEDs. Two cops stayed with Walt while the others checked for signs of life in the bodies on the ground. The place looked like war zone because it was. Four bodies were in the middle of the parking area, the original two and the two others that tried to rush him. Two were by the SUV that were blind sided by the first birdhouse explosion. The other was by the garage. Seven people were hit for sure and maybe one or two others that drove the ATV down the driveway were hurt as well. The ATV was disabled with 4 flat tires and abandoned at the County road by Walt's mailbox.

Walt took the two deputies in the cabin and showed them his guns on the kitchen table. Sparky was barking up a storm and still locked in the bathroom. Walt showed the deputies the bullet holes in his front door and then took them into the radio room to watch the security footage of the incident. Some video was taken when the lights were on and some was taken with the lights off but with the night vision the video clearly showed the deputies what had happened.

The officers outside were setting up lights where needed to photograph the crime scene. Since they were in a rural area they didn't need to use police tape but they did set out numbered plastic cards to identify areas where shell casings and other items of interest could be found. About an hour later two detectives showed up to have a look around. They took more photographs and measured key distances and identified the bodies and recorded serial numbers from their weapons.

The detectives also looked at the security camera video and took the DVD disc with them. They also seized Walt's rifle and shotgun telling Walt that they needed these to perform ballistics tests and to be sure that the weapons had not been stolen. They assured him that he would get them back shortly.

They were also very interested in the ATV down at the road and did put police tape around this until they could check it for finger prints. Because it was licensed for use on the road they noted the plate number and looked the ATV over for signs of blood but they didn't find any that was obvious. By 7:00 am the County Coroner's office arrived and removed the seven dead bodies from Walt's yard. About 7:30 a tow truck showed up so the deputies and detectives moved their vehicles so that the ATVs could be towed down the hill where all 4 vehicles were loaded onto a flatbed trailer. A little after 8:00 Chip arrived after hearing what happened when he got to work. He visited with the detectives and other deputies and everyone left except for Chip who went over to talk to Walt. "I told them that you were a friend of mine and they agreed that you could give them a formal statement sometime in the next few days. There are no plans to charge you with anything at this time but you never know what a District Attorney will do. So how are you doing?"

"Well I'm alright. It was a helluva night. Now that everyone is gone I need to let Sparky out. She has been in the bathroom and has had a helluva night as well." Walt let Sparky out back and she ran around and barked even though there was nobody left to bark at.

"Come on in, I made a copy of the security video and you can see what happened." Chip followed Walt in the house and noticed the bullet holes through the door. Walt played the video. It was pretty good quality for security cameras but it would have been better with audio. " Too bad you can't hear the gunfire, it was pretty hectic for awhile."

"I know what you mean but I can see the muzzle flashes. So where were you shooting from?" They went out front and walked over to the shooting bench. "Wow you took some fire over here. It's a wonder you weren't killed."

"I would have been but this is filled with sand over 20 inches thick, Walt told him.

Chip finally understood that this was A fortified shooting position and not simply a Bar-B-Q area. Then he looked over where the lead ATV would have parked and said, "What happened over there?" as he pointed to the tree.

Walt explained to Chip that the birdhouses were filled with 2 pounds of Tannerite.

"I don't know if that is legal but you are lucky you had this." Chip told him as he looked around and saw the damage to the two trees and the other birdhouses. Chip rolled his eyes and thought to himself, "He doesn't look like Rambo. Who does Walt think he is, Grandpa Rambo?"

"Oh you are probably wondering what happened to the tires on the ATV that was down at the road. Come down here and I'll show you." When they got about 1/2 way down the driveway Walt asks, "Do you see it?'

" See what? What Am I looking for?" Chip asked.

Walt stepped over to the side of the road and pointed, "This, be careful don't cut yourself. This is sharp."

Chip took a close look and saw the black paracord going through the woods to the house. Then he noticed the lag bolt pivot on the base of the shredder tree and figured out how it worked. "I don't think this is illegal but I can see that it would be very effective. Of course if somebody hurts themselves on this you better have some really good home owners insurance." He rolled his eyes again.

"I understand but it may help you solve the case. Without it the fourth ATV would have been long gone."

"That's for sure I'll let you know what we come up with and when they want you to go in and give them a statement."

"OK not a problem. I am anxious to get my guns back."

"I can understand and will see what I can do. You are a one man crime stopper Walt."

"I just hope there aren't any more Batmen to deal with, now that they have seen my defenses."

"You know what they say, dead men tell no tales." The two walked up the driveway and Chip got in his vehicle and left.

Wow that had been some night, Walt was beat but he remembered that Sparky had not been fed so he got her some fresh water and some chow. Then he looked in the bathroom and saw that the inside of the door was pretty well scratched up. Understandable considering what she went through. Walt remembered the bullet holes in the door and plugged them with bolts, washers, and nuts. He looked at the bullet holes in the wall and decided to deal with these later. He was just glad that Sparky had been locked in the bathroom. Otherwise she might have been hurt.

Walt was so glad that he had prepared for trouble as well as he did. Without the shooting bench, the LED lights, the birdhouses, and the tire shredder things could have turned out much differently. He had survived a gunfight with 8 gang members who came to his home to do him harm. Seven were dead and the status of the other man was unknown. But if he came around again, he could expect more of the same. Just in case someone would try to ambush him, Walt doubled down on the idea of being armed at all times. Whether he was getting wood or walking the dog, he would be alert and he would be packing.

Walt realized that he was also lucky to have Chip on his side. He could easily be in jail right now and waiting to see a judge if it wasn't for Chip. The local Sheriff was a good guy and had approved Walt's concealed Carry permit but the District Attorney was up for re-election and nobody could guess how he might react. One thing was for sure, after last night there were seven less bad dudes in the neighborhood, and that was alright with Walt.

The next day Walt was called into the Sheriff's department to give his formal statement and answer a few questions. The Sheriff's Office had been moved a few years ago near the Fairgrounds and was no longer located in downtown Sandpoint by the Court House so he didn't need to use a detour to reach it.

It didn't take too long to give his statement or answer questions. They did have questions about the explosive birdhouses and the District Attorney was not happy about this. But when the Sheriff pointed out that Walt had been attacked by eight armed men at his home in the middle of the night, the DA knew that no jury would convict him anyway. By then the ballistics tests had been done on Walt's guns and they were returned to him that day.

To get home Walt had to drive past the Box Mart store and could see by the empty parking lot that they were still closed. When he got to Highway 200 intersection he turned right instead of left to see if the gas station was open. It was closed as well so Walt turned around and went home.

When he got home the let Sparky out back and placed his rifle and shotgun on the kitchen table. He strapped on his fanny pack holding the Ruger LCR .357 and went outside to bring in some wood. Then he filled his generator with gas and started it to charge his battery bank. After checking his security cameras he saw that he had no new visitors while he was gone.

He went outside and got a ladder from the garage and took down two of his bird houses out front and put them up where the two that had been detonated had been before. Then he put his ladder back in the garage and took a close look at his shooting bench where he counted sixteen bullet holes in the plywood. That was amazing. He would have been hit or likely killed if the bench would not have been filled with sand. He was surprised the cops didn't dig out the slugs for evidence but apparently the security camera video was enough evidence for them.

Walt went inside and spread some newspaper on the kitchen table and got his gun cleaning supplies and cleaned each weapon thoroughly and gave them a light coat of oil. He took them out to the shooting bench, reloaded them both and put them back in the hidden compartment. After picking up the kitchen table and putting his cleaning supplies away he took Sparky for a quick walk down to the mailbox.

He didn't expect to have any mail yet but he wanted to walk past the tire shredder and mentally thank it for its service. When they got back to the cabin he let the generator run for another hour until the battery bank had been topped off. When they got back inside Walt took his fanny pack off and took another look at the bullet holes in the walls. Each had hit an interior wood covered wall and gone through to the other side and were lodged into the log wall. Walt couldn't think of a good way to patch these so he decided that he would hang a few pictures and a calendar to cover them up.

The last bit of snow was in his ice chest so Walt put a couple of beers inside since he didn't know when he would have cold beer again. While the beer was cooling he made some canned chili for lunch but this time Sparky was out of luck since chili wasn't good for dogs. After he finished the chili Walt sat back in his chair to enjoy his beer and ponder what had happened in the last few days. After his second beer he decided that he was ready for round two, if there was one. Just then the phone rang and it was Chip. "Walt I wanted to tell you that we found the guy that got away in the ATV, when they tried to serve the warrant, he opened fire and wounded one of the deputies and the bad guy was killed in the gunfight. When they searched his home they found that he had been trying to tear down a marijuana growing operation. We checked his phone and he couldn't have called anyone because the cell tower is still down. The detectives will be looking at his phone log to see if there any more Batmen in the area and to see who his contacts are. Just wanted to let you know."

Walt was relieved that he didn't have to worry about a lone wolf seeking revenge for his pals. "Sorry to hear about the deputy but I am really glad to hear about the news about taking down the grow room."

"We don't know for sure but I don't think there are any more Batmen. We think it was only a local club. The gang unit is still trying to figure this out."

"That's great. I gave my statement this morning and got my guns back. The DA was upset about the birdhouses but the

Sheriff talked him down so I am just having a couple of beers and relaxing at the moment."

"OK, sounds good, just wanted to let you know. I have got to get back to work now. Talk to you later."

"Thanks for calling." Walt hung up the phone. That was good news, and cause for celebration, but he had already had his two beer limit for the day. He decided that he would still be vigilant. Just because there were no more Batmen on the Creek didn't mean that some of their friends wouldn't try to make him pay.

Walt turned on the radio just in time to hear the local news. "The Sheriff has reported an attempted home invasion up Rapid Lightning Creek Road. Seven armed men were killed and the homeowner is OK. More information will follow when the investigation is complete and no charges are expected." Walt was pleased they didn't mention his name or address. "In other news the Federal Government had announced that tax payments and reports normally due on April 15 are now not due until August 15." That's decent of them since they don't even have office space yet and can't pay people their social security or retirement checks. Walt just shook his head. "And finally bread lines and food riots have been reported in many major cities. See video coverage on our affiliate TV stations or their websites." Well, Walt thought, at least they saved the best story for last. Walt tuned to the classic rock station and kept the radio on for awhile longer.

Overall Walt was pleased with the effort he had put in regarding home security but one thing that could be improved would be to put his electric fence charger and timer on a battery so that it would work during a power outage, he had a spare battery that he could use but he didn't have a 12 volt timer. Also if he did this he would either have to remember to charge the battery regularly or install a small solar cell. Since he didn't have the timer or solar cell, he put this on his list for later.

The next morning Walt looked out the window and saw that the skies were still dark and cloudy. The lack of sunshine has been known to affect people's mental health and maybe this explained much of the public's malaise. Sure there was lots to feel bad about lately but the lack of sunshine didn't help. Like the old saying, this isn't hell but you can see it from here. Just thinking of this made him smile and feel better. His batteries were fully charged and so was he. Walt was ready for a new day. He knew that people would be asking him about the shooting and he wasn't sure what he would say or how he would react. One thing was for sure, he didn't feel badly about it. Some bad men came to his home in the middle of the night and they got what they deserved. At least the taxpayers were not stuck with feeding pond scum like this. Rush Limbaugh used to use the term human debris and this described them perfectly.

Sparky was eager to go outside and she was even more eager to come inside because she knew her chow was waiting. She didn't show any bad affects from being locked in the bathroom while all the shooting was going on. Maybe dogs were better at forgetting and forgiveness than people, Walt didn't know. He did know that if people in general were as good as dogs, the world would be a better place to live. He had always wondered if she would be happier if she had another dog to play with or if she would resent having to share his time and attention. If he got another pup she could show him the ropes, he wasn't sure if this was a good idea or not.

For breakfast Walt thought that pancakes would be a good change of pace. They were easy to make and good to eat. Besides he had lots of pancake mix and syrup on hand so he heated up the cast iron pan on the propane camp stove and made a regular international house of pancakes breakfast. One thing he couldn't tell Sparky is that pancakes were bad for dogs. Syrup maybe, but not a silver dollar size pancake.

After breakfast and his third cup of coffee Walt got on the internet and emailed his out of area radio friends about what happened with the Batmen. He didn't want to give details about this over the radio and he knew that they would want to know. He sent another email to the CB net group mentioning

248

that he had some trouble with the Batmen but that he and Sparky were fine. He reminded everyone that the reason he had survived was that he was prepared and encouraged others to do the same. Have a plan and be prepared ahead of time, that was his advice.

He had some more web work to do for the Pacific Northwest Remote Viewers and for the toymakers as well. This would take his mind off recent events and he could always use the extra money. Since he was thinking of money, Walt thought that it would be a good idea to take Sparky down by the creek to see how high the water was and if it was covering the sandbar or not. The water wasn't that high yet so he knew the big melt had not started. It would probably be another month or two before he could get his truck to the sandbar, but he wasn't concerned, just curious. His gold wasn't going anywhere.

He did see evidence that some critters had been feeding on the dead fish and mostly they had cleaned things up pretty well. The ground was beginning to thaw and it would be interesting to see if this would be a bad mud season or not. In some years you could walk and the ground ahead of you would ripple as you stepped on it. In other years the mud was not much of a problem at all. During spring break up the highway department would post signs restricting heavy truck traffic and limiting speed limits to 35 mph.

Walt guessed that this would be done soon because of the earthquake regardless of the mud. Mud season was tough on people who lived off of the county road. Many would park their cars and walk home so they didn't rut up their roads and driveways. Some people would block the roads so that UPS and FedEx didn't cause ruts in the roads but that would probably not be an issue this year since so much of the Sandpoint area was closed already.

One thing Walt could do this time of year was to spread some of the processed sand that he had stored in his woodshed. He hauled this out in buckets to the parking area and dumped in piles and then spread it with a rake. This made room for the new sandbar material, covered up the blood stains, and leveled out the area as well.

Another thing he could do in the next few days was to walk the property and look for down trees and mushrooms. It was probably to early for morels but it never hurt to be on the look out for this annual delicacy. Morels were the only kind of wild mushroom Walt ate because they were easy to identify and wonderful to eat, especially when fried in butter. They could be found in a variety of wooded environments and especially liked to grow in an area after it has been burned. During prime mushroom season bands of pickers would scour the hills and forests collecting morels by the truckload and selling them to local stores. Usually these would be three to five inches tall but sometimes they would be much larger. After late June the season was over except at high altitudes where it was a little cooler.

Knowing where the dead trees were down ahead of time made collecting firewood a little easier. Some years Walt cut all of his wood but most years he bought a load of wood or two to supplement the wood he collected on his property. Running out of firewood was a greenhorn mistake and most people only had to do this once before they learned their lesson. Cutting and collecting firewood was a lot more pleasant when it was T-shirt weather and the wood was dry.

Walt was not a wood snob, he burned anything that he could find. Some people would only burn Tamarack or Birch and would laugh at the idea of burning white fir, cottonwood, and less desirable species. But part of the idea of cutting your own wood was sound property management and fire protection so it made sense to cut anything that needed to be cut.

If you lived in the woods it was important to have a reliable chain saw whether you cut your own wood or not. Otherwise a windstorm could knock down trees so that you couldn't get to town, or if needed, help like fire trucks and ambulances could not get to you.

After supper Walt turned on the CB radio to see if anyone was on. It wasn't Sunday so there was no scheduled net but maybe some people would be on the radio. He gave out a call,

"This is Walt, is there anyone listening tonight? Over."

"Hey Walt, this is Chip, just got home from work. How are you doing tonight?"

"Sparky and I are doing well. Got caught up on my chores and my sleep. Over."

"Roger that. Not a lot new going on in town. Still haven't heard anything about the roads or power. Over."

"When I went to town I saw that the gas station was still closed. Where do you get gas?"

"We have our own pumps at the Sheriff's office so this isn't a problem. Over."

"That makes sense. How about you? Are things slowing down a little?"

"Not busy for me today but the other guys had some calls."

"Yes OK, I haven't listened to the scanner lately. In fact I haven't been on the radio at all. I could use a day chasing some DX if the bands are is in good shape,"

"I heard the propagation report and 20 and up sounded like they would be pretty good for the next few days."

"That's good news. I was thinking of trying some QRP with the hexbeam."

"Good idea. The hexbeam can make up for the lack of power in those peanut whistle radios."

"Roger that. I know that Tony is really anxious to get his call signs. I hope he gets it soon."

"I am sure he understands why this is taking a little longer but it still must be frustrating. I remember when you had to go to an FCC office to take the tests. Over."

"Me too. How would you like to drive four hours just to take the test? That must have been awful, especially if you didn't pass."

"Well at least they make it easier now with no code test and giving you all the questions and all of the answers in the study guides."

"The only reason I got my extra class is that they no longer required 20 words per minute for a code test. I passed it at 13 wpm and that was enough for me."

"I know what you mean. That's why lots of people never went beyond CB."

"You got that right. But a lot of hams got their start on CB as well."

"I know that I did. Have you heard channel 6 lately?"

"I sure have. They call it the super bowl with lots of guys running extremely high power and shooting skip. Over."

"I just heard about that the other day. Somebody told me that the FCC was looking for a guy who supposedly was running 50,000 watts."

"Amazing. I would hate to pay his electric bill. They'll catch him someday if he keeps it up."

"I am surprised his neighbors don't turn him in."

"Know what you mean. If people still had analog TVs he would be making a lot of enemies."

"That's for sure." Walt could not imagine that much power. Most AM radio stations don't use that much power except for the clear channel stations.

"Hi guys this is Tony. Over."

"Walt responded, Hey Chip do you know what they call a new ham?"

"Let me guess, how about a piglet?"

"Very funny. Anyway how are you two doing?" Tony asked.

Good answer Chip. I am doing fine. What are you up to?" Walt asked.

"I heard you both and just wanted to tell you how cool it is to listen to some of the Hams. Over."

"Tony this is Chip. You are really going to have fun with this. If you ever can't sleep get up and listen to the Ham bands. You'll hear stations from all over the world."

"Chip is right Tony. Not only is the propagation better, but more DX stations are on at night over here because it is daytime over there." Walt wanted Tony to understand this.

"I never thought it much but this makes sense, more people are operating during the day," Tony realized that when it was noon in London it was only 4 am here.

"Another thing you will find is that sometimes 20, 17. and 15 meters can stay open much later than normal so it's worth it to check those bands out even if you think they are closed." Walt added.

"One thing I do Tony is to listen to channel 6 and a few others channels on the CB. If you hear stations from far away, that means that 10 meters is probably open as well." Chip told him. Old hams are always trying to help new hams.

"That's a good point Chip. I should do that more often myself." Walt agreed that this was a good tip.

"Hey Guys this is Mary."

"Go ahead Mary, this is Walt."

"I just wanted to thank Tony for loaning Beth and I the study manuals. We just started but the manuals are pretty thorough and I'm sure this will be fun. Over."

"Your welcome Mary, Sherri and I are glad we could help. At least we have two hams who can answer our questions."

"Elmer One and Elmer two, right Chip?" An Elmer is an experienced ham that helps a new ham learn the ropes.

"That's right Walt. I remember when I was just starting out. Like they say, there is no such thing as a stupid question. Go ahead Mary."

"That's great. I'm sure we'll have a lot of them. When we get closer to taking the tests we'll get some advice about what kind of radio to start out with. Over."

Walt couldn't help himself, "There is an old adage that says if you have $500 to spend, spend $400 on antennas and $100 on a radio. It sounds silly but it is true. You can get a lot farther with a low power radio and a good antenna than you can with a lousy antenna and a more powerful radio,"

"Very true. A lot of hams don't understand this. They think all that matters is more power." Chip wanted to emphasize the point.

"Oh Chip, I wanted to ask you about the Airstream down at the falls. Is it legal to camp down there?"

"I don't know, I'll look into it." Chip had seen the trailer but didn't know anything about it.

The falls was a local treasure about 3 miles up the road from the Country Store. All you could see from the road was a small parking area. If you just drove past this, you would have no idea what was only a few feet away. A small and steep footpath took you down to Rapid Lightning Creek where there was a beautiful waterfall and a nice big bowl of water below the falls. It was a favorite swimming hole on a hot day and many fishermen tried their luck there as well. If you were lucky in the spring you could watch the fish try to migrate up the creek and jump the falls in order to get farther up stream. When you were at the creek all you could hear was rushing water. Both sides along the creek were rocky and steep. Even though it was in the northwest it reminded people of a movie set with Tarzan standing on the cliff, ready to dive into the water below.

"We love the falls too. It's a great place to cool off on a hot summer day. I hope they don't stay long." Mary remarked.

"It's not that they are camping that bothers me," Tony said, "It is that they look like they are moving in and blocking everyone else from enjoying the falls."

"I know what you mean Tony. We just wanted to say Hi to everyone, I guess Beth and I will sign out." Mary was glad to talk with the guys.

"OK Mary. Sherri and I are out of here too. Good night everyone.

"Me too. I have to get some dinner. See you all later." Chip replied.

"OK, sounds good fun to talk with you all. Have a good evening. I am out of here to. 73." Walt signed off and turned off his CB. It was just in time for the news as Walt turned on his portable radio.

"National and Local News Headlines are brought to you this evening by Traders Realtors in downtown Sandpoint. 1.The State of Texas has announced that it is considering

254

withdrawing from the Union because of the total lack of federal help in securing the southern border. 2. A record number of drug overdose deaths have been seen over Spring Break. The DEA says the majority of deaths are caused by Fentanyl coming across the border from Mexico. 3. The Joe Bama administration has signed an executive order canceling all student loan debt."

"Now for Local News Headlines. 1.The Bonner County Sheriff has broken up a marijuana grow operation in the Rapid Lightning area. The suspect opened fire on police and has been killed and a deputy was injured in the raid. 2. A mass exodus of people are fleeing many major cities across the U.S. but so far, Sandpoint has been spared because road access has been closed due to earthquake damage. 3. Bonner County Road Limits are now in effect. We return to our regularly scheduled programming."

Walt loved his radios but lately he had been addicted to the news. And there seemed to a lot more bad news than good news, especially lately. He had heard the phrase, "If it bleeds, it leads," referring to the news business and this was certainly true. That was one nice thing about ham radio, you heard a lot of good stories and not a lot of bad news. He knew a few people who had totally disconnected. They stopped using their radios and stopped using the internet. Although he could never do this there was something to be said for the idea that ignorance is bliss.

Walt let Sparky out one more time for the night and went to bed It rained hard that night and the sounds of the rain on his metal roof made him fall asleep quickly. In the morning he woke up and Sparky was still sleeping. She was sleeping so soundly that she didn't hear Walt get up. When he looked in at her she was sleeping on her back and Walt thought that she looked like she was having a wonderful dream. When she realized he was staring at her she rolled over, got up on her feet, and was all hugs and kisses, a regular wiggle butt.

After breakfast Walt got the radio and waited to see who would be the first to come on. After 10 minutes or so he heard a voice, " This is AM7DX, is there anybody on frequency?"

Walt brought the desktop microphone closer to him, pushed the transmit bar and said, "Hey Jeff, this is AP7ZMT. Good signal this morning."

"Roger, I have you about an S7. It didn't freeze hear but rained most of the night. How about you?"

"We had a hard rain last night. No idea how much for sure but it must have been at least 1/4 of an inch. 38 degrees right now. Over."

"OK, got your email. Sounds pretty exciting. Over."

"No doubt about that. I've got some bullet holes in my door to prove it."

"Roger that. It sounds like you were pretty well prepared. Over." (AM7DX)

"That sounds too close for me." (AU7PM)

"Roger that Frank. The driveway alarm more than paid for itself." (AP7ZMT)

"Did they haul you down to the station? Are you facing any charges?" (AM7DX)

"I had to go in later but no charges were filed and I got my guns back already." (AP7ZMT)

"You are lucky that you live in Idaho. They only put the good guys in jail here in Washington. AU7PM."

"One of the neighbors is also a deputy. That helped a lot. They knew no jury would convict me anyway." (AP7ZMT)

"Sounds like you were ready for them. Would have made a good movie. Morning guys. AY7OM."

"I have some pretty good video from the security cameras but it doesn't have any audio or background music." (AP7ZMT)

"Things are getting pretty crazy over here too. I don't even want to think about going to town." (AU7PM)

"I know what you mean. We're getting lots of campers over here." (AY7OM)

"That's a high class word for homeless people isn't it? (AM7DX)

"I think you are right Jeff. It wasn't a problem here until lately. AP7ZMT"

"You can't blame people for not wanting to be around crime." (AU7PM)

"Do you have power yet Walt?"

"No power or cell service yet Ray. There are some detours so that people can get to town but the stores aren't open."

"Remember when people made fun of preppers? I'll bet a whole lot of people will be getting into it now."(AM7DX)

"It will be a lot harder and more expensive than it used to be, that's for sure." (AY7OM)

"Did anybody check the bands out this morning?' (AU7PM)

"I was on 17 meters till a few minutes ago. I heard England, Germany, and Italy. Made a short SSB contact with France. AR7QRN.

"Morning Dennis, I should get on and start working some DX. Haven't done that in awhile. AP7ZMT."

"I worked South Africa yesterday morning on 15 meter CW." (AP7PM)

"It's nice to know that the bands are coming back. AY7OM."

"I worked a couple stations on 10 meters yesterday afternoon. One was in Texas and the other guy was in Florida." (AR7QRN)

"Wasn't it nice not to have to pay our taxes for another few months?" (AM7DX)

" Can you imagine getting a pass on your student loan debt? Some of those people saved a couple hundred thousand dollars."

"And not one of those bastards will thank us for it either. What do you think?" (AP7ZMT)

"It's kind of hard to pay it back when you can't even get a job flipping burgers." (AM7DX)

"Well if they would take off their nose ring and show up on time I'll bet they could get a job. Over." (AY7OM)

"Why get a job when you can stay in Daddy's basement for free? Over." (AM7DX)

"It sounds like another vote buying scheme to me. AU7PM."

"No doubt about it. Did anyone hear his speech the other night?" (AY7OM)

"There must be something wrong with him telling people that their kids would foot the bill anyway. Over." (AR7QRN)

"I liked the part about the Windy City. AP7ZMT."

"I liked the fact that he couldn't remember the name of his own secretary of defense." (AM7DX)

"You would fail a debate class if you looked at your notes that many times. Over." (AY7OM)

"Like I have said before we would be better off picking somebody out of the phone book. Over." (AR7QRN)

"Did you hear the report that the Government knew the voting machines could be hacked as early as 2018? Nothing to see here folks. AU7PM."

"You're right Frank, if they don't fix the voting machines we will never have another fair election. AY7OM."

"That's the problem, the voting machines are already fixed. AM7DX."

"What if voting was like buying a fishing license? You buy a lifetime license and never have to vote again?" (AR7QRN)

"They would like that. It's getting too crazy for me this morning. It's always fun. See you guys later. 73. This AP7ZMT clear."

They all wished Walt well and continued solving the world's problems. Walt turned off his radio. At least nobody pressed him for details about the shooting over the air. There was no reason to broadcast this for everyone to hear.

That afternoon Walt and all the members of the Rapid Lightning Creek CB Net were sent the following email from Chip. "I told you that I would check into what was going on with the Airstream trailer parked at the falls. The people who are staying there say that they have just purchased the property and that they will be staying by the road until they can access the rest of the property on the other side of Rapid Lightning Creek. This got me to ask some questions about the law.

If your property is not posted with No Trespassing signs the police cannot remove squatters. This would have to be done by court order and the process can take months or even years. If a squatter remains on your property long enough they can gain ownership of the property by filing for adverse possession.

One example that occurs in this area is with respect to access. Lets say that you grant someone the use of a road through your property to access their property. If they continuously access their property through your property they can eventually get legal access to use the road through your property (without your permission) and if they sell their property, the access through your property would transfer as an easement to the new owners. The only way to prevent this is to block the road once a year and document this with pictures that this has been done.

The bottom line is that if you expect the Sheriffs Department to help you evict squatters without going to court you must post No Trespassing signs on your property. I am not an expert but this is what I was told about the law. I hope this helps. Chip."

When Walt got Chip's email he wished that he had bought a couple of No trespassing signs when he had the chance. Until he could get some metal signs, he decided to make his own. He looked at several styles on line. Some read, "No Trespassing" in bold black type with red colored bars above and below the letters. Others read, "No Trespassing – Violators will be Prosecuted." Most were the size of a piece of paper and some were a little smaller. Walt took a screen shot of the one he liked the best and enlarged it in Photoshop and printed this on gloss photo paper. Then he put his homemade sign in a clear plastic sleeve put some stiff cardboard in back of the sign to make it more rigid. He knew this wouldn't hold up outdoors because the colors would fade but when needed, he could always make some new signs. He put one half way up his driveway and another on the entrance to his parking area.

He got an email that evening addressed to the group from Stan and Nancy. They said that they knew the woman who owned the property at the Falls and they would try to contact her to see if she had sold the property or not. The last time they saw her she was adamant about not ever selling and wanting to ensure that people could access the Falls without restrictions. Most of her property was on the other side of the river anyway and she had talked about the idea of donating this to Idaho Fish and Game when she passed.

Walt thought this would be interesting to find out if she had sold the property or not since, at least at one time, had strong feelings about not selling and allowing the public to access the Falls.

The next day, as he was making lunch, Walt heard the driveway announcer alarm. A minute later a small Ford pick up truck pulled into his yard. An overweight younger man got out of the truck and Walt and Sparky went out to meet him,

She was barking at the man when he asked Walt, "I left my tree stand up here somewhere and I wondered if you had seen it?"

Walt was shocked. This kid put up a tree stand on his property and had the nerve to ask about it. Sparky was still barking when Walt replied, "I found your illegal tree stand and got rid of it. Are you ignorant, stupid, or what?"

The man stepped up to Walt and said, "I didn't know it was private property and I want my tree stand back." When Sparky saw the man had got within a couple of feet of Walt she was having a fit.

"You can get back in your truck and get the hell out of here," Walt shouted. Just then Sparky tried to get between them barking louder than ever. The man kicked Sparky and she went flying and crying at the same time.

Without hesitation Walt waived his left hand out and near the man's face to distract him and Walt delivered a powerful web hand knife strike to and through the man's throat and knocked him flat on his ass.

Walt had taken some Aikido a few years back, This is a Japanese soft martial art that teaches mostly defensive hand to hand techniques. Walt hadn't been in the dojo for years and had forgotten much of what he learned. The throat strike is often taught in jujitsu and other martial arts as well. The problem with it is that most people think that a simple strike to the throat will bring a man to his knees. Like a kick to the groin, sometimes it does and sometimes it doesn't.

One problem with a throat strike is that once a confrontation begins, most people naturally put their head down and try to protect their throats using their chin. Walt had learned that the best way to use this technique was to strike first before the opponent could prepare himself. The other thing that made the web hand throat strike effective was the follow through.

With your strong side hand at your side, the hand is spread like getting ready to draw a pistol in a western movie. Then the hand is brought up on a diagonal toward the throat, rotated 90 degrees toward the inside, and then the throat is struck with web part of the hand between the fingers and the thumb. This makes it easier to get your hand under his chin and on his throat as if you were trying to choke him. But it is not enough to just hit the throat, you must step into and past him as you strike, and throw the web hand through his throat. When done properly, this will bring any man to the ground. Even if the strike misses the throat and hit the chin, face, or, forehead, if done with a good follow through, this would still put a man on his butt.

Unless a man is as hard as nails, he will usually be choking, coughing, and in so much pain that he does not want to fight anymore. But if someone who is a trained fighter or high on drugs may attempt to get up off the ground and continue to fight,

When the man was on the ground, he was choking and attempting to get up. Sparky was back and barking wildly in his face. Walt stood over him and waived his pointed finger as if scolding him and shouted, "Don't get up, I've got the feeling

261

that you have never been in a dojo. If you do get up, I'll put you in the hospital."

The man was startled and considered that even though Walt was older, his military hand to hand experience might be too much for him. Walt stepped back and never took his eyes off him until he put Sparky back in the house. He then walked up to the man still on the ground and said, "OK Soy Boy, back in your truck." He pointed to his security cameras and said, " I've got your picture and I have your license plate. If there is any more trouble of any kind, me and my friends will come looking for you. Now get out and don't come back or I'll have you arrested for trespassing."

The man got in his truck and went back down the driveway. Walt went back inside to make sure Sparky was OK and she didn't seem to have anything hurt but her pride from being kicked.

The man had made a terrible mistake by kicking Sparky. One thing Walt couldn't tolerate was people who were cruel to animals or children. In his view they didn't deserve to live. Walt was glad that he hadn't pointed his pistol or threatened the man with his gun. If he complained to the Sheriff, Walt's security video would prove that no weapon was used and no jury would convict a man defending his dog from a bully.

In a way Walt wished the man would have gotten up and continued the fight. He still wished he could take some teeth well after the man was gone. Anyone who harmed Sparky would have hell to pay, and then some. Walt went in to finish his lunch and Sparky was close by to see if he dropped anything.

It was a little too early to harvest sand from the sandbar but Walt got a crazy idea. He has seen a landscaper pick up rocks that had been thrown on a lawn by a snow blower with a shop vacuum. He wondered if a shop vac would pick up rocks, why wouldn't it pick up ash? The only problem of course was that he would need to use his generator and a 100 foot extension cord. There was plenty of ash near the porch that he could reach with his extension cord so he decided to give this a try. It worked really well and in a very short time his shop vacuum was so heavy with ash, he could hardly lift it.

Walt emptied the shop vacuum into 5 gallon buckets and filled up the shop vacuum one more time. Then he set up his automatic gold panning machine and processed the ash for the rest of the afternoon. As before, he did recover a little gold but he did not bother to weigh it.

This was great, Walt thought, since he could make money at home while waiting for his retirement checks to resume. He did feel a little guilty about this but he had decided that keeping his mouth shut was the still the best choice. After all, a fisherman doesn't tell everyone where his best fishing hole was or it wouldn't be a good fishing hole any longer. The same was true for hunting, mushroom collecting, and firewood gathering. There are some things a man should keep to himself.

Walt picked up his gold panning equipment and cleaned up the living room. He took the processed ash and spread it lightly across the parking area. If he kept processing ash he would need to find a better spot to put the ash that was already processed. He put his shop vacuum and extension cord away topped off the generator with gas so that it would be ready to go when he needed it.

It was still early enough in the afternoon so he took Sparky for a quick walk up the road to make her feel better about the way that she had been mistreated. She didn't show any signs of being sore and Walt was happy about that. One thing about dogs, they were tough. If people were as tough as dogs they would be a lot better off.

Walt thought that he should celebrate having thought to use the shop vacuum so he tried to make a really good idea. He decided on fried spam and rice with some canned peaches on the side. Sparky knew she didn't stand a chance of getting any of this for dinner so she just laid down under the table while Walt had supper. She knew that he was enjoying his chow because he never stopped eating until his plate was empty.

It was Saturday night and Walt didn't feel like getting on the radio or watching YouTube videos online. Instead he found an old radio program, Radio Mystery Theater, being broadcast on AM station KSL out of Salt Lake Utah. This show usually calmed him down and got him relaxed enough to go to bed.

Walt always had plans on Sunday. In the afternoon he liked to listen to the Alex Jones Sunday show on 9.350 Mhz. Even though it was only a two hour show it summarized what he had been reporting in more detail the week before. In fact, it was the only news show that he both listened to and also bothered to take notes. Alex had good sources for his stories and seemed to not get sidetracked with small distractions and was always looking at/the bigger picture. And unlike other hosts, if he was wrong he would freely admit it. The world was lucky to have him. This weeks show concentrated on the Big Pharma companies that hid test data concerning the effectiveness and safety of their Covid vaccines. He also did stories that day about how only a handful of people controlled 90% of the media news in the United States and how big tech and social media companies had influenced our elections. On that note he pointed out that our government knew as early as 2016 that the voting machines could be easily compromised online but did nothing about it.

When the Sunday show was over at 4 pm Walt only had a couple of hours to take care of Sparky and make supper before it was time for the Rapid Lightning Creek CB net.

Walt turned on his CB at 6:10 pm and began taking check-ins soon after that. By 6:25 pm everyone was checked in and Walt opened the net. "Once again I would like to thank you all for checking in tonight. From what I have heard we may be seeing some light at the end of the tunnel soon. Let's see we'll get started with Mary and Beth, then go to Tom, and next to Peter, then Bret, then Chip then Susan, Stan and Gloria, Steve, Tony and Sherri, Jane, Jim, Fly Boy, Scott, Robert and Nancy, Charles and Megan,then back to me. Go ahead Mary and Beth,"

"Hello everyone. We don't have much news over here. We have just started studying for our ham tests and are looking forward to taking the exam. We haven't studied for a test in years. Over to Tom"

"I can only imagine what it would be like to study for a test. I haven't taken one in a long time myself. Not much new here except I saw a mosquito today and that must be a sure sign of spring. Up to Peter."

"I can't say I have seen one yet but the tree swallows are showing up everyday to survey the bugs. When there are enough of them they will start to nest. I love to watch them fly. Down to Bret."

"Not much new here either. I sure hope the power comes back soon. Can't tell you how much I miss having it and I know you do too. Over to Chip."

"Amen on the power Bret. I have some news for you. I just heard that the Washington State Police busted the gang that has been hitting small stores like our Country Store. They have been advertising their stolen food items on Craig's List. Thought you would want to know. Over to Susan."

"That is good news. I am sure the people at the Country Store are happy to think that this bunch will be behind bars. When they stole from our store they stole from all of us. Up to Stan."

"That's for sure Susan, That's why they haven't been open. We have some news about the squatter. We talked to the owner and she did not sell her Property at the Falls and will be contacting the Sheriffs department to see what can be done. She wants the Falls to be enjoyed by everyone. Over Steve."

"I guess you can camp anywhere you like until someone throws you off. Some people have a lot of nerve. I hope they take their trash with them when they leave. I am betting that they have California plates on their Airstream trailer but you can't see the plates from the road. Over to Tony."

"That is good news. The thought of not being able to go down to the Falls was a real bummer. It's always a treat on a hot summer day. Still haven't got our ham calls yet but glad you are having fun studying for the test Mary. Down to you Jane."

"Speaking of Craig's List I saw a local listing advertising solar cells for sale. It didn't mention how many he had but I think I will give them a call. I'll let you know what I find out. Up to Jim."

"I've got some news. I drove by the Country Store today and saw that they were open, and hoping, for business. That should make a lot of people happy. I am low on gas and propane. Up to Fly Boy."

"That's great. I heard that the Farm Store was going to be open tomorrow. They brought in a big generator to run the store and they have baby chicks for sale. Over to Scott."

"Yes I'll bet they had to open when the chicks arrived. Just wanted to remind everyone that Fishing Season Starts on Saturday in case you need to get a license. And if you don't have a license, Free Fishing Day is the Saturday after that. Up to Robert and Nancy.

"Thanks for the reminder. I'll pick up a license at the store. Hopefully the bear have left a few fish for the rest of us. I can't believe it is almost May. Time flies when your having fun. It will be nice when we don't have to make a fire in the mornings. Down to you Charles and Megan."

"Thanks for the reminder about the fishing season Tom. And great news about the Country Store being open too. I'll bet that a lot of people will be buying chicks this year. I'll bet they sell out soon. I have thought about this too but until the power comes on I wouldn't be able to deal with baby chicks. They need heat until they get some feathers. Over to Mary and Beth."

"That's true, they also need chick feed. I hope the Farm Store has plenty of that. We have thought about getting some laying hens but we're not ready to deal with chicks either. Go ahead Tom."

"I think it may be hard to find laying hens this year. You might have to start with chicks. You know it wasn't too long ago that you could buy baby chicks and have them delivered by the Post Office. The trouble was that they would often remove the cardboard box tops to give the chicks air in the Post office.

Then some would jump out and end up going back into other boxes so you couldn't be sure about what kind of chickens you really had until they were a little older. Over to Peter."

"That's funny Tom. I can see that this would be a problem. I have thought about getting some meat birds like Cornish Cross for the freezer but with the power going out all the time this doesn't seem practical. Over to Bret."

"I would rather have some baby ducks. They are so cool. I am sure that if I did they would all be pets anyway. Same thing with rabbits. I know they are a good source of meat but I like bunnies too much to even think about it. Over to Chip."

"I am too busy to do anything like that but if you had the time it would be a good idea. Oh I just heard that most of the main roads will be open tomorrow but the side roads will still have weight restrictions. Over to Susan."

"That will be great to see the roads and some of the stores open up again. I just remembered that our State Property taxes are due in June. I hope the government checks get here by then. Up to Stan and Gloria."

"That's what it is going to take to get the economy open, that's for sure. We stayed with some folks for a couple of days who had baby chicks in the house. They never sleep and let me tell you, you can't either. Boy do they make a racket. Down to Steve."

"I'll bet that was exciting. It's almost time to start thinking about a garden but it's too late to start most plants from seed. It's a lot cheaper that way. Over to Tony."

"That's for sure. Sherri starts a lot of things from seeds in March but we don't dare put them outside until Memorial Day. This year it might be a lot later than that. Go ahead Jane."

"I wonder how they are doing down at the greenhouses on Selle Road? I'll bet they spent a fortune trying to keep them heated this year. I usually get my garden plants and a few flowers there every year. Over to Jim."

"I don't know how they are doing but I did drive by a week ago and they looked like they were open. I don't know if you have bought any seeds lately but some only have a dozen tiny seeds in a pack. Up to Fly Boy."

"Lately everything is that way. Cereal boxes are about the same size as they have always been but there is not as much in inside. They must think we are all stupid. Over to you Scott."

"Has anyone noticed the price of propane lately. What used to cost a little more than $3 here now costs $9 and in Europe the same amount costs $27! Makes you think twice about using the Bar-B-Q. Over to Robert and Nancy."

"That is outrageous. We haven't bought any since last fall. That Green New Deal sure is something. Over to Charles and Megan."

"You mean the new raw deal don't you? We haven't bought any lately either. Makes our wood heat look like a better choice all the time. What we really need in this country are more windmills and solar cells. Of course they only work if the wind is blowing and the sun is shining. Go ahead Walt."

"I agree Charles, more windmills, solar farms, and lots more laws will fix everything. Maybe if we repealed the law of gravity things would fall up instead of down. Anyway it's been fun and I have learned a lot tonight. Want to thanks everyone for not blabbing about what happened at my place all over the airwaves. And it sounds like things are looking up. Thanks again for checking in and thanks Stan for calling the owner about the situation at the Falls. I'll say 73 and catch you all later. This is Walt and I'll be clear.

Walt didn't leave his radio on to see if some of the others chose to stay a little longer and visit. He let Sparky out one more time before bed and installed the light shades in all the windows and thought that he would get some sleep.

Chapter 8. May

"Here comes the sun, and I say it's all right
Little darling, the smiles returning to the faces
Little darling, it feels like years since it's been here
Here comes the sun do, do, do"
The Beatles

When Walt woke up late even though he had gone to bed early. He looked out the window and it literally was a new month and a new day. The dark clouds were gone and it was too early to tell for sure but it looked like they were going to see some blue sky for the first time in months. Walt let Sparky out and pulled the light shades from the rest of the windows.

When Sparky came inside, she was ready for chow and so was Walt. He made some mashed potatoes from a box and then fried them with some cubes of Spam. A few cups of coffee later he complimented himself on a tasty breakfast creation. Not bad for a prepper with no refrigeration, he thought. Then he saw the strange light in the sky. It wasn't a UFO, it was the sun, rising and blessing everything that it touched with bright yellow light and penetrating warmth.

Walt wasn't a particularly religious man but he certainly believed in God. At that moment he held his hands together and prayed for the first time in years. He thanked God for helping him and Sparky to get through the last few months and especially for the blue sky and yellow sun. If this wasn't a sign from Heaven after all he had been through, he didn't know what was. He was sure that everyone who could see this felt exactly the same way. This would be a May Day for the record books. The times, they were a changing as the old song said.

Finally the solar cells people had in their yards were beginning to earn their keep and this first dose of sunshine was a better mood lifter than any drug could ever be. At this point he would not have been surprised to see Jesus descend from the sky and come to rescue mankind. The last few months had been as close to hell as he ever wanted to be. Hallelujah the sky is clear and sunshine has returned to Idahome. It was better than hitting the lottery. What could be better than this?

The next day Walt got another surprise when the power came on. This was great news to be sure. He plugged in the refrigerator and put his well and inverter back to grid power. He set the timer on his water heater and turned this on as well. He reset the clock on the electric stove and the microwave and also turned on his air cleaner that hadn't been run in months. Since he has no food on hand that required refrigeration, he put some jugs filled with water inside and filled his ice cube trays and put them in the freezer portion of the refrigerator. Then he remembered that he did have something he could put in the refrigerator, beer. So he brought up six of his prized bottles He decided that it was better to run the freezer than not run it so he added some water jugs to it as well.

Walt figured it would take 2 hours for his water heater to heat the water for a shower so he made a mental note of the time. Now that he had power, he started to pick up ash with the shop vacuum.. He was able to put about 6 or 7 gallons of ash in the woodshed so at least he was being somewhat productive. Just for fun he put a battery charger on the tractor since he hadn't run this in some time.

When Walt stepped in the shower he adjusted the temperature so that it wasn't too warm but the longer he showered, he increased the temperature a little at a time. When the hot water was about gone, Walt stepped out and felt like a new man. His hillbilly hot tub was great but it didn't compare to getting a hot shower anytime he liked. Sparky licked his legs as he was drying off and Walt reminded her that now, she could have a shower too. She must have understood him because she stopped licking his feet and laid down by the stove.

That evening Walt was able to make supper with his electric oven. This was quite a treat because up until now he would cook on his camp stove or occasionally on the Bar-B-Q. He boiled some noodles and made what resembled a lasagna with the limited ingredients on hand. He also baked some corn bread muffins so this was a nice change of pace.

Because the neighborhood had power, Walt decided that he no longer needed to put up his light shades. This made the cabin feel a little less like a cave and he liked being able to look out of the windows until it got dark. If the power grid didn't hold at least he had a hot shower and some baked muffins to be happy about.

Before he went to bed he turned on his computer and checked his email and then looked at his favorite news sites and a few YouTube videos as well. It sure was nice to do what he wanted without worrying about conserving power or counting electrons. Things were looking up.

The next morning he woke up and enjoyed being able to look out of the windows while still in bed. He could walk to the bathroom without a flashlight and didn't need to add water to the tank in order to flush the toilet. He took a look out the window and realized that he wasn't dreaming. The power was on and it looked like another clear day.

While making breakfast he was listening to the local news on the radio. They reported that mail delivery would begin again next week and asked people to meet the carrier at their mailbox, if possible because people would likely have more mail than would fit into the box. Walt thought this was great because now that the roads were open, and rural mail service was being resumed, he could order a few things online again.

After breakfast Walt thought that he would try something new. He had seen a YouTube video about making bread. He took some notes and thought that he would give it a try. It was a simple recipe and he has everything he needed. After he mixed the dough he put it in his a pan and let it rise.

While the dough was rising he got on his ham radio and thought that he would see what was happening on 20, 17, and 15 meters. The upper HF bands were not open yet so Walt went down to 40 meters. He heard Asia, Indonesia, and Hawaii coming in pretty well he waited for one of them to sign. The Hawaiian station cleared first and began calling, CQ, CQ. CQ.

CQ North America, this is AS6KY in Oahu, Hawaii calling CQ, and standing by."

Walt had already turned on his amplifier. "AS6KY this is AP7ZMT. Over."

"AP7ZMT, thanks for coming back you are 10 over 9 in Oahu this morning go ahead."

"AS6KY roger that you have a very strong signal here as well. I have you 15 over 9 into Sandpoint, Idaho. The name here is Walt. Over."

"OK Walt, my name is Philip and I am running a 7610 with about 900 watts into a butternut vertical. Over."

"I am running a 7300 into a 40 meter dipole with about 500 watts. I wanted to ask you how are things going in Hawaii since Kilauea? Over."

"I have friends on the Big Island and things are getting a little more back to normal now but I lost several family members. Over."

"Oh man, I know it was a bad one and it also affected Southern California as you know. But Oahu was spared. Is that right?" (AP7ZMT)

"Roger, the winds were on our favor up here. We've seen Kilauea blow before but nothing like this. Over." (AS6KY)

"Roger that, Are any tourists coming over now?

" We are just starting to get some tourists here and on some of the smaller islands but Hawaii had to rebuild the airport and there are a lot fewer hotels than there used to be. Over." (AS6KY)

"So if people aren't coming by air are they coming by boat? AP7ZMT."

"Roger, most of our tourists here now are from Japan and the Philippines. Over." (AS6KY)

"Roger, how has your weather been? Over" (AP7ZMT)

"We have had a pretty normal winter and spring here. The fishermen are not doing well. Over." (AS6KY)

"We saw the sun for the first time in over 3 months the other day. The volcano at Yellowstone really darkened the

272

skies for months. We got 3 inches of ash up here. Over."
(AP7ZMT)

"That was even bigger than Kilauea I think. AS6KY."

"I'm not sure, both were pretty bad. I think Kilauea might have had more casualties all together. We also had an earthquake south of town and we just got our power back."

"Let's hope that Mother Nature gives us a break for awhile Walt."

"I think that we can all use a break. At least we have more to talk about than the weather. People are going to remember this year for a long time Philip. So how long have you lived in Hawaii? AP7ZMT."

"My wife and I retired here about 10 years ago, We moved out here from San Diego. Over." (AS6KY)

"You wouldn't want to be in San Diego now that's for sure. So what is it like to operate from your QTH? I imagine you get a lot of DX from there." (AP7ZMT)

"It's really good for most stations. As you might expect Europe is a little tough, mainly because of the time difference."

"That makes sense. Africa is the toughest place for me to work but that's ham radio for you. Well Philip it's been fun and I hope we can chat again sometime. I am going to have to say 73 now. I have to make some bread. I am not talking about making money, I am trying to bake bread for the first time. Wish me luck. This AP7ZMT. Over."

"OK Walt you take care as well. Good luck with your baking. Sounds like we are both lucky campers. I'll be clear. 73. AS6KY. QR Zed?

Walt turned on his computer and checked his emails. He got an email from Tony who said that the FCC had notified him that a copy of his new license and call sign was available online, He was AW7GHK and Sherri was AW7GHL so now they could start shopping for some equipment. They decided that they wanted to spend about $1000 on a radio and tuner.
Walt thought that this was great and told him that he would start looking around online and give him some suggestions.

He also got an email from Stan telling him that the squatters had been evicted and that they were trying to organize a Rapid Lightning road clean up for two weeks from Saturday at 9 am.

Once a year people would pick up trash along the road and put it in plastic trash bags in front of their place. Then people would pick this up and take it to the dump. It was more than a clean up, it was a social event and a chance to see the neighbors after a long winter.

While online he checked the local newspaper's website and saw that the Bonner County Schools would remain closed until Fall. He also read a story that listed a lot of business that would re-open next week. A few businesses were advertising a grand re-opening with special sales prices to bring people into town.

By this time his dough had risen so he put it in the oven at 350 degrees and hoped for the best. Just before the timer told him to check it, he was already tasting it in his mind. When it was time he opened the oven and it looked pretty good. It had not fallen and it smelled great.

After it cooled he cut a couple of thick slices and made a fried spam sandwich with mustard. It was quite good. In fact it was so good he had another 1/2 slice while the bread was still warm. The other 1/2 of the slice went to Sparky who indicated that she thought it was excellent. After it cooled a little he put it in a 2 gallon freezer bag and got a small glass and a cold beer to wash it down.

Walt turned on the classic rock station on his portable radio and sat in his chair with a notebook and began sipping his beer and making a list. He was pretty pleased with how prepared he had been for winter but there was always room for improvement. His list wasn't in any particular order but in the order that he thought of things;

1. Process as much sand from sandbar as possible while gold prices were still high.
2. Collect Ash to process later
3. Firewood, kindling, pine cones, birch bark
4. Get some solar cells
5. Buy spare electric water pump and pressure switch

6. Get Canner and Canning Jars
7. Build Smoke House and get fruitwood
8. Buy handheld CB radio
9. Find out about CB simplex repeaters
10. Buy CB amplifier
11. Get 12volt cooler/freezer
12. Buy small propane bottles
13. Buy wooden matches
14. Get Battery and solar cell for fence charger
15. Buy meat for Canning
16. Restock Pantry / Dog Food
17. Make Some Beer
18. Get extra beer making supplies
19. Fill up gas and diesel jugs
20. Restock Pantry items like TP, paper towels, paper plates, quart and gallon zip lock bags, wax paper, freezer paper, plastic wrap, etc,
21. Get some help around here

Just as he wrote the word "help", an old Todd Rundgren song started playing on the radio:

"Leroy, boy, is that you?
I thought your post-hangin' days were through
Sunk-in eyes and full of sighs
Tell no lies, You get wise
I tell you now, we're gonna pull you through
There's only one thing left that we can do
We gotta get you a woman
It's like nothin' else to make you feel sure you're alive
We gotta get you a woman..."

The End.

About the Author

Steve met his wife Cindy while serving in the Army in Augsburg, Germany. Soon after that they were married and moved to Ft. Collins, Colorado where they lived for two years. When they got the chance they moved to the mountains of North Idaho where they bought some land in the mountains and began building a log cabin, where they still live today. Neither had any building experience but, this didn't stop them. They moved back to the land with almost no money, no experience, a willingness to sacrifice, lots of youthful energy., and a stack of *Mother Earth News* magazines to inspire their back to the land adventure.

Over the years they brought in power, built a wood shop, developed a homestead, and began making wooden toys that they sold at area craft fairs for twenty years. When gasoline prices began to skyrocket and it got expensive to travel to art shows, Steve taught himself to be a webmaster so that he could spend more time at home. Little by little they kept working on their homestead and making improvements as time and money allowed.

Their property is mostly covered in evergreen trees so they spent a lot of time cutting trees and clearing the land. Now Steve is mostly retired and Cindy grows lots of food in her greenhouse and garden. They enjoy being at home, and only go to town once a week. Steve enjoys his ham radio hobby and they both try to play a few games of pool everyday in a carport that they converted into a billiards room.

Years ago they wrote several books about marketing artwork and craft products and hadn't thought anymore about writing for years. But when Steve turned 70 years old, he began thinking of writing again. At age 70 he knew that his best days were behind him and he decided to write his first novel. *The Adventures of Walt and Sparky - Hunkering Down* is his first book in the series. Hopefully the second book in the series will be available early in 2023.

If you would like to be notified when other books in the series are available you can contact the author at the mailing address listed on the copyright information page in the front of this book.

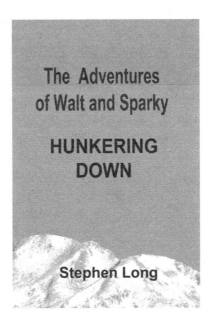

If you have enjoyed this book, we hope that you will suggest it to your friends. It will be available at better book stores and online. Also please take a moment to submit a book review so that others may enjoy it as well.